Grandmother Carried Her Pearls

Kirk House Publishers

Grandmother Carried Her Pearls

PATRICIA CARNEY

First Printing: May 2024
First Edition

Paper Back ISBN: 978-1-959681-54-0
eBook ISBN: 978-1-959681-55-7
Hardcover ISBN: 978-1-959681-56-4
LCCN: 2024908251

Interior and Cover Design by Ann Aubitz
Front Cover Photo by Lynton L. Hansen
Author Headshot by Kathryn J. Jursik Krueger

Published by Kirk House Publishers
1250 E 115th Street
Burnsville, MN 55337
kirkhousepublishers.com
612-781-2815

Epigraph

Grandmother Carried Her Pearls
Our earthmother, Gaia, very first
of our universal birth, being formed
by Gaia's union with her sea spouse
transforming thru birth a pure pearly
essence of her inner luminescence

Oyster secreting her calcium around
a grain of her very earth, ingesting
simple sand and transforming herself
into a birthing seed, spewing mother-
of-pearl into this outer light-world

Her earth daughters, gone from the sea,
the primordial sea, still carry this salt
water amid pearls within their ovaries
giving to each new daughter, *in ute*ro,
the seeds of Eve's granddaughters

As all the mothers-of-daughters carry
their own grandchildren, *in utero*, within
the folds of the ovaries, layer upon layer
of evolving life, and most precious of all,
a perfect pearl, a mother-of-daughter-girl

~Patricia Carney

Dedication

For my daughters, my pearls, Kate and Leigh.

Prologue

September 1977

"This is where you grow up. Nothing like learning to swim by jumping right into the deep end. You will have an easy time here, no need to walk the streets or find a middleman to do your bidding. These guys are all horny; you'll have an easy time asking your price. When you learn your trade, move on, Trudy. Go to California the way your boyfriend suggested, lots of money there."

Faust nearly lifted Trudy out of her seat. She was trying to understand what Faust was telling her. By the time she realized that she was standing in the parking lot of a truck stop, Faust slammed the passenger door and walked around the front of his car. A trucker walked out of the truck stop food counter as Faust was opening the driver's door. He shouted to the grizzly, overweight trucker, "She's all yours!"

Looking at Trudy, Faust added, "We had a great time last night, didn't we, Babe!" Looking back to the trucker, Faust smirked, the final remark intended for him. "Ask her for a quick date before you roll out! She won't be available for long!"

Faust got back into the car and drove off. Trudy was stunned. Was he going to turn around and come back for her? Frozen in place like a young doe at the side of the road, mesmerized by the headlights of oncoming traffic, Trudy watched the Jaguar speed off, taking the ramp on the opposite side of the interstate back toward Milson.

The fat trucker also watched and asked Trudy, "Where you heading?"

Trudy ignored the man. She was still standing in the empty parking spot. Another trucker stepped out the door and observed momentarily. The fat man stepped into the parking space next to Trudy, purposely standing in front of the second trucker, and asked Trudy, "Need a ride? I see your sugar daddy left you behind. I've got a really nice rig out here. Or if you don't want a ride, we could just talk for a while, see what happens."

"Give it up, she's way out of your league," quipped the second trucker wearing a blue work shirt with an embroidered truck logo on the pocket. He was taller and much more fit.

The fat guy responded, "I saw her first, shove off!"

The second trucker only laughed. "You're lucky it's early Monday morning and I've got a deadline; I can't stay." Turning to Trudy and also stepping into the empty parking spot, he added, "I'll be rolling back in here tomorrow afternoon. If you're still around, I can show you a really fun time."

Trudy didn't understand why these men were talking to her, much less trying to outdo one another. The fat trucker didn't appreciate the interruption. As the second trucker turned to leave, the fat guy took Trudy's left arm and tried to lead her in the direction of his truck, telling Trudy they should get out of the parking lot.

"Let go of my arm!" yelled Trudy.

"How much do you want? Okay? But we can't just stand here; the management won't let girls pick up truckers out front. Come on, I'll take you to my cab before you get in trouble."

"No! No!" screamed Trudy.

A third trucker stepped out from inside the counter. He observed the struggle and walked over to the fat man as he was grabbing Trudy's arm, trying to drag her over to his cab.

"Let her go!" He grabbed the fat man by the collar of his shirt and yanked him closer, then, grabbing his neck, got into his face and finished his comments: "I suggest you go to your rig before I shove your face into the blacktop!"

Fatso looked up at the big man and decided it was not in his interest to fight. He had already let go of Trudy's arm. He turned and walked away before he got shoved away.

"Trudy? What the hell are you doing here?"

Chapter 1

One year earlier...August 1976

"Let me see your hands." Trudy lifted her hands, palms down, for the middle-aged woman wearing a white dress.

"No fingernail polish, good. Clean, short nails. Turn your hands over. Well, here's something I don't see much anymore, calluses. I can't remember when I last saw a girl with calluses. You're hired." Jackie turned toward the customer sitting on the other side of the counter, "The girl has calluses."

Mac merely nodded, smiling at Trudy, who was blushing at this unwanted attention on her hands.

"Do you want me to fill out a form or give you more information?" Trudy inquired meekly. Before coming, she had practiced in front of a mirror, answering imagined questions and hoping to make a good impression, really needing to get a job—and soon.

"Look, honey, I'm not hiring a secretary. You're going to start off as a dishwasher and busing counter, then if that works out, waitressing. I'd be happy if you didn't pretend to have experience, cause I'm going to train you my way. How did you get calluses? Most of the Barbie dolls I see around this college neighborhood have hands softer than my earlobes."

"I grew up on a dairy farm," Trudy offered reluctantly, since this was not what she wanted to offer about herself.

Jackie was notably pleased. "A farm girl! I thought the farm exodus ended twenty years ago. Not so many farm families left, not like when I was young, and we all moved to the big city right after high school."

Jackie was still addressing her comments to Mac, who silently nodded to her. He looked over at Trudy and smiled as if to say, "Just bear with her comments."

Mac was a huge man, probably well over six feet; even though he was seated on a counter stool, he towered over the other customers. He must have weighed over 250 pounds. His enormous hands maneuvered his coffee mug to his mouth, ignoring the O-ring handle since even his pinkie finger could not have fit through it.

Yet Trudy saw kindness in Mac's eyes. He could see that she was embarrassed by this unwanted attention, and he nodded to encourage her.

"Come in tomorrow morning at six o'clock prompt, get a white uniform. I'll have a hairnet for you."

Speaking in short, clipped phrases, this woman was clearly in charge, not one to waste time on niceties. Trudy was too inexperienced to know what else to ask. She agreed to Jackie's instructions and left the café, smiling back at Mac and taking a quick look around.

The café had a long, horseshoe-shaped counter around a stainless steel grill with multiple burners. At the back of this horseshoe was a sink and long drying rack. The floor was freshly washed. Square, four-by-four-inch tiles lined the four walls to shoulder height with plaster up to the ceiling. Everything was white and sparkling clean, even the Formica countertop. What wasn't white was stainless steel, including the appliances, the sink, and grille hood.

The front entrance led out to the sidewalk. Next to this door, a large window offered a clear look out onto the street. The window was also spotless . This woman ran a tidy, no-nonsense place, not a greasy spoon. Trudy now understood her "no fingernail polish" remark.

It was late August and the leaves were already beginning to fade. As Trudy stepped out onto the front sidewalk, a warm wind whipped her long brown hair over her face. With full lips and hazel eyes set wide over high cheekbones, Trudy's beauty was natural, needing no makeup. Years spent on the farm had kept her fit, not from working out like city kids, but from manual labor.

Jackie's Counter was an old storefront café, one of several along a street of two- and three-story brick buildings. This was Milson's campus section of town within a larger Midwest city. These businesses along the street catered to transient students who lived in the many duplexes and small apartments nearby. The side neighborhoods were mostly single-family homes of white-collar and upper-middle-class families.

This upper east side encompassed the university, art galleries, music studios, and bookstores, along with diners, laundromats, and bars serving the college kids. The permanent residents contrasted sharply with the students in age, dress, and lifestyle. Yet they resided in a symbiotic relationship, the residents owning the early day while the students, released from class, partied nights.

Upon her arrival just a few weeks before, Trudy had found a small efficiency apartment near the university. Unlike most of the tenants, she was not a student, at least, not yet. Her romantic notions of life in the big city had drawn her to the city and to the university. Besides, she'd had to leave; it had not been an option for her to remain at home following high school graduation after her grandmother's death.

On her way back to her apartment, Trudy had passed a bar called The Spot, which also had a "Help Wanted" sign for dancers. While Trudy had noticed this employment opportunity, she had quickly concluded she was not a trained dancer and instead went farther down the block to inquire at Jackie's Counter.

Inside The Spot, Terrek was enjoying a cold beer after spending his afternoon moving into the freshman dorm on campus. It was a warm day for moving, and the icy brew was just the ticket, the first of several more to come. Something he remembered from his introductory class on economics from high school made him smile: "Beer drinking, like economics, followed the law of diminishing returns." Terrek's thoughts added, "It was most rewarding on first sip."

It was dark inside even though outside the day was bright and sunny. The darkness covered the shabby carpet, worn bar stools, and general dirtiness. It also enhanced the black lights illuminating the iridescent orange, purple, pink, and lime-green of the stage. He watched the dancers gyrating and twirling around poles. The dancers wore scant costumes, more fringes and ribbons than cloth that glowed under the lights.

Loud, pounding music, heavy on the bass and drums, blasted from the sound system tower of speakers next to the stage. The stage was just a raised platform, six inches off the main floor with long poles standing floor to ceiling in the center. This was not background music and was meant to dissuade conversation, in favor of drinking and leering at the dancing girls.

Males frequented The Spot—not only students, but by businessmen, truckers, working men, and winos off the street—as varied a population as the college section of town. It was the only place in an otherwise provincial city that offered partly nude female dancers. Terrek leered at the dancers. Their gyrations and outstretched arms seemingly beckoned only to him, the other patrons hidden in the dark. The erotic dancers aroused him. He floated away in a time warp of rhythm and alcohol.

Unseen by Terrek and farther away from the blasting music, one of the regulars sat at the bar. A world apart, Mr. Harold Faust, Esq., wore a bespoke Italian suit, white shirt with his initials embroidered on the cuffs, a patterned silk tie, and Allen Edmonds shoes impeccably polished. His equine face, with its strong, square chin and straight nose, were set off by a full head of white hair that shone like a halo under the blacklights. Disputing his white mane, he appeared trim and youthful. He kept his distance from the other men but knew the dancers, having stopped in almost daily for his Perfect Rob Roy.

When a dancer saw Faust enter for his afternoon break, she always knew to begin her dance, a tip would await an exotic, athletic performance though he never wanted the dancers to come over for small talk. He talked to no one at The Spot; not even the bartender who knew his regular order and would have it ready when he walked in. No one was to interrupt his afternoon interlude.

As the music ended and black lights flashed off, fluorescent lighting splashed over the men like a cold shower. The exotic dancers were transformed into middle-aged, sweaty females glad to take a break.

At the break, Terrek saw the bar was getting crowded and decided to leave just as Faust was also stepping out. Terrek watched the elegant man step into a '74 green Jaguar XKE and pull away. Terrek knew cars and understood the status they represented.

~ ૨ ~

Trudy returned to her efficiency apartment, leaving the door ajar and immediately opened the two windows across the room. She was not accustomed to the closed-in feeling of the city or this small room. Sun rays of late August poured in, casting a yellow glow through the open door right into the hallway. She was preoccupied with obtaining a white uniform by the next morning. Trudy still didn't know where department stores were. Unlike her small rural town, this big city seemed to have many main streets where she surmised stores might be found. She decided to ask the college girl across the hall. Trudy had met Leslie the day she moved into the building.

She walked across the hall and paused to read the new poster hung on Leslie's door. The initials "VOW" in red, white, and blue, with a fist and two raised fingers forming the letter "V" as if in a victory salute, filled the poster above a subtitle that read, "Voters of Women."

Trudy knocked on the door. As Leslie opened it a draft created by open windows in both rooms and the open hallway doors forced a green and orange maple leaf to float down the wind draft and come to rest just inside Leslie's room.

"Oh, sorry, I've got my windows open, let me pick it up."

Leslie laughed, "Don't, it's a welcome color among all my paper clutter."

Her apartment was filled with papers, notebooks, textbooks, and more posters like the one hung on her door. One bookshelf was filled with books but many more book towers were set on the floor.

Trudy started bluntly: "I found a job today. I have to have a white uniform by six in the morning, and I have no idea where to get one. Do you know where I can buy one?"

"Really, what kind of job?" Leslie asked.

"Working at that small restaurant several blocks away called Jackie's Counter. I was told I'd start off washing dishes, but the owner said later I might waitress."

"My sympathy. Don't get stuck there too long. But you're in luck. I worked last year as a nurse's aide. What a bummer that job was, cleaning bedpans mostly." Leslie winced at the memory. "You can have my old uniform."

She went to her overstuffed closet and pulled out a white polyester uniform in a plain shirtdress style.

"You must be about my size, except you're a few inches taller. You'd be doing me a favor getting this out of my cramped closet."

Trudy was grateful and began to express her thanks, but Leslie stopped her short.

"Look, let me give you some sisterly advice. These white uniforms are slave's clothing. Women who wear them do menial work for lousy wages. And there are too many ways women get trapped in those jobs. The white uniform marks you. It proclaims, 'I'm a menial, I work cheap.'"

Trudy had no idea what Leslie was going on about. She needed a job if she was going to live here in the city, pay rent, and buy food.

Leslie pointed to the poster on the door, "I belong to VOW. We are an organization made up of women, mostly college students, involved in getting women elected to public office. The only 'vow' for us is either an oath of office or an oath to vote for progressive women candidates on the ballot. Women need power. It's the only way to end the enslavement of women in our society."

Trudy thought Leslie already sounded like a politician. Though not particularly attractive, her passionate speech gave her face a certain energy that animated her plain looks with energetic intelligence. Trudy found her interesting, but she continued naively: "Who's going to wait-ress then?"

Leslie shook her head, "I'll take you to one of our meetings. You'll learn about women's liberation and the hard-won battle for voting rights for women."

Leslie sounded patronizing, but Trudy was grateful for the uniform and wanted to be pleasant. She thanked Leslie again and told her she was a lifesaver.

Trudy went back to her apartment to try on the uniform. It fit her loosely with the skirt well above her knees. She wondered how Jackie would react, but at least, she had the uniform before the next morning.

The next day, Trudy started her new job. Her tasks were explained one at a time by Jackie in between customers. Trudy quickly learned how to use the dishwasher which required more hand work than machine work. This routine consisted of rinsing the dishes in hot water with bleach, rinsing again, placing them on a rack to move through the washer, rinsing again, and transferring them to a drying rack. The last step involved returning the dishes to shelves under the counter for re-use. Dishwashing was a chore that was constantly repeated.

Trudy soon learned that Jackie's Counter was a restaurant where everything was at hand and utility was the purpose of its organization. Not a place for atmosphere, décor, themed dining, or even a coffee house vibe. It was also utilitarian in pricing, service, and food preparation. The food was fresh and well-prepared. Customers included students, businessmen, truckers, working folks of all stripes. Everyone appreciated the quick service.

Within a couple of weeks, Trudy started recognizing those who came almost daily. Jackie treated these regulars to a pleasant greeting, playful teasing, and sharing the general news of the day.

Mac, the man Trudy saw at her job interview, was one of the regulars. He was a trucker, and between his long-distance runs, he took all his meals at the restaurant. Trudy soon realized that Mac and Jackie were sweet on each other.

A few weeks went by before Mac broke Jackie's rule that Trudy was not to converse with the customers when washing dishes. "How's the new dishwasher workin' out for you, Jackie?"

Her response was short, "She's working."

Mac winked at Trudy who had looked up. "Congratulations! On Jackie's scale of two, you're either workin' or you ain't!"

Jackie smiled and cut Mac off. "You leave the help to their business. I didn't hire her to jaw with the customers. You want to talk with ladies hired to talk, go over to The Spot."

"Okay, okay, don't get your dander up."

But Mac was smiling, and Trudy smiled back, knowing that he was only teasing. Trudy knew what Jackie expected and understood she was to get the work done promptly. She kept to her corner of the restaurant with its two stainless steel sinks and long drain board. Steam rose, condensing on the white tiles and the small back window. Trudy found this corner a perfect steam closet for daydreaming while doing her repetitious job which required little thought.

After work, Trudy had started to walk through the campus quad. She was fascinated by the older buildings, many from the 1800s looking like castles. They made her think of the fairy tales her grandmother used to read to her at bedtime as a young child, a beautiful princess in distress always saved by some handsome Prince Charming.

Trudy loved walking among the many students around campus. Many male students were perfect models for a Prince Charming. They were often out playing tag football or throwing a frisbee. Trudy would sit on a grassy hill overseeing the campus.

Trudy wanted more than anything to enroll at the university. She would need to earn money to pay tuition and fees, but she dreamed of being on campus one day and attending literature classes taught in these medieval buildings.

While at work, the routine allowed Trudy to daydream in the misty cloud overhanging the sinks. Trudy imagined the handsome campus guys were her fairy tale princes.

"Trudy, Trudy, TRUDY!" Jackie had to shout since Trudy wasn't paying attention. Trudy's spell was broken as she looked over to see Jackie calling her over to the counter.

"I need you to start paying attention to what's happening at the counter. When we're busy like this, I want you to help out with serving, especially coffee in the early morning. Today, I'm going to start you filling coffee cups, and we'll see how it goes."

"Hang in there, Trudy," Mac interrupted, holding out his mug for more coffee. "Once you start helping at the counter, you get to share tips. Ain't that so, Jackie?"

"She'll get her share when she's done her share," Jackie retorted.

Trudy filled several cups and returned to her corner, sorry that her fantasy world had been so sharply interrupted. But the thought of earning tips was encouraging. Maybe she could start saving now and find a way to enroll at the university. Her high school grades were excellent, and she was an in-state resident. She was sure that she'd be accepted. The money had been the only thing holding her back.

Terrek walked into Jackie's Counter around 9 a.m., having failed to get up early enough to eat breakfast before class. The counter seats were filled, but just as he had walked in, a patron using a stool near the door stood to leave. Terrek nabbed the seat even though several customers had been standing and waiting.

He saw Trudy at the sinks and called out, "How about some coffee?" Trudy looked over and saw from his backpack that he was probably a student. Blonde with blue eyes, he was gorgeous and impatient. She set a coffee cup in front of him and began pouring coffee, but his rudeness had not escaped Jackie.

"Look here, 'College,' you wait your turn. Others were already waiting for that stool you grabbed, and don't go telling my dishwasher to serve you."

"It's okay Jackie, I got it."

Trudy smiled at Terrek as she poured his coffee. He asked: "Are you a student at Milson U.?" "Not yet," Trudy apologized.

Jackie came over and told Trudy to go back to the sinks. The rush hour was waning and other customers were starting to leave, opening up many seats at the counter. Jackie never asked her regulars to move on, but she had little patience for college kids who seemed spoiled and expected prompt service even though they tipped little, if at all. She took Terrek's order, promptly served him, and started to clear his plate as he took his last bite, wiping up around his place. Terrek got the message. He paid and left, leaving no tip.

Trudy watched him leave. He glanced over to the sinks and smiled as he opened the door. Trudy thought maybe she'd see him again on campus; her imaginary prince now had a new handsome face for her steamy daydream world.

Chapter 2

October 1976

Trudy's days started to gain a certain regularity through her job routine. Her workday began at six in the morning until two in the afternoon. The rest of the day was her own, as was Saturday when Jackie had part-time help and Sunday when Jackie's Counter was closed.

Jackie started to rely on Trudy to take more of the orders and serve the food, and as promised, she got to share the tips. Tip money was placed in a tin box next to the cash register and at the end of her shift, Jackie generously split the tips 50/50. Trudy soon realized that on a good day she could earn more than triple her minimum wage. She began saving as much as half of the tip money. She just might be able to enroll in classes next semester, at least part-time. This was no longer just a menial dishwashing job; it was the key to her dream of enrolling at the university.

Trudy also realized that Jackie's short, clipped commands were not meant to be cruel. Trudy and Jackie worked well as a team. Trudy followed directions, did her job, and stayed out of Jackie's way. But she did start to observe her boss more closely. Jackie was attractive in her own way, middle-aged, probably pretty as a girl and maybe still was except that she chose to wear a plain white uniform, no makeup, hair pulled back off her petite face. Yet her hazel eyes were intense, set off by her auburn hair. Notwithstanding her petite stature, all her customers understood she was in charge. Trudy also respected Jackie and feared her as well.

Jackie could be a fireball if a customer got out of line, as a few early morning drunks had experienced. Trudy admired the way she never let one of them swear or get rowdy in her place. Jackie gave the local police free coffee, and she could count on them to watch her café even though Trudy never saw Jackie make a 9-1-1 call. The mere presence of the uniformed officer having his daily coffee was enough to keep the peace.

In her free time, Trudy explored the college campus until it became a familiar place. She found the student union, which was open to visitors, and often purchased a light supper or just coffee while she read a novel at one of the small tables. She liked being around the students; many studied here so that being alone at a table was not uncommon.

The oldest Tudor buildings of Milson University were her favorites, especially one red brick building that had a turret, making it resemble a medieval castle. She explored the old hallways, with wooden floors that creaked. Stained glass windows illuminated the high ceilings and old plaster walls. This building was perfect for an imaginary world where she became one of the literary students reading romantic literature of British lore. Trudy loved reading Gothic novels.

Trudy had seen Terrek on campus several times, and she began to return to this same campus quad in hopes of an encounter. One bright sunny day, Terrek saw Trudy and recognized her, saying hello. After several encounters, Terrek returned to Jackie's Counter even though he'd sworn he would never return after the earlier rude treatment. Trudy was pretty and seeing her on campus had made him change his mind. He would just ignore that older woman and hope that Trudy might serve him.

When Trudy saw Terrek, she immediately got his coffee before he ordered. She didn't understand why Jackie gave Terrek such rough treatment. While often disparaging about the college kids, others ate here without such rude treatment. Her fiery temper was on display one morning when Terrek stopped for just coffee. She felt that he was loitering too long at the counter and didn't ask but demanded that Terrek move on. He'd sat with his coffee long enough.

This eruption surprised Trudy. Terrek hadn't done anything to cause the outburst. Many customers sat much longer. Terrek clearly did not like Jackie either. "Get off my back," was his retort on leaving.

One Indian summer day later in October, after a hurried late lunch at Jackie's Counter, Terrek left but waited outside the door. Trudy would be leaving soon since it was nearly closing time. He waited outside to avoid irritating the witch, a name Terrek now used for the owner.

When Trudy left, Terrek was still outside on the front walk. "Hi! Are you heading over to campus today?" Terrek was friendly.

"Uh, yes," Trudy answered hesitantly. She usually went home first to change out of the white uniform.

"I'm going that way; mind if I walk along?"

Trudy merely nodded. She was too surprised and too flustered to make small talk.

"How can you stand working for that witch? I'd stay out of there except for…."

Trudy wanted to defend her boss, but it was obvious Terrek saw a different side of Jackie than she did. She merely answered that she needed the job.

As the two walked toward the campus, they exchanged simple questions and answers about where they were from, which high school they attended. Terrek did most of the talking. He seemed quite willing to tell Trudy all about himself.

"My dad has some big ideas about my future. He owns a salvage yard, actually a couple of them. You might think a junkyard is a junk job, but Dad tells everyone he's in the right place at the right time. Scrap metal is becoming an important component in manufacturing. He also got a major towing contract with the city. He now gets most of the towing jobs. He takes the cars right into his scrap yard for storage, and if they are not picked up by their owner, he cashes in on a percentage of the car's value."

"Anyway, to make a long story short, my old man thinks I should study engineering or environmental sciences, take over his business, and develop it into some kind of recycling or reclamation center. Sometimes I think he forgets it's just a junkyard and that his dreams are not my dreams. He says I've got an inside track, not like the way he had to start from nothing. I'm supposed to help him turn the junkyard into a gold mine or something. But, you know, he never asks me if that's what I want to do. The old man thinks because he's paying my room and board plus tuition at school, he gets to tell me what to do."

Trudy wished Terrek had been a poetry or English lit. major, but alchemy was also part of an old medieval world. Trudy knew that was a stretch, but it accommodated her imaginary dream world. It could be that Terrek might be on top of the world one day as his dad wished. She offered encouragement:

"You're lucky to have your dad care so much. I would love to have someone pay my tuition."

"I just wish he'd get off my back. I'm glad to be away at school though."

Trudy was happy to let Terrek do most of the talking. It was such a lovely day. The bright orange and gold autumn leaves brightened the green campus lawn. Several students were playing tag football. Terrek knew them, and they threw him the ball in a welcoming gesture. Terrek playfully handed the ball to Trudy, and to his surprise, she took it; handling the oblong shape familiarly, she threw a perfect spiral back to the guys. They were obviously impressed.

"You are different than these college girls," Terrek said in admiration. Waving his friends off, Terrek put his arm around Trudy's shoulder.

"Come on, I'll take you over to the student union for beer and popcorn. We can sit by the lake around the back patio and enjoy the sun."

Trudy settled for a Coke while Terrek got a beer. Trudy wished she wasn't wearing a white uniform, but no one seemed to pay any attention. No dress codes applied here. This gorgeous late afternoon had brought most students outside. It felt wonderful to be part of student life as Trudy pretended to be one of them.

As daylight waned, Terrek walked Trudy to her apartment. He wanted to see where she lived. But he didn't linger. He didn't want to be overbearing with this pretty girl. Trudy was sweet, and he liked the way she listened without being judgmental.

After that first pleasant afternoon, Terrek started waiting around for Trudy to finish work, even if he didn't eat lunch at Jackie's Counter. Trudy was always glad to see him. He was introducing her to many parts of campus that she did not know about. They often spent time in the student union. Terrek showed Trudy the pool and ping-pong tables, the arcade and pinball games. When he played poker with his buddies, she sat off to his side, just watching.

Terrek seemed to do little in the way of schoolwork. He never carried books or spent time at the library. Trudy assumed he was going to classes and studying when she was working. He was fun to be with, easy to talk to, and he introduced her to some of the other students. Terrek hung out with a tight circle of guys, many from his same high school and some guys from his dorm and their girlfriends. Trudy felt she was becoming part of the crowd.

As midterm of first semester rolled by, Trudy began spending most of her free time with Terrek. They sat in the designated student section of Saturday football games in the crowded stadium, watching cheerleaders and the marching band along with football. Unlike the small high school Trudy had attended, everything here was super-sized. After the game, the student body packed University Avenue, the main street that fanned out from the campus. This area included beer bars and collegiate gift shops selling Milson U sweatshirts, T-shirts, and college souvenirs, all catering to the students along with pizza parlors, burger places, and fast-food stops. Young, beautiful students populated University Avenue; this was utopia for the college-aged generation.

As the days turned colder, daylight growing shorter, Trudy and Terrek spent more time inside, hanging out at the union. Terrek often had several beers, but he never got ugly, the way she had seen her dad get when she was very young. Trudy excused the drinking since all the guys Terrek hung with did the same—it was just something college guys did.

Terrek walked Trudy home, telling her, "I really like you Trudy, even your name, so different, not like the college broads on campus."

Trudy blushed at the double-edged compliment. She didn't like him calling women "broads." She wanted to be one of them soon, and she asked him what he meant by "different."

"You're fun to be with," was his only response. Trudy thought about Leslie and thought maybe she saw Terrek's point. Leslie was always so serious and preoccupied with her causes. She smiled and returned the compliment. "You're fun to be with, too."

As the days became weeks, what started as a simple goodbye kiss had become long, intimate kissing, first outside Trudy's door, then progressing to French kissing inside Trudy's small apartment with petting and breathless arousal. When Terrek went too far, she stopped him, saying she wasn't ready for a sexual relationship, as if all their kissing and groping was not sexual. But Terrek knew exactly what Trudy meant.

Terrek always stopped when she asked, so she allowed him to come into her room most of the time. Trudy knew she liked Terrek a lot, but she refused to give her feelings a name. When Terrek told Trudy that she was his, it was enough for her. Trudy enjoyed the intimacy as much as he did. But she did not want anything, even Terrek, to sidetrack her dream of going to college. Her grandmother had always encouraged her to do well in school, telling her she could be the first in their extended Irish clan to go on to college and get her degree. She had often told Trudy she was smarter than anyone else in the family.

As they walked into her apartment, Trudy began telling Terrek about her grandmother and her encouragement to go on to college. But Terrek wasn't interested in small talk now. He pulled Trudy close and kissed her warmly, slowly putting his hand up the back of her blouse and adroitly unhooking her bra. He slipped his hand over her breast, playfully pinching her nipples. Terrek steered Trudy over to her bed and pulled her on top of him as he continued petting her breasts and French kissing and pulling her blouse completely up. Terrek turned their coupling over. He was now on top, kissing her breasts and running his tongue around her erect nipples.

Trudy was becoming very aroused. He placed his hand under the elastic of her panties and down the smooth skin of her hips and fanny. She felt her body grow hot and moist as Terrek climbed fully on top of Trudy. As he began to unzip his pants, Trudy panicked.

"I'm not ready for this!" She shouted louder than she had intended. Trudy abruptly pushed Terrek off and stood up, pulling her blouse down. "You must leave, right now!" Terrek had always stopped when she asked. But this time he was aroused and growing frustrated. He stood up next to Trudy, leered at her, frowning, but did not say a word. He finally turned and angrily stomped out of the apartment, slamming the door loudly to punctuate his feelings.

On his way out, Terrek saw Leslie's door across the hallway with the VOW poster tacked to the apartment door. Terrek, not only frustrated, now grew angry, and he grabbed the top of the large poster and ripped straight down. He then ripped it into pieces, throwing them on the floor.

Leslie heard the tearing of the poster and threw open the door. "You bastard! Get your filthy hands off my poster." Terrek panicked, turned, and ran down the hallway.

Trudy heard Leslie shouting and opened her door. Watching Terrek flee, Trudy stood there as Leslie turned on her:

"Look what that bastard did! How could you go out with a jerk like that?"

Trudy was shocked. She couldn't believe that Terrek would do this even though she knew he was angry with her, but Leslie had nothing to do with it.

"There must be some mistake. Terrek wouldn't do that on purpose. Maybe he slipped or something."

Trudy knew that sounded lame, but what could she say? She didn't want to explain to Leslie why Terrek left in anger. Leslie raged on, "That's what you think? You know what I think? He saw the message and didn't like it. Guys like him are afraid of women gaining power and moving in on their built-in advantages. They're all chauvinists; they've been told all their lives that men inherit the world while women are here to serve them. Your guy didn't like what he saw! Why do you go out with him?"

"I'm sorry it's torn," Trudy apologized, "I'll pay for the poster."

"Money is not the issue," shouted Leslie.

Leslie retrieved a new poster from the stack in her room and posted it on the door so as not to let the jerk have his victory for long. The "V" fingers on the poster for victory now had a literal message. Leslie was the vanquisher of a chauvinist. Trudy went into her room to get the promised payment.

She returned to the hall as Leslie finished hanging the replacement. "I'm going to hang more posters around campus, too. You just tell that jerk, if he's not man enough to talk about it, I'll find where he lives and hang one on his door."

Leslie turned to Trudy, calming down a bit. "Really, what do you see in this guy? You told me you wanted to enroll at Milson, but this guy will just use you. He'll interfere with your plans if you keep spending all of your time with him."

Trudy resented Leslie's personal tone. "Terrek's not like that, and I don't think he did this on purpose. He's really a sweet guy. Maybe he thinks too many college women have an attitude against men, that you're more interested in causes like your club."

"CLUB! This isn't a CLUB," Leslie shouted, "Is that what you think we are, just some jaunty bridge club?"

Leslie gave Trudy a nasty look and stalked back into her room, closing the door. Trudy regretted having such harsh words with her neighbor. Leslie had always been kind. She went back to her room, found an old mailing envelope, and slipped the five dollars inside. She wrote, "Sorry," on it and slipped it under Leslie's door.

A few minutes later, Leslie walked across the hall with the envelope in hand and gently knocked on Trudy's door. When Trudy opened it, Leslie began apologetically, "I know this wasn't your fault, please keep your money. You don't understand what VOW is about. I really don't care what your boyfriend thinks, but I'd like to take you to one of our meetings—you could see for yourself what it is really about. You are still planning to enroll next semester, right?"

"Yes, nothing has changed that," responded Trudy, "I stopped in the bursar's office and picked up a course catalog and inquired about open enrollment."

Leslie was pleased to hear she was still serious about enrolling. "What majors are interested in?"

"I've always wanted to study literature. I've been reading the catalog and found I could choose British or American Literature as my major. I've always loved Gothic novels, but I'm leaning toward American Lit. I want to read more contemporary works, learn what authors are writing about now." Trudy was enthusiastic. Somehow, telling Leslie made these dreams seem real, something that she could really accomplish.

"Remember that menial job at the café you warned me would be a dead-end job? I'm not just a dishwasher now, I'm a waitress. And the owner splits the tips with me. I never dreamed I could earn so much money in such a short time. I don't have enough saved for full tuition, but I'll be able to pay for two or even three courses next semester. I'll start slow, keep working, and see how it goes."

"Good for you, Trudy! Really, I'm happy to hear you're going to be a student soon. I really want you to stop and meet some of my friends at VOW. Get to know a few of the serious women here."

Leslie was trying to make peace, and Trudy was relieved, agreeing vaguely that she would go sometime. But Leslie was serious. The next meeting was on Saturday morning, and Leslie hoped she would really come.

Chapter 3

December 1976

Pleased with Trudy's work habits, Jackie made her position a "meal job," as Jackie called it. Trudy would stay after closing at 2:00 and eat a hearty bowl of homemade soup and a sandwich. Marna, the elderly woman who rented an upper apartment, always came down to eat with Jackie and Mac, if he was in town, and now Trudy. Marna's heavy European accent made Trudy think this older woman was very proper and ladylike. She always wore a dress and often came into Jackie's Counter after attending daily mass. Jackie treated her more like her grandmother than a tenant.

"Will you be going home for the holidays?" Jackie asked Trudy, adding, "I need to know when you're not available." Trudy replied that she was staying in town and offered to work through the holidays and on any of the days Jackie was open.

Jackie was surprised, knowing little of Trudy's home or family, but she did not want to pry. "Good, you can come to our celebration on Christmas Eve."

"You'll be in for a real treat!" Marna told Trudy, adding, "Jackie's closest friend, Sandy, always comes to Milson for Christmas, along with most of her regulars that have no other plans. Then, best of all, Mac invites his buddies, and we all become a lively bunch for the holidays."

"Who is Sandy?"

Jackie had gone into the back room to start her homemade soup for the next day; it would simmer all night. Marna quietly answered the question, knowing it was very sensitive to Jackie.

She prefaced her answer, "I know very little since Jackie doesn't say too much, but Sandy had been her best friend since high school. She left Milson after meeting a rodeo bronco rider and went to Oklahoma with him to open a restaurant. They married and, according to Jackie, were wildly successful running a dude ranch, as Jackie calls it."

Trudy was amazed. "Wow, a bronco rider and dude ranch!" Trudy thought that this was a side of Jackie that she had never seen before. Like when she was in first grade, she once thought her teacher lived in school. She realized that she thought Jackie had always run her little restaurant.

"Sshh!" Marna signaled to Trudy to be discrete, putting her index finger in front of her quieting lips. She whispered, "Something had happened to Jackie involving her own boyfriend—he left her or something awful happened. I'm not sure. But it left Jackie deeply depressed and lonely. Sandy came into town and helped Jackie. I'm not sure of the details, but Jackie tells everyone it was Sandy that helped her open the counter and taught her how to run a restaurant. On Christmas, Jackie always tells everyone that Sandy saved her life. This is all I know."

Terrek kissed Trudy outside Jackie's Counter on the day the semester ended, telling her he'd call after Christmas. He was on his way home for the holidays. Terrek was surprised to learn that Trudy wasn't also going home to be with family, but he was pleased she'd be able to spend some time with him. He promised to call and set a date during the break.

On Christmas Eve morning, Trudy did come to work as promised but saw a window sign, "Closed." She tried the door and found it locked. Next, she peered through the large front window. The café was empty, but Jackie saw her and came to unlock the door to let her in.

The sterile white restaurant had been transformed. Twinkling lights illuminated a small spruce tree decorated with Christmas ornaments, candy canes, tinsel, and a bright silver star at the top. Pine boughs with red ribbons tied in bowties were draped across the mirrors. A manger was set up on the back work counter with the figurines of Mary, Joseph, and the Child. Porcelain animals of sheep and a donkey were standing on top of straw.

But most unusual was the sound of Christmas carols playing on an eight-track. Jackie never allowed even a radio to play inside the café—customers who walked in with portable transistor radios were asked to turn them off. Trudy burst out laughing while Jackie helped pull off her coat, cheerfully greeting her, "Merry Christmas!"

"Jackie, what's going on? I thought you said, 'You'd be open on Christmas Eve'?"

"I am! We are celebrating Christmas—I do it every year this way. I am open, but only for my people today. Our guests will be along soon; you can help me get ready."

"No customers then?"

"The regulars are my guests, not customers for today, like Mac, of course, and Marna, my best friend Sandy is coming from out of town. Then our regulars will be here like Professor Stevenson, Mac's trucker friends, Pig and Tag, and sometimes a few other truckers that Mac knows, guys that didn't get home for the holiday, and anyone else the others might invite."

Trudy knew Marna was like family, and Mac was Jackie's boy-friend. But she recognized most of the other names as regular customers of Jackie's Counter.

Jackie continued, "All of our customers that have no family. This is our 'family' tradition over the years. And what about you, Trudy? How come you're not going home to family over the holidays? The entire campus has already cleared out."

"Both my parents are gone. I was raised by my grandmother who died last year. I could go back to the farm. My uncle runs it now, and I will call him later today. But it wouldn't be the same without my grandmother. Also, I'm trying to save money for tuition so I can enroll at Milson U. I'm getting my application in for next semester. That will be my Christmas treat. It'll be just a few courses, not full-time, but I'm excited to start."

Jackie had never heard Trudy offer so much information about herself, and though she was curious about where her parents had gone, she knew better than to pry. Trudy would share in her own time.

"Well, you can celebrate with us this year. We are going to prepare the finest brunch served in any restaurant in this city, even the fancy hotels. We have fruitcake, fresh strawberries, and melons, omelets, a ham, Christmas cookies, of course, and homemade candies."

Following Jackie's instructions, Trudy began to bring out dishes of food, setting them along the counter which just for today was a buffet table. Mac showed up wearing a Santa hat and bearing a big red bag full of wrapped gifts. If he'd had a white beard, he could have passed for Santa; he was a big man and also jolly.

"Merry Christmas," shouted Mac, adding, "Ho, Ho, Ho. Look who I've brought in with me!" Jackie looked over and saw Sandy walk in with Mac. Jackie quickly went to the front door and hugged Sandy warmly. Mac insisted on hugs as well.

"When did you arrive?"

Sandy answered, "I just got in and came directly from the airport." Mac went back out and brought in her suitcase from the taxi.

"We'll talk more later—help me get ready for our party!"

As Sandy picked up where Jackie left off, it was obvious that she knew the counter. Trudy studied Sandy with interest. She was dressed like a cowgirl in a red flannel shirt and jeans. She was taller than Jackie, pretty, but less petite, more like a tomboy. Trudy liked her immediately.

With Christmas carols playing and Mac's good humor, Trudy thought all of it was as joyful as the old-fashioned traditions in *A Christmas Carol*. Trudy loved reading Elizabethan and Victorian novels, and Dickens was an author she admired because of his unusual characters. She thought to herself that this café had its share of Dickensian characters.

"It's starting to snow," Mac proclaimed. "Since I'm not driving my truck, I can enjoy snow for once. I'll go out and push a shovel around while you gals get out the treats. I'll be hungry when I'm done."

Mac retrieved a shovel from the back room, carried it out the front door and began singing, "I'm Dreaming of a White Christmas" along with the music. It was so contagious Trudy, Sandy, and Jackie chimed in.

As Mac left, Sandy asked Jackie how their relationship was getting on. "Well, I'm not some giddy high school cheerleader dating the star football player if that's what you're hinting, but Mac's one of the finest men you'd ever meet. He has a heart of pure gold that's nearly as large as that brawny body. Mac would do anything for a friend in need. He's got real street-smarts, driving all over this country. He's seen plenty. Underneath that tough-guy street-smart act, he's really a sensitive, caring man. Mac likes to call me his home base." Jackie paused, "Maybe not very romantic, but I'll take it. It's solid just like Mac. He keeps me grounded." Jackie blushed and quietly added, "He's moved upstairs since your last visit."

"Sounds like Mac's a gem. You're lucky to have him, then. I hope I get to know him better while I'm here," Sandy added, "And who's this new gal?" Jackie introduced Sandy to Trudy, telling her Trudy was her new hire, and a hard worker, too.

"Keep her then, not easy to find good restaurant workers." Sandy smiled warmly at Trudy.

Marna was next to arrive through the rear door, having walked down the back stairs. With her white hair pulled back in a bun and slightly stooped, she always sat down on the end stool, nearest the grill. Yet Trudy always saw a twinkle in her eye and genuine kindness in this older woman. She reminded Trudy of her own grandmother since they were of the same generation, an era of manners and propriety.

Trudy could not place Marna's accent—maybe German or Slavic. She always sat out of the way at the end of the counter. On weekdays, she came in for coffee before going to morning mass at St. Mary Magdalene Catholic Church down the street. On church days, Marna wore a lace scarf on her head, open at the neck following the old traditions when women covered their heads in church. She appeared frail, but she always had a smile and liked her coffee black and strong.

Marna brought a stollen with her, and she placed it on the buffet counter. She wanted to help with the preparations, but Jackie gave her some coffee and ordered her to sit down at her usual stool near the sinks where they could easily talk. The Christmas stollen was a traditional coffeecake from her homeland, filled with nuts and fruits. It was clearly homemade.

Professor Stevenson, a man appearing to be in his early fifties, entered, stomping snow off his boots. Trudy thought he always seemed bookish and shy, and he always sat down next to Marna finding her to be an excellent source of information on old European traditions and history. The professor taught European history at the university, and both enjoyed discussing antiquity.

Jackie and Trudy set out the usual plates and flatware on the counter, but the festive food and holiday serving platters along with the red and green napkins gave the institutional dishes a holiday cheerfulness. More regulars were now coming into the café, exchanging greetings, joining the conversation, and singing along to the carols. The food was ready, and Jackie insisted that everyone begin eating. She continued to work the grill, making extra egg omelets while Trudy poured coffee, but Jackie soon insisted that Trudy sit down and enjoy brunch.

While she ate, Trudy watched the festivities and thought this was as strange a collection of people as she'd ever been with. But their warmth and good cheer made Jackie's Counter feel like home away from home during the holidays.

After most had finished eating, Mac brought out his big sack and started to hand out presents. Those he didn't know well got a gift candy box, but for each of his closest friends, Mac had something special. The largest, beautifully wrapped box he gave to Jackie. He gave a small, well-wrapped gift to Trudy. She protested, saying she did not have a gift to give in return. Mac laughed and told her it would be impossible to find a gift for him unless she knew how to buy new tires for his truck. But he said he'd take a hug and a kiss and call it even, and Trudy readily complied.

Trudy unwrapped her gift. Inside, she found a small gold bracelet with a tiny gold heart charm. "It's for your wrist," Mac proclaimed, as if Trudy didn't know where a bracelet was worn, and he added: "I thought it would match that gold heart necklace you're always wearing."

Trudy's eyes got teary. Not only had Mac bought her a Christmas gift, but he also found one that was very personal, just for her. The others were opening gifts and did not pay attention to their exchange. Mac was dumbfounded by her tears and asked if the gift wasn't right.

"No, Mac, it's beautiful. It is a perfect match for my heart necklace. The heart is actually a brooch I received for Christmas just last year from my uncle. It was a gift from my grandmother. She'd set it aside with instructions that it was to be given to me. Let me show you."

Trudy unhooked the gold chain from around her neck. She showed Mac the beautiful heart-shaped brooch, which was obviously old and had traditionally been worn as an ornamental pin on a dress or sweater. The brooch was yellow gold and didn't quite match the newer gold of the chain which her grandmother had added so that she could wear the heart as a necklace. The brooch had "T" engraved in an ornate calligrapher's script with tiny diamonds outlining the letter.

Trudy opened it to show Mac. The brooch was made with a tiny hinge on one side and a small latch on the opposite side. Inside, two tiny pictures were placed, one in the front cover and the other on the back plate of the brooch. On the right was a headshot of a handsome soldier dressed in a WWII army uniform, on the left side, a beautiful bride wearing her wedding dress and veil. The pictures were in sepia tone and obviously old but lovingly preserved inside the brooch.

"It's my grandmother's wedding brooch that she wore on her wedding dress. The officer is my grandfather. He came home from the war to marry my grandmother. He wore his uniform for the ceremony. I was named for my grandmother. That's how I got this old-fashioned name. The brooch is incredibly special to me. My grandmother mostly raised me, and she died just a little over a year ago. When she was about my age, she kept this brooch near her heart to pray for my grandfather, hoping he would return home safely from the war. She added her bridal picture and the chain after they married."

"Mac, you are so thoughtful. The bracelet is a perfect complement. I don't know how you even noticed the brooch; it's usually inside my uniform when I'm working." Trudy gave Mac another hug with tears running down her cheeks. "After the brooch, this is the nicest gift anyone has ever given me."

Mac got choked up as well, and he noticed that now everyone was watching this exchange. To cover his embarrassment, he looked over to Jackie. "Well, woman, are you goin' to open your gift, or not?"

Jackie opened the large, gift-wrapped box. She pulled out a black leather jacket. Mac explained, "It's so you can ride behind me on my Harley!" Jackie smiled, but Sandy proclaimed, "That's a great jacket for riding horses!"

Trudy watched the others open gifts but concluded that Mac had given her the very best gift, one that brought back sweet memories of her grandmother. She really missed her, especially today.

Trudy spent Christmas Day alone. She found the solitude peaceful, still enjoying the memory of the surprise party the day before. She listened to Christmas carols on the radio and saw that it was snowing again, just fluffy flakes gently falling. She decided to walk over to Milson U and enjoy the pristine quiet and beauty of the snow-covered, undisturbed campus quad.

The quietness of the campus compared sharply to the preholiday hustle. Her favorite medieval buildings took on a magical quality shouldering the freshly fallen snow. Trudy took a meditative stroll, deeply absorbed in planning for her life as a student. When Terrek was around, she could not contemplate in this way and was glad to be alone for a while. She was not missing Terrek and glad he'd gone home.

Trudy felt a new resolve to enroll, determined to do it in the coming week as soon as the administrative office reopened. Late in the afternoon, after having returned to her apartment, the phone rang. Trudy answered, wondering who might be calling her on Christmas Day since she had already talked to her uncle and cousins.

"Hi, sweetheart, I really miss you, Merry Christmas." It was Terrek. "Christmas at home is awful. I don't think I can take another day of this. My old man got drunk. Mom argues with him nonstop. They both treat me like I'm still in high school living at home, as if I'd never left. Can I see you tomorrow?"

Trudy's mood was rudely interrupted by his litany of complaints. "I'm working tomorrow. I didn't think I'd see you until later in your break."

"Please don't say no," he pleaded. "Look, I'm playing cards with some buddies for the next few days before the New Year. We planned this get-together before we all left for fall semester. And my folks expect me to stick around for a while too, but how about I pick you up on Saturday? I don't want to wait until after New Year's. Please say yes."

Trudy thought for a moment. She'd still have time to enroll, and after a few quiet days, it would be nice to see Terrek. She had no plans for New Year's Eve or Day.

"Okay, pick me up on Saturday around ten in the morning. It's New Year's Eve—we can celebrate." "Great. Can't wait to see you!" Trudy wished him well and hung up. She couldn't shake her feeling that she wished Terrek had not called at all. It was odd because she had spent so much time with him, dreaming about him and always looking forward to being with him. But her fantasies were dimming as she contemplated her very real chance to go to college at last. Terrek had so much to be thankful for, his tuition was fully paid, and he didn't have to work while he was a full-time student. Trudy didn't want to be resentful, but life would be so much easier if she had both her parents providing such benefits.

Terrek picked up Trudy as planned in his army-green Jeep with a canvas top and plastic windows. He kissed Trudy warmly, and his good cheer warmed her. His leather jacket and khaki pants went with the Jeep and reminded Trudy of her grandfather in WWII. He'd shown her pictures of himself in an old army Jeep, dressed in his army fatigues.

"I've got great plans," Terrek began. "I'm taking you to my secret world headquarters."

He handed Trudy an olive-green army blanket and told her to put it over her lap because the Jeep never got very warm in winter. Trudy was enticed by the idea of driving to Terrek International, as he called it.

They drove away from the city for well over an hour. The ride was stiff, the wheels bouncing over every pothole. Freezing air whistled through every crack and seam of the plastic windows. The heater, cranked all the way up, fought a losing battle with the cold.

Terrek finally exited the expressway onto a two-lane road that turned into gravel and seemed to lead to an open field. The road hadn't been plowed recently and the Jeep bounced madly in the ruts. A couple of miles in, Terrek turned into a driveway. A large fenced-in area was posted with signs that warned trespassers, Keep Out, Guard Dogs on Duty.

"This is it," he announced. They were outside his father's reclamation yard. "No workers are here today. They have off the entire week from Christmas 'til New Year. You and I will be the only ones here."

Trudy read aloud the large sign above the gate: "Auto Paradise."

"Yeah, my old man's idea of humor. That's his name for the junk yard, the final resting place for many cars. But don't be fooled." Terrek held out both arms as if to embrace the property, "This is the home of Terrek International."

Trudy laughed. "Okay, you laugh now, but wait until you see my secret headquarters."

Terrek opened the gate and drove into the yard. It was large. Comparing it to a farm, Trudy estimated it was over eighty acres, the size of two small farms. Piles of scrap were everywhere. Lanes just wide enough for a truck to pass separated the mounds of old junkers. Terrek drove slowly, shifting into four-wheel drive to maneuver around the icy ruts. There seemed to be some organization to the heaps. Metals were separated from old upholstery-covered seats and the chrome bumpers from trim. Farther back, car frames were piled four and five high, and all the way back, entire cars were parked next to one another without space enough to open a door. Terrek stopped the Jeep.

"Come on, we'll play King of the Hill." He playfully pulled Trudy out of her seat near a pile of whole frames that had been flattened and piled on top of one another. He hopped onto the hood of the car at the bottom. The flattened cars had been piled alternating back to front, like sardines in a can. He jumped up onto the next trunk and then to the hood of the third. The cars started to rock.

"Don't get hurt!" Trudy shouted. Her heart was pounding as she watched Terrek jumping up the dangerous heap of teetering old cars. "Almost there," he yelled back.

At the top, Terrek beat his chest, proclaiming, "I'm King of the Hill. Come up and challenge me."

"I'm not climbing on that junk pile," Trudy answered firmly.

"If you don't challenge me, I'll always be the king!"

"That's fine with me. You can be the king of this place. Now come down!" Trudy shouted as if she were the one to give orders. The king obeyed and climbed down, to her relief.

Back on the ground. Terrek kissed Trudy in triumph. Her heart still pounding from the fright, she lingered and kissed him back. Terrek drew back, giving her a long, admiring glance and then told her he wanted to show her the real surprise.

They got back into the Jeep, and Terrek drove past the old heaps, explaining the junk business. Most frames were bent beyond repair, but their parts and sometimes entire engines were sent all over the country to dealers, repair shops or collectors. Eventually they'd be scrap, but a lot of value would be reclaimed first.

"The secret headquarters of Terrek International is right over here." He pulled up next to a black stretch limousine. The rims sat up on blocks without tires, as if a dethroned chariot. Other than the missing tires, the limo looked brand new. It was sleek, with no dents or scratches, and looked as if it had just been washed and waxed. The snow and ice had been wiped away recently.

"Madam, your car is waiting." Terrek bowed as he opened the passenger door for Trudy. She peered inside before entering. The car's interior was the antithesis of everything she'd seen so far. This limo was plush: two long seats against the side walls, a driver's seat in front of a panel separating back and front, and another smaller sofa at the back under the rear view window. All were covered in white leather with soft overstuffed cushions. The floor and walls were covered in red velvety carpeting. The ceiling had a full-length mirror front to back between the moon roofs, and a narrow mahogany table with drink holders beneath stood between the side couches.

Accoutrements not found in most sedans included a small built-in television, a sound system, and even a bar with tiny sink behind the driver's seat. The windows were tinted, and courtesy lights behind mahogany panels illuminated the side walls.

After Trudy climbed into the limo, Terrek connected the battery that powered the lighting, heater, and sound system. Following her into the car, Terrek put on an eight-track tape, tuning the quad speakers low. He told Trudy that he had installed the sound system and many of the extra features himself, explaining that this was his one private place away from everything—his parents, his home, school. Trudy saw how proud he was of this limo.

He'd also brought in a bottle of sparkling wine, cold from sitting outside in a snowbank. Terrek popped the cork and poured two flutes, handing one to Trudy. Sitting on a side couch, they listened to the music and sipped champagne. Terrek bragged that he had spent a good part of the last few days dubbing special music onto a tape for their celebration.

Terrek turned to Trudy: "Happy New Year." He clinked his glass to hers, slid closer, and kissed her again, more sweetly than they had outside. "I really missed you."

"This is a fun surprise," Trudy responded.

As it grew darker outside, the limo started warming up. The cushions and carpeting offered plenty of insulation. Terrek shared small talk about his family's holiday. He filled a second glass, kissing Trudy again.

Unaccustomed to sparkling wine, Trudy felt a bit giddy and encouraged Terrek to tell her more about the limo. He explained that the body and frame had been damaged in an accident and he had asked his father if he could repair the body, keeping this beautiful interior for his getaway. His father was reluctant at first, but Terrek started repairing the dents himself and painting the newly repaired body.

Terrek poured another glass for Trudy and then paused the Christmas music, forwarded the track to his special mix of theme music, and turned up the volume: "Bad, Bad Leroy Brown" by Jim Croce came on first, which made Trudy laugh as she listened to the lyrics, "And meaner than a junkyard dog!" She found it appropriate for this place. "That song always makes my buddies laugh, too. We hang out here and play poker," added Terrek.

He went on about the limo, bragging that his father had been impressed with the quality of his work. He thought it might be a clever way to get Terrek interested in the business, so he agreed to leave the limo in Auto Paradise, at least for now, but no guarantee.

"That was over three years ago," Terrek said. He paused to pour each of them a new glass. It was warm enough now to remove their outer coats. "This is my palace. Your wish is my command."

Unwittingly, Terrek struck the right chord. Trudy loved her daydream world of castles with a handsome prince. Inside this plush limo, she could easily imagine the prince's throne room inside his palace. She returned his kiss and told him that she really liked his limo.

The next song was the Beach Boys' "California Girls." Terrek, making another New Year's toast, explained that he dreamed one day he'd go to California and surf, adding that he thought of her when the Beach Boys sang about the Midwest girls all being farm girls, wishing they could be in California.

Terrek said they could celebrate New Year's Eve right here in his favorite palace with his favorite girl. As Terrek proposed another New Year's toast for a grand year of fun, the music changed from the Beach Boys to Bob Dylan singing, "Blowin' in the Wind."

Terrek finished the New Year's wish, "To a wonderful year!" He kissed Trudy again and longer, holding her close. As they continued to drink their champagne, Dylan began singing, "Lay, Lady, Lay."

"One more thing to show you about the limo." Terrek scooted over to the back seat and pulled a lever underneath. The seat eased forward and flattened into a bed. Terrek pulled Trudy over, taking her drink and placing it on the table with his own.

Petting passionately, Terrek unbuttoned Trudy's blouse to fondle her breasts, kissing her nipples. Trudy groaned and allowed Terrek to remove her blouse and unhook her bra. She felt his erection as he stroked her inner thigh. Trudy wiggled out of her bra.

The effects of the champagne and petting relaxed her normal caution. Trudy did not want to be practical or coy. Experiencing a slow wave of arousal crescendo into an orgasm, Terrek began placing his fingers into the warm moist lips of her vagina, and she came again. She had never been so aroused. Terrek unzipped his pants and removed them.

Dylan's song lyrics continued as if a medieval minstrel were accompanying erotic fantasies. "Just Like a Woman" began playing. Terrek slowly entered Trudy in rhythmic extension of the aching in the Dylan song. It was Terrek who was just like the man of the song lyrics playing in the background. And yet he also became like the little boy in a make-believe world in his father's junkyard. On the other hand, Trudy began the night as the little girl, a virgin, but she'd become the woman of Dylan's song, her virginal garden with her beautiful luminescent pearls seeded with millions of microscopic sperm.

The final song in Terrek's mix began to play. The English version of "Auld Lang Syne" capped off their romantic evening. As Terrek held Trudy in a satisfied embrace, they listened to the old lyrics: *We two have paddled in the stream from morning sun till dine / But seas between us broad have roared since auld lang syne.*

With both spent and inebriated, Terrek retrieved a red down quilt from a lower drawer and flipped off the lights and tape player. The lovers fell into a deep sleep, wrapped within the red cover and embrace of each other's arms.

Chapter 4

January 1977

Trudy spent the rest of semester break enrolling in introductory English and sociology courses, two prerequisites for most majors. The routine of her job and school preparations took most of her time. She had gone to the bookstore for her required textbooks and began reading. Her job seemed less tedious now that she had a purpose, and she began to feel like part of the circle of regulars since the holiday party.

When Terrek returned for the first week of second-semester classes, he was not pleased to learn that Trudy had enrolled. While she had always told him she wanted to be a student, he just assumed this was her fantasy. Now that she had actually enrolled, he worried she would have less free time to hang out with him.

Terrek complained, "I'm not doing well in school and didn't pass all my courses last semester. "I'm thinking about dropping out altogether. Remember we talked about California! I want you to be part of the new plans—live life on the beach, learn to surf!"

"That's your resolution, not mine. I've come to Milson to go to college. This has been my dream, and now I have a chance to see it through!"

When Trudy added that she wasn't going to college to please her parents but to see if she could measure up to her own dreams. Terrek just stormed off and headed to The Spot to watch the dancers.

Late one afternoon toward the end of January, Terrek went to meet Trudy after her English class. He'd had a few beers at The Spot, killing time until her class ended. When Trudy walked out of the classroom, she was talking with a guy in her class. Terrek became enraged. He approached Trudy abruptly, took her arm, and led her away before she could finish talking.

"Terrek, don't be so rude. He was just asking about our homework assignment."

"Yeah, right, and I wonder what 'assignment' he was planning."

They walked to Trudy's apartment without speaking further. Trudy was embarrassed and growing angry as well. When they reached her building, Trudy told Terrek she had homework. As they walked through the hallway, she stopped at her apartment door and told Terrek straight away that he could not come inside. Her face flushed as she overcame her usual manner of going along rather than insisting on her own way, but this was too important to her, and she could also smell the alcohol on his breath.

"I don't know why you don't take school seriously. You have such a great opportunity and the full support of your parents. I spent most of my savings to pay tuition, and I'm not going to waste this chance."

Blushing from the outburst of emotion, Trudy's beauty fueled Terrek's desire to go inside and make love again. At the same time, he resented the unrequested advice she was giving. Trudy stood her ground, refusing to open her apartment door. In anger, Terrek grabbed Trudy's books, slammed them onto the floor of the hallway, and stormed out.

Leslie heard the loud commotion and opened her door to see Terrek leaving and Trudy kneeling on the floor, gathering her texts and scattered papers.

"Do you need help?"

Trudy, still too angry to talk, did not respond.

"That's the same guy who tore the poster, isn't it?"

Trudy nodded as she got up and faced Leslie. Seeing how flushed Trudy looked, Leslie grew more concerned.

"Do you want to come in for a while to make sure he doesn't come back?" queried Leslie.

"No, I'm okay," was all Trudy could say.

Leslie was not convinced.

"Look, I'll keep my door open just in case. It really is time you come to the VOW office. We've got literature about how to deal with an abusive relationship. You don't have to handle this alone; you can get support. Please, say you will come. We could go Saturday morning when you don't work."

Trudy could see that Leslie was concerned for her, more than she felt the need. But to placate Leslie, she finally agreed. She didn't want a long conversation with Leslie right now, and this was the easiest way to avoid any further explanations. Trudy turned and went inside her apartment. Leslie left her door open, still concerned for Trudy's safety.

On Saturday morning, Trudy woke to the peeling alarm clock. She wanted more sleep, and it was Saturday! Trudy wondered why she had agreed to go with Leslie; this was her day to sleep in. And she felt so tired even though she'd had a full night of sleep.

Normally, Saturday was her carefree day, saving homework for Sunday. This day was usually spent with Terrek and their circle of friends. Football season was over, but basketball was just starting.

Thinking of Terrek, Trudy regretted the way they parted; she wanted to let Terrek know that she wasn't upset and to spend a carefree day with him.

She considered telling Leslie that she didn't feel well and would pass on the trip to VOW. But she knew that if she skipped it, Leslie would be more concerned and would ask more questions. Trudy decided just to go and get it over with. Trudy dragged herself out of bed and got dressed.

Leslie led the way toward campus. Fresh snow covered the lawns and walks. Since it was a sunny morning, the light reflected brightly. Trudy told Leslie about her new classes and how excited she was to finally get started.

"Good for you, Trudy! I'm really happy you got accepted to go to Milson."

It was a joy to hear words of encouragement. Hearing Leslie, Trudy felt like she had a right to be on campus—that she belonged. As they walked through the campus quad, Trudy thought maybe getting involved with VOW wouldn't be so bad if she was going to meet other students.

The VOW office was just across from the older part of campus. Storefront buildings stretched the length of the city block with businesses that served students, including a bookstore, office supply store, bike repair shop, a family planning clinic, and several fast-food restaurants. On the corner, Trudy saw a red, white, and blue banner, VOTERS OF WOMEN, stretched across a window. Leslie opened the front door and waved Trudy inside.

Leslie began a tour, "This big open area is our meeting room, and along the sides, there are workstations with various information about women's topics. We concentrate on elections and registering women voters, but we also have information on domestic abuse, federal programs that help students, and health information for women." Are you registered to vote in Milson?"

Trudy responded that she wasn't, so Leslie said that they could start there. She handed Trudy registration forms with instructions. "I've got to set up for a meeting but look around at the pamphlets and see what's available for help."

Leslie encouraged Trudy to fill out her voter registration form. And she especially wanted Trudy to get the domestic violence call-center pamphlet. She walked over to pick one out and handed it to her. While Leslie began to set up, Trudy kept an eye on her and dutifully sat down at a side table and began to fill out the voter registration form.

As more women came into the office, Leslie introduced Trudy to them as a new student on campus. Though delighted with her new classification, Trudy was more interested in observing the members than reading the pamphlets. They all dressed and acted like Leslie, mostly wearing jeans and school sweatshirts. No one wore makeup, but there was something else that she couldn't quite put into words, just that they acted differently. Terrek would probably call them "college broads." Maybe it was that they seemed more forthright. These women knew where they were going in life, what they wanted—they had a mission of sorts.

As Trudy turned in her voter registration form, Leslie told Trudy they were starting the meeting soon. "You're welcome to stay. The most important function of VOW is to get women elected to political offices: local, state, and national. The meeting will be about getting more voters registered and information for election strategies."

"Last year, we got the first female ever elected alderwoman to the city council," bragged Leslie. "Do they have to belong to a certain party?" inquired Trudy.

"No, we are nonpartisan. We have to be to get our tax exemption as an organization," answered Leslie knowingly. "Well, what if the women don't agree with your members on some of the issues?" Trudy asked.

"We've had those debates. But first we have to accomplish a power base. We have to have women in office. Those that can represent women's voices."

Trudy didn't come here to have a debate with Leslie, and her instincts always informed her to avoid confrontations. But in her heart, Trudy didn't think she would fit in with these students. Did these girls really want to be in school to learn? Or were they trying to prove something? Trudy supported women wanting to seek office, but voting for someone just because they were female, or even male for that matter, seemed frivolous somehow.

Leslie concluded, "Trudy, you just didn't understand how power works." Trudy shrugged, thinking she often felt powerless except for the few things she could control. She could work, earn money, go to classes, do her homework. For now, that would be enough for her. But Trudy saw how important all of this was to Leslie and respected that.

The meeting started, and Trudy observed for a short time from the back of the open area, but once she realized it was going to be a long meeting, she decided to leave. Trudy made eye contact with Leslie, waved, and quietly left.

It was late morning, and she had the rest of her day free. Trudy wondered if she should try to find Terrek. He was fun to be with, not like these serious women at the VOW office. Despite the domestic abuse pamphlet Leslie had given her, Trudy was not afraid of Terrek.

Instead, Trudy walked over to Jackie's Counter. Since she wasn't scheduled to work on a Saturday. It would be nice to sit at the counter, have a bowl of homemade soup, and enjoy a casual conversation with some common sense folk who just went about their own business. She walked in and sat down.

"Hi, Trudy." Jackie greeted her. "Be with you in a minute."

"If you don't mind, I can get my own coffee." Trudy smiled to herself, thinking she was beginning to sound like old Marna.

It was not the noon hour yet, and the café wasn't too busy—Saturday mornings were usually slow. Jackie came over, wiping her wet hands on the terry-cloth apron she always wore, one that would be changed a half dozen times during the day.

"What are you up to today?" questioned Jackie in a friendly manner.

"Not much. Got some homework for my new classes," Trudy responded.

"Good, that will keep you off the streets and out of trouble," Jackie chided. "Want some chicken dumpling soup? You can't study on an empty stomach."

Jackie's homemade soups were delicious. The regulars always had a cup of soup with their sandwich, unlike the students who mostly wanted a burger and fries. Jackie set down a cup of soup for Trudy just as Mac walked in. His presence was always as large as his frame. He yelled out to all those he knew at the counter, and when he saw Trudy, he came over and sat down next to her.

"You're on the wrong side of the counter, ain't ya kid? What'd Jackie do, fire you?" Mac said this loud enough so that Jackie heard every word. "Don't worry, I got an inside track with the management here, maybe I can smooth things over for you."

Trudy loved how Mac carried on. He always livened up the counter and had a way with everyone. "No, I'm just stopping for lunch. I don't work on Saturdays."

But before Trudy could go any further with her explanation, Jackie answered Mac with her own witticism: "Anybody getting your reference had better check out their unemployment benefits and start reading more help-wanted ads. Trudy came in here because she knows where to get a decent meal, which I can see you haven't missed too many yourself."

Mac, appreciating the come-uppance, called for peace, "There's not a man livin' who can spar with the wit and tongue of a woman with Jackie's talents," he said, winking at Trudy and smiling broadly.

Mac shared the small talk of the week on the road with Jackie and included Trudy in the conversation. Whenever he returned from a road trip, he would tell Jackie what kind of load he was trucking, the cities he had stopped in, and any unusual highlights of the trip, sometimes just bad weather. As Mac said, Jackie was his home base.

The weeks passed quickly with so much to do. Trudy also noted that she started to feel nauseated on waking. She tried to rationalize that it was just a nervous stomach because of her new classes. The feeling always passed once she had eaten and started her routine for the day. But one morning at work, Trudy was feeling particularly punk. Many smells were making her nauseated—freshly brewed coffee seemed to be the worst—one whiff made her nearly vomit. She tried to stay over the steamy sinks and avoid the coffee area. But this morning was particularly busy.

Jackie called on Trudy to refill coffee. Trudy picked up the carafe, turning her head and holding the pot out away from her. She grabbed a napkin and held it over her mouth and nose as she refilled the coffee cups. One customer watching her said he'd pass, and Professor Stevenson asked if something was wrong with the coffee this morning.

Jackie heard this and watched Trudy. Finally, she told Trudy to put the coffee down or she'd have the health department in here. "Is something wrong, Trudy?"

"No, I'm…I am maybe getting a cold or something and didn't want to spread germs. I was just being careful," tried Trudy unconvincingly.

"Do you need to go home? I can manage myself if you are ill."

Trudy said she could stay, but for today, she wanted to avoid serving the food if that would be alright. Jackie consented, but she continued to watch Trudy, and Trudy forced herself to keep working. Somehow, she made it through the morning.

When she sat down and began to eat a light lunch, Trudy told Jackie she was feeling better now and not to worry. The color had returned to her face, and Jackie thought she looked better. Jackie quizzed her about working and taking classes. Was it too much for her to handle? But Trudy disagreed with the thought. They both let the incident pass without further discussion.

After work, Trudy went to her apartment and to bed, even though it was the middle of the afternoon. She felt better after a long nap, but still felt tired. She went to work the next day, and she went to her English class but continued to feel nauseated and very tired. Other than work and classes, she was spending most of her time in her apartment, isolating herself and avoiding any other activities.

Trudy then missed her second menstrual period. She could not rationalize her fears now—not the second month in a row. She knew that she was depressed and sleeping a lot. She did not want to give thought to her fears, but they washed over her. Was she pregnant? As she asked herself the question, she burst into tears, pulled her pillow to her chest, and curled into a fetal position. She had never felt so alone.

Like a robot, Trudy forced herself into work each morning. She struggled through the earliest hours and quietly worked through the morning until her nausea eased. Some days were better than others. Jackie noticed the change. Trudy was pale and seemed sad. Though always quiet, Jackie noticed that Trudy never smiled anymore. Even Mac was no longer able to get Trudy to smile. Yet Jackie left her alone, not wanting to pry.

Trudy stopped going to her classes. She was too depressed to study and now really felt like a failure. She sent a letter to the administration that she was dropping her courses. It was too late for a refund, but at least she would not be graded—counted as a failure. Her records would just record two dropped classes.

Isolating herself, she had no one to talk with, and she didn't know what to do. She knew she should probably see a doctor but didn't know any in this city. Trudy managed to get to work each day, and to eat a small amount before holing up in her room again. She was angry with herself. How could she be so stupid? She had one dream, to go to college. And now she was turning her back on that. She clung to her heart-shaped brooch and cried herself to sleep.

Chapter 5

March 1977

The ugly weather of March intensified Trudy's depression. She cut off all contact with school and friends. Her work ethic, instilled during her upbringing on the farm, was the only reason she kept returning to the café. Though daylight was lengthening as winter waned, bitter rain, gray clouds, and dense fog reinforced her sense of isolation. On Saturday, Trudy stayed in bed. She knew she had to start making plans and tried to force herself to come up with a list of options.

Terrek saved her from having to track him down—she had not seen him since January. He knocked lightly on the door. "Trudy, it's me," Terrek announced in his familiar way.

Trudy was shocked at the unexpected visit and called out, "Hold on!" Terrek checked his watch. It was late morning, and Trudy was usually an early riser, but it was Saturday. Trudy finally opened her door.

Terrek was struck by her disheveled appearance. It was not like Trudy to leave her hair in disarray, tangles hanging down the side of her face. She was pale, with the look of a snow princess with pearly white skin. But Trudy always had high color from being outside and active. She was not smiling, and her eyes appeared glassy. He looked around her room. The shades were pulled, the bed unmade, clothing scattered on the floor.

"What's wrong, are you sick?" Terrek charged ahead, "I'm sorry I've not been around for so long. I had to sort some things out. We've got to talk. I think I've got things sorted out, but I need to check with you first. But let's get out of here!"

Trudy studied Terrek, dressed in faded jeans and his leather bomber jacket. He was strikingly handsome. Trudy thought he was right; she needed to get out of this room. She had been entombed here for too many days. She grabbed her jacket.

They headed toward the campus union where they had spent so many carefree days. Finding an empty booth, they sat down and ordered lunch. Terrek began to tell Trudy why he came.

"I want you to know why I haven't been around. We left off badly last time. I'm sorry. I lost my temper. Knocking your books to the floor was dumb. I just really wanted to talk with you after class, and I lost it when I saw you talking to that guy. But it was wrong, and I apologize."

Trudy had so much on her mind, she'd forgotten about their last encounter. As always, she sat quietly, giving him an audience, but she wasn't really listening. She was thinking about how she would tell him she was pregnant and that he was going to be a father.

She kept getting stuck on the word "father." If someone was a father, then there was a mother, and Trudy avoided that label. Terrek certainly was not father material. She could not get past those words, couldn't personalize this.

"Trudy, I said, 'I'm sorry!'" He could tell she wasn't listening. It was as if she was in a trance. It had taken him some time to muster the nerve to tell her he was wrong. The least she could do was listen.

Repeating his apology, he finally broke Trudy's spell. She looked up at him.

"I'd forgotten all about that," she said dully. "It seems like a long time ago. I'm not angry, and you don't have to apologize."

"I don't?" Terrek grinned. "When I saw your eyes so blurry, I thought you were crying or angry, maybe because I hadn't come around for so many weeks?"

He didn't wait for her answer. "I want to tell you where I've been, what I've decided. You're the *first* to know." As if telling her first was a big deal, and if Trudy wasn't angry, his hesitancy about telling her all but disappeared.

Over burgers and fries, Terrek launched into a long narrative since their misunderstanding, as he called it. At times he went further back, talking about summer when they first met and the fun times they shared. He talked about his first semester classes, how his father expected certain things of him, how unfair it all was.

Finally, he blurted out: "I failed two classes last semester. I was allowed to re-enroll for the spring semester but on probation. If I don't turn my grades around, I will flunk out. I tried going to classes when I got back, but I hated it. I don't want to be in school anymore. I'm done with it."

"I can't let my father make my decisions. I'm an adult now and I need to sort things out for myself. Even though I enrolled in classes, and my second-semester tuition is paid, I've been skipping all my classes. My parents think I'm a full-time student, and they're still sending money. But I took off. I've been spending time with some old buddies, sometimes staying with them, other times just traveling around parts of the state, or going to some of their dorms just to hang out in a new place, nothing specific."

"Everywhere I went, I kept trying to figure out what to do. Finally, I went back to my limo to think. During this whole last week, I avoided my dad who rarely comes to the junkyard, so it wasn't hard. But I finally got my thoughts sorted out. I've thought about this before. Only this time you were always in my dreams. You were wonderful on New Year's Eve, and I want you to be with me. I know I've got to level with my folks, but before I do that, I had to have a talk with you. I want you to be with me, be part of my new plans."

Frustrated and not sharing Terrek's enthusiasm, Trudy blurted out, "What plans, Terrek? What plans are you talking about?"

"Leave school, this city, this state. We go to California! I'll call my father when we get there and tell him what we've decided. We can both get jobs near the beach. We're young, let's not waste our chance to be beach bums, learn to surf, get out of this awful weather here in Milson. Who wants to live here? It's terrible weather for half the year."

Trudy listened, not sharing his enthusiasm. He sounded like a little boy planning to run away from home. He was complaining that he couldn't let his father make his plans, yet here he was trying to make *her* plans.

Listening to Terrek talk about running away made her painfully aware of the folly of getting carried away in his dream world. But his fantasy world collided with her reality. California sounded more like hell than the garden of paradise.

As these thoughts occurred to Trudy, she thought about her problem. This was a real problem, not the frivolous one Terrek was describing. Suddenly, Trudy grew impatient with his willfulness. It occurred to her that he probably never had to deal with real adversity — something not in his control, like the deaths of loved ones, like an unplanned pregnancy!

"Trudy, you're so distant," complained Terrek. "You're the first person I've told about dropping out of school. I thought all week about coming to talk to you. Don't you have some reaction? Please, say you will come with me!"

"I've got something to tell you too, but not here," was Trudy's only response.

They finished lunch and started walking back to Trudy's apartment. Once outside, Terrek continued rambling on about California, about researching the best beaches and the kind of jobs that were hiring now. Maybe he could even find a job working right on the beach.

He got really excited about surfing, about the kind of surfboard he thought he should buy, or maybe he should rent, try out different boards before making the purchase. Terrek told her the weather was in the 70s there now, and if they go further south in the state it gets even warmer with lots of beaches to choose from.

"You will be the hottest babe on the beach like that Beach Boys song about California girls. Well, wait until they see the Midwest farm girl!" Terrek laughed at his play on words from that song. "Wait until you've got this great tan, sunning on a sandy beach in your bikini. I'll have to fight those guys off. Maybe some Hollywood agent even discovers you right there in the California sun!"

As Terrek rambled on about his fantasy world, Trudy thought about how her steam-sink fantasy dreams were gone, no more Prince Charming, no Gothic novels or castles, no poetry, but worst of all, no dreams.

Terrek continued to prattle on, "I haven't been this happy in a month. Telling you about the plans makes them seem real. Say you'll go, and not next month because I'm thinking the end of this week. I can help you get everything squared away and help you pack. You can give notice at the counter, drop your classes. I can get a truck. We just load up a few things and head off to California. Just say yes!"

They arrived at Trudy's building and went inside. Terrek persisted in getting Trudy to agree, finally stopping and facing her directly as she opened her apartment door and stepped inside.

"Trudy, what do you say? Let's do it," he begged.

"Terrek, I'm pregnant!"

"What!!" Terrek's eyes narrowed, and he glared at Trudy.

"I said, I am pregnant."

Terrek lost it. He started shouting, "Why did you let that happen? You will ruin everything. What were you thinking, Trudy? What a stupid thing to do!"

Trudy grew angry. "I didn't plan this. How many times did I tell you, no! Why didn't you protect both of us? It's not like I knew about that damn limo or the champagne or anything else you were planning that night! What were YOU thinking?"

Terrek moved away from Trudy, turning back toward the door. "You're not going to pin this on me! No one gets pregnant that fast. How do I know how many guys you've been sleeping around with since New Year's? Maybe that guy from class, how would I know?"

Trudy's anger boiled over: "Get out! Get out of my life, now!" She couldn't think. She was nearly hysterical, could not even believe he was accusing her of sleeping around. She only wanted him out of her room, now!

Terrek was glad to go. He raged into the hallway, leaving the door open. Seeing the VOW poster pinned back up on Leslie's door, he attacked the poster again: "I thought I got rid of that already!" Tearing it off the door, he ripped it into many pieces, flinging them to the floor and stomped on them, adding: "You're becoming just like them, Trudy, ever since you enrolled. Just another college broad. What a fool I've been. I thought you were different! I was wrong!"

As Terrek stormed down the hallway, Trudy was left with her anger. She was fuming and could not entomb herself in the small apartment any longer. She slammed her door and marched down the hallway, taking the back exit. She stepped outside into light drizzle.

Looking through the icy sleet with teary eyes, she squinted at the crystal stars and began to walk aimlessly into the unknown.

The next morning, Leslie picked up the poster pieces that had been kicked up and down the hallway. She knocked on Trudy's door. But when she saw Trudy had been obviously crying and was not dressed, though it was late morning, she forgot about the poster pieces. Trudy looked desperate.

"What's wrong?" Trudy looked down at the poster pieces in Leslie's hands and started crying again. Leslie came in and closed the door, hoping she could get Trudy to tell her what was wrong.

"Did your boyfriend attack you?"

Trudy just shook her head, trying to collect herself and stop crying. Finally, she said, "I don't know what to do. I'm trapped, just totally trapped."

Leslie looked around the room. It was messy, but there was no sign of a fight, no overturned table or broken lamps.

"Trudy, what do you mean? No one else is here, is there?"

"No, not like that, I just wish I knew what to do?"

Leslie, ever the true believer in sisterhood, took charge: "Trudy, you don't look so well. Get dressed, and come to my room, I'll make you some oatmeal. Eat, and maybe you'll feel better. If you can tell me what's wrong, maybe I can help you figure it out. Okay?"

Trudy saw that Leslie was trying to be kind, and she agreed. She changed into jeans and a sweatshirt, rinsed her face, brushed her hair. It made her feel a bit more normal. She recalled Terrek's taunt that she was becoming just like Leslie. *Well, maybe I am,* she thought and walked across the hall into Leslie's open apartment.

Leslie spooned hot cereal into a bowl, cut some fruit, and made toast. Sitting at Leslie's small round table, Trudy declined coffee but took the food with juice and began to eat. She started to feel better, less nauseated, and was able to collect herself, stop crying. When she finished eating, Leslie asked again, "Why do you feel trapped?"

Trudy wasn't sure where to start, "I dropped my two classes, I had no choice. The only thing I'm doing now is working. Terrek is out of my life, forever! We had a terrible argument yesterday. I'm sorry about the torn poster. He is so immature."

"Well, if you ask me, Terrek being out of your life is good news, not bad. I don't see what that has to do with dropping your classes?"

"I was stupid. I played Russian roulette, and I got the bullet."

"Trudy, what are you talking about?"

"I'm pregnant!"

It took Leslie a moment to understand the Russian roulette comment, but she got that Trudy did not want to be pregnant.

Finally, she looked kindly at Trudy: "That doesn't have to be a trap. You still have choices. You are in control of your own body. If you don't want this pregnancy, do something about it."

"Like what? Kill myself?" chided Trudy, thinking that was easy for Leslie to say, she wasn't pregnant.

"Come on, Trudy. You have options, the same options any pregnant woman has. Haven't you heard about *Roe v. Wade*? The landmark Supreme Court case giving all women the constitutional right to choose? Women get to make their own decisions about being pregnant: You can keep the baby, you can get an abortion, and there are options in between.

"I can't keep a baby. I don't have any way to take care of a baby."

"Of course you do. If you choose to be a single mom, you can get the father to pay child support, get government benefits that pay for medical and support costs. I can take you to the health clinic. They'll explain the benefits and even help you apply. But wait, did you do a pregnancy test? Have you even confirmed you are pregnant?"

Trudy just hung her head, she had not seen a doctor, but she'd missed two menstrual periods and was having morning sickness, so she just assumed she was.

Leslie got some paper and a pen and started to make a list, beginning with using a test kit, and a trip to the clinic to get some information about benefits. She left spaces under benefits, reminding Trudy she was not an authority and only knew second-hand what might be available. Then she split the list into separate columns: "Keep baby," and "Terminate." Under each, Leslie left more blank spaces, but telling Trudy that the clinic visit would help complete the missing information for each choice.

Leslie added, "I've got a pregnancy test kit from a friend at the clinic, it's not yet available over the counter, but I wanted one, and she sort of took one and gave it to me. I did pay for it, but without a doctor's prescription, so it's sort of an under-the-counter test kit. Keep that part quiet, okay?"

Trudy readily agreed, she didn't want anyone to know about her pregnancy, so keeping a test kit secret was easy. Trudy appreciated Leslie's advice. Her thinking was organized and rational.

"You can take the test right now!" Leslie went into her bathroom and came back with an oblong box. She opened it and read the instructions from the test kit. It required a simple urine test with instructions for using a small slide panel that would be marked after being placed in a small cup of urine. Leslie encouraged Trudy to go into the bathroom, take the printed sheet and to follow the directions. The kit included all the equipment needed to follow the instructions. Trudy agreed.

As Trudy returned to the kitchen with the testing stick in a small vial of urine. The directions told them to wait several minutes. Leslie took Trudy's hand while they both sat at her kitchen table and waited. After the prescribed time, Trudy was instructed to read the test window on the stick by looking for two or more red lines across the grid. Trudy closed her eyes as she pulled out the stick, but she knew in her heart what the test results would be. Finally, she looked and held it up for Leslie to see: two lines crossed the window grid, the confirmation of pregnancy underlined in bright red.

"Okay, that's enough for now, you'll still need to see a doctor to do a real test. But for now, go back to the list to help make a choice, keep or terminate." Trudy finally expressed her concern about the first choice for keeping the baby:

"I'm not married. Where I come from, women don't have babies unless they're married."

Leslie thought Trudy was being provincial, but she knew not to lecture her so she changed gears: "You make a good point. You should talk to your parents, ask them for help. They might not be happy, but maybe they would still help you. I know my parents wouldn't be happy, but they would help. Have you talked to them, Trudy?"

Trudy shook her head. "Both my parents are dead, have been since I was a young girl," responded Trudy sadly.

"Well, who raised you, then? I don't want to pry into your life, but don't you have someone that you call family?"

Leslie had noticed that Trudy seemed to be alone since she moved to Milson, except for her boyfriend. She never seemed to have visitors, and she knew that Trudy stayed over Christmas when most students had gone home. She had been curious but didn't ask.

Trudy knew Leslie was trying to help, she paused and finally opened up a bit to Leslie: "I don't talk about this much, but my grandmother raised me. Her name was Trudy Clare, she was a wonderful woman, and she loved me unconditionally. My grandfather was around too, but he was a farmer and kind of distant. It was my grandmother who took care of me and, you could say, was my parent."

Trudy's eyes became teary again. "My mother got pregnant before she was married, too. She was a senior in high school, and my dad was older but was her sweetheart. After graduation, Dad got drafted to fight in Vietnam. Mom had gotten pregnant, and she wanted him to marry her before he left. I have both of their high school graduation pictures—they were both so beautiful, and I've always imagined they were truly in love."

Trudy stopped. Leslie was listening intently and asked, "But lots of girls got pregnant before their guy went off to war. That happened in WWII, even in my own family! Didn't your dad come back for you and your mom?"

"That's the hard part of my story," Trudy continued: "I only know what my grandmother told me. I did ask questions, but she said it was too painful for her to talk about it much. She only told me enough to answer my questions. I never really got to know either of my parents. I was just a toddler. I was told that Dad was never the same after the war. He came home shellshocked, according to my grandfather, whatever that meant. But Dad took up drinking heavily, and Mom started to drink, too. I guess they argued a fair amount. Grandmother said the Vietnam Veterans weren't treated very well after they came home."

"Dad was angry, couldn't hold on to a job, didn't want to be a farmer and started beating my mother. I was told that my grandfather stepped in and forced my mother to come home with her baby—that was me. Dad committed suicide. I don't know any details. Mom couldn't face living home with her parents after losing my dad, and I guess she partly blamed my grandfather. I don't know, she just took off and abandoned me, I guess. I was only five years old. When I was older, my grandmother just said Mom was dead, too. They wouldn't tell me what happened. Maybe she committed suicide, too, but I don't know."

"I'm sorry, Trudy. That's really sad, but you have no other family, no one to help you?"

"My grandfather died before my grandmother. My uncle moved onto the farm and took over; he was their eldest son. Grandmother told him she would take care of me. I always helped with farm chores—milking cows and stuff. My uncle and his family were always kind, but I always knew that I was not one of theirs. Grandmother was every-thing to me. She was in her eighties by the time I was a senior in high school. She died that winter. My uncle said I could stay, but I wanted to move on with my life. I graduated—made my plans. I wanted to go to college, and I think you know the rest. Here I am."

As Trudy finished, Leslie sat quietly for a moment deciding not to press Trudy about getting any help on the home front. She thanked Trudy for opening up to her and told her that she would try to help.

Chapter 6

Mid-March 1977

Trudy finished her shift at Jackie's Counter. She had agreed to meet Leslie at the VOW office and she went directly from work, still wearing her white uniform. The weekend fog had lifted; it was cold again but sunny.

Leslie had made an appointment for Trudy at the family planning clinic next to VOW and agreed to go with her for the first appointment. Trudy was concerned about the cost but Leslie assured her the initial visit would be free. She'd get some basic information and counseling from a professional about her options.

"Trudy, you need to do this right away, the longer you wait, the greater the expense, of that much I'm sure. Maybe you can ask your boyfriend to help pay. He was a partner in all of this."

"No," Trudy responded flatly. "I'm really grateful for your help, and you've done so much to help me get organized. But one thing I do know is that I will never ask for Terrek's help." Leslie dropped the suggestion as they walked inside the clinic.

Trudy filled out forms that asked for basic information. Answering no to the question of whether she had consulted with a doctor regarding the pregnancy. She was worried about whether she was supposed to have seen a doctor already. She left all the questions about family blank.

Trudy gave the form to the receptionist and sat down. Leslie pointed out all of the informational pamphlets, but Trudy was too nervous to concentrate. She told Leslie she would just wait. Leslie offered to pick out a few that seemed appropriate, and Trudy agreed that would be helpful.

She was finally called by a friendly looking, middle-aged woman dressed in ordinary street clothing. Even her office was ordinary, not too clinical looking, and Trudy was relieved by this. Introducing herself, the counselor picked up Trudy's form and asked a few easy questions. Trudy relaxed a bit, though she couldn't remember the woman's name even having just heard it. She hoped her lack of family history wasn't going to be a problem.

The counselor eased her mind: "It's your choice not to disclose information about your family and boyfriend," and then changed topic. "I see you did take a self-exam. If you don't mind, we will do a blood test. Once in a while those over-the-counter exams give a false reading, positive or negative."

Trudy readily agreed. Next, the counselor said they would go through her options and answer any questions she might have. "If you do want to keep the baby, it might be helpful to have the father here. But that's up to you of course.

"I don't know who the father is." Her face turned red. Trudy was a terrible liar. The counselor did not believe her. This lie was so very common since pregnant women lied about this all the time for many reasons—thinking they were protecting themselves or their family, or sometimes even the father. The counselor assumed this attractive young student was not promiscuous. Girls like that knew the routine; they came in and demanded abortion services at the outset.

The counselor wisely avoided any confrontation. "My counseling changes once you've made a choice. You basically need to give the clinic direction of either wanting to have your baby or terminating the pregnancy." The counselor concluded that since Trudy had not yet seen a doctor, she should start with a medical exam and have a blood test. She made an appointment for Trudy the following day since she was already far into her first trimester. The counselor said Trudy could not afford to waste time and wished she would have come into the clinic sooner. Trudy merely agreed to the appointment, remaining silent.

Walking out with Leslie, Trudy was a bit disappointed. Nothing had changed. She was still in the same place as before. But Leslie had chosen a few pamphlets to take along, and she gave them to Trudy. She tried to cheer her up, pointing out that with a doctor's appointment, she did make some progress. Leslie suggested that Trudy read through some of the pamphlets so she'd have a better understanding of her choices.

Trudy undressed. She removed everything except her brooch and put on the paper gown, open to the front as instructed. Dr. Singh entered the room. He was dark-skinned with straight black hair and kind brown eyes. With his heavy accent, Trudy couldn't always understand him, but his female assistant would repeat a question if Trudy failed to answer.

When the doctor asked when she had her last menstrual period, she became embarrassed. She was not accustomed to discussing such personal information with a man, even if he was a medical doctor. She quietly muttered not since December. The doctor raised his eyebrows, wondering why she waited so long, but quickly changed gears and reassured her that she would be all right.

Then he washed his hands and put on plastic gloves. His assistant instructed Trudy to lie down and place her feet in the raised stirrups. Trudy stripped of her clothing, covered only in paper like wrapped sausage, put her feet up in the stirrups. Spreading her legs before unknown staff, Trudy had never felt so vulnerable. She stared at the ceiling, wanting to get this over with as soon as possible. Trudy clutched the sides of the table with both hands while the doctor told her to just relax. He might just as well have said to levitate in thin air, both were equally impossible.

After the exam, Trudy was told to get dressed and wait in the doctor's office. The blood and urine test results would be obtained soon, but the twenty minutes Trudy had to wait seemed like hours. Dr. Singh finally came back and routinely recited the results. The blood test was positive, confirming the pregnancy. He told her everything else was normal and she was a healthy woman. Finally, the doctor asked Trudy what her plans were regarding the pregnancy.

Trudy nervously looked down at the floor and mumbled that she wasn't sure. Dr. Singh didn't hear her and asked again. Still avoiding any eye contact, Trudy repeated that she wasn't sure about her plans.

Dr. Singh stood, in a hurry to leave, but kindly told Trudy not to worry. He explained that his medical exam was completed and that Trudy would get another appointment for counseling to help her through her decision-making. He left the room. Trudy, still nervous, now also grew impatient.

The counselor that she had seen the day before came into the room after having talked briefly with Dr. Singh. She sensed Trudy's mood, "I know you'd like to be done with all of this, but you do need to understand all the implications of your decision. Dr. Singh indicated more counseling, but your time for making some of the choices is getting short, so I'll give you an expedited appointment, okay?"

Trudy was glad to hear someone else understood her frustration. Her next appointment was set for two days later, but Trudy realized this was going to entail many appointments and procedures, whatever she decided. Trudy went home and read the pamphlets Leslie had given her. She started a list of questions to ask. She wanted to get on with all of this. Her first months were spent in denial. Now she wanted the opposite: to affirm and act. But what action?

Looking at the list, she berated herself for not asking questions that were now obvious. Why couldn't she take charge? This was her life, not Leslie's, not Terrek's, no one's but hers. Trudy had always been reticent. It was her nature to sit back and observe. But for once she felt that she needed to grow up.

Two days later, Trudy returned for her counseling appointment determined to make sense of what she should do. She'd read and re-read the pamphlets. The same counselor again called her into an office. Trudy still did not catch the woman's name, but the counselor acted as if they were both familiar, calling Trudy by her first name. This time, there were no forms to complete, no preliminary information, just a statement of facts.

Trudy was nearly three months pregnant, single, and had no insurance. The counselor stressed that the clinic was here to serve women and could help with many requirements, but first Trudy needed to decide what she wanted to do. The counselor listed various programs and support groups available. Trudy remained distant, only vaguely hearing the list of programs.

The counselor saw that Trudy was not engaged and stopped, asking instead: "What do you want, Trudy? It is extremely important that any decision you make is the right one for you, but I can't make it for you. Do you understand?"

Trudy focused, "I understand. I just want this to be over with."

"Do you mean the pregnancy? Or do you mean giving birth to your baby? What is it you want to be over?"

"I . . ., I'm not ready to have a baby, to be a mother!"

The counselor took it slow, using Trudy's words, not wanting to get ahead of her thought process. "Okay, that's an honest statement. You don't want to be a mother, but you still have choices. Do you want me to spell them out again?"

Using the word "mother" connected with herself had a strange impact on Trudy's psyche. She still did not connect with the word, not in a rational, I-could-be-a-mother sense.

The counselor patiently waited. Trudy finally said, "I think I know my choices: abortion, having the baby and keep it, or allow someone to adopt it. I did read the pamphlets."

"Yes, basically. There are some nuances to the last two, keeping the baby with programming and financial assistance or waiting for a while, with your baby in foster care until you can take the baby back into your own care, or the choice of adoption. There are gradations in these choices. You can get the help you need, and our clinic can help you apply for services. Do you have any questions about this?"

"No. No questions. I mean. I'm not ready to be a mother, and I don't want to be pregnant."

"Are you saying you want to end your pregnancy? Do you want an abortion?"

Trudy cringed. This was the word she had been avoiding, "abortion." Trudy thought of her grandmother—the woman who had raised her. Trudy had once complained that boys had all the privileges in school. Now she clutched her brooch and remembered her grandmother's words: *Girls have the most precious job of all, and grandmothers have a special job of helping their granddaughters.* Her grandmother called it *"Grandmother Carried Her Pearls."*

She recalled her grandmother explaining her bit of wisdom: When a woman is pregnant with a girl, that girl receives all the ova, the eggs, she will ever carry in her lifetime of fertility. In other words, a mother not only carries her own daughter, but she also carries her grandchildren, as the ova formed within the mother. Like a mother-of-pearl, her grandmother said, birthing a daughter is special. Her eggs are as precious as pearls. Grandmother proudly told Trudy that she had once carried her during her pregnancy when she had carried Trudy's own mother, as the little eggs forming within her daughter's ovaries. Trudy wondered if she too was carrying a pearl, a baby girl, growing the eggs for her own granddaughters, and for the legacy of her grandmother, the family matriarch.

The counselor brought Trudy back to the immediacy of deciding: "Trudy, if you are going to terminate your pregnancy, you have to make this decision soon. I won't get into the legalities now, but the current law, which came down from the highest court just a few years ago, is formulated in a case called *Roe v. Wade*. The Supreme Court held that a woman has a constitutional right to make her own personal health decisions regarding pregnancy in the first three months. You are getting close to the end of your first trimester. Once you are in your second or third trimester, your rights change. I don't want to make this any more complicated now than needed. You'd still have rights, but other factors start to come into consideration." The counselor concluded, "In other words, if you want to have an abortion, you have to make this decision very soon."

Trudy nodded, "Yes, I understand. I just don't want to be pregnant. I am not ready to be someone's mother." Disconnected again, Trudy knew that she was pregnant.

"I want to end this pregnancy."

"Are you asking to abort your pregnancy, then?"

"Yes," Trudy responded with finality.

The counselor then explained to Trudy that while many of the services provided at the clinic were without charge to the patient—the medical care, counseling, well-baby care and more, were all paid by grants, charitable donations, and government aid. But abortion is the one service that was not supported by grants or taxes. The clinic was able to get some private support for this service, but the patient is also required to pay.

"I'm always sorry to have to explain this, but it is the real world we live in. There is no free abortion. Politicians are adamant about not using taxpayer money for abortions. We try to keep the cost as low as possible, but you will be required to pay a $500 deposit to schedule an abortion."

Trudy turned white. She did not have $500, not after using all her savings to pay for her two college classes. The counselor saw that Trudy was having difficulty accepting this. But everything would become more complicated and more costly if she waited any longer.

"I'm sorry, I don't like placing conditions like this on your decision-making, but this is not something I can control. It's clinic policy, and I must follow the policy adopted by our governing board. If we don't comply with the law, we'd cease to exist at all and couldn't offer any services."

"Perhaps you could ask your family or the father's family to help? I've also known women who decide to sell their car or get an advance from an employer. You need to explore all your options."

Trudy remained silent. She had no idea how she'd get the money. Since Trudy had no other questions, the counselor concluded by suggesting that Trudy schedule an appointment now to reserve a clinic appointment while she got the money together. Technically, this was against clinic rules, the counselor explained. The money was supposed to be paid before scheduling, but she knew that Trudy needed to act soon. The counselor wanted to do everything she could to help, even bend the rules if she wasn't violating board policy. She left to get the appointment book from the receptionist.

On returning, she told Trudy she'd set up an outpatient procedure for her "clinical appointment on termination" — the buzzwords used in the office for an abortion. The earliest date was two weeks out, which Trudy agreed to take. The counselor wrote the date down and handed her the slip.

"You have the date. I know you are anxious about this; I made a big exception to our rules, but this is as far as I can go. When you come in for this next appointment, you'll have to have the $500 paid up. Do you have any questions?"

Trudy shook her head and thanked the counselor. She wondered how she'd get $500 in just two weeks. Trudy walked back to her apartment disheartened, wondering how she could find this money in such a short time.

When she got into her room, Trudy first got her checking book. After paying April rent, she'd only have $136 and change in reserve. She double-checked her receipt from school obtained after dropping classes, wondering if at least part of her tuition could still be refunded. As she feared, she had waited too long to withdraw. The money was only refundable for six weeks.

Later in the afternoon, Leslie stopped by, knowing Trudy had gone to the clinic that day. Trudy told Leslie about her appointment, about the decision she'd made to terminate the pregnancy. She explained there was one problem, coming up with the $500 deposit.

Leslie was determined to help: She first suggested again that Terrek be asked to pay. He was also responsible for the pregnancy.

"That's the least he can do after everything you have to go through," Leslie argued.

Trudy was testy, "Well, so much for women's equality. Terrek denied having any part of this, and I'm left to deal with everything by myself."

"You should still ask. Maybe he'll be glad to know you won't be seeking child support. Five hundred dollars is getting off cheap for him."

"No, I won't ask. Terrek was awful the last time we talked. I don't know if he's even here anymore. He dropped out of school and said he was leaving for California. I don't even know where he is now."

Leslie saw Trudy was serious and changed her tone. "I can lend you $50. That's all I have. Who else can help? Do you have any money at all?"

Trudy explained that after paying the rent, she had only $136. "Add that and my fifty, and you are close to $200. Maybe you could ask your boss for an advance on your wages?"

Trudy really, really didn't like this idea. She did not want to involve Jackie—she was already getting tips and free meals. Besides, she did not want to discuss her pregnancy with her boss.

Leslie suggested maybe Trudy could skip paying next month's rent. Lots of college kids did that and made it up by paying a bit more each month. Landlords usually took the approach that they'd get paid eventually. They usually didn't evict college kids after just one late payment.

Leslie did the math. "That's another $200, for a total of $386. You only need to find another $114. There must be some way we can find that in two weeks!"

Trudy told Leslie about the counselor suggesting selling a car, but she didn't own a car or anything else of value. But Leslie liked the idea,

"What about that necklace you're always wearing? That looks valuable—and old too. Good jewelry and gold chains are always worth something."

"My brooch!"

Trudy wrapped her hand around her grandmother's heart brooch. This was more valuable to her than a mere $100. It represented her one connection to the woman who had raised her, loved her unconditionally. The idea of selling it was so horrifying to Trudy, she began to cry.

Trudy didn't try to explain the significance of her brooch to Leslie. It was priceless as far as Trudy was concerned, and she felt ashamed for putting herself in such a circumstance. What would her grandmother have said to her? Although Trudy knew that her grandmother would have given her the $500 if she was in trouble. She had been a generous woman. Trudy now missed her more than she had known or admitted. She tried so hard to be mature, to be self-supporting. All this plus her fear of skipping a rental payment seemed overwhelming. What if Leslie was wrong? What if she did get evicted, then what?

Leslie comforted Trudy, telling her she knew all of this was difficult. She encouraged Trudy to be strong. Maybe there was another way to get the value from her jewelry without an outright sale.

"There's a pawn shop near the campus. You could pawn the brooch, use it to get a loan, and get some time to buy the necklace back. College kids pawn guitars, amps, watches, all kinds of stuff. Being near a campus is a good location for a pawnbroker." Leslie concluded, "We could at least look into this—you only have a few weeks to get this money, but you'd probably have many months to repay and reclaim your necklace."

Leslie continued, "Let's go Saturday morning to the pawn shop and see what you can get. I'll go with you so you don't have to do it alone." Trudy could think of no other solution and agreed.

Arriving at the pawnbroker's storefront, Trudy read the large, gold-leaf lettering on the window behind rusty metal bars: **INSTANT CASH**. Just below, in a smaller font, single words ran the length of the window: **Diamonds * Gold Rings * Jewelry * Coins.**

On the opposite side of the middle door, another large window posted the name: **DOC'S HOCK SHOP,** below, in the same gold-leaf lettering, **If in doubt, bring it in, Get a Quote, Same location over 35 years,** invited customers to make an inquiry. The pawnbroker's trade symbol, three globes hanging from a tri-level bar, hung over the door.

Trudy did not like the metal bars and crass messaging. If she had been alone, she'd have left, but Leslie encouraged her. "Look, it says to come in for a quote. We can at least ask some questions."

They walked in. Old hardwood floors blackened from years of neglect squeaked with every stop. A horseshoe counter took up most of the space, leaving a small center aisle. Display cases with thick glass windows displayed myriad items: Watches, gold chains, bracelets, necklaces, money clips, eyeglasses, small electronics, and more, all for sale. Behind the counter, larger items were hanging on the wall or sitting on shelving, including musical instruments, mostly guitars, televisions, stereo equipment, small appliances, and sporting trophies. Trudy had never before seen such a peculiar collection of goods displayed in one store.

Behind a center teller-like cage sat a fat, balding man with thick eyeglasses. The remnants of his scalp hair stood on end, with longer hair growing inside his nostrils and over his eyebrows. A stubble beard gave his round face the appearance of a porcupine. He bit a stubby cigar between his teeth as he bent over a watch face with a magnifying glass held between his fingers with dirty nails.

Doc, presumably, finally looked up. He observed the two young women, peered over his glasses, asking, "What can I do for you girlies?"

Leslie did the talking. She explained that they had valuable jewelry and wanted to get a quote, adding that it also had a gold chain.

Doc laughed sarcastically. "I determine value. Let's have a look."

Leslie looked to Trudy, waiting for her to remove the brooch from around her neck. But Trudy held it tightly inside her clasped hand. She disliked everything about this man. Instinctively, she felt he was not trustworthy. She did not want his dirty fingers pawing her grandmother's brooch. Every fiber of her body told Trudy to turn around and get out of here.

"Well, I don't have all day, and I can't give you a quote without seeing it," sneered the pawnbroker.

Reluctantly, Trudy lifted the gold chain over her head and laid the brooch on the glass tray that the man pushed under the teller window. Doc pushed his thick lenses up on his nose and lifted his magnifying glass.

Bending over the brooch, Doc verbally cataloged what he saw. "The heart's an old piece. The engraving and inset diamonds show its age. Not chips, very tiny cut diamonds. Chain's not as good, newer piece. We can talk. What do you want?"

Leslie explained that her friend wanted to take a loan for a short time, not sell. She would reclaim the necklace and wanted to know what Doc's terms were. Doc smirked, knowing he was dealing with a couple of inexperienced college kids. He explained that there were holding costs and an outside limit on how much time he would keep the piece before it would be placed for sale. If they did come back, they'd have to pay the holding costs plus interest for the time held. He charged 25 percent of the loan amount and would only hold it for ninety days. Leslie tried to haggle, telling him the interest rate was too high.

The pawnbroker continued to smirk. "Look, I'm not a banker. You want better terms on a loan? Go see a banker, go see the guys in white shirts. What's your problem? Why are you hocking this old jewelry?"

"None of your business," Leslie replied. "What will you give us for the jewelry?"

"Fifty bucks," Doc responded.

Leslie was growing angry, "Fifty! You know that jewelry has antique value besides being gold with diamonds. We want $150, and you hold it for six months."

"I'll give you a hundred bucks, and the ninety days is not negotiable," Doc replied.

"We have to clear $125 if we are going to do this loan," insisted Leslie.

Doc stared at Trudy, looking her over. It made Trudy's skin crawl. She wanted to run out, but this man now held her most cherished item in his grubby hands.

"Add that gold bracelet to the deal, and I'll make it $125."

Doc had noticed the bracelet that Mac had given Trudy for Christmas. The brooch was her most cherished possession, but giving up the bracelet would make Trudy feel disloyal and cheap for hocking a present from a friend. Her eyes filled with tears. This haggling was so humiliating .

Leslie mentally did the calculation: Trudy needed another $114. This last offer would be more than enough.

"We'll take it, but only as a loan. We are not selling this jewelry," Leslie emphasized, nodding to Trudy to give the pawnbroker Mac's bracelet as well.

"That will depend on whether you reclaim it within ninety days," Doc replied dryly.

He took the jewelry and slipped it into a paper envelope. He wrote a receipt with the terms. To get the jewelry returned, Trudy would need to repay the $125 plus $31.25 interest and $10 handling fee for a total of $166 and change.

Doc counted out $125 in small bills, and he counted it again in front of the girls, placed it in a small envelope and slid it under the bars along with the receipt for the jewelry. Leslie and Trudy departed. Doc went back to poring over the gold watch. He didn't care about their troubles or their urgent need for money. Doc did not want to know. Everyone who came into his pawn shop had a tale of woe. Like King Midas, all the pawnbroker cared about was the gold.

Chapter 7

April/May 1977

Trudy no longer woke up feeling nauseous and felt a new surge of energy. Her skin was soft and smooth, her body flowering with spring. But she had been so taken up with her plans of late she had not noticed these physical changes, except that her morning sickness was not as intense. She was relieved at this.

She'd paid her $500 to the clinic as an advance and asked off from work. She hadn't eaten anything since midnight as instructed. The day for the termination, as the clinic called it, arrived. All the details had been handled. But Trudy could not calm her racing pulse or ease her headache as she headed to the clinic. She had not slept well during the night. Arriving much too early for her appointment, she was irritated at having to wait. She could not sit still.

She fidgeted with her hair, paced around, and looked for some way to pass the time. She grabbed one of the clinic pamphlets and sat down again. As she paged through the introduction, she realized that she was reading about fetal development throughout the stages of pregnancy. This was not one of the pamphlets Leslie had chosen to give her.

Trudy became absorbed in the progress of the fetus. At the beginning, the fetus looked like a tadpole. She was fascinated by the idea that the stages of gestation were not unlike the stages of evolution, starting with a single cell dividing and becoming more and more complex. Mentally she noted her progress was at about week twelve. She paged through the pamphlet and began reading, "At week twelve, the fetus is recognizable as a human baby, with a large head and a small rump."

Trudy stopped reading and closed the pamphlet for a moment. But she was curious and opened it again. *At sixteen weeks the face has developed human features. This is the earliest stage at which a mother may be aware of movements.* Next to this text was an illustration. Small hands and feet were clearly apparent. The caption stated, *At this stage, the baby is starting to suck.*

The terminology had changed, not "fetus," but "baby." She closed the pamphlet and returned it to the rack, not wanting to read any further. She sat down and tried to calm herself but broke into a cold sweat and began to hyperventilate. She looked around the waiting room. The fluorescent lights glared, and a buzzing that came from the long tubes grew louder. Her senses were magnifying the light and sound. In a panic, she ran out the door of the clinic. Once on the street, she kept running. The fresh air renewed her, relieved her headache. She kept running without attention to direction.

Breathless, she slowed and began walking rapidly, not willing to stop. Her mind was racing. What was she supposed to do next? There were no answers, only questions. When she looked around, she had no clue where she was. Seeing taller buildings and larger storefronts, apparently this was downtown Milson, but nothing seemed familiar. She began to inventory her options outlined by Leslie but this was no help. Trudy berated herself for not taking charge. What was she supposed to do now?

Should she go back? It was past the time for her appointment. Trudy pictured Dr. Singh pulling on his plastic gloves. The clinical aspect of the exam room made her pulse race all over again, but now she was also hungry. She had not eaten since early last night. Trudy instinctively reached for her brooch as she had done out of habit hundreds of times. The brooch was not hanging over her heart, and she thought of the disgusting guy from the pawn shop pawing at her grandmother's treasure.

What would her grandmother have done? In her day, a pregnant girl got married, no matter what, even if her father had to get his shotgun and force an unwilling boy to decide that marriage was his best option. A baby born illegitimate, her grandfather would have said, *Is a bastard.*

Trudy tried to imagine Terrek forced at gunpoint to walk into a church and get married. The thought sent chills down her spine. His idea of providing for a family would be to ask his father for money to buy diapers. Trudy pictured herself kept somewhere, maybe in the junkyard limo, while he took off, maybe never coming back. She was thankful there were no shotgun weddings anymore.

Try as she might, Trudy could not visualize herself with a baby. What would Leslie do? Trudy imagined she would make having a baby her project. She'd find all the programs and assistance available. She'd make single parenthood all about young women maximizing their own lives while also raising a child.

Her time warp unraveled as hunger pangs reminded her that she had not eaten. She found a fast-food place and hungrily devoured a burger with fries and a thick chocolate shake, comfort food. Eating helped her to calm down.

Alone in a booth toward the back of a mostly empty dining area, Trudy snagged the phone books on a shelf below a pay phone. The books included the Yellow Pages which listed business entries as opposed to the White Pages, the book that listed residential phone numbers and addresses. Trudy began to page through the subject headings of the Yellow Pages.

PLUMBING, POLICE, POULTRY SUPPLIES, POWER, PREG-NANCY. Bingo, Trudy was surprised to find this word in the pages of a phone book. Under pregnancy, the sub-listings included: ***See Abortion Services. See also Birth Control Information & Family Planning Services. See also, Physicians & Surgeons, Gynecology.*** Trudy read down the column and stopped at ***See also, Pregnancy Counseling, Adoption.***

Below this caption, a single entry read: *Pregnancy hotline, call 24 hours,* with the listing of a single phone number. Trudy finished her fries and shake and stared at the phone number, wondering what a hotline might provide. She took a coin from her purse, walked over to the hanging wall phone, dropped the coin in the slot and punched the phone numbers telling herself that she could always hang up.

She was in an unknown location with few people. This gave her a strange sense of privacy and control. Now anonymous, Trudy convinced herself that there was nothing to lose by making this call.

"Hello, thank you for calling the pregnancy hotline, how may I help you?" The woman's voice was sympathetic, sweet-sounding:

Trudy merely responded, "Hello?" It came out more as a question than a greeting.

"Hi, my name is Jill. May I ask if you are calling for yourself?"

"Yes," Trudy responded.

Jill asked, "Are you in any immediate danger or trouble?" Trudy responded in the negative and Jill continued offering to spend as much time talking as needed. Her voice was friendly, even easy to talk to. She asked if the caller could give her first name.

"Trudy." Jill thanked her. She grasped the name and began to speak directly, as if they knew each other. "Trudy, why did you call and what might I do to help?"

Trudy found herself opening up a bit more. She said she had run away and was confused. Jill asked if Trudy was alone and quizzed her in this same friendly way as Trudy gave some details of her story. Jill told Trudy that there was an attorney in the office who was very experienced. Trudy's voice stiffened, she didn't need an attorney, she wasn't in trouble with the law or being chased by anyone or anything like that.

Jill's voice softened, telling Trudy that the attorney was truly kind and took an interest in helping young women who were pregnant. He could answer questions that Trudy might have, help explain her options. Jill asked Trudy if she could transfer the call to Attorney Harold Faust. Trudy reluctantly agreed, reminding herself she could hang up the phone if she didn't want to continue. But she was curious. She needed to hear about her options.

Attorney Faust came on the line. His voice was deep but friendly and concerned. He said hello, calling Trudy by her first name, and explained that Jill had given him a short summary. He reiterated the offer to help her explore her options. Faust possessed her name, calling her Trudy each time that he addressed her. He told her that he helped many young women and said he knew that she probably felt confused and unsure of what to do. He told Trudy this was normal for a young woman facing an unplanned pregnancy. Trudy found this kind male voice comforting. He seemed to understand that she was frightened and confused.

He assured Trudy that she could tell him only as much as she felt comfortable sharing. First, he asked if she was an adult, over 18. Trudy told him she was nineteen. Then he wanted to know how long she had been pregnant. The questions slowly got more personal, but Trudy kept answering his questions, like had she seen a doctor. The attorney finally asked where she was calling from?

Trudy described the fast-food restaurant. Faust asked which one, but Trudy couldn't answer and did not know the location. She had run a long way from the clinic. He asked for the phone number that she was calling from, and Trudy gave him the number of the pay phone. He asked if she could see a street sign outside the restaurant. Trudy looked out and saw a corner street sign.

"I'm on Milson Street," Trudy replied.

"Okay, Milson Street and what's the cross street?"

Trudy looked again, Fifth Street. She gave the information to the attorney, and he responded that she was downtown about five miles from his office. Then he asked Trudy where she lived. Trudy stopped. She did not want to give that information to a stranger. He sensed her hesitancy from the pause and immediately backtracked.

"You don't have to answer that question, but would you be willing to come to my office and talk? Jill is here and can help answer your questions. I've been doing pregnancy counseling and adoption work for many years. You do not have to pay any money and can leave any time you want, but you are obviously lost. I can help you find your way back to familiar ground. Okay?"

Trudy knew she was lost and so did the attorney. But she also didn't know where this office was and told him she didn't know if she could find it.

"That's easy, I'll come pick you up, it won't take long, and my office is near the campus so you'll be able to find your way, okay?"

Trudy agreed reluctantly. This man had a friendly voice, but he was still a stranger. She looked around. A fast-food place is a great place for coming and going without knowing anyone, not like Jackie's

Counter. But it was not a good place for finding help or making sense of things. Trudy knew she couldn't just keep running. Somehow, she needed to sort things out and get a new plan.

Trudy had never before admitted to herself that she could not just terminate her pregnancy. Why did it take running away for her to understand this? And now what? Was she starting over, again?

Trudy went out and stood on the corner as instructed looking for a green sports car with the full bright headlights shining. As the Jaguar approached, she was frozen in place like a doe staring into oncoming traffic. She was picked up by the attorney as promised. He drove her to his office.

Since Faust had an afternoon filled with client meetings, Jill showed Trudy around taking care to be friendly and supportive. She told Trudy that she could ask her any questions. After spending many minutes familiarizing Trudy with the offices and conference room, Jill scheduled a meeting for the next day with Atty. Faust and reassured Trudy that no money would be required for her appointment.

The next day, Trudy worked at Jackie's Counter as usual, but she left quickly after a light lunch to keep her appointment. Faust's office was just a few blocks away, within walking distance of work and home. Trudy was furious with herself now. She'd wasted $500, hocked her most prized possession, dropped out of school which had been her one real dream, and now she was keeping an appointment without knowing anything about this attorney or the services that were being promised. She could have just run away again, but she knew that would only lead to more doubt. Trudy forced herself to walk to the office in time for the appointment, going past The Spot on her way.

Meanwhile, Harold Faust was in The Spot enjoying his afternoon Perfect Rob Roy. He was also thinking about the pregnant young woman he had picked up the day before. He'd been caught off-guard by how beautiful she was. She will have a beautiful baby, he surmised. He could assemble a résumé of his wealthiest clients waiting for a private adoption and put them at the top of his waiting list. The thought gave him satisfaction as he enjoyed his cocktail.

Faust looked at his watch and drained his glass. Trudy's appointment was in fifteen minutes. He was unaware of a coincidental connection to his thoughts. Terrek was also sitting at the bar finishing a pitcher of beer and leering at the stripper. Terrek, however, did notice the well-dressed gentleman with the full mane of silver hair and remembered the car the man drove off in last summer. He never forgot unique cars. Terrek poured another glass of beer, promising himself that he'd own such a car one day.

Whether happenstance, coincidence or destiny, this river of life flowed through the same timeframe, like a riverbank overflowing with a surging spring thaw. Faust walked out, paying no attention to the other men at the bar.

Trudy, true to form, arrived early for her scheduled appointment. Jill greeted her telling Trudy that Mr. Faust would be along shortly and offered to get Trudy something to drink. She then took Trudy to a conference room that was nicely appointed with art and lush green succulents. A long table stood in the middle with maroon leather chairs around it.

Trudy studied Jill: she was a middle-aged woman smartly dressed in a tight suit and spiked heels. Her dyed-blonde hair and makeup were impeccable. Her well-managed appearance compensated for her average looks, and she had a figure that would catch a man's glance on any street corner.

The expensive décor contrasted sharply with the metal desks and plastic chairs at the family planning clinic. Everything here suggested warmth and comfort as well as wealth. It made Trudy apprehensive. This was not her world. Jill sat down with Trudy and set about trying to make her feel at ease. She began telling her about Attorney Faust.

"Attorney Faust has been sponsoring the pregnancy hotline for many years. He has helped hundreds of young women, and he's earned several awards." Jill pointed to the nearby wall displaying a row of plaques from different community groups. She stood and pointed to a large, engraved plaque.

"This one is from Life is a Right." Moving to the next ones, Jill recited the groups, "Here's one from Fraternity of Christian Fellows, and Mothers of Charity. And this one is his favorite: District Attorney Distinguished Service Award for Community Service."

Trudy was impressed. Jill continued telling Trudy that he was great friends with the district attorney who appreciates his work, knowing he would go to the end of the world and back to help any young woman calling the pregnancy hotline. She concluded by telling Trudy that she would be in good hands.

As if just introduced, Faust entered the conference room. He, too, was well-dressed in a blue suit, white shirt, and silk tie. These rich surroundings felt intimidating, and now that Faust had walked in, Trudy felt out of place. But Faust sat down at the conference table and immediately put her at ease:

"You look better today. I was really worried about you yesterday. I'm glad we got you home for some rest." Trudy felt like a lost child being protected by her father. Faust smiled at her as he expressed his concern. Trudy had not known her own father, and Faust's father-like attention was a comfort she had not known as a child.

Jill left the room. Faust picked up his yellow legal pad and explained that he wanted to get some history about her pregnancy and also to make a list of Trudy's most pressing concerns. They'd work together on finding solutions for her problems so that her pregnancy would be less troublesome. He explained that in his experience most young pregnant women had many concerns beyond the fact of an unplanned pregnancy.

Trudy was confused, not sure what he was getting at. Faust pressed her: "Am I right? What's bothering you right now?"

"You mean, like being behind in my rent this month?" Trudy queried.

"Exactly! That's the kind of thing I want you to tell me. Let's get those irritations listed so that I can really help you."

Faust continued, "In all of my years of practice, I've learned that a crisis pregnancy always involved other concerns, that all the problems need to be considered." He continued, "Don't think about the pregnancy for now, just name everything that's causing tension in your life."

He took the yellow pad and gave the page a title in the top margin: Trudy's Hit List. Then he wrote on the first line below the heading, "1. Behind one month's rent."

"Okay, that is your first concern. Let's keep going, what else is troubling you? "Trudy nodded and began to name her concerns while Faust wrote them down:

TRUDY'S HIT LIST:

1. Behind one month's rent.

2. No health insurance; how to pay for medical bills?

3. No doctor, needs referral and appointment.

4. Has not told employer, what about job during pregnancy?

5. Paid deposit of $500 to family planning clinic, can Trudy get refund?

6. Jewelry at pawnbroker, reclaim before 90 days.

Trudy paused. Faust encouraged her telling her that she was off to a good start and asked, "You've not listed any problems regarding your boyfriend or family? In my experience, these are usually on the list."

Trudy answered, "Both my parents are deceased. I was raised by my grandmother who died just before my high school graduation, last year."

"And your boyfriend?" Faust prompted. Trudy paused, but then emphasized, "My ex-boyfriend is no longer part of my life and will not be involved under any circumstances." Faust did not press further. He knew he'd get more information later as Trudy got to know him better.

"Let's solve problem number one today," Faust suggested.

"How?" Trudy asked.

"That's easy, we go pay your rent."

"If I had the money, I would have done that already," she protested.

"Trudy, you just have to trust me for now. We will work this out so that in the end it will be good for you, good for your baby, and even good for me. I'm going to give your landlord his rent money so you don't get evicted."

"I'm already in debt—I can't repay you."

"You won't be asked to, Trudy," Faust replied.

Trudy was confused. In this world as she knew it, one does not get something for nothing. Her grandmother was a practical woman and always told Trudy never to trust unsolicited offers from strangers. Now Faust was confronting her with two contradictions to this wisdom, an unsolicited offer made by a stranger. Trudy unconsciously reached for her brooch, her hand closing to an empty fist.

Faust smiled kindly. But her instincts told her to turn down this offer.

"Just trust me for now, Trudy. I know you're confused or you wouldn't have called yesterday, but if I'm going to help you, we've got to set aside these minor issues first."

Hal stood and pointed to the plaques.

"Look, important people have commended me for services provided, not just to young women like you, but to this community. I have a good reputation you can trust. Over the next few months, you'll see how this will all fit together."

Faust called Jill in and told her to photocopy Trudy's hit list. He gave Trudy one copy and told her they could check off each problem on the list as it got solved. He also had Jill schedule their next appointment.

Faust then drove Trudy to her apartment building, noting her address. Trudy pointed out the manager's office. She watched as Faust became her advocate, following him into the office. Faust introduced himself to the manager, gave him his office card, and informed the manager that they came to pay the delinquent rent.

"I understand Trudy is behind," Faust began.

"That's right. I've got her eviction notice right here. I'm tired of these college kids skipping rent payments."

Ignoring the notice, Faust asked, "How much?"

"Two hundred dollars," was the manager's reply.

Faust pulled out his money clip, counted out four, crisp $100 bills and handed them to the manager.

"That's for April—and May in advance,"

"I don't know," the manager hesitated. "The owner wants me to evict anyone who is late before they skip out for summer. He's tired of these kids taking advantage."

Faust pulled out one more bill. "Give me the notice to tear up, and this one is yours."

The manager looked Faust in the eye and met understanding. He handed over the eviction notice in exchange for $100. Faust turned, put his arm gently on Trudy's shoulder, and walked her out of the office.

"Check off your first problem. We'll work on the others next time. Okay?"

Trudy watched Faust leave. She wondered if all of life's problems were that easy to solve in his world. Maybe she just magnified everything too much. She made a mental note to herself. *Be an adult!* Trudy went up to her apartment. Leslie heard the unlocking of her door and poked her head out.

"Come over for a moment. Let's talk. I've been worried about you since yesterday. How did your clinic visit go?"

Trudy stepped into Leslie's apartment but refused to sit down. Leslie stared at Trudy, noting how wonderful she looked. She had expected the abortion would require some recovery time and was confused. Seeing Leslie's puzzled look, Trudy stopped her before she went further, explaining that she had not gone through with the termination.

"But why? You worked so hard to get the money. You told me you couldn't go through with the pregnancy."

"I just couldn't do it. I did go to the clinic, but I panicked and ran. Don't worry, I will repay your fifty dollars."

"It's not the money!" Leslie could not believe Trudy had failed to follow through. She'd been so desperate to raise the funds. "What are you going to do now?"

"I called a pregnancy hotline and met this attorney," Trudy began. "He helped me make a list of my problems and says he'll counsel me."

"What's his name?" Leslie was skeptical.

"Attorney Harold Faust." Trudy pulled out the card Faust had given her and showed it to Leslie, telling her about all his community awards for helping pregnant girls.

"Never heard of him. But what's an attorney going to do? The clinic already told you about your rights. You're in control of your own body—any decision to be made belongs to you. You have the right to choose."

"I know all that. But I've still got to understand the consequences. I need to know what happens after I've made my decision. That's the hard part. This attorney runs a pregnancy hotline. I found it in the Yellow Pages. He agreed to help me. He even got my late rent paid today and got the manager to tear up the eviction notice."

"What does he get?" Leslie was suspicious.

"I don't know," hesitated Trudy. Leslie's words were echoing her own thoughts.

"You're losing the chance to take care of the big problem. You don't have a lot of time."

"It's not that easy, Leslie. I left the clinic yesterday by myself. No one made me run. Ending the pregnancy means getting rid of a growing baby. And the baby's nearly sucking its thumb."

"I'm not following you, Trudy."

But Trudy went to the door, telling Leslie she did not want to discuss this anymore. But before she left, Leslie told her that she would check out Attorney Harold Faust. She'd ask the counselors at the VOW office what they knew of him and the hotline. Trudy was already out the door. She did not want to hear any more about Leslie's organization.

Lying down on her bed, Trudy felt as if she'd been like a sapling wedged in the ice during the winter freeze, Trudy's early months of pregnancy had been spent in denial of her truth. With the spring thaw, the riverbanks swell and what was once a frozen stream becomes a torrent, and so it seemed to Trudy. Now that she had faced terminating the pregnancy and rejected the act, she was being swept downstream in the current, no longer in control of the forces moving her.

⸺ ℓ ⸺

Trudy kept her appointment at Faust's office as scheduled. Jill took her into the same conference room as before. When Faust walked into the room, he greeted Trudy warmly and thanked her for being prompt, apologizing for keeping her waiting even though it had only been a few moments.

He started by asking for a bit more background information from Trudy, her health status, school attended, some family history. Trudy answered his questions without hesitation. When Faust again asked about the father of her baby, guessing that perhaps he was her high school sweetheart, Trudy avoided giving a direct answer. She did offer that the father was not a boy she knew from high school. Meekly, she told Faust that she didn't really know the father, that it had been a brief encounter. Faust didn't believe her, but he also knew that now was not the time to press. Trudy was becoming irritated with these questions about a boyfriend.

Faust changed the subject. He pulled out the yellow worksheet with Trudy's hit list and put a check mark in front of number one: rent problem solved. He went to the next items:

"Problems two and three are related. No health insurance, no money for doctors, right?"

"Right," Trudy agreed.

Faust asked if she had seen a doctor at all or had any tests, and Trudy told him about her clinic visits and the brief services they had provided. She explained that she had intended to terminate the pregnancy but couldn't do it and ran. "That's how I got here," she concluded.

"Glad you did," Faust responded.

He told her they'd solve these next two problems by making a phone call to get started. Faust picked up his phone and dialed a familiar number. He looked across the conference table and smiled at Trudy. The call was picked up, and Faust began a familiar conversation with the person who answered.

When he hung up the phone, he told Trudy she had an appointment with the finest ob-gyn doctor in the business. He got her an appointment this week even though the doctor's office said he was booked up for the entire week, but because of his connections, the office agreed to extend hours. It was important for Trudy to get regular doctor visits and begin a vitamin routine to be sure the baby is healthy. Faust told her he knew the doctor always wanted the mother to take calcium supplements and other needed nutrients.

Trudy began to feel like a little girl again: A child who had her doctor appointments arranged by a parent. She knew she needed to go along with this planning, but she nonetheless berated herself for not acting like an adult. Faust wrote down the date and time for the appointment and told her to come directly to his office. He would take Trudy for her first time.

Trudy returned to Faust's office on the day he had scheduled for her first doctor's appointment. He drove Trudy to Dr. Wellstein's office and stayed long enough to introduce Trudy and make sure she was comfortable before leaving. Dr. Wellstein examined Trudy and gave instructions for routine care including vitamins with extra calcium. Trudy was also given a schedule for routine check-ups during her pregnancy.

Early the following week, Trudy returned to Faust's office. He asked her how her doctor's appointment had gone. Trudy merely answered, fine. As he continued with his interview and instructing Trudy on her options. He continued to be supportive, encouraging Trudy. She found him to be a good listener, and she began to share more and more of her background.

As Faust finished for the day, he told Trudy, "I'm taking a short vacation over Memorial Day weekend. I'd like to suggest that you have a nice break as well, give all of this a rest for a few days. We'll set up our next appointment right after. Okay?" Trudy merely nodded.

～ ᐁ

Memorial Day weekend marked the unofficial start of summer in this heartland city. The semester ended and most of the students had gone home. Milson now belonged to the local residents once again.

Trudy stopped at Jackie's Counter for breakfast on Saturday. She had a renewed appetite and wanted a hearty breakfast, and Jackie had often encouraged Trudy to stop on her free days. This holiday weekend, Trudy found the restaurant was very quiet with only a few diners.

Mac arrived shortly after. He was dressed in leather pants and vest. Trudy had never seen him dressed in anything other than his usual black T-shirt and jeans.

"Woman, it's beautiful outside! Let's have a nice breakfast and close the place down, I'm takin' you for a ride on my classic Panhead Harley!"

"You know I can't do that. We've got Sunday and Monday, isn't that enough?"

"Blast it! Did you look outside? That's not my regular Harley, I've even got the sidecar attached. You can't count on this weather stickin' around!"

"Take Trudy. She's free. I work on Saturday." Jackie stood her ground and pulled Trudy into this good-natured skirmish.

Mac looked over at Trudy and took a seat next to her at the counter.

"What's all this about, Mac?"

Mac waxed poetic telling Trudy about his love of Harleys and the collector 1950s era Panhead Harley that he had just gotten out of winter storage. He explained all the special features and the need to have a passenger if he was taking the sidecar.

Mac and Trudy finished a hearty breakfast while Mac assured Trudy that she'd love the ride. He was a very safe rider. Trudy remembered Faust telling her to take a break. She got excited listening to Mac and thought this would be a fun way to spend it. She readily agreed to be Mac's passenger.

Outside, Mac helped Trudy get into the sidecar, he handed her an old form-fitting leather helmet with ear flaps. The helmet matched the era of the motorcycle and sidecar. He also gave her a pair of goggles to wear. Trudy felt like she was putting on a costume. Mac even gave her a long white scarf and adjusted it so that one end was much longer. He told Trudy it would tail as they rode, like the tail on a kite.

Trudy felt like she was in a parade as they drove out of town. Mac headed down the rustic rode that followed the river. Willow trees grew along the bank with weeping branches draping low over the roadway. These lacy branches formed a long tunnel of shade, dappled patters of sun and shade danced on the road before them.

The throaty, potato-potato, sound of the Harley engine made it impossible to talk so Trudy let the sidecar carry her forward as if riding a raft down the meandering river. Mac finally pulled into a little root beer stand where orders were filled at an outside window.

As Mac walked over to get two root beer drinks, Trudy removed her helmet and unwound the scarf just as Mack was returning.

"Where's your pretty heart?" Mac asked as he handed Trudy a root beer. "You told me that you never took it off."

"How do you remember things like that?" Trudy thought that was particularly unusual for a guy to notice such a thing.

"I don't usually pay much attention to women's bangles. Could care less unless Jackie wears it of course! But you were so broken up over the whole thing at Christmas, I couldn't forget. I'm concerned you lost it in the sidecar."

Mac downed his root beer and began searching though his sidecar looking on the floor and seat.

No! Don't look for it. I didn't lose it."

Seeing how confused Mac looked, Trudy added, "I needed money a while back. I used my brooch to get a loan at that local pawn shop. But, I'm going to get it back, it was just for a loan."

"A pawn broker!" Mac bellowed, adding: "Please tell me you didn't go to Doc's Hock Shop!"

Mac's concern was frightening to Trudy. She had to get her grandmother's brooch back, had to! She told Mac not to worry, she had gotten a receipt, and Doc told her he'd hold it for 90 days.

Mac said nothing more but to hurry up and finish her root beer. He helped Trudy back into the sidecar and hurried back into Milson, dropping Trudy off at her apartment. Mac then roared off down the street with an empty sidecar.

Chapter 8

June 1977

Leslie knocked on Trudy's apartment door and called out her name. Hearing Leslie's voice, Trudy opened the door, inviting her in even though she was already in her nightgown.

"I got a line on this Harold Faust guy," Leslie began. "He's quite the silk-stocking lawyer, comes from an old family with money, prominent in the community."

"That's nice, I already guessed that much," responded Trudy, disinterested and resenting Leslie's know-it-all tone of voice.

"But listen to this. His practice is mostly private adoption, representing some of the wealthiest clients, not just here, but all over the country."

Trudy's interest heightened. "How do you know all this?"

"A lawyer at the public defender's office is also one of our volunteer advisers at the VOW office. The lawyer didn't know the name right off, but she checked through her legal contacts. Lawyers working for the public defender don't travel in the same circles as your guy."

Leslie paused, "Are you going to give your baby up for adoption?"

Trudy hesitated, not knowing if she should share her feelings. "I've not made any decision, except that I couldn't do the termination," Using the clinic's euphemism for abortion, she added, "Faust has that hotline number for helping with an unplanned pregnancy. That's all we are doing now, just doing some planning."

"He's been very helpful since I never had a game plan and didn't know what to do." Leslie listened but wondered who was doing the planning. She offered more information from her investigative work. "We checked out the hotline, too. All the crisis centers told us that Faust is not part of the network. He's not a licensed social worker and doesn't get any community funding like the accredited agencies. Faust listed his hotline number in the Yellow Pages under adoption services, but it goes directly to his attorney's office. Did you know that?"

"Yeah, I found that out."

Trudy sat down on her bed. She was confused, not sure she wanted to talk further. Leslie pulled a chair over facing Trudy.

"What's Faust been telling you?"

"He's been helping me. Really!"

Trying to convince herself as much as Leslie, Trudy continued explaining that Faust helped her focus. Giving examples, Trudy listed rent paid, doctor referral, appointments for well-baby care, vitamins for a healthy pregnancy, and more to do.

"Well, are you paying him?"

"No, of course not, I don't have any money," Trudy responded.

"And what about the delinquent rent?" This was a question that Trudy had already been asking herself.

"I don't know. Faust just told me not to worry about it." Trudy knew that sounded lame.

"Come on, Trudy, Faust must be getting something for all this. He makes a lot of money. Do you think he's just a Good Samaritan?

"Why not? He's gotten community awards. I even saw the plaques. One was from the district attorney for community service. Faust has never asked me to do anything I didn't agree to do. Why do you and that VOW lawyer have to be so suspicious just because he doesn't work through your women's network?"

Leslie understood that Trudy was getting impatient and didn't want to argue with her. "You just don't understand much about the women's movement. But I didn't come here to discuss that with you. I am really concerned that this lawyer might be doing something that's not entirely on the level. I just want you to make sure you know what you're getting into, that's all. Maybe, ask him a few more questions to get to the bottom of what he's planning."

"I've asked questions," Trudy responded.

Leslie saw she was irritating Trudy and changed gears. "Forget it. I won't talk about the lawyer. Let's just talk about what you're planning to do. I know you don't have much family; I'd like to help if I can."

Trudy saw Leslie was trying to be a friend. She'd always been generous, even kind.

After a moment of silence, Trudy told Leslie about Faust meeting with Jackie at work. Trudy felt she had betrayed the kind-heartedness of Jackie who had done so much for her since she came to Milson. Finally, she wrapped her loose nightgown tightly over her body.

"I'm starting to show!"

Trudy began crying. Leslie truly felt sorry, not knowing what more she could do to help. She went over to the bed and sat next to Trudy, putting her arm around her. She let Trudy cry for a while.

"I'll help any way I can," offered Leslie gently.

Trudy just shook her head as if to say there was nothing else to be done.

"You are going to need some maternity clothing. I have an idea. We can do something I love to do, which can help you, too." Leslie offered, trying to cheer Trudy.

"What's that?" Trudy asked through her tears.

"We'll go rummaging."

Leslie explained that the beginning of summer is rummage sale weekend for their neighborhood community near campus. She had seen posters tacked on grocery store bulletin boards and a local ad in the weekly shopper.

"I already planned to go. Maybe we can find some maternity clothes or just loose blouses for you," Leslie said, "Let's do it. It'll be fun!"

Trudy was afraid Leslie might be onto one of her "projects" again. But as usual, she hadn't planned for this herself, and Leslie was offering some solution. She had nothing to lose by going along, agreeing to go on Saturday.

The aroma of beef soup with fresh vegetables saturated the air inside Jackie's Counter. Marna stepped in for her morning coffee before going to mass. The first rays of sunlight flooded the Counter as Marna took her first sip of java. This routine shared by the two women started their day most mornings.

Marna knew instantly that something was bothering Jackie and asked what was troubling her. Jackie told Marna about yesterday's visit from the attorney, adding her disappointment that Trudy had not trusted her enough to talk with her alone. She told Marna that she had already guessed that Trudy was pregnant, but never said a word, waiting for Trudy to broach the subject.

"When Attorney Faust asked to speak with me about Trudy working during her pregnancy, Faust insinuated that I'd just fire her if she had to take time off. I've never said that to Trudy! Then he continue to lecture me about Trudy's rights. I only want to help Trudy, but he just assumed that my only concerns were about her work hours."

Marna listened patiently. Seventy some years had taught her to listen when a friend shared frustrations. Her attention allowed Jackie to vent. Marna finally offered, "Seems to me that Trudy's the one with the real trouble. Such a pretty girl, but so alone, doesn't she have any family to help her?"

Jackie explained the little she knew after having asked Trudy why she had not gone home for the holidays.

"When I was young, an unmarried pregnant girl was sent to live with an aunt living far away, or if no aunt, maybe a convent. These young women today claim to be independent. But not much has changed; it is still only *her* problem."

Jackie just nodded. She'd had her own connection with the "abandoned woman" problem. Jackie added: "But where does this lawyer come in? He wasn't your typical ambulance chaser. He was dressed in expensive clothing and walked in here like he owned the world. No way Trudy can pay for a lawyer like that."

Marna advised Jackie to forget her hurt feelings. "We need to find some way to help Trudy. I'll start by praying for her when I'm at Mass today." Jackie nodded, adding: "I wish Mac were in town. He's always better at figuring out problems than I am."

Marna left as Jackie unlocked the front door and hung up the open sign. She passed Trudy arriving for the day, smiled, and greeted her warmly. Trudy smiled warmly back at Marna. When she entered, she was careful not to make eye contact with Jackie. She quickly walked inside and went about her familiar routine. The two women worked side-by-side with efficiency and without talking. As the morning rush ended, Jackie finally broke the silence:

"About yesterday, it's okay. You can work as long as you like. Let me know if I can help in any way."

Tears welled up in Trudy's eyes. She only managed to nod her head, saying, "Thanks."

When Marna returned, she was cheerful and talkative as always. Today, she made a special attempt to engage Jackie and Trudy in her small talk. By the end of the morning, the tension had eased. But Jackie was disturbed by the deep sadness that she sensed in Trudy.

After work, Trudy was still considering all the questions Leslie had raised. She was supposed to go see Faust for another appointment this afternoon. Trudy decided to skip it today. As her conscience tugged against this decision, she concluded that she was in charge and free to come and go as she pleased. Trudy walked over to campus, something she had not done in many months. It was a warm day, and she enjoyed the return to this familiar place.

On Friday morning, the routine of Jackie's counter gave Trudy a sense of normalcy. When she left at the end of her shift, Faust was waiting curbside in his sleek Jaguar.

Faust knew the meeting he had with Jackie had been uncomfortable for Trudy, but he was puzzled that she had skipped her appointment. He had expected her to follow through with his instructions as she had always done. When Faust saw Trudy, he sprang from the car and opened the passenger door for her to get in. Trudy was conflicted, but on seeing Faust, she complied rather than argue.

"Good news! I've accomplished the next item on your list," announced Faust.

He handed Trudy a white envelope. Inside, Trudy found five one-hundred-dollar bills.

Faust continued: "The family planning clinic agreed to make a complete refund with a little persuasion. I told them that after interviewing you, I determined that you had not been given complete information about your risks in having such a procedure. You could not give 'informed consent' as we call it, meaning you never knew all your risks and all the side effects of an abortion. Also, you never received the service that you paid for. The clinic gave me no trouble. I got your refund. The clinic just wanted me to go away. I'm sure you can use the extra money," Faust concluded, smiling. "Let's skip the office for today and celebrate."

Trudy felt numb. At one time, she would have considered five hundred dollars a lot of money. It had been so hard to get it all together in the first place. Now with Faust, it was just freely given. She couldn't make sense of how everything was so easy for Faust while everything had seemed nearly insurmountable for her.

Faust drove Trudy to the fast-food restaurant where she had once stopped to make her hotline call to Faust's office. He suggested she could order a milkshake or whatever, and they could talk. Fate had once drawn them together here; they could relax and see where it would lead today.

Trudy allowed Faust to order a double chocolate milkshake for her while he had coffee. They sat across from one another in a booth in the back where it was quiet. Faust was friendly, but he finally got down to the point, asking Trudy why she'd missed her appointment.

Trudy sipped on her straw and considered her response. She finally said: "My friend Leslie told me you are not a licensed adoption agency and that your law practice represents women in adoption cases, is that right?"

"Yes, I do adoption," responded Faust. "What are you getting at?"

"Am I your client, then, or someone you are just helping, like you said?"

Faust smiled, "You are whatever you want to be," replied Faust, adding, "I don't determine who my client is—you do that."

Trudy was puzzled, but she summoned her courage and continued.

"Do you want my baby for adoption?"

"That's up to you," returned Faust. "It is up to the client to tell me what they want to do, if you decide to be a client." Faust then redirected the question to Trudy: "Have I ever asked you to give up your baby in an adoption?"

"No," shaking her head in response.

"Is there any reason you don't trust me? If so, just tell me why."

"I guess not," Trudy admitted, but remembering Leslie's words, she pushed on, "I am wondering why you are helping me like this. What do you get? How do you get paid?"

Faust sat back in the booth, taking in the scope of her concerns. He finally responded: "I am a fortunate man. I have more than I need and can obtain anything that I may wish to have. I am in a position in life that brings respect. I was born into it; it's not something I had to earn from scratch like you do. I really don't have to work if I don't want to; my father was remarkably successful and wealthy. I learned that the real accomplishment life offers to someone like me is to help others who don't get all these benefits. I know you may not be able to understand my position, but I decided a long time ago that my only opportunity for feeling successful is in helping others who have not been as fortunate.

"There's a whole world out there, Trudy. Tell me what you want to do. I know you are in an unfortunate circumstance with this unplanned pregnancy. I get that young women can be trapped. Your young man, whoever he is, is off scot-free while you deal with this alone. I want to help you."

Trudy listened but was still puzzled and not sure he was answering her question. Faust saw that he was not making his point clearly. He changed gears:

"You could ask, 'why does anyone give money to charity?' There are millions of dollars given every year to all kinds of worthy causes. Do people ask why? Of course they do. Many suggest the worst motives: so and so needs a tax deduction, or so and so hates their own kids so everything is given away. This can be a sad world, Trudy. No one trusts simple generosity anymore."

After his speech, Faust looked at Trudy and challenged, "If you don't trust me, you are free to go your own way. You don't have to see me. Remember, you called the hotline seeking help. I didn't call you."

His efforts were not lost on her. She now felt a bit guilty for questioning him, everything he said was true. Out of habit, Trudy reached for her brooch, but it was not there. Then she looked at the envelope of money and realized that it could give her a way to get her brooch back. She looked at Faust.

"I do appreciate what you've done."

Trudy never had a real father. Her grandfather had been her closest father figure, but he was from an age where men left the raising of girls to women. She wondered if maybe Faust felt somewhat fatherly to girls in her kind of trouble. He did talk as if he did, even taking her side when Terrek left her. She had never been comfortable talking to older men. Maybe if she could think of him as fatherly, maybe she could be more comfortable with his offer to help. She decided to take Faust at face value. He was really trying to help her.

Saturday morning, the day Trudy agreed to go rummaging with Leslie, was also the first meteorological day of summer, but Milson was already in full summer bloom. Flower gardens and hanging planters adorned residences and business doorways. Restaurants offered outdoor seating with round patio tables blooming with colorful umbrellas. Summer, the season of color, is the glorious time of peach, lilac, pink, strawberry red, blueberry, and many bright hues wrapped inside the warm yellow envelope of the sun. Children, let loose from school, were out flying purple and green kites, riding bikes, blue streamers tailing on handlebars. Some were blowing rainbows of bubbles, all framed between beautiful pink dawns and orange sunsets. Now that the daylight hours were longer and the temperatures warmer, everyone seemed to emerge from hibernation.

Also outdoor rummage sales season, tables had been set up in driveways or front walks with the most elaborate assortment of goods: furniture, toys, dishes, mementos, and much more.

Leslie had scouted the rummage sales before Saturday, finding ads on supermarket bulletin boards or the local paper. She selected one where an entire neighborhood was participating. As they arrived, it all reminded Trudy of the medieval fairs in her Gothic novels, held outside the castle walls. Countryside folk sold crops and handmade crafts while buying silks and spices, enjoying the music of roving minstrels.

At first, Trudy just tagged along, taking in the sights as they moved from table to table, going house to house. Leslie's good mood was contagious. She explained the unwritten rule of rummaging: never seem too interested in an item, especially if it was one that you really wanted. She was keeping an eye out for gently used maternity clothes. At the fourth house, she found baby furniture and toys. She thought this might be a promising sign and was pleased to discover that indeed it was.

With two toddlers in tow, the seller had maternity clothing to sell. Leslie saw that the woman was about the same height as Trudy and probably about the same size before her babies were born. She had several boxes of maternity clothes. Leslie haggled over the price and finally offered twenty dollars for the whole lot. Trudy found this exchange embarrassing, but she noticed both the woman and Leslie were greatly satisfied with the result.

A good part of the morning had passed, so Leslie and Trudy took a break at a picnic table, enjoying lemonade and homemade cookies. They surveyed their purchases. One item was still missing, something white needed for work. Leslie pressed on to the other sites on her list. Finally, they succeeded in finding a white maternity outfit, a blouse to be worn over white polyester pants. The clothing was being sold by a registered nurse who worked at a hospital during her pregnancy. It would be perfect for Jackie's Counter.

At their last stop, an old maple rocking chair caught Trudy's eye. It was very nearly identical to the chair her grandmother had owned. Trudy remembered sitting in her lap, listening to Grimm's fairy tales while being gently rocked. Trudy told Leslie about her grandmother's chair and wondered what the price was for this one. She still had almost no furniture in her sparse apartment and plenty of room for the rocker. Leslie's eyes gleamed at the challenge to barter.

Trudy had the money from recovery of her clinic deposit and was overjoyed to hear the lady only wanted thirty dollars for the chair. But Leslie said it was too much for such an old rocker. That's the point, Trudy thought, old like grandmother's. Leslie sat in the chair and rocked it a bit while the lady reconsidered, and said she'd settle for twenty-five. Trudy was ecstatic. But Leslie said she'd have to think it over. She moved on to another table, pretending to look over other items.

Trudy kept staring at the rocking chair, and soon, another woman began to look it over. Trudy really wanted that rocker. She walked back and told the seller to mark it sold. She'd pay twenty-five dollars. Leslie shook her head, but she smiled at Trudy.

They tied the rocker onto the top of Leslie's Volkswagen Beetle. Leslie kept telling Trudy she overpaid for the rocker and likely could have gotten it cheaper if she hadn't jumped the gun like that. But Trudy was satisfied, happy to own it.

Since they had such good luck at the rummage sale, Trudy asked Leslie if they could complete their morning by going to the pawn shop so she could retrieve her grandmother's brooch. Trudy imagined herself sitting in the rocker with the brooch around her neck. It would give her much peace. Leslie readily agreed. They stopped at the apartment so that Trudy could retrieve her receipt and headed to the pawn shop with the rocker still tied on top.

Doc's shop was wide open, a heavy brick holding the door open. As Leslie and Trudy walked in, they realized the shop was sweltering. An old rotating floor fan was blowing down the aisle but did little more than circulate the warm air.

Doc was behind the teller's cage, seated just as before. He had removed his outer shirt, his sleeveless undershirt soaked in sweat. Trudy found him even more disgusting than last time with his kinky body hair coiling through the V-neck. The sweaty odor was nearly enough to make Trudy turn around as she felt a wave of nausea overtake her. If not for the brooch, she would have fled to the fresh air outside.

Trudy glanced at the glass cases, searching for her brooch and mentally comparing the plethora of items to the rummage sales they had walked through that morning. Lots of items for sale, but the similarity ended there. While the rummage sales seemed folksy and gay, the hock shop was dingy and dusty. The rummage sales were an occasional weekend frolic. This place would never cease to exist as long as there were homeless people, drug addicts, winos, and the poor. If this had been a Grimm's fairy tale, Doc would be a fat troll living under the toll bridge.

Doc was not in good humor, probably because of the heat. He looked up at Leslie and Trudy, removed the cigar butt from his mouth, and gruffly barked at them, asking what they wanted. Leslie spoke up, telling him they'd come to reclaim an item he was holding.

"What's the number?" Doc snarled.

Trudy pulled out her receipt and handed it to Leslie, who read the large red numbers at the top corner: 77223. Doc began looking through bin "2" and labeled "1977," reciting: "20, 21, 25," ending at 29. "Nope, 23 is not here."

"Look again," Leslie insisted. "It has to be there. The 90 days hasn't expired!"

Doc looked again, confirming that the item number was not in the bin and then glared at Leslie. Shouting, rebutted, "I NEVER PROMISE to hold anything 90 days."

"But you did—the receipt even spells it out. Right there at the top of the page."

Doc sneered at Leslie, "I hold it for UP TO 90 days in the shop, after which I dispose of it if I want and if it's not sold. Look at the fine print at the bottom. It's standard language."

Leslie and Trudy looked at the bottom of the receipt. Under the lines filled in with the handwritten notes describing the item, they found infinitesimally small print. It nearly required a magnifying glass to read. Leslie held it up closer.

"Merchandise will be held unsold for 30 days. After 90 days, bailsman is no longer responsible for merchandise not reclaimed."

"But you said 90 days!" protested Leslie.

"90 days is how long I keep it in my shop. I hold it for 30 days to be reclaimed, and if not, I can sell it if I get an offer. After 30 days, it becomes my choice to sell it if you haven't reclaimed it and if I get another offer. Obviously, someone else bought it after the 30 days expired."

Trudy's head was spinning. Her grandmother's brooch was gone, the pictures of her grandparents gone, her very last memento gone! With tears in her eyes, she choked out her question.

"Who did you sell it to?"

Doc's red boiler face finally blew. He began bellowing, "How the hell do I know! I sell hundreds of items week in and week out. I don't give a damn who bought it. You didn't reclaim it after 30 days. If that item was so valuable to you, why did YOU hock it. Both of you, GET THE HELL OUT! It's too hot for me to hold your hands and wipe your runny noses. Grow up and wise up."

Doc sat down, pushed his glasses back to the top of his head and picked at some gold watch parts, ignoring both young women, still standing in the aisle dumbstruck. They finally turned and left, unable to deal with Doc further and not knowing what else they could do.

On the sidewalk, Leslie told Trudy how sorry she was. Looking again at the receipt still in her hand, she tried to understand how Doc had tricked them. Trudy didn't respond. Through teary eyes, she gazed at Leslie's little car with the rocking chair tied to the roof. The car looked like a little turtle carrying the weight of the world on its small shell.

Later that evening and alone in her room, Trudy sat in the chair, rocking back and forth. She wished that she could regain the serenity of her grandmother rocking her before bedtime. As she rocked, trying to regain this equilibrium, Trudy felt kicking from deep inside her womb. She held her hand over the kicking, realizing that she was now the one doing the rocking—trying to give comfort to this new life coming into being from deep within the formless cosmos of life, new life with a new heartbeat seeking the rhythm.

Chapter 9

July 1977

Trudy dragged herself out of bed. Working would pass the time. It was all Trudy could do now. She'd decided to see Faust again and didn't want to think about her lost brooch. She noted only her numbness and her self-imposed abyss of indecision.

After work, she mindlessly walked over to his law office. Faust had just returned from his afternoon break at The Spot and smiled when he saw her. He knew she'd be back. Though she hadn't made an appointment, Faust greeted her cheerfully and welcomed her into his conference room, telling Jill to hold his calls.

With steely resolve, Trudy began, "I just want to know where I go from here. What do I do now?"

Faust sensed her urgency but also knew that Trudy needed to think through her options one step at a time, to feel she was making her own choices.

"As I said last week, you must instruct me—it's not the other way around."

"I know. I don't want to be pregnant, but I am; I can't just terminate the life of this little baby growing in me that's even kicking and letting me know he or she wants out someday, too."

Trudy placed her hand over her expanding waistline to show Faust she was feeling the baby kick.

"But I'm not ready to have one. I have no way to take care of a baby. I really wanted to go to college. I did for a little while, too. I loved my English class, and I hated dropping out. I used to wonder if I'd be smart enough to go to college. Now I think I could really do it. And not having any money to pay for tuition, I got through that, sort of. But not if I have to take care of a baby. I always make everything I do seem hard, like I'll never be able to do it. You helped me sort through my hit list—now I need to figure out where I'm going. You seem to make sense of it so easily, but…"

Trudy was doing all the talking, but now she stammered to a halt. This was as far as she had gotten in a rational, thought-out sense of where her life was heading.

"But now what?" she finally concluded.

Faust saved her the trouble of saying anything further. "Don't be so hard on yourself! You can still go to college if that is your dream. You've only suffered a setback, not an end."

"How?"

Faust took over. "List your choices from here, and how to make them work. I can help. You decided not to have an abortion; that's been your choice so far. Your dream is to go to college. Yet there is still something you never told me, and it's got to figure in here."

"What's that?" asked Trudy.

"Who is the father? You need to plan for the baby now that you've decided not to have an abortion. You have to consider this baby's father. There is no way around that, as much as you have tried to avoid it."

Trudy got quiet. She did not want anything to do with Terrek. Why should she? He had abandoned her when she told him about being pregnant. At first, she was hurt, but now Faust's words were making her angry. It was already Terrek's choice not to help with his child.

Why was she being forced to consider him? Terrek hadn't considered her needs.

Trudy decided she really did not want to talk about him and repeated her earlier lie.

"I don't know who he is, I told you that."

"Come on, Trudy, I know that's not true. You are a nice girl, and I have dealt with many pregnant girls; I know you are not someone who is promiscuous, someone who sleeps around. You know the father, and probably quite well, too. Tell me who he is."

Trudy had done her best to put all of this out of mind. Remembering the last time she saw Terrek, she began to tear up. He'd made her feel cheap and dirty, his words just the opposite of Faust's judgment. Terrek claimed she did sleep around and with lots of other guys, and that he was not responsible for her pregnancy. The sense of abandonment washed over her again, and she began to cry.

Faust observed her changing emotions and adopted a sympathetic tone, comforting her like a parent. Gently, he asked her to tell him about this boy, saying he wanted to help, but that she'd need to tell him about the baby's father.

The floodgates opened. Trudy told Faust about Terrek. Faust guided her along, asking a few questions but letting Trudy do most of the telling of her story. She explained how they met at the café where she worked, how Terrek had taken her to campus, showed her around, included her in social events with his friends—football games, hanging out at the student union, college activities. She talked about how handsome Terrek was, how lucky he was to have his parents pay for school. She described the adventures in his Jeep, the fun of being with him. She explained how he started coming to meet her after work, that it was Terrek who'd helped her think she could be part of campus life, go to college. It was all part of her dream.

She told Faust about the Christmas holiday, how she did not go home but stayed in town, working and enrolling to start school the second semester. It had been her happiest time in Milson.

"Trudy, tell me how you became intimate?"

Trudy had never discussed this with anyone, not even Leslie. She stopped, not knowing what to say. Faust assured her everything was confidential.

"Did he force you?" Trudy shook her head, no.

"It began with just holding hands, which moved on to kissing, then he started to come into my apartment. But I'd always told him that I was not ready to have an intimate relationship, that going to college was my dream. Terrek had said he respected that, and he'd never forced himself on me."

Trudy then described the trip to Auto Paradise and Terrek's limo, which he called his International Headquarters, which had seemed like a palace room for a princess in her daydreams. She told Faust how they'd celebrated the New Year with champagne and music. Trudy remembered the Dylan song, "Lay Lady Lay," but she skipped describing those details.

"I was not being careful, not after the champagne. I was so stupid, just another fairy tale gone bad. But no, he did not force me."

Faust was a bit confused, and even a little amused at how this guy had set this up, but he kept his expression serious. "Is Auto Paradise a junkyard, then?"

"Yes, I got pregnant in a junkyard. My grandfather would have said I was used goods being sold cheap."

The thought of her grandparents set her off crying again. This story would have been impossible to tell her grandmother. Her disappointment would have been more than Trudy could ever bear. But her grandmother had passed. There was no one who cared anymore. She was totally alone, and she was talking about her most private thoughts with a lawyer of all people. Her grandmother would never have let Trudy do this alone. But this was her reality, now.

Faust was kind. He went to get her a glass of water himself, not wanting Jill to interrupt them now. He brought a box of tissue so Trudy could wipe her eyes. He began again, gently.

"Trudy, you are being very hard on yourself—give yourself a break, just this once! You did not intend to get pregnant, and under those circumstances, New Year's Eve celebration, semester break—besides, it takes two, so stop taking all this on yourself. Tell me more about Terrek, do you know where he is now?"

Trudy composed herself, sipping the water, wiping her eyes, somehow feeling some relief getting all this out. She told Faust what she knew about Terrek, how he resented his father and all the big plans that his father had for the recycling center and starting a new business. She related how Terrek had dropped out or flunked out of school, that he did not tell his parents. But as to where he was now, she really didn't know. She told Faust Terrek had plans to go to California, but she did not know if he had actually made the move.

"Where did he plan to go in California, did he say?"

"Terrek was so unrealistic," replied Trudy. "He was just running away, in my opinion. He talked about hanging out on the beach, surfing. But I knew it wasn't an actual plan. I knew being real wasn't being a beach bum. I couldn't just run off like that, no real planning. Before he knew of my pregnancy, he kept telling me to quit my job and run off with him."

"After I knew I was pregnant, I decided to burst his bubble. I just dumped it on him, telling him I was pregnant. He didn't take it well. He didn't want to hear that and accused me of sleeping around. That's when I kicked him out and told him I never wanted to see him again. I haven't seen him since. I really don't know where he is."

Faust gave Trudy a few moments to gather herself. He spoke slowly and kindly, "Terrek's reaction was not that unusual. Terrek's young, just a year out of high school. His actions were immature." Faust added, "He did what most immature, confused guys do. They run."

Faust stressed to Trudy, "Don't let Terrek's nasty accusations reflect on how you feel about yourself. You're way more mature than Terrek. You're actually dealing with this." Trudy merely listened, nodding in agreement. It was a relief to hear an older man explain that this boy was immature, but it was still folly for her.

"Can you see now, why Terrek can't be a part of any decision that I make?" Trudy asked.

Faust smiled, "Okay, let's move on today as if you had just walked into my office, and I didn't know anything about you other than a request to hear your legal options spelled out."

Trudy nodded. Going back to the starting point, Faust reiterated, "One, get an abortion. Two, get married and raise this baby as a family with a mother and father. Three, don't get married, be a single mother with the father helping to pay child support. Four, get temporary care for the baby in some type of placement until you are ready to assume parental care, and lots more but we'll keep it simple for now. Five, give the child up to be adopted by parents that are ready to assume parenting."

"This is very sketchy, but it gives you a summary. If you do keep your baby, the father must at least pay support. He has other rights, but let's keep this focus on your choices. Once you decide, I can inform you what else remains. Okay?"

Trudy appreciated this approach. If she hadn't been mulling over all her hurt and turmoil, the uncertainty of it all, she might have been clearer about the ultimate question.

"I really have only two choices now. I keep my baby or I don't."

Faust agreed. He explained that if she chose to keep the baby, she would no longer need his services, and he would refer her to a family planning clinic for assistance. If she chose adoption, his office could help.

"You're near the end of your second trimester and need to make a decision soon," Faust emphasized.

Trudy nodded but added, "If I do keep the baby, Terrek has to be involved, right?"

"Yes, you both have the same rights as parents, and you both must be responsible for the baby."

"And if I decide on adoption, Terrek just has to go along? Or what?"

"Good question. If you decide to let this baby be adopted, both you and the father must have your rights terminated by a court. As I said, both parents have the same rights to be a parent. Hearing you describe how Terrek acted, most boys like that just sign off on their legal rights and never have any more to do with the adoption."

"And Terrek could disagree?"

"Yes, but until you decide, these are all unanswered questions. Look, Trudy, make your own decision. Don't think about Terrek's rights for now."

Trudy stood up. It had been a long conference. "I'd like to think about this. You really helped me today. Thank you."

Faust knew Trudy was done for the day. He was disappointed that she still hadn't decided. But he knew that Trudy was a careful person; it would be a mistake to push her now. On her way out, Faust reminded Trudy she was scheduled for another well-baby check-up with Dr. Wellstein. Jill normally accompanied her, but he asked if she thought she could go alone this time and then come back next week with her decision.

"You need a deadline, Trudy. This gives you a week. You can talk to your doctor again if you want. Can we set up an appointment for next week after your appointment?"

Trudy hesitated, not knowing if she'd be able to decide in a week. Trudy flinched suddenly; the baby was kicking harder and harder. It was as if the baby wanted to kick her into reality. Trudy agreed: decision to be made by next week. Faust called Jill in with his appointment book, and their next appointment was scheduled.

Trudy spent a nearly sleepless night tossing in bed. She could not get comfortable, and her thoughts kept racing around the baby decision. How could she make a life-altering decision when nothing was known—a girl or boy, smart or talented, healthy or colicky or worse— it was all a blank slate.

Trudy headed to work. She kept promising herself that she'd decide later, after work. As her work shift was nearly over, Marna came into Jackie's Counter, sitting down on her usual stool. Trudy finished cleaning for the day, and Jackie served her a bowl of ham and potato soup, the day's homemade special.

"Trudy, will you come up to my apartment just for a few minutes after you finish eating? I promise not to keep you too long," Marna asked.

Trudy was caught off-guard by the unexpected question. She'd never been to Marna's apartment, although she knew that Marna lived upstairs in the small unit to the back of the building while Mac and Jackie lived in the front unit. Trudy agreed, knowing she couldn't turn down Marna's kindness. Jackie treated Marna like family, and Trudy had learned to be as respectful as her boss. Marna went upstairs while Trudy finished lunch. After eating, Trudy walked up the back stairway and knocked on Marna's apartment door.

"Thank you for coming up. I have something to give you." Marna handed her a white box tied with a pink ribbon and bow. Trudy barely had time to look around the small kitchen as Marna led her to the table and asked her to sit down to open the box. Trudy did as asked, sitting at the tiny round table, holding the box.

"It's for you—go ahead and open it," Marna prompted.

Trudy felt self-conscious but complied with the directions. She quietly opened the box, carefully untying the ribbon and cautiously lifting the top cover. White tissue paper wrapped the contents, and Trudy slowly lifted the tissue. Inside, she found a beautiful white blouse. Trudy pulled the garment out. It was intricately woven linen that almost felt like silk. Recognizing the hand-sewn stitching so like her grandmother's handiwork, she unfolded the blouse. It was skill-fully decorated with mother-of-pearl buttons and lace threaded with a pink ribbon around the collar with a tatted edge for threading the ribbon. It was amazingly beautiful and delicately feminine. Holding the blouse up, Trudy saw that it had a billowing hem. It would be a perfect maternity blouse.

"Marna, it is beautiful—it is too fine for me to wear!" Trudy commented without thinking, simply saying what she felt.

Marna smiled gently and spoke with her old-world accent, "No, you are just as wonderful as any young mother that bears a child. You should have a special place because of this. Think of yourself in this way."

"I haven't felt beautiful," Trudy confided.

"I could tell by the way you hung your head. I want you to have this pretty feminine blouse so you know that you are beautiful. I wish I could do more." Trudy sat speechless and near tears.

Stepping closer, Marna hugged Trudy. "What else can I do to help?" she asked, adding, "I hope you don't mind, I asked Jackie to come up—we both would like to offer our help. You don't say much."

Almost on cue, Jackie knocked quietly on the back door and walked in without waiting. She saw the blouse and asked Trudy to hold it up. For a few minutes, the three women talked about how lovely the blouse was, admiring Marna's fine tatting and needlework.

Trudy smiled through tears, embarrassed by all the unexpected attention. Jackie picked up on what Marna had been saying when she came in, asking again how they both might help her.

"I know I'll miss work. You may need to get some new help, and…"

Jackie cut Trudy's words short. "I'm not talking about restaurant work. How can we help you? What will you do with a baby?"

Trudy wasn't prepared to talk with her boss about this. She was still grappling with all of it herself. But she answered, "I haven't decided. I've narrowed it down to two choices. Attorney Faust has been advising me."

Jackie frowned. Marna, looking confused, asked, "What do you mean, Trudy?"

"Oh, Marna, I haven't even thanked you. This maternity blouse is beautiful. It is so much finer than my rummage sale clothing. I know I must look like I don't care how I look. But you are so thoughtful!"

Jackie steered the conversation back, picking up Trudy's words. She asked, "What choices?" Trudy hesitated and then simply answered, "I don't know if I will keep the baby or allow the baby to be adopted. I'm still talking this over with the attorney."

Jackie remembered Faust. It sent a chill down her spine. She wondered what he was up to and how he came into the picture to advise Trudy, who had no money. But she could also see that Trudy was reluctant to talk with her. She had come upstairs because Marna wanted to give her something. Jackie genuinely wanted to help, but Trudy had not asked for help or advice. She knew that Trudy saw her as a boss, not as a friend she could turn to for help.

Trudy focused on Marna: "You remind me of my grandmother. I don't mean because she was older, but because she was kind." Touched by her words, Marna encouraged her. "You will do what is right for your child. A mother always does. Deciding to keep your baby can never be wrong. Nature already determined this for you."

Trudy smiled warmly at Marna, sounding so much like her grandmother in everything she said. But she believed that neither Marna nor Jackie understood what she'd been going through these last six-plus months.

An unexpected voice began shouting from the bottom of the stairs: "I could walk off with every penny in this cash drawer!"

Jackie rushed downstairs at the familiar voice of Mac reminding her that no one was watching her restaurant after she had forgotten to lock the front door. "With the paltry prices that I charge, there's not enough money to make it worth anyone's effort!"

Marna and Trudy burst out laughing. Trudy turned to Marna to thank her again before leaving and this time warmly returned Marna's hug. Trudy knew she was surrounded by good, hard-working folks as her grandfather would have judged them. Trudy stepped out the back door at the bottom of the landing without going into the restaurant or talking further to Jackie.

At home, Trudy was glad to catch an afternoon nap since she had not slept well the night before. The hearty soup meal had also made her sleepy. On rising, Trudy sat in her rocker thinking over Marna's words of wisdom that a mother always does what is right for her baby. Marna had put this in a way that Trudy had never before considered. How would a mother choose? The rocking provided an orderliness to her thought process.

The baby needs a mother who will do what is right. Trudy's perspective was changing, not just what was right for her, but for this little life. As she considered this, Trudy remembered the appointment with Faust the following week. She knew he expected her to make a final decision.

After work on the next day, Trudy walked into the reception area of Faust's office with new resolve. Jill was surprised to see her and asked if Trudy had a problem, her appointment wasn't until the following week. Trudy assured her that there was nothing *else* wrong.

"Could Attorney Faust step out to talk ? It won't take long," she promised. Jill began to put her off, telling her Faust had another client. Just then, another young, pregnant girl walked out of the inner office with Faust. Trudy overheard Faust tell the young girl she would not regret choosing adoption.

When Faust saw Trudy, a look of irritation crossed his face. He instructed her to go sit in his office and turned to escort the pregnant girl to the outer door. When he returned, he was rather short, "Your appointment is set for next week."

Trudy responded, "I won't take much time, I know that my appointment is next week, but I came to cancel it. But I wanted to thank you. You spent a lot of time helping me."

Faust sat silently. He finally spoke and not with the friendliness Trudy had come to expect from him.

"I'm going to ask you not to cancel that appointment. I know you may think that you've reached some decision. But I also know, from many years of counseling, you may also feel differently tomorrow. Keep your appointment, go see the doctor, think this through, come back as planned, and then we will see if you've really made a final decision. Can you do that much, Trudy, after all the time you and I have spent on this?"

Trudy resented Faust was making this about *his* time. But he stressed one week would not change anything for now. After a long, difficult pause, Trudy finally agreed. She'd come back next week for her scheduled appointment.

After Trudy left, Faust got on the intercom and told Jill to get Tony Papia from New York on the phone. After a few minutes, Jill reported that she was able to get Maria, but not her husband. Faust was annoyed. He'd have to talk with the wife.

"Maria, I'm going to have to ask you to delay your flight. Next weekend is going to be too soon."

"What's wrong?" Maria was nearly shouting, her voice shrill.

"The young woman is hesitating right now, and I'll need more time."

"Do you know how frustrating this is for us! Tony will be disappointed. I'm going to get him to call you back—I can't talk about this anymore!"

Maria hung up without a goodbye. Faust shook his head, thinking these wealthy, East Coast clients were always the worst—pushy, demanding, and expecting everything their way.

After just a few minutes, Jill's voice came over the intercom to say that Tony Papia was now on the line.

Faust picked up the phone, and without getting a word out, a deep male voice with a New York accent took over:

"Hal, do you know how frustrating this is for Maria? What's going on, now?"

Faust explained again that the mother was hesitating and that he needed more time. "Just wait a few more weeks. It's important not to rush this meeting."

"Let me tell you something, Hal. This waiting is driving Maria insane, do you hear me? First, she can't have a baby. We had years of going to the doctor. Then she finally decides to adopt, I thought we were over the worst. Now this adoption is turning into another roller coaster. I want you to get this done. You came highly recommended even though you're out of state. I am not going to watch Maria get disappointed again."

"I am only asking for a few more weeks. If you push at the wrong time, the mother will bolt. I know my work," replied Faust.

"Well, what's it going to take?" demanded Tony.

Faust sat back and smiled. He could hear desperation. He now had the upper hand. "It will take more time and more money," Faust replied.

"How much more time?"

"Give me another two weeks," replied Faust. "I have the mother coming in next week, I'll give her intensive counseling."

"And how much more money? I've already paid a hundred thousand. I expect results for that kind of money."

"Another ten thousand for now," replied Faust.

"Damn it, I'll pay, but if you screw this up, I'll ruin you. You won't have a law license when I'm done with you. Do you hear me?"

Faust loved these threats. He knew that when a party begins to threaten, it meant they had no real alternatives left. But Faust was conciliatory:

"Tony, you have my word, we'll get this done. But you have to work with me, I'm just asking for two weeks. I'll call you next week, and we will set a new date for you to come in."

Tony was still not happy, complaining that he'd now have to deal with his unhappy wife for two more weeks, but he finally agreed to wait and ended the call. Faust buzzed Jill and asked her to remind him of Trudy's next appointment, date, and time. As she responded, he merely smiled, thinking this could be better for him in the long run.

Chapter 10

August 1977

The hot weeks of summer ran like melted butter down the streets of the city, sticky and sweltering. Insects from the surrounding farmlands swarmed into the city, having fertilized the harvest and reproduced exponentially. The life cycle of summer was nearing fulfillment.

Trudy found the heat particularly uncomfortable, unable to sleep well at night and never able to find comfort during the day. Her body weight had shifted her center of balance, making her unusually uncoordinated. Worse, she had never felt so embarrassed about her appearance, so she sought anonymity, staying inside her apartment except when working. At work, she tried to hide in her corner near the sinks. Jackie sensed her need and left her alone.

Marna came in on Monday after church and tried to cheer her up. Trudy smiled at her, largely to put Marna at ease. Her appointment with Faust later in the week was all she could think about. As Trudy neared the end of her shift, Jackie insisted she have soup and a sandwich before leaving.

After Trudy left, Jackie talked with Marna about the gift to Trudy, wishing it would have allowed them to learn more about Trudy's plans. It was hard to get Trudy to open up. Still in the dark, Jackie had thought all weekend and finally asked Mac to delay his weekly trucking run for a day or so. She asked him to come down when she closed, knowing Marna would also be present. Almost on cue, Mac walked through the back as Jackie locked the front entrance door and placed the closed sign in the door window.

"We need to try to help Trudy, somehow."

Jackie explained her worries about the attorney Trudy had mentioned. What was his involvement with Trudy? She had hoped Trudy might tell them more today, but Trudy had been even quieter than usual.

"I could go out and find this kid that's supposed to be the father, corral him, hog-tie him, make him take on his responsibilities."

"No, Trudy's been abandoned by him, that's obvious even though she doesn't talk about it, and if it is who I think it is, it's just as well. That might be the best thing that's happened to her."

"Well, you're bein' pretty rough on men today, I better watch myself," quipped Mac.

He knew about the kid who'd been hanging around the counter but hadn't thought much about it other than the kid waited around for Trudy.

"This is no time for joking, Mac. This is serious."

Marna asked, "Well, what can we do, what do you have in mind?"

Mac was impatient, wanting to get to the point: "You gonna' let Trudy keep workin' here after she has that baby?"

"Of course she can. And we can accommodate a newborn for a while, too, but then she'll need to find some childcare."

"That's the spirit," cheered Mac. "Have you made that offer to Trudy?"

"No," Jackie hesitated.

"I could offer to rock the baby if it's fussy," said Marna. "I could ask Mac to bring my rocking chair down from my apartment while the new baby is here. Maybe, you'd allow me to put my rocker in the back room. Trudy could nurse if she is planning to breastfeed, or I can even help with giving the baby a bottle. Then I could gently rock the baby to sleep."

"I'll carry that rocker down right now, if you like," quipped Mac. "Look, Jackie, you have to be direct with Trudy! Make this offer to her. We can all help!"

Marna smiled broadly, thinking about how having a baby around would add life to her slow routine. "I'd treasure such a time. Young women never understand how precious these few months can be. It takes a lifetime of experience to know how quickly everything moves on. Before you know it, the baby is a toddler and then running off to play with other children, and then all grown up."

Jackie, Mac, and Marna sat for a while lost in daydreams about how they might help. Mac agreed to stay in town one more day. Jackie wanted all of them to show Trudy how they could help. It seemed clear that Trudy would probably not bring this matter up herself without some prompting. After Marna's gift, Trudy just ran off, unwilling to talk further. Jackie knew she'd have to take the lead on offering to help, and she felt supported now that all three of them agreed to help, to figure it out as they went along.

Mac summed it up: "Well, woman, that's part of your problem, Trudy's not a mind reader! You've got to talk to her. And if it's money she needs, short term, I can help with that, too!"

Jackie was proud of Mac for offering. He was a good man, and he helped her think things through, as did Marna, but in a different way. Jackie resolved to talk with Trudy and offer to help.

At work the next day, Jackie and Trudy worked efficiently through the lunch hour. Trudy was somber and quiet, but they were a good team, keeping the lunch hour rush running smoothly. As Jackie began to clean up, she got Trudy a bowl of the chicken dumpling soup.

Trudy was always grateful, making this her main meal of the day. But today, when Jackie asked her to stay after closing, telling her that she would like to talk, Trudy became nervous.

Both Marna and Mac came in just as Jackie was locking the door. Trudy had finished her lunch and, as she looked up, wondered why Mac was still in town. This was unusual. She stood to clear her soup bowl, but Jackie took it from her and asked her to sit down again. Jackie cleaned meticulously while talking; she needed to keep moving. Trudy, already anxious, noticed that Jackie also seemed nervous.

Without wasting a single working moment, Jackie sprayed the counter with a bleach solution and started to wipe away the cooking grease, all the while talking almost faster than Trudy could listen. Jackie began describing how a baby could sleep in the back room between feedings. Mac would carry Marna's rocking chair down, and all three of them could rock the baby when awake.

Marna picked up on Jackie's narrative and told Trudy the baby would be a joy to rock. Jackie described a perfect little spot in the back corner for a little bassinet. As Jackie cleaned the mirrors, she explained how caring for a newborn might work as the baby slept; when she got a little older, they might even bring in a small swing for the baby. The white tile began to glisten, and the mirrors sparkled.

Trudy took a few moments before she understood what Jackie and Marna were telling her. They were trying to envision how to help with her baby here at Jackie's Counter.

"You can look in on your baby as often as needed. We'll make it work," offered Jackie.

Trudy was deeply touched. She never dared to think about asking for anything like this. The baby had always been just her *problem*, but Marna kept calling her baby a blessing, not a problem. She didn't know what to say.

Mac finally spoke up, "If you want me to go out and find your guy, just give me the word. I'll go hog-tie him and bring him in!"

Jackie gave Mac a dirty look and piped in, "Trudy's too good for him!"

But Mac held his ground, addressing Trudy, "Just give me the word."

With tears in her eyes, Trudy laughed nervously, "No, Mac. Thanks for offering, but I don't want Terrek around, not now."

Jackie knew her suspicions were correct. The father was that brash, young college guy who had been hanging around. He had abandoned Trudy when she got pregnant. Marna took Trudy's hand when she saw the tears and told her they wanted to help. Jackie followed Marna's lead, stopped cleaning, and implored Trudy to let them think through how they might help once her baby comes.

After nearly an hour of making plans for a baby at the restaurant, Trudy left. Her head was spinning. She had a lot to think about. At home, washing her working clothes and hanging them to dry in her small bathroom shower, Trudy considered the new offer and wondered what Leslie might think. She had always been a good sounding board and always seemed to think of new angles that Trudy had never even considered.

Trudy knocked on the poster covering Leslie's door to see if she was home. Leslie had just returned from summer break. She was just getting out of the shower as she opened her door. She was happy to see Trudy, noting how pregnant she now looked. Leslie told Trudy to come in while she finished drying her hair.

Trudy looked around at the furniture in the room as Leslie finished, trying to imagine the rummage sales that had produced such a hodgepodge. Trudy then considered whether a bassinet or crib might be available—Leslie would be just the one to help find them.

Trudy began excitedly, sharing with Leslie the new ideas she had talked over with Jackie, Marna, and Mac at the counter. After she finished describing how they envisioned the early months with a new baby, Leslie sat down on her bed opposite Trudy.

Trudy explained that she had another appointment with Faust the next day and was supposed to think through her final decision, keep the baby or give the baby up for adoption.

"It's crunch time," Trudy explained. "But now that my boss has offered to help, I'm leaning toward keeping the baby.

"What do you think? You've always been able to help me think through my options."

"It sounds like an awful lot of hard work: you will be a single mom, work all day and then come home to a small apartment and care for your baby all day and night. A baby does not sleep through the night, you do know this, don't you? Then, you'll probably not be able to go back to school, or if you somehow did, you'd wear yourself out."

Trudy was disappointed that Leslie wasn't sharing her enthusiasm, but she was not going to be easily discouraged.

"I'm not afraid of hard work, that's always been part of my life."

"But are you being realistic? Little kids get sick a lot, runny noses, teething, earaches. You have no help so everything is on you. Trudy, if your real dream, which you always told me was your dream, is to go to college, there could be another way."

"What way?" wondered Trudy.

"Don't work, Keep your baby if you want, but go back to school."

"How would I pay my rent, food, and all my other bills?"

"You get assistance. There are programs for women that have an unplanned pregnancy. Talk to the counselors, Trudy, they can tell you about Aid to Families with Dependent Children, even childcare options. Look, I'm no expert on this stuff, but I know several of the women in VOW who applied for benefits, go to school, keep their babies. They don't work."

"Of course, you'd have to quit your job. You can't get benefits if you're working and earning money."

Trudy didn't like this idea; it went against everything she had been taught. Her grandfather had refused to cash his Social Security checks, calling them a government plot to make everyone dependent on handouts. Her grandmother had quietly opened an account and deposited them without ever spending that money. Her grandfather kept guns around, saying he'd fight off all the freeloaders when the economy collapsed because everyone had forgotten how to work. After grandfather died, her grandmother used that money to pay the estate taxes so her son wouldn't lose the family farm.

"Both my grandparents always told me, you don't get something for nothing." Leslie just shook her head. Trudy's grandparents were living in the past, and most people don't live on farms anymore. She pointed out that women no longer have shotgun weddings anymore, either.

"I'm going to do what feels right for me," insisted Trudy.

"Okay, it's your right." Leslie added, "But at least consider filling out an application for benefits. You can always change your mind later."

Trudy thanked Leslie for listening and for giving her more to think over. She was glad Leslie was back in town and then remembered the other reason she wanted to see Leslie. She asked her to go to another rummage sale. Leslie liked the idea and readily agreed.

After work the next day, Trudy was supposed to keep the appointment with Faust, but she talked herself out of keeping it. She had gone last week and thanked him for his time and advice. That's enough, she concluded. With Jackie's offer to help, she didn't want Faust to take over her planning.

Instead, Trudy walked through campus and over to the VOW office. She looked through the front window to see if Leslie was inside. Not finding her, she went next door into the family planning clinic. She made a beeline directly to the display pamphlets. The receptionist looked up and asked if she could help. Trudy picked up the AFDC brochure and asked if she could get an application. Noting her advanced pregnancy, the receptionist selected the required application and financial disclosure form that Trudy would need and gave her the paperwork.

Trudy headed back to her apartment, thinking that had been easy enough. There was so much to think through. She hoped looking over the financial application would help to organize her thoughts. Suddenly, her baby kicked, causing her to stop. The baby's kick was getting stronger and nearly took her breath away, it was so emphatic! She smiled, quietly telling the baby to just wait a little while longer, she needed to get some planning in place.

As Trudy walked into her apartment building nearing dusk, she was startled by a shadowy figure—her eyes had not yet adjusted from outside to the darker hallway. She stumbled slightly just as Attorney Faust emerged from the hallway shadows. His unexpected appearance frightened her, almost as if he had materialized from the ether. Trudy stood speechless.

"Trudy, you missed your appointment today. Not good! You're so close to your baby's due date. It's important to stay in close contact these last few weeks."

Trudy did not reply. Faust stood firmly, staring at her, and finally suggested they go into her apartment to talk. She reluctantly complied, walked down the hallway, and unlocked her door. Faust followed. Inside, he motioned Trudy to the rocking chair as if he owned the place.

"What were you thinking, Trudy? Why didn't you come in as we agreed?"

Trudy began to rock slowly. She unconsciously reached for her brooch; it was not there.

Trudy finally answered Faust, "I'm keeping my baby."

Faust looked down at her, still standing, "Okay, it's your decision. I've always told you that."

He continued, changing tactics, "Look, if you're upset that I couldn't spend more time with you when you came in last week, I want you to remember that I was not expecting you. I do have other clients. You do know that. But that doesn't mean I'm not concerned or have stopped wanting to help you. I really want to know if you've thought all this through completely. Trudy, have you?"

Trudy did not want to have Faust help her think this through. She didn't want to follow along this time.

"You should leave. I'm sorry that I let you in. I know I have a lot to think over, and I don't need to talk with you while I'm doing it.

Faust sat down on the edge of Trudy's bed and began slowly, "Have you really looked at all the requirements for keeping the baby? I know you have no family to help you here."

Trudy was transfixed by Faust's gaze. In the dimly lit room, his eyes appeared yellow, like a predatory wolf about to pounce on his prey. Trudy could not take her own eyes from his. She felt like a trapped animal waiting for him to pounce. If only Faust would divert his stare, just for a moment, she could make her move, escape from the room. An involuntary spasm ran through her body as she pushed farther back in the rocker.

Faust continued, "You need to be seeing the doctor weekly now. We need to get you booked for the final weeks. I know you haven't done any of that. Trudy. I know you haven't made real plans for these final weeks."

Trudy tried to hold her ground. "I have a plan: Jackie and Mac will help me.."

Faust narrowed his gaze. "And the delivery? Your medical care? Who gets you to the hospital when contractions start? And then home again after the baby is born? And gets everything the baby will need?"

Faust stopped and finally looked around the room, diverting his gaze, but the trap had been sprung. Trudy began to consider his points. She watched him look around her room, knowing there was nothing here for baby care. He made her nervous, and she knew his points were legitimate concerns.

"Dr. Wellstein has been giving you excellent care, but he never agreed to deliver your baby. Did you ever think to discuss that with him?"

Trudy merely shook her head no, looking down so that Faust could not see her tears.

"The actual delivery needs planning, a hospital has to be notified, informed of your approximate due date, and quite frankly, how they get paid."

Faust looked back at Trudy and leaned forward, "Yes, we do need to talk money, now. Not for me, I told you that you would not need to pay for my time; but the hospital, they are a business, you know. They will need to know how your bill will be paid if they are going to reserve a room for your delivery.

"Trudy, I know you aren't thinking about money and entering into a contract with the hospital, but this is a fact and must be considered. I'm sorry. I want to help, but you can't just avoid all this because you've suddenly decided you don't want to come in and talk about it."

"Then there's the baby. The baby has to have a doctor. Did you think about any of this, Trudy?"

Faust kept repeating her name, the same way he did when she first called the hotline number. He possessed her name.

"Well, did you, Trudy? Did you get a doctor for your baby?"

Trudy's tears flowed freely down her cheeks as she mumbled, "No!"

Faust gave Trudy a moment and then continued with his voice gentle now: "How will you pay for everything? It's getting late and your baby is going to have many needs."

"I don't know!" Trudy sobbed.

She felt crushed. Earlier today, everything seemed to be falling in place. She thought she had plans! How could she have missed so many obvious points? Even Leslie had not brought up any of this, and she could usually count on Leslie to be an honest voice.

Trudy gathered her courage and tried one more time. "Maybe I can get some assistance; I went for some applications today."

"Maybe?" scoffed Faust.

Taking the upper hand as if her father, Faust became the adult talking to a child.

"Sure, there's government assistance out there. But are you thinking about what's best for your baby? Do you think a welfare patient gets the same medical treatment as a private pay case? Faust pronounced "government assistance" as if it was roadkill, something even a predator would not want. He continued. "Are you even considering the welfare of the baby? Do you want to have your baby at County

General, where they put you in a ward, not even a real hospital room? Don't you want better care than that for your baby?"

"How would I get better care?" Trudy saw there was no escape. There never really was.

"The baby gets that care by having the money to pay for it, that's how. This is how the world works. People get what they pay for—you should know that."

Trudy could hear her grandfather's voice: *"You get what you pay for."*

"There's more, Trudy. The baby needs a good home with a full nursery, a family life, a mother and a father, a good education—the best of everything. At least if you care about your baby, that's what most parents want."

Tears rolled down Trudy's cheeks. She looked around her tiny apartment, realizing how pathetic it all looked for bringing home a new baby.

Faust watched her. He knew she was helpless, and he said softly, "Trudy, please, let me help you."

"What do I do now?" she pleaded.

"Come with me; you shouldn't be alone in your last weeks. You need someone to be around now. Pack a few things in an overnight bag. I'm going to take you to a safe place; it will be safe for you and your baby."

Trudy gathered a few items, a night gown, personal items, a toothbrush, just basics. It took only a few minutes. Faust waited, took the small suitcase from her hand, and told her to follow him. They left the small apartment, turning off the lights. Trudy didn't look back.

Driving out of town in Faust's XKE, Trudy remembered her two previous trips away: the first in December in Terrek's Jeep, an adventure with all her hopes and dreams before her. The second, in Mac's sidecar as if in a parade, celebrating the start of summer. Now it was night, the oncoming headlights blurred through her tears, and Trudy did not know what nightmare awaited her, much less where Faust was taking her. Trudy thought about the disparities of each trip: from a Jeep to a Harley classic sidecar, to an expensive European sportscar, all transportation dictated by the choices of men. Trudy walked everywhere she wanted to go.

After nearly an hour, they turned off the interstate onto single-lane county road and then onto a dirt road built for logging. Finally the Jaguar turned into a packed dirt driveway and stopped next to a log cabin. A dimly lit path led to the side door. Faust took Trudy inside and led her to a small bedroom suite. He would stay with her through the night, and they would talk further in the morning.

Trudy awoke, surprised she had actually slept through the night in a strange bed in a strange place. She had not slept through the night in a long time. She was stiff and struggled to get to her feet. She went into the small bathroom inside this suite and then dressed before venturing out of the room.

Still not fully awake and terribly hungry, Trudy wandered around inside the cabin. Faust was gone. In the kitchen, she drank a glass of water and found a note propped up on a saltshaker on top the kitchen table: *Getting coffee and supplies, back soon.*

Trudy stared out the window over the kitchen sink. Pine trees surrounded the cottage. In a clearing, a narrow path led to a little lake amid the Jack Pines. A single pier jutted out over the water. She was drawn outside, where the smell of pine scotch hung in the late summer air. The juncos and thrushes were singing sweetly. The sunrise over the lake was so lovely that Trudy could not help but walk to the shoreline and out onto the pier, trying to get closer to the dawn.

A few clumps of white birch leaned out from the shore. The lake surface appeared more mirror than the surface water. No wind penetrated through the forest. The lake reflected each bough in repeating shapes as if lying flat on the still water. The vision was so intoxicating that Trudy lost herself in the mirrored images.

She walked to the end of the little pier, struggling with her off-centered weight. Lowering her body, she managed sit on the end to dangle her bare feet in the water. Unknown to Trudy, a yellow Labrador retriever had been standing on the shore just behind the pier. The dog cocked her head waiting for the human to move. The Lab finally gave a quiet, gentle hum-like whiny sound and ventured closer to Trudy, putting her nose into the air to catch the human's scent. Her tail wagged as she recognized the scent of a non-threatening female.

The Lab could wait no longer for the human's invitation and trotted out to the end of the pier, approaching carefully. As the dog approached within six inches of Trudy's back, Trudy remained absorbed in her thoughts, failing to note the dog's presence. The Lab whined softly and Trudy finally became present to the moment. The dog immediately sensed the sadness, she lowered her head as a gesture of submission. Trudy, long accustomed to farm dogs, understood the Lab's body language. She reached out her own hand to make acquaintance and then patted the back of the dog's neck. Their greeting complete, the Lab licked Trudy's tear-stained face as if trying to help cure these ails.

Trudy heard the Jaguar's wheels coming down the logging road and struggled to get to her feet. The dog heard the car as well and ran off back into the forest. Faust got out of his car carrying a large grocery bag in one hand and a carton of drinks in the other. Steam rose from the hot coffee.

"Good morning!" yelled Faust. "Lovely day for sitting on the pier, isn't it?"

Trudy did not respond, but she wiped her eyes and walked toward the cabin. She was hungry and hoped Faust brought breakfast. Faust greeted her warmly, asking how she had slept. Trudy didn't feel the need for a little chit-chat and responded curtly, "Fine."

"I'll make some eggs and bacon if you like; here's some coffee."

Trudy winced. She didn't drink coffee anymore, not since her morning sickness. But Faust remained cheerful, getting her a glass of water instead, frying up eggs and bacon and putting bread in the toaster.

Trudy looked around the cabin. Now that it was daylight, she could see it was a cheerful little place with the outside logs also visible inside. The kitchen had modern appliances though, and cheerful yellow curtains.

Faust had breakfast ready in no time and served Trudy at the wooden table centered in the middle of the kitchen. While she ate, Faust made himself eggs and told Trudy about the cabin; he owned all the forest land around the small lake, allowing for complete privacy.

As he sat down across from Trudy, he chattered on as if she were interested, apparently assuming that Trudy wanted to know where she was. But Trudy didn't care anymore—nothing seemed to matter.

Faust cleared away the breakfast dishes and got a second cup of coffee. He sat down facing Trudy, determined to have a serious conversation.

"You look better this morning, Trudy, I was very concerned yesterday when I saw how hopeless you appeared."

Trudy did feel better having eaten and having slept through the night. Maybe it was the quiet.

Faust continued, "Let's make a plan, okay?"

Trudy only nodded; she still didn't like the way Faust always seemed to take control.

"As I said last night, I don't think you should be alone anymore, not this close to your due date. I do need to go back to my office, but I'll ask Jill to come out and spend the day with you, for now."

Trudy considered what her own day was supposed to be about before Faust took control. She would have been at work, and she hadn't called in an absence.

"I'm supposed to be at work right now."

"I know, but Dr. Wellstein thinks you should not be standing all day, not this late in your pregnancy. Most working women would be thinking of taking a leave by now. I can call your employer, but you have more pressing things to think about right now."

"Like what?"

"Come on, you know, Trudy, we need to think about your baby. The baby will need a home. I want you to think seriously about this now. Maybe staying at the cabin will give you time. I can have Jill bring out some files for you. They contain the resumes of parents who want to adopt a baby. You can at least look through them and think about a private adoption—one where you get to select the parents. You'd have the final say as to what home your baby could go,"

Faust had only vaguely told her about private adoption, but she knew nothing about how it worked.

"Well?"

"I look through files? What's in them?"

"Everything, a complete resume: first names, ages, education, employment, home ownership, other children, basically all the information about a prospective family, everything except last name and exact address, just a general description of an area where they live."

Trudy wondered if she even wanted to consider this. What would it mean for her, for her baby?

"Trudy, you never got much past the general idea of adoption. What I'm describing is called a private adoption, not one done by an agency. If you place the baby with an adoption agency, they make all the decisions for the baby. You'd never get to know who the parents are or anything about them. But I don't work with agencies. I do private adoptions. You, the mother, get to decide after reviewing the files of prospective parents. You can even meet the applicants if you want. You decide."

"I do?"

"Yes, the only qualification is that no one gets last names and exact addresses, not yours, nor theirs. If you want to meet with them and talk about what you'd like for your baby, you can choose to do that, or write them a note, or not. It would be up to you how much involvement you want. Once the adoption is complete, you would not have any rights to see the baby, so you must know that before you make the final decision. But you have much more control than if you were just terminating your rights altogether and letting an agency handle it."

Faust sat back. He saw that Trudy was taking all of this in and knew better than to push forward until Trudy considered this idea. He had intended to introduce these ideas at the appointment Trudy skipped. Now he knew she'd need time to think this through. But time was getting short.

"Let's do this. I'll go back to the office and send Jill out here with three private adoption files. You can review them, take your time, see what a prospective family might offer your baby. No pressure, just look through the files, see what it's about. Okay?"

Trudy hesitated, but Faust persisted.

"Come on, Trudy. Time is getting short, you can look, can't you?

"All right, I'll look at the files," Trudy answered, quietly wondering what she'd find.

"Great. Take a shower, enjoy the cabin. It really is a pretty little place. Jill will be here in a little over an hour and I'll come back later today."

Faust left. Trudy was glad to be alone to think all this over. But as soon as Faust left, she realized that she had more questions than any real answers. She realized she had never finished her thoughts on wanting to tell Jackie and Mac about her plans. She began to worry once again about her own responsibilities. Trudy looked around the cabin again. She found only a small radio, no television, no phone. This cabin must have been Faust's getaway; it seemed really isolated. She felt so alone and had no idea where she was and no way to contact anyone.

Chapter 11

Mid-August 1977

Leslie walked into Jackie's Counter and found a clean, sparkling restaurant. It was small, just a horseshoe-shaped counter with stools circling around it and not what she expected. Having imagined that Trudy worked in a greasy spoon place, Leslie was impressed with how bright and clean it appeared. The breakfast rush was winding down. There were two open stools near the sinks, but one had a coffee mug still full so she took the second stool from the end and sat down.

Leslie looked around but did not find Trudy. She hadn't seen her since before last weekend when the two planned to go rummaging again. She assumed the woman in the center was Jackie. Trudy always spoke about Jackie with great respect—but always in a proper way, not friendly. Jackie's appearance was also not what Leslie had imagined. Listening to Trudy, she thought Jackie was tall, overbearing, a no-nonsense person. But this woman was attractive, middle-aged, and petite.

"Marna, sit down and drink your coffee," Jackie ordered.

"Just a few more dishes to rinse and stack," replied the older woman at the sink.

"Breakfast rush is over. I can manage those now. Sit down."

Marna gave up and walked around the edge of the counter to the stool next to Leslie, smiling at the younger woman. Jackie, wiping her hands on her terry-cloth apron, approached Leslie to take her order.

"I'm looking for Trudy. Has she been working at all this week?"

Both Marna and Jackie stopped short and studied Leslie.

"I live in the apartment across from Trudy. My name is Leslie. I'm concerned because I haven't seen Trudy all week. I've been watching for her, I even left my apartment door open last night waiting for her to come home, but I don't think she ever did. We had plans for last weekend, but she never came, and I don't know where Trudy is. And now I'm worried."

"Trudy hasn't worked all week," Jackie replied. "Her attorney called on Monday to inform me that Trudy's doctor wanted her to stop working and stay off her feet. But I assumed she was staying in her apartment. You haven't seen Trudy at all this week?"

Leslie could see that Jackie was puzzled.

"Oh, dear!" Remarked the older woman seated next to her.

Jackie took Leslie's order and began preparing it for her. Leslie relayed her last conversation with Trudy, telling Jackie and Marna that the two planned to go to rummage sales to find baby furniture, blankets, and clothing.

Marna also shared their last conversation with Trudy of offering to help so Trudy could work. She explained how they'd planned to help with the baby. Marna stressed that she looked forward to helping care for her newborn. Jackie added that she didn't like getting the call from Faust, wondering why he was calling and not Trudy.

"That's strange. Trudy told me last weekend that she wasn't going to see him any longer," added Leslie.

Marna finally expressed the obvious. "Where is Trudy?"

As Jackie served Leslie's pancakes and coffee, she thanked Leslie for telling them about Trudy's absence. Then turned to Marna, "I'm wondering the same thing! Mac is home tomorrow, we need his input."

"Who is Mac?" asked Leslie.

Jackie responded simply that Mac was her friend and had good sense about problem solving, especially if this attorney was involved. Marna shared that Mac cared very much about Trudy and had offered to help her, even giving her money, if needed.

As Leslie finished her breakfast, she and Jackie exchanged contact information and agreed they'd keep each other informed if Trudy did show up. Leslie had no better plan. And told Jackie that she'd stop again after the weekend.

Faust steered his sleek green Jaguar around the sharp turns of the country road, enjoying the drive and pleased that he'd gotten Trudy out of Milson. He was now in control. He'd have Jill staying with Trudy during the day and had sent out three files with her yesterday for Trudy to review. The files contained resumes of prospective adoptive parents.

Driving out, Faust knew that Jill was getting irritated and he'd have to smooth things over with her. But he knew how to handle Jill. Working for him for over ten years, Jill did whatever she was told. She was not only his secretary, but also his secret fiancée. Faust required this secret arrangement since he was already married. But he spent little time with his wife and children, mostly weekends. He had told his family he slept in a back room at his office suite preparing for court trials or working on files when he was super busy. Instead, he often spent the night at Jill's quiet apartment or at the lake cottage. Faust also knew that a long weekend with Jill in Las Vegas would smooth everything over as it always did. He had proposed to Jill on one such trip, but he had been vague about when and how he'd be finally free to marry her.

Faust turned onto the logging road and drove down the lane, pulling in and parking near his cabin. Inside, he found Jill filing her nails.

"Where's Trudy?"

Jill gave him a surly response. "Trudy is outside, as she has been most of the time that I've been out here babysitting. And I want to leave. This is not part of my job as a legal secretary. Hal, you're pushing me too far this time."

Faust looked out the window. Ignoring Jill's complaints, he asked if Trudy had gone over the three files. "Trudy has not even looked at them, not once in spite of many reminders.

"I'll take care of it," and Faust walked outside.

He found Trudy walking along the shoreline path of the small lake. The yellow Lab walked at her side. Faust swore at Jill under his breath for failing to watch Trudy and failing to get her to go over the files. He stopped to pick up a large branch fallen from one of the birch trees and approached Trudy and the dog.

When the dog saw the man, she laid her ears back, the fur along her spine standing on end, and began snarling. Looking up at Trudy, the dog wanted both of them to retreat, but as Faust drew near, she backed away growling. Faust raised the branch in a threatening gesture, and the dog turned and ran off.

"Damn bitch," swore Faust

"What did you do that for? She's a sweet dog!" objected Trudy.

"Stay away from the dogs out here, Trudy. I don't want you to get hurt in your condition. Those dogs carry fleas and ticks, and probably have never had their rabies shots. I don't let them on my property."

"You don't know much about animals," Trudy protested.

She stared back at Faust, angry that he had picked up a stick to threaten the dog. The short hairs on the nape of her neck were also raised. Trudy thought the dog was a good judge of character, more than she had been.

Faust told Trudy to go back to the cabin—that they needed to talk. Once inside, he asked her why she had not looked at the files. Trudy looked at Jill, resenting her presence, and did not reply. Faust followed Trudy's eyes and ordered Jill to go outside.

Finally, Trudy responded: "I don't want to stay here. I want to go back to my apartment."

Faust swore again under his breath, now really irritated. This was not what he'd anticipated. He walked around the kitchen table, got a drink of water, looked outside. Finally, he changed gears.

"Trudy, I know you are tense. You're close to the end of your pregnancy; you can't get comfortable, no matter how hard you try, but you are here to rest and prepare for the birth of your baby."

"Look, you have a doctor's appointment tomorrow. Jill is going to drive you into town. I will come back after you see Dr. Wellstein. But I want you to go over the files, first. Can you do that? Please!"

Trudy kept her eyes down. She was tearing up again, but she was tired of crying and did not want Faust to see her crying, not again. Faust waited. It was apparent that he would not leave until he got an answer.

Trudy finally lifted her head, "Alright, I'll look at the files."

"Today, Trudy, you need to look at them today! Okay?"

"Yes," Trudy surrendered.

"That's the spirit! I'll go talk with Jill and bring supper later. This will all be over soon and you can go back to your apartment, school, work, whatever."

Faust walked outside, knowing he'd have to deal with another unhappy female.

Once outside, Jill began her own complaint.

"I can't stay here with Trudy. She doesn't listen to me, doesn't even talk to me. And I repeat, I am not some babysitter, Hal."

"Not now, Jill!"

Faust knew Jill was near her breaking point, and he was getting impatient, but he knew how to handle Jill.

"Look, Babe, I know the days must seem endless out here, but this won't last long. Once we get this adoption done, we'll take a nice long weekend, go to Vegas, do whatever you choose. Go shopping. I'll treat you to a nice spa, the one you always like, take in a show, go out to eat, have some time together. Can you be patient for just a few more days?"

Faust took Jill's hands and made her face him, waiting for her to calm down and consider his offer. As usual, she softened. His touch always made her hopeful. She met his eyes and smiled.

Faust told Jill he'd bring back dinner for the three of them. He'd return before dark, they'd eat and then he would talk with Trudy.

"But make sure Trudy reads the files this time."

His abrupt change of tone irritated Jill.

"I told you, Trudy doesn't listen to me," But Faust had already turned toward the cabin.

As Faust re-entered the cabin, he told Trudy again to go over the files, instructing her, "Do not go out of the cabin until finished." His tone of voice irritated Trudy, but she made no reply.

After Faust drove away, Jill went back into the cabin and placed the three files on the kitchen table where Trudy was still sitting. But Trudy stood up and told Jill she was tired and needed to lie down for a bit. She went to her room, ignoring Jill.

More than an hour later, Trudy finally went back into the kitchen. Jill tried to be pleasant. She poured a glass of milk and gave Trudy a plate of oatmeal cookies. The three files were still on the table. As pleasantly as Trudy had ever heard her speak, Jill asked Trudy to look at the files as Faust had instructed, repeating her plea and implying they were both subject to Faust's demands. Trudy knew this was inevitable and finally pulled the first manilla file, simply marked, *A,* and opened the file to an introductory letter.

Trudy quickly scanned it, noting the grammatical errors. Liking its tone, she reread it more carefully, reminding herself not to be an English major:

Dear Birth Mom

Our names are John and Karen. We are instructed to write a letter of introduction to you. On why we would like to adopt your baby.

Our family includes our son, Sam, who is an active, happy three-year-old. We hope to adopt another baby to make our family complete, a baby we would love and also Sam can have a brother or a sister.

Karen is a full-time mom and will be for your baby too. She loves being a stay-at-home mom. John is a firefighter for the city that we live in and works really hard. While we don't have a fancy house, we do own a nice home with three bedrooms so our new baby would have his or her own room.

John makes enough money to provide a comfortable living for us although we are not wealthy, we have everything a baby would need, especially our love. We don't think money is our main selling point, a baby in our home would spend a lot of time with family. Play with Sam and would have a wonderful extended family full of grandparents, aunts and uncles and cousins. Our entire family would all love this child.

We would go to the park and the zoo. We take a lot of family walks, and Sam plays with the neighborhood kids. Because John has days off after working a shift of 24 hours, we can plan family outings like camping in the State Parks. We believe in strong family values including church on Sundays.

Your baby would receive a good public education. We are active in the school parents' association, scouting, sport teams and whatever else our children find an interest in doing. We are hands-on parents giving our full support to our children. Most of all, we promise to love your baby. We'd love to meet with you.

Sincerely, John and Karen

Trudy tried to picture John and Karen in the park with Sam. She pictured her baby in a little stroller. She imagined the dad pushing Sam on the swing. Karen stayed with the baby. Trudy liked this imaginary scene. She finished looking through the file, which largely included documents supporting their information, including their tax return. Last names and address were redacted. Trudy liked what she read so much that she was tempted to ignore the other files. But Jill encouraged her, sliding file *B* across the table after Trudy closed the file on John and Karen.

Trudy sighed but pushed on. She opened to another introductory letter. It was apparent that the files were arranged in a certain format. Trudy read on:

To Whom it May Concern:

My name is Priscilla, my friends call me Sally. I am a single woman, age 38. I am a successful career woman. I climbed to a top position in my corporation and make an excellent salary, details are attached in the file.

I have advanced degrees and sufficient experience to allow me to pick any position or employment in my field of expertise. Headhunters contact me often. You may be wondering why I am placing my resume with Attorney. Faust for your consideration.

Woman to woman, I think you may understand. I've attained my lifetime career goals, and I realized that I have more to offer. I would like to have a child and start my own family; I can provide handsomely for a child. It would give real meaning to all of my success.

I do not wish to marry. Men find it difficult to accept my success; but I do have many men in my life to provide a role model for a child, I have two brothers and many male friends who know that I want to adopt a child and have promised to make the baby part of an extended family.

I can provide many advantages for a child. I own a beautiful condo with a full bedroom suite for the baby. I would spend a full half year at home with a new baby and then hire the finest nanny while I continue to be the provider for our family. The child would attend wonderful schools, take dance classes, or music lessons, or drama classes, whatever their interest dictates. I can provide many privileges for the child.

In closing, I consider myself to be a modern woman. I can make many dreams come true for your baby, and my dream as well.

I remain, Priscilla

Trudy barely looked at the supporting documents. She wanted a real family for her baby if she couldn't keep the baby herself. She wondered if Priscilla knew Leslie. Maybe she had been once been part of VOW. But Trudy knew that file **B** could not compete with file **A** in her mind. Sally could find some other soulmate to have her woman-to-woman talk; it did not move her in any way.

Trudy looked out the cabin window, wanting some fresh air. She told Jill she needed a break before reviewing the last file. Without waiting for permission, she stood up from the table and walked outside, hoping the yellow Lab would return. She started to walk down the dirt road but didn't get far. Her ankles were swollen and her back began to hurt.

Trudy turned and walked down to the lake instead. She sat on an old Adirondack chair facing the water. It was a warm day in late August, also late in the afternoon. The stillness soon gave way to an incessant sound of mosquitoes buzzing in her ears and amplifying her discomfort. She headed back to the cabin where Jill was waiting. She handed file **C** to Trudy, reminding her that she had to review it before Faust returned.

Trudy considered refusing to look at it. She had already decided on the first file but decided not to argue with Jill. She would give this file a cursory look and be done with the homework. At least she could avoid Faust's haranguing.

Like the other two, file **C** began with a letter.

Dear ____:

Our names are Tony and Marie, our tale is a bittersweet story. We are happily married, but Marie has been unable to have a baby even though she has seen the very best doctors that money can buy. We have experienced great disappointment in not fulfilling our one unmet wish to have a child.

After many years of trying, we finally decided to complete our family through adoption. We can offer your child a wonderful life. Tony works as an investment banker on Wall Street in a firm started by his father and earns an excellent salary. We can provide handsomely for a family.

Marie is an art dealer and works from home although she is affiliated with a gallery on Fifth Avenue and is also a curator at MOMA. Marie has many contacts in the art and theater world and can open doors for a child most parents could only dream about.

We have an apartment in the city and a country home. Both have a fully appointed nursery for a baby. We would provide private schools, tutors, and the best Ivy League education for our child.

Since we live in a large east-coast city, we chose the heartland to seek an adoption, knowing both of us would appreciate privacy. We would welcome meeting you. We promise that you would be providing your baby the absolute best that life can offer.

Trudy found it ironic that Marie tried so hard to have a baby while Trudy had one fling and got pregnant. Clearly, Tony and Marie offered better financial advantages and education than the other files. Yet one thing was missing. While file *C* documented at length the advantages for her baby, not once did Tony and Marie say they would love the baby.

Trudy thought about her grandparents. They had often talked about farmers being the breadbasket for this whole country while the wealthy East Coast crowd profited off their labor. Her grandfather complained often about this when he'd had a bad crop year. But for Trudy, not offering to give love could not be offset by all this wealth. She still preferred the family that offered to love the baby, the file of John and Karen.

Under the watchful eyes of Jill, Trudy paged through financial disclosure statements, letters of reference from trusted friends and the like, but her opinion did not change. She would choose file *A*. As she closed the last file, she heard Faust's car driving down the forest lane, returning with their supper.

Trudy had eaten little of her supper, telling Faust she was not very hungry. She went outside before he and Jill finished eating. While Trudy was outside, Faust asked Jill if Trudy had reviewed the files, and Jill confirmed she had. He was pleased. He quickly finished eating, planning to go outside to talk with Trudy. Before walking out, he reminded Jill that Tony and Marie were scheduled to be in town the following week and planned to stay over the Labor Day holidays.

Faust saw Trudy sitting in the Adirondack chair near the lake. He casually walked over and sat down on the ground next to her. He stretched his legs out and made small talk about how beautiful everything looked in the light of the setting sun. Trudy sat silently.

Faust finally asked her if she had any questions about the files. Trudy refused to be engaged and merely responded that she had no questions. Seeing that he was wasting his time, Faust took a more direct approach,

"Well, Trudy, have you made a choice? You've read about three sets of prospective parents, did you pick one?"

"One file was of a single parent, not 'parents.'"

"Okay, but the other files were two parents," agued Faust, "Clearly they offered different choices—that was the point of having three. But did you prefer one over the others?"

"Yes, I like file *A*, I don't want my baby to have a single mom."

File *C* was the one for Tony and Marie. Faust thought it was clearly the best offer. He had labeled it the last file so Trudy could see how much more file *C* had to offer than the other two. But he knew better than to argue with Trudy.

"That's fine, I'm glad you made a choice. I'm going to go back to the cottage and leave some instructions with Jill, but come in before it gets dark, okay?"

Faust walked back into the cabin. He shouted at Jill:

"Where are those files?"

Jill pointed to the kitchen counter. Faust retrieved them and quickly confirmed the files were labeled in the correct order. Tony and Marie's file was *C*. Faust reviewed file *A* again, wondering why Trudy preferred it. Trudy returned to the cabin. It was getting dark quickly now, near the end of summer.

"What did you like about file *A*? Clients often ask me what it is in a file that makes a birth mom choose one over others." Faust tried to sound unconcerned and businesslike. Trudy sat down on the chair and considered the question.

"Three reasons, I guess. John and Karen sound like nice people. Karen stays home and will actually be the mom taking care of the baby. Then, I like that they have little Sam; it would be nice for my baby to have a brother. Mostly though, John and Karen said they'd love my baby—no one else said that."

Faust realized that he had miscalculated. Trudy wasn't thinking about the real world that runs on money and power, the real world as he knew it. Trudy lived in a fantasy world of happily ever after endings. His mistake was in forgetting Trudy was still young and naïve. He smiled: "Good reasons! I'm glad you could make a choice. Thanks for explaining it to me."

Faust told Jill to come out to the car with him as he was getting ready to drive back to Milson. Outside, Faust told Jill to get in the car with him. He wanted to be sure that Trudy could not hear. But Jill had anticipated the problem and asked Faust what he was going to do now, knowing that Tony and Marie were scheduled to come in next week. Trudy hadn't chosen their file. Faust admitted that he miscalculated but said he'd find a solution.

Faust explained his plan. He would go back into the cabin and get information from Trudy about finding Terrek so he could get his waiver for terminating the rights of the putative father, one never legally confirmed. His waiver would be required by the court. He would also talk with her about meeting the prospective adoptive parents next week. Jill was to keep quiet about who it would be for now. Faust would figure that out before any meeting.

Jill was irritated that Faust was going to leave again; she thought he was staying the night. Faust reached over and kissed her, telling her he knew this case was particularly trying, but it would be worth a great deal in the long run. He asked Jill to bear with him and kissed her again, passionately and convincingly.

Faust returned to the kitchen, where Trudy still sat at the kitchen table. He told her that he was pleased that she had finally come to a decision. He explained the next procedures for the adoption included getting Terrek to sign off on any rights he had as the father. Trudy protested, but Faust told her it was required. When he asked if there were any other men that he needed to consider, Trudy became angry and told him again that there were no others.

"Then tell me how I can find Terrek—give me some help. If Terrek is the only one, I don't need anything else, except how to find Terrek."

Trudy saw his point. She told Faust that Terrek liked to hang out at The Spot. She also described his father's business. While she did not know exactly where it was, she reminded him it was called Auto Paradise, and it was about an hour's drive from Milson.

Faust smiled. He knew where The Spot was, and he could find the salvage yard knowing the business name. For now, that would be enough. If not, he could investigate further.

Faust told Trudy that he would arrange a meeting with the prospective parents she had selected and needed to get this done soon. Her due date was in early September and they did not have much time left. Faust told her he would set up the meeting for next week and reminded her that no one would learn last names or home addresses.

Jackie anxiously waited for Mac to wake up and come down to the café. She had just closed for the rest of the weekend and finished cleaning the grill. For the rest of Saturday through Sunday, the café was closed. Normally, she and Mac would have time to themselves, often ride through the countryside, meeting Mac's biker buddies, or just spend quiet time in their apartment. Mac usually took Jackie out for dinner on Sunday evening so that she'd get a break from cooking.

Jackie knew better than to ask Mac to listen late last night when he had rolled in from a long week on the road. Mac needed to catch up on his sleep, which usually meant at least twelve or more straight hours in bed. It usually worked perfectly into their weekend routine, Jackie working while Mac was sleeping. She had not yet told him about Leslie's visit and their concern for Trudy, now missing.

Jackie kept going over the conversation with Leslie. Prior to this visit, Jackie had been irritated that Trudy had not called herself to ask for time off during the last weeks of her pregnancy, especially after she and Marna had offered to help. But now her irritation changed to one of deep concern. Jackie feared Faust was behind this. She needed to know what Mac might think.

Mac finally rolled out of bed, still somewhat disheveled, and walked down the back steps and into the restaurant. Jackie was cleaning as she always did on Saturday. He was hungry, and Jackie gave him some desperately needed java and prepared a hearty breakfast.

Marna walked in and sat down near Mac. Jackie had asked her to come down. Jackie served coffee as she and Marna shared the story of Leslie's visit. Jackie always did her best thinking while working, so she carried on, pulling the smoke screen off the hood to soak in the sinks.

Mac ate and listened. Marna began by describing Leslie and explained why she had come into Jackie's Counter. Jackie explained how Faust had called about Trudy needing to stay off her feet. She and

Marna both assumed Trudy was resting at home. But once Leslie came looking for Trudy and explained she never came back to the apartment, they became suspicious.

"I don't trust him, Mac. He came in here before with Trudy, telling me what my duties entailed as her employer. Faust talked the whole time as if Trudy didn't have anything to say. Now, he tells me Trudy won't be working these last weeks of her pregnancy, but we've heard nothing more from Trudy. After our talk with her last week, we thought Trudy was going to work here after her baby was born. This doesn't make sense. Why didn't Trudy call? Where is she?"

Both Jackie and Marna watched Mac take his final bite, sip his coffee. Mac was slow and deliberate when thinking through anything, showing no emotion, which often irritated Jackie. She prompted him, wanting some input.

To calm her down, Mac replied, "Seems to me you need to talk with Attorney Faust. It all leads back to him. Maybe he knows where Trudy is and we can ask him and then talk to Trudy."

Jackie was hesitant, "Talk with Faust?"

"Yup,"

"But how? And when?"

"Look, I'll delay going to work on Monday. I could use the extra sleep anyhow. After you close, we'll walk over to Faust's office. It's just down the block from here. I pass it often and noted the name. We will sit in his office until he agrees to talk to us—seems pretty obvious that this is where we start. We ask Faust where Trudy is."

Jackie considered Mac's proposal, "You will go with me? To his office?"

"Yup."

Jackie knew she wouldn't have the nerve to do it alone. But if Faust was going to speak to anyone, it might just be Mac.

Chapter 12

End of August 1977

Faust pulled over into a root beer stand on his way back to Milson, unaware that Trudy and Mac had stopped there earlier in the summer. They had sought root beer as a summer treat, filled with expectations of good times and the promises of the season. Faust stopped to use the Yellow Pages hanging inside a plastic binder, which dangled from a chain in the tall cube of a phone booth in the corner yard.

Thumbing through the Yellow Pages, Faust found many entries under **AUTO & AUTOMOBILES,** but nothing for auto salvage. He also found nothing under J except **JUNK, Rubbish & Scrap Metal**. Faust swore and decided to try the White Pages for a name listing. He pulled up the other book and ran his finger down the column from AAA Auto Repairs to the listing for Auto Paradise. Faust smiled, jotting down the phone number and address.

Deciding it was too late and too dark to find Auto Paradise now, Faust drove back into Milson. He'd stop at The Spot on Monday and try to find Terrek, thinking he might not need to drive all the way out to this business address. Perhaps some of the dancers would be familiar with his habits for coming and going.

On Monday morning, Faust finished drafting the legal documents for Termination of Parental Rights by Putative Father. At noon, he walked over to The Spot for his usual Perfect Rob Roy. The Spot opened just before the noon hour, the slowest time of day. Its busy time didn't start until late afternoon unless Milson U had a football or basketball game. Other events might also bring the students in earlier to start celebrating or if the fraternities had some event.

Today was particularly slow. The school semester had not yet started. It was Monday, and the weather was too nice to be inside. Faust found only a few older men seated around the bar. As his drink was served per routine, Faust asked the bartender to send Tanya over as he wanted to ask her something. Tanya was busy cleaning and waxing the pole in the middle of the low platform for her later routine. When she was called over, Tanya was happy to oblige. She had gotten tips from Faust in the past.

Faust took his drink and walked over to one of the side cocktail tables, inviting Tanya to join him. Faust put twenty dollars on the small table in front of her and told her he needed some information. He got right down to business, asking her if she knew a young college guy named Terrek. Her disapproving smirk answered his question. She told him that she knew Terrek. He hung out often at The Spot. He was demanding, but tipped little, if he bothered at all. She called him a young punk, always wanting attention and pawing the strippers if the bouncers weren't looking.

Faust explained that he needed to talk with Terrek, and he pressed her for more information. She told him that she never saw Terrek until later in the afternoon and didn't know if she'd see him this day as he seemed to have no regular routine. He'd just show up, drink too much beer, and leer at the dancers.

Faust pulled out his business card and gave it to Tanya. "I'll make it worth your while to give me a call the next time you see Terrek, okay?"

Tanya readily agreed; she didn't care why Faust wanted so badly to see the punk. She had no loyalty to him and would be happy to earn easy cash. Having gotten Tanya's promise, Faust drained his cocktail and left.

Mac arrived at Jackie's Counter after closing time to accompany Jackie to the lawyer's office as promised. He was fully rested and nicely dressed, not in his usual black T-shirt and jeans but in a long-sleeve shirt, open at the collar, and dress slacks. Jackie quickly changed out of her white dress and put on her best skirt and blouse for their visit to the lawyer.

The two walked Into Faust's office, and Mac told the receptionist that they were here to see Attorney Faust. With Jill out of the office, Faust had hired a temp from the employment agency. Not familiar with Faust's regular clients, she politely looked through the appoint-ment register, but not finding an appointment, the receptionist told Mac there was no appointment booked for this hour. Mac then in-formed her that they had no appointment.

"I'm sorry Mr. Faust only sees clients by appointment," the recep-tionist responded, asking if Mac would like to schedule one.

Mac was direct, "We are going to take a seat right here until Atty. Faust talks with us. This is too important, and we will wait."

Mac steered Jackie to a seat in the waiting area, and both sat down. The receptionist became flustered. She picked up the conference phone and buzzed Faust's inner office, telling him that a man calling himself Mac, and a woman came in without an appointment but would not leave until they got to talk with him. Faust hung up the phone telling her he'd take care of it, irritated by the interruption.

Several minutes later, Faust walked into the small waiting area, trying to recall if he knew anyone by the name of Mac. When he saw the two people seated, it was the woman he recognized. Trudy's employer had spoken with him several times. He'd even stopped one time at her small café. The unfamiliar man sitting next to her could have been a football lineman. He was huge. The office chair was barely large enough for his frame.

Faust became cautious, knowing their connection was Trudy. As he approached the seated couple, he changed gears from being upset, even disrespectful, to being cautious and deliberate.

"What is it you want? My receptionist tells me you plan to sit here until I speak to you."

Mac answered, also direct and deliberate: "That's right. We want to talk to you about Trudy."

"I don't normally meet anyone without an appointment, but I will give you five minutes, I do have *real* appointments this afternoon. Follow me, we'll use my conference room."

Mac permitted Jackie to follow Faust, walking behind her into an inner conference room with a long table and chairs. Faust directed them to side chairs and then sat at the head of the table opposite the open door.

"What about Trudy?" Faust began. Mac turned to Jackie and nodded. He knew her concerns were paramount and wanted her to speak her mind.

"I want to know where Trudy is. You called last week to tell me she could not work on doctor's orders, but I've learned that she has not returned to her apartment, and I am worried about her."

"How do you know that?"

"Because one of her friends named Leslie, who lives across the hall from Trudy, came into the restaurant looking for her. Leslie was worried, and now I am too. Where is Trudy?" Jackie repeated.

"And just who is this Leslie?"

Mac interrupted. "Look, you've been asked a question, twice now. You answer that question, Where is Trudy?"

Faust stared at Mac. He was a good judge of character and knew this man was not to be toyed with. Jackie was wise to bring him along. He also knew that Jackie was also a very direct person. She wanted answers.

Looking at Mac, Faust replied, "I know only a few things about you: your name is Mac according to the receptionist, and you came into my office unannounced along with Trudy's employer. You know that I'm an attorney, and I represent Trudy, but her employer already knew this, didn't you?"

Jackie only nodded. Mac spoke again:

"Where is Trudy? Now, answer that question."

Faust smiled. "What I am telling you is that I represent Trudy. I can't share client information with you."

As a trucker and a biker, often treated as one unwelcome by the elite, Mac had little time for game playing with people. He'd learned to speak softly because of his size. He knew that he intimidated folks. For real friends, like Jackie or Trudy, Mac did not want to be the cause of their fear; but for snobs, he used his size and outsider persona to ensure he'd be left alone. This was not his world. Mac rose from his chair, gently pulled out Jackie's chair and took her arm, telling her they were done. He turned his back on Faust, and led Jackie out of the conference room, through the small waiting area, and out the door.

Once outside, Jackie complained. "We didn't get an answer! We need to go back in there and get Faust to tell us where Trudy is."

Mac steered them along the sidewalk back toward Jackie's Counter. After they were a full block away from the lawyer's office, he finally spoke: "Faust is not going to tell us where Trudy is."

"But we could have tried harder. There must be something he could tell us about Trudy," Jackie objected.

"Look, he told us everything he was going to tell us. I wasn't going to sit there and play his game. If we tried asking more questions, the answer would be the same. He played his lawyer card. He doesn't care one whit for Trudy's well-being, she's just a client to him. My only question is, What's in it for him? Guys like that care only about money and influence."

"Trudy doesn't have any money!" Jackie objected.

"Exactly, so what's his game? How does a lawyer like that make money off clients like Trudy?" replied Mac.

Jackie was really upset, but she tried to fight her tears. Mac saw how upset she was, and her tears wounded him deeply. Jackie was the one woman he truly loved, his world revolved around her. All the hours on the road, trucking coast to coast, it was all centered around returning to Jackie. They had known each other for many years, and recently, he had moved in with her. Mac knew Jackie did not cry easily.

There was a small pocket park on the way back to the café. Mac steered Jackie over to a park bench and suggested they sit for a while so that Jackie could regain her composure. It was a beautiful, end-of-summer day which they had scarcely enjoyed. Even their lovely end-of-summer weekend had been filled with worry about Trudy. Jackie cared very much about her young employee. Trudy had become one of Jackie's inner circle, people she cared about. Mac knew this was very hard for her, especially given her history.

Jackie, like Trudy, had made her own mistakes when she was young and before she knew Mac, but Mac knew her story. They shared all of their inner thoughts. Mac also knew that Jackie dealt with her own issues by being in total control of her surroundings. Her little restaurant was her way of controlling her world—be the best little café in the world, the neatest, the cleanest, the best food. Then her world was in its proper orbit. Early on, Mac resented the overwhelming routine and lack of spontaneity, but he slowly began to understand this was how Jackie learned to cope and to overcome her own sense of loss.

As they sat on the old, wooden park bench, Mac wrapped his arm around Jackie. She tried to control her tears, her fears, and the hurt of not getting more information. Knowing Trudy was eight months pregnant, she wanted to help. It all seemed out of control, all left unresolved and without any certainty. Jackie hated the feeling of not being in control, but she couldn't just write it off the way Mac did. Trudy was at that age that Jackie once was. The age when she made her critical blunder that had changed her own world. She had also been young and naïve, but Trudy was more than just an employee now especially since she had no real family herself. Feeling powerless, Jackie cried openly.

"Oh, Mac, what are we going to do?" The flood gates opened, and despite her efforts, Jackie cried uncontrollably. Mac remained quiet. To speak would have been to join Jackie in crying. Mac did not cry. He remained silent, he pulled Jackie closer, and allowed Jackie to vent, to have her cry. The birds in the old sugar maple stopped singing, momentarily. Everything seemed to get quiet in the little park, even the insects seemed to allow Jackie to grieve her loss of equilibrium.

After a long wait, Mac gently put his oversized fingers under Jackie's chin and pulled her face up to look at him. He wiped the tears on her cheeks with his thumb and then gently bent down to kiss her, to show her that he was here for her, that he loved her. Jackie rested her head against his broad shoulder and finally composed herself.

"Mac, I don't know what I'd do without you."

"I know, babe, me too. I'm here for you. I love you so much."

"I love you, too,"

Jackie kissed Mac again, fully on his lips. Mac was her world, and after their years together, Jackie knew it was enough for her, too. Regaining her composure, Jackie asked Mac again, what she should do, just ignore everything?

They lingered on the bench for a bit. Finally, Mac told Jackie he did have one idea. It was obvious that Faust knew where Trudy was. If he hadn't known, he could have merely said so and ended their unexpected visit. Jackie reminded Mac that Leslie told her that Trudy said she wasn't going to go back to see Faust anymore. She wondered why Trudy would change her mind.

"Maybe she didn't," replied Mac.

"How do you mean?"

"Well, maybe she didn't go see the lawyer—maybe he went to see her. I still think the way to find Trudy is through Faust."

"But he won't talk," objected Jackie.

"I have an idea, but I've got to talk to Pig and Tag. Let's go back to the apartment so I can give them a call."

Jackie didn't know how Mac's biker buddies were going to help. Mac told her to let him formulate an idea. If his buddies would help, he'd explain it to her. They left the park bench, and the birds began to sing goodbye to summer once again.

Faust left his office by midafternoon, but before returning to the lake cottage, he planned to stop at Auto Paradise to see if he could get more information on Terrek, maybe even get lucky and find him. Faust put the briefcase holding the termination documents into the trunk of his Jaguar, not knowing exactly where he'd finally track Terrek down. Auto Paradise was a bit out of the way, but like the lake cottage, it was north out of Milson.

Faust drove up to the front gate of Auto Paradise. It was late in the afternoon. Two German Shepherds and an intimidating black Doberman barked loudly on the other side of the gate so Faust remained inside his car. Eventually, a yardman walked out of a smaller side gate and approached the Jaguar. Faust opened his window and asked if a young fellow named Terrek was on the premises.

"You must mean the owner's kid. Who's asking?"

"I was told a nicely appointed limo is available, I'd like to take a look," lied Faust.

"Didn't know that kid was selling the limo, I got no instructions,"

Faust pulled out a twenty-dollar bill and offered it to the yardman, responding, "Just let me take a look. Do you know if Terrek is in the yard?"

Sneering, the yardman answered, "I don't keep track of that spoiled kid. I got real work." But the yardman smiled. He took the twenty and instructed Faust to pull up next to the small office after he opened the gate. Once inside, Faust was told to take an old pickup and given directions on where to turn among the rows of junkers. He'd have to leave the Jaguar by the front office.

Faust grabbed his briefcase from the trunk and began driving through the interior of the junkyard, turning through rows of wrecked cars until he finally spotted the limo sitting up on blocks near the center of the acres of heaps. The limo stood out like a thoroughbred in a pasture full of old workhorses. Hoping to find Terrek, Faust climbed out of the old truck and approached the driver's side front door. With tinted windows, Faust could not see inside the limo. He knocked on the window and waited. No answer forthcoming, Faust walked around the stretch limo and tried the back passenger door—happily it opened and he peered inside.

He paused to appreciate all the appointments and then stepped inside. Finding the bar behind the chauffeur's seat, he opened the liquor cabinet and looked at the offerings. Surprised to find what he called the good stuff, he poured brandy into a snifter. Sitting back, he sipped his drink and leered at the red velvet interior with the bench seat still pulled out as a flat bed. He imagined Terrek and Trudy here last December. Trudy told him she had gotten pregnant in the limo. He grinned and raised his glass in his own toast:

"Trudy, to your misfortune, and to my good fortune!"

Not finding Terrek, Faust left quickly and drove to his lake cottage, arriving shortly after dusk. He saw Trudy down at the lake, fishing with the Lab sitting next to her at the end of the pier. Jill stepped out of the cabin, wanting to talk, but he angrily growled, "Not now. I need to talk with Trudy—alone."

Resenting his tone, Jill retreated into the cottage, now pouting. Faust marched down to the lake and began swearing at the dog. The Lab promptly retreated from the pier and ran off into the woods. Trudy resented everything about Faust's approach but had some difficulty standing up fast enough to grab the dog to give her protection.

"Trudy, I told you to stay away from that dog."

"I know dogs; she's no threat to me. Not like you!" retorted Trudy, now angry herself. Faust walked out on the pier wanting to help Trudy, seeing her struggling to get to her feet, but she refused his hand and stood on her own. Faust stepped back and allowed Trudy to have her way. Realizing he was off to a bad start with both Jill and Trudy, Faust tried to start over, suggesting that Trudy sit on the Adirondack chair on the shore so they could talk.

But Trudy was still irritated. "I want to go back to my apartment now."

"Trudy, I'm sorry. I just didn't want you to get hurt. We need to talk. Please sit down for a moment. I have good news and some bad news to share."

Trudy stood her ground. Faust's idea of talking always led to Faust getting his way. Trudy repeated, "I want to go home!"

"Please, we need to talk."

Faust walked over to the Adirondack chair and moved it closer for Trudy to sit down. The sun, already setting behind the cottage, cast long shadows. The last daylight settled over the lake, reflecting in pale pink and yellow hues like a soft bedside quilt. The evening offered a downy quiet as well, a perfectly lovely ending to a beautiful day, but no one was enjoying the weather.

"Please," Faust repeated, holding the back of the chair for her.

Trudy relented and sat down, asking what the good news was, ignoring that Faust had said both good and bad news.

Faust started by first asking Trudy to remember the three files that she reviewed. He tried to placate Trudy, telling her that he knew she put a lot of thought into her selection and telling her that he had gone right back to his office to set up the meeting so they could all meet and discuss the baby's adoption. Finally, Faust explained the *good news* was good for this couple.

"Karen is pregnant," he lied. "When I called to set up the meeting, Karen was just bubbling over with the news. She told me she was pregnant, and that she and John were so happy to be having their own second child. But the *bad news* for you is that Karen also said they were no longer able to adopt, not with a new baby on the way. I congratulated her, of course."

"Trudy, if you had talked to Karen, you'd know how happy she was. You do still have the two other files to pick from."

Faust tried to sound enthusiastic, hoping Trudy would now select Tony and Marie's file, remembering that Trudy insisted that she would not choose the file of a single parent. But Trudy repeated her earlier demand.

"I want to go back home. You told me I came here to be safe but look how far it is back to Milson and the hospital if something did happen. I would be much better off closer to the hospital in Milson."

Faust paused. He pulled a second chair over next to Trudy and sat down.

"I hear you, Trudy, I really do. But there is not much time left. You do have another doctor's appointment tomorrow. Let's do this. Jill will drive you back into Milson. Jill wants to get back home as well. I will set up a new appointment from one of the other files, whichever one you choose. While you're seeing the doctor, I'll try to get a new appointment set up as soon as possible with new adoptive parents. As to staying in the city, whatever the doctor thinks about staying in town will guide the choice. I don't think he will want you to be staying alone, but we'll let the doctor advise you. Okay? Can we do that?"

Wondering if she really was making any progress with her insistence on returning to Milson, Trudy knew she needed to see Dr. Wellstein. He had made it clear that he wanted to see Trudy weekly now, to make sure her blood pressure was stable, that the baby's heart rate remained stable, and whatever else he was keeping track of. She didn't remember all the technical stuff, but she did understand that both her health and the baby's needed close monitoring now.

"We go back to Milson?" Trudy repeated.

"Yes," Faust confirmed, "Now tell me which file so I know who to call for the meeting."

Trudy hesitated, remembering the other two files.

"I guess, file *C*, I don't want a single mom for my baby, I did tell you that already."

"I know, but I didn't want to presume. It is your choice. I'll call Tony and Marie first thing tomorrow."

The last light of the day sent horizontal rays over the water. Pinks and yellows skipped off the surface like an angelic aura, bedding the day under pastel loveliness much like an evening prayer softens breathing before sleep. Trudy followed Faust back into the cabin, his planning finalized for now.

On Tuesday, Mac, accompanied by Pig and Tag, walked into the counter just prior to closing time. The three had met for a short ride that morning, ending at their biker's hangout, an old garage they rented. Mac explained his concern for Trudy. Both Pig and Tag remembered her from stops at the counter as the pretty young helper that Jackie hired. Mac explained Jackie's concerns and told them about the visit to see Faust.

"I think Faust knows where Trudy is, but he's not talking. I need help; I plan to follow him to see if he'll lead me to Trudy. She's not been home for over a week, and I think Faust has her holed up somewhere. But I can't follow him 24 hours a day on my own. I need help."

Pig and Tag readily agreed to help. They formulated plans and finally made some decisions, which concluded with the three going over to Jackie's Counter to get lunch and to explain their plan to Jackie.

As the three bikers walked in just before closing, they attracted quite of bit of attention. Mac was well-known, but Tag, a very tall, very husky Black man with a shaved head, and Pig, much shorter and less husky than Tag, but also dressed in leathers, appeared intimidating to Jackie's customers. They quickly finished eating and cleared out. Mac and Tag were used to having such deference paid to them, and Pig enjoyed being included in the large shadow they cast. All three were army veterans, having served in Nam together, and they were as tight as any band of brothers.

Mac asked Jackie to make hamburgers for them and asked her to call Marna to come down. He wanted her to hear the plan, the more eyes watching out for Trudy, the better. The bikers sat around the counter while Jackie served burgers and soda.

Leslie had also stopped in just before closing time, having agreed to stay in touch with Jackie. She reported no contact all weekend and wanted to know if Jackie knew more. Jackie reported the same but told her to stay, hoping Mac had some ideas.

Jackie introduced her to Mac and his buddies, telling Mac: "Leslie is Trudy's neighbor. She's the one I told you about who came in last week, looking for Trudy."

Mac took charge. "I'm happy to meet you, Leslie, Trudy's friend, is our friend."

Mac introduced Tag and Pig to her. Leslie, the graduate student and member of VOW, lived in a different orbit than these bikers. But for one brief moment, their orbits were eclipsing. Such a meeting would have been as unlikely as a full lunar eclipse, but with Trudy being their common concern, they all wanted to help, giving them all a common cause.

Mac began telling everyone that he and his two buddies had formulated a plan. They guessed that Faust had something to do with Trudy's disappearance and likely could lead them to her. All three decided to take off from work the rest of this week; it was nearly Labor

Day and they all had a long weekend coming up. The three planned to put a tail on Faust, taking round-the-clock shifts to follow him.

Mac asked Leslie to continue watching the apartment and call if there were any signs that Trudy had returned. Marna was asked to keep praying for their success and safety. But Marna spoke up:

"You know that I always pray for my dear friends, each and every day. But I've already figured out how I can help. My niece is a nurse at Milson General Hospital. I asked her to keep track of the maternity admittances. She's supposed to keep patient identity private, but since I'm the one who told her Trudy's name and an expected delivery date in early September, my niece agreed she could confirm if a person named Trudy was admitted to the hospital, but nothing more. I will keep calling every day, and if I hear something, I will report to Jackie."

"Good work!" shouted Mac, adding, "Jackie's Counter will be our command center. If anyone finds out anything about Trudy or her location, we all contact Jackie, who will pass the word."

Mac told his buddies he'd do the first shift. "If Faust is in his office, I can start tailing him from there. We'll stay in touch with our CB radios, so stay vigilant and get some sleep. The next shift will be tonight, I'll call Pig first and Tag can go next."

With the planning set, Mac rode his Harley the few blocks over to Faust's office. Mac knew about the green Jaguar, having seen Faust driving around in this car. Mac had laughed the first time he saw Faust in the Jag but figured it was the perfect car for him, showy and pretentious. Now Mac knew he'd be able to watch not only for Faust but his car. It would be easy to tail.

Mac cruised around the block of the attorney's office and spotted the Jaguar parked in the alley. Faust was probably inside his office. The attorney was in fact at that moment confirming an appointment with Tony and Marie. The couple had agreed to come into Milson before

Labor Day weekend to meet Trudy and prepare for the temporary placement of the infant in their home, pending the final adoption. Faust advised them they would need to finish the out-of-state adoption compact needed to remove the baby from the Midwest to the East Coast state where they lived. He was preparing all the various documents and just needed to get the alleged father to sign off.

Faust finished up his checklist for all the work he needed to complete on the Termination of Parental Rights. The adoption involved a lot of document preparation, and Faust did not want any slip-up with this wealthy client. They were paying top dollar for a private adoption, and Faust considered himself the premier lawyer in the field with a national reputation. He wanted this done with perfection. But he still had to find Terrek and get his waiver of rights. Faust did not like loose ends and vowed to himself he'd have this finished before Tony and Marie got to Milson.

Jill had been instructed to drive Trudy into Milson in her car to see Dr. Wellstein. Faust had already talked with the doctor and confirmed the doctor wanted Trudy to rest as much as possible and stressed it was not a good time for her to be alone. Faust would use the doctor's advice to get Trudy back to the cottage for at least one more night, promising to get her a place close to the hospital until her delivery date. He'd make plans for Trudy's stay in town near Tony and Marie so that all the planning would flow smoothly. Faust did not want Trudy to go back to her own apartment and lose control.

Faust made a final call to the client and asked Tony to book two rooms and to be in town tomorrow. He wanted them to stay in the airport hotel, which was quite close to the hospital. Tony readily agreed, and Marie was overjoyed to hear that she'd get to spend time with the birth mother. She wanted very much to meet her. She even hoped she might be allowed to stay in the birthing room with the baby's mother during the delivery. Marie could barely contain her excitement. Tony stressed to Faust that he expected him to get this done smoothly, no more complications.

~ ℮

Just as Faust finished his checklist, the receptionist buzzed his office telling him a woman named Tanya was on the line. Faust smiled. He hoped it was the lead he needed to find Terrek. He took the call, and Tanya informed him that Terrek had just walked into The Spot. Faust hung up, telling her he'd be over directly.

Faust hurriedly left all his documents on top of the desk and rushed over to The Spot. He didn't want to lose this chance at finding Terrek. As he pulled the Jaguar out of the back alley, Mac kicked the Harley into gear and followed the green roadster.

They'd only gone a few blocks when Mac was surprised to see Faust park the car, grab his brief case from the trunk, and walk into The Spot. Mac pulled over and decided to follow him into The Spot. It was always dark inside, and even Mac could keep a low profile. Mac didn't much care for this strip joint. He had stopped several times with some biker buddies, mostly to drink a few beers. Jackie was Mac's woman, and he always felt sad for the dancers. But he figured they knew how to entertain the men and get tips.

Mac spotted Faust sitting on the opposite side of the horseshoe bar and took a seat on the far side near the door. A dancer approached Faust but did not sit down. She pointed out Terrek to Faust, sitting on the same side of the bar as Mac, but closer to the dance floor. Mac watched Faust slip her a twenty. He then picked up his briefcase, which he had retrieved from the trunk of his car. He walked around the bar, over to the stool next to Terrek.

Once seated, Faust called out to the bartender to fill a pitcher of beer and to bring an extra glass. Terrek ignored Faust, more interested in watching the dancers. Faust poured himself a glass and asked if he could refresh Terrek's mug, which was nearly drained. Terrek looked at Faust, shoved his mug over, and uttered, "Sure, thanks."

Terrek went back to watching the dancers, thinking little of the gesture, just another guy wanting to watch the dancers while being friendly. But Faust continued to address Terrek,

"Cheers! Glad to finally meet you, Terrek!"

Hearing his name, Terrek diverted his attention back to the man buying him a beer, taking a closer look this time. Terrek saw this was no ordinary student and not a typical strip joint patron. This man was well-dressed, silk tie, business suit, a handsome, middle-aged man. Terrek vaguely recalled seeing him before.

"How do you know my name?"

"Not only your name. Your father owns Auto Paradise, you were a student at Milson last semester, and you drive a Jeep."

Terrek was not the only one interested after Faust stated the name Terrek. Mac knew this was the name of Trudy's boyfriend. Now that Faust had walked over to his side of the bar, Mac was watching and listening closely. Faust's back was toward Mac, and facing Terrek, but Mac could hear everything.

In response to Terrek's question, Faust pulled out a business card, handed it to Terrek, and told him that he was representing Trudy.

"You and I have some business to do."

Faust set his briefcase on top of the bar, clicked open the two front clasps, and pulled out the Termination of Parental Rights document that he had prepared. Terrek responded with the question Faust knew he would ask: "What business do I have with you?"

"I represent Trudy in a private adoption. She is going to give your baby up for adoption."

Already knowing how Terrek would respond, Faust waited momentarily.

"It's not *my* baby, if that's what Trudy told you. It could be a lot of guys.' I told her not to try and pin this on me, I told her that already," Terrek sniveled louder than he should have.

"Yes, I know. You deny that you are the father of her baby, right?" "That's right!" Terrek declared loudly and adamantly, drawing attention.

Listening from his dark corner, Mac wanted to walk over to Terrek, grab him by the scruff of his neck, and tell him he wasn't fit to even say the name Trudy, much less be her boyfriend. Yet Mac stayed put, controlling his temper. He disliked both of these men, but he was on a mission and kept his low profile.

Faust continued to control their exchange: "Trudy told me the same thing. You deny being the father, but you don't deny knowing Trudy, do you?"

"So?" was Terrek's retort.

"Not only that, but you also had sex with Trudy last year, celebrating New Year's Eve."

"That's what she says. I'm not telling you anything."

"You don't have to. I've already been out to Auto Paradise. I sat in your limo—even enjoyed some of your brandy. Get some scotch though if you want to have a fully stocked bar. But it all matched pretty well with what Trudy described."

"Hey, that's private property! You had no right to go into my limo!" objected Terrek.

"You mean Terrek International, right?"

Terrek stood up. He was angry and was about to turn and leave. Faust grabbed his arm and told him to sit down again as he softened his tone:

"Look, I didn't come here to be unpleasant. Sit down, have another beer, I can make this go away and no one, not even your father, needs to know about our conversation here or anything else."

As Faust poured a fresh glass for him, Terrek sat down again.

"I know you deny being the father. This document is only a Petition for Termination of Rights for a Putative Father." Faust pulled the paperwork out of his briefcase. "Putative is a legal term that means the signee is possibly the father, not proven. We could do a blood test to prove fatherhood, but why bother? Trudy decided to terminate her parental rights and allow her baby to be adopted. You can also just sign off—no need to do anything more."

Terrek barely looked at the document. "I'm not signing anything— why should I?"

"You could get an attorney, of course, but I could also bring a paternity suit against you. I could get a court to order you to do a blood test. Once it is confirmed that you are the father, and I have no reason to disbelieve the mother on this account, I can get court orders to force you to cooperate. If you don't terminate your rights, you could be ordered to search for employment, pay medical bills, pay child support, provide benefits like health insurance, and more. But sign this, and you are free of all these responsibilities. Unless, of course, you want to be a father to the baby. It's your parental right, and it's the reason you must give consent to allow the termination and adoption."

"You're not my attorney."

"That's correct," replied Faust, adding, "I represent the adoptive parents and for now, Trudy. Both parties agree on an adoption."

"Let's get real. You don't need all these entanglements, and Trudy doesn't want to be involved in a lawsuit proving a paternity claim either. You cooperate, sign the consent, and you're done. It's that easy."

Terrek leered at Faust. He did not like hearing this lecture about his responsibilities and thought Faust was starting to sound like his old man. Terrek always rebelled when told to do things that he didn't want to do.

"I told you, I'm not signing papers. I know my rights—you can't force me to do it."

Faust poured another beer for Terrek. He paused, irritated at having to be rational with this immature kid. Recalibrating, Faust changed gears: "I see you are not easily convinced, very smart, but you are also miscalculating. I will do what I said. I will see you in court if I have to, but why? It is just wasting your time."

Faust pulled out his money clip, "I'm willing to pay for your time and the drink that I had in the limo, courtesy of Terrek International." He peeled off a hundred-dollar bill and handed it to Terrek, adding, "It would be unethical to pay you for signing the consent, but I can pay for these courtesies. I know the girls here. How would you like to have Tanya spend the night with you? I can arrange it. You have quite the hangout in that limo. I'm sure one of the girls would love to go there with you. Signing this consent will be worth your while. Now, what do you say?"

Terrek's eyes widened, "You know Tanya that well?"

Faust smiled. He saw that he had found the right temptation this time. "Sure, I know her well. She gave me the tip that you were here. I can call her over right now. You go home, freshen up and come back. When Tanya's shift is done after her dance routine, I'll make it worth her time to go with you. Is it a deal?"

"Deal," Terrek drained his glass as Faust picked up the pen to hand to Terrek.

Refusing to accept the pen, Terrek replied, "Not so fast. How do I know Tanya will come with me when I return?" Tanya, still on her break, was watching Faust with interest, having identified Terrek to him. Faust now made eye contact with her and motioned her over.

Like Tanya, Mac was also watching all this with intense scrutiny. He was not sure what Faust was doing but overheard the proposition made to Terrek. He saw Faust nod to Tanya and watched her approach the two men.

Faust checked around the bar, making sure neither the bartender nor the bouncer were watching what he was about to do. It was something strictly off limits at The Spot, but the girls knew how to manage their own entertainment, all done on the side with savvy customers. Like so much else in Faust's circle, it was a matter of knowing who and how, but not the why, of following rules.

Lowering his money clip below the drink rail, Faust turned away from the bar and faced Tanya. He pulled out two crisp hundred-dollar bills and handed them to her. He looked around to see if anyone was watching, and spotted Mac for the first time, just down from where he was sitting, and realized that Mac was at his back when he faced Terrek. He also speculated that Mac was close enough to hear them. Faust also noted that the bouncer was sitting outside on the sidewalk, not currently watching inside. The next music set had not yet started, and it was still early—not much activity inside to warrant vigilance. The bartender was pouring a drink on the other side of the horseshoe.

Faust quietly whispered to Tanya, "Terrek really likes the way you dance; he'd like to show you his plush limo and spend some time with you tonight. Can he entertain you there?"

Tanya took the two bills, folded them, slipping them into her bra, fully understanding. She looked over to Terrek, "See you at seven."

Terrek smiled, turned back to the bar, picked up the pen, and signed the consent. Meanwhile, Faust conjectured that Mac might have followed him into the bar. He did not want to be followed if Mac was in fact watching him, which would lead him to Trudy.

Terrek got up to leave as instructed, planning to return later to pick up Tanya. He smiled at her, anticipating a fun evening. As he walked out, passing Mac on the way to the door, Faust watched Mac. He stayed put. Just as Terrek was about to step outside into the sunlight, Faust called out after him, loud enough for Mac to hear: "Say hi to Trudy for me!"

Terrek did not hear Faust's parting comment with all the street noise. But Mac heard. He turned to watch Terrek stepping outside. He made a quick calculation. If this young guy was staying with Trudy, maybe he was following the wrong man. He wanted to find Trudy. Just as Faust had calculated, Mac stood up and followed Terrek out of The Spot.

Faust watched him leave, then quickly gathered the signed consent form, returned it to his briefcase, and thanked Tanya, assuring her he'd make her time with Terrek worth her efforts. He then left through a side entrance away from the street. He walked through an alley and back around to the front sidewalk. Before stepping onto the front walk, he peered around the corner of the bar in time to see Mac following Terrek, walking down the sidewalk. As Terrek got into his Jeep, Mac ran back to his Harley, kicked it into gear and pulled out to follow the Jeep. Faust waited until they were several blocks away, then quickly got to his Jaguar and headed back to his office.

Jill was waiting at the office with Trudy after her appointment with Dr. Wellstein. To finish the day, Faust told Trudy about the plans to meet with Tony and Marie and return to the city the next day as he had promised. He also explained that Dr. Wellstein insisted that Trudy not be alone for her remaining time before the baby is born. They'd have to spend one more night at the lake cottage. Trudy was disappointed and about to object when Faust assured her this would be her final night at the cottage. She was too tired to argue further. And Faust assured her he would stay as well. Tomorrow she'd meet the adoptive parents and would remain in Milson until the baby comes. Reluctantly, she agreed to go back to the lake cottage for one night.

Chapter 13

Labor Day Weekend 1977

Mac called Pig and told him how he lost Faust's trail, having made the wrong decision to follow Terrek out of The Spot. He'd stopped the kid near his dorm and asked where Trudy was. When Terrek refused to answer any questions, he threatened to tie Terrek behind his Harley and drag him the way cowboys did to cattle rustlers. Terrek caved easily and claimed that he had no idea where Trudy was. He had just signed a consent to terminate his parental rights to the baby at The Spot.

"I believed the kid," Mac told Pig.

Mac continued, explaining that Faust saw him at the bar just as Terrek was leaving. He correctly assumed I was tailing him. When the kid left the bar, Faust called out to him to say, "Hello to Trudy for him."

"Faust was manipulating me. He knew following the kid would throw me off his trail. Faust knew I wanted to find Trudy," Mac complained to Pig, adding, "I was stupid for taking the bait." But Pig told him he would've done the same.

"I didn't know! When I heard Faust, I thought maybe Trudy had gone to live with her boyfriend; it made some sense at the time. Now, we do know one thing for sure, Faust knows where Trudy is, and he also knows that I'm watching him. But he doesn't know about you and Tag."

Mac suggested Pig go back to Faust's office first thing in the morning to see if he could spot the Jaguar. Meanwhile, they could all get some sleep tonight. I'll explain what's going on to Tag. Hopefully, we can pick up Faust's trail again. I might stop at the courthouse to see if I can get any information about this paternity action that Terrek had mentioned.

Faust hated driving Jill's Chevy sedan but decided to trade cars with his secretary. He'd drive Trudy to the meeting with Tony and Marie who had flown into town and checked into the airport hotel as planned. Faust feared Mac might be watching for his green Jaguar as he drove into Milson. He knew it could be readily spotted. Instead, Jill would have a joy ride back to the office and be relieved of her babysitting duties.

Trudy was thankful to finally leave the cottage, having been assured by Faust that it would be her last night at this remote location. But she was nervous about meeting this new adoptive couple.

Never mind this beautiful September day, Trudy was not enjoying it. Her ankles were swollen, and she was tired since she could not get more than a couple hours of sleep, unable to turn over easily in the small, single-bed at the cottage. As they drove along, Trudy noted the birch leaves were already turning gold along the edge of the forest road. Had she been home on the farm, she'd be helping her family bail hay.

The memory saddened her, feeling homesick and alone. Faust noticed how sullen Trudy had become, and he tried to cheer her explaining that she would have a beautiful room at the absolutely best hotel in the airport, which was also near to the hospital as her doctor wanted.

He explained, "Tony and Marie know how to live well; they booked a suite for you with your own jacuzzi in the room. Marie said that she wanted to share some 'pamper time' with you. Those were her words, 'pamper time.' Knowing Marie, you can have anything you need, just ask."

Trudy wasn't impressed, "I can't use a jacuzzi, I was specifically told not to do that by Dr. Wellstein's nurse."

Faust laughed. "There you have it, I don't know those female things, but Marie will be attentive to your needs, that's my point. Cheer up. Your ordeal is nearly over. I know you must feel like these days are endless, but soon you'll be able to get your life back in order, take up whatever it is you want to do, finish school, whatever."

His words irritated Trudy, but she thought he was right about one thing: this was an ordeal, her ordeal, not his. Now that Dr. Wellstein had given her literature on what to expect during the delivery, how to breathe, how not to panic and how her body would react during the hours before delivery of the baby, she was in fact beginning to panic.

Trudy had seen many calves born in the barn, but this was her body, experiencing birth for the first time. Dr. Wellstein talked about well-baby classes for expectant mothers. She didn't have much time left, but she was told to enroll in several sessions. Trudy had not bothered to tell Faust this. She was reading the literature on her own and trying to decide if she wanted to be part of a class with expectant mothers all planning new nurseries and having baby showers. She wasn't doing any of that, and Trudy would not have a husband as her "coach" as the literature defined the father's role in the delivery room. This was indeed Trudy's ordeal.

Faust pulled up to the front door of the Grand Hamilton Hotel, handing his keys to the porter. Opening the passenger door, he assisted Trudy, taking her arm to guide her into the front lobby. Once inside, Trudy felt very pregnant and conspicuous in this grand hotel lobby. She stood under a sparkling chandelier lighting the marble flooring and Persian carpets.

The guests were impeccably dressed in beautiful summer linens while she wore the same oversized gray sweatshirt and jeans she'd worn all week at the cottage. Feeling self-conscious, she hung her head, not wanting to be seen. Her uncombed hair hung like strings over her face. She tried to balance her baby weight by tipping her center of balance to the back of her heels, feeling like a freak.

Faust walked up to the reservation desk and was about to ask for the room number of Tony and Marie when a voice called to him from the staircase that descended from a balcony into the majestic lobby. Tony, tall, with olive-toned skin, wearing a cotton polo shirt and light tan linen slacks, walked over and shook Faust's hand. He announced that they were already checked in, and he would take them up to the rooms.

Faust turned to introduce Trudy, but she stopped him, saying she needed to use the restroom and quickly walked down a side hallway. She left hurriedly, not wanting to be introduced to this handsome man with impeccably styled black hair.

Trudy stayed inside the bathroom as long as she could, splashing cold water over her face. The image starring back at her in the mirror as she tried to smooth her hair was a disaster, a stranger in her once trim body.

When she finally walked back into the lobby, the two men were waiting for her at the bottom of the staircase. As she approached, she asked if there was an elevator she might use. Tony immediately apologized for being so thoughtless. Arriving at adjoining suites, Tony motioned them through the open door, allowing Faust and Trudy to enter the room. Marie was anxiously awaiting them inside.

Trudy glanced up ever so slightly to see this woman, possibly the future mother of her baby. Marie appeared to be thirty-something, slim and attractive. She had the same olive-toned skin and brown eyes as her husband, but her hair was long and blonde, beautifully coiffured. She carried herself as if she were a model. She was wearing a crisp aqua linen pantsuit, with a cream silk shell, and wearing a gold necklace with turquoise stones. Her nails were manicured and her makeup professionally applied. Though not a natural beauty, her clothing and makeup maximized all of her best features, particularly her eyes. Her figure was stunning. Trudy felt unworthy to be in their presence and wished she could just leave.

Marie stepped closer to Trudy and gently placed her fingertips below Trudy's chin, gently asking her to lift up her face.

"Hello!" Marie began with a jubilant, friendly greeting, adding, "I've been so anxious to meet you and spend time with you, get to know something about you. Plus, you have to get to know us!" She turned to Faust, "Hal, you never told me how beautiful Trudy is! A natural beauty!"

Still never formally introduced, Marie dismissed the men. Tony, taking his wife's cue, suggested to Faust they return to the lobby to discuss their mutual business. Marie took Trudy's hand and kindly led her into her suite.

Marie guided Trudy to a pair of overstuffed chairs near the balcony of her suite that overlooked the airport tarmac. Trudy, feeling like a slave inside the queen's palace, obeyed. Marie criticized Hal, telling Trudy he should have taken better care of her, noting her wrinkled clothing.

"Tell me something about yourself, Trudy, I'd like to get to know you—hear some stories about your family."

But Trudy had no idea what to say; she had nothing that would interest her. Marie tried to fill the silence, to get Trudy to open up to her. She explained how happy Trudy had made them when she selected their file for the private adoption. She told Trudy how she had wanted to be a mother for a long time but was never able to have her own baby.

"One day, I will be able to tell your baby how beautiful you are, but I'd like to share some stories about you, or tell the baby whatever it is you'd like me to say! You already know about Tony and me from all the information we had to complete, but beyond that, I want you to ask me anything else."

"We will give your baby the best care, the best schooling, music classes, whatever talents this little one has will be amplified by the best coaches or artists or teachers that the East Coast has to offer," Marie added, "But what is it you want the baby to know?"

Trudy had not thought of anything to say to Marie; she didn't even want to be here, but Marie was trying so hard to be kind. She finally offered the little she had:

"I'm nineteen. I got pregnant after starting college, and I would really like to go back to taking classes. I come from a small farming town north of Milson. I grew up on a farm with my grandmother and grandfather who raised me. Really not much to tell you,"

Marie kept trying to prompt Trudy to say something, but she only succeeded in making her more uncomfortable. Trudy's eyes began to tear, thinking about this strange woman informing her baby about the "birth mother."

Marie was moved by Trudy's tears. While striving to make Trudy comfortable enough to open up, she realized all the questions were overwhelming. Finally, hoping to soothe both of them, she retrieved her hairbrush from the powder room and began to brush Trudy's long, tangled hair. As she brushed Trudy's hair, she told her that her own mother used to do this for her just as she would like to one day do it for her own child.

"You have such beautiful hair, Trudy. I can see Hal didn't give you enough time to get ready this morning."

With more encouragement from Marie, Trudy shared more of her history, remembering her own grandmother brushing her hair and shared with Marie a few memories of her beloved grandmother. This flowed into more stories as Trudy explained to Marie that she barely knew her own mother or father but that her grandmother had raised her. Telling Marie how kind and wise her grandmother was, Trudy explained how hard life had been for her grandparents, working the farm, nearly losing it several times in bad years, and enduring the death of a child, Trudy's mother. She talked a bit about her uncle and her cousins, sharing some of the fun times playing on the haystack in the barn or trekking through the woods in the snow.

Marie thought it sounded idyllic, but Trudy emphasized the harshness of her grandparents' lives. Marie shared more details about Tony and the home they lived in. She told Trudy about the nursery that she had already decorated.

Trudy finally interrupted Marie's litany of promises, asking, "Will you love my baby?"

Marie stopped brushing Trudy's hair. "How thoughtless of me!" Marie exclaimed, adding: "Of course, I will love the baby. I understood that, first of all, I thought it was understood. Both Tony and I will love this baby with all of our hearts."

Trudy did want to actually hear this promise spoken in words as if it would be a sealed agreement between them. This was the most important promise of all to her, not all of the things that money could buy. Yet Trudy felt in her own heart that no one could really love a baby the way a mother could. Trudy could never get beyond that realization. It was part of her own sadness growing up.

Marie gently asked if Trudy could talk about how she lost her mother. Why her grandmother was the one who raised her. Trudy quietly answered that her mother died of a broken heart. Her father had been drafted into the Vietnam conflict. He died from injuries he suffered after serving in Vietnam, and her mother was unable to cope with losing the love of her life. Trudy left out the details about her father's spiral into death from combat fatigue and exposure to agent orange and other chemicals, along with his use of drugs and alcohol. He suffered from guilt and the ugliness of the treatment he and all the Vietnam veterans endured. Her mother went down the same rabbit hole of abusing drugs and alcohol with him.

It had taken Trudy a long time to come to grips with her family history and didn't believe that Marie would be able to relate to any of this ugliness. Trudy decided to let this end with her. Why have any grandchild of these Vietnam vets live with this nightmare any longer? It gave her some comfort to keep this secret. She could save her baby from this ugliness.

"Trudy, we only have a few days together. Can I set up a spa treatment for both of us? We can get a facial, have our hair done, get pampered. I really would love doing this with you! Please say yes!"

"Now?" She panicked, not having slept well all week at Faust's cottage. She explained to Marie she was tired and not up to going anywhere right now. Trudy had no idea what a spa treatment might entail but didn't say this to Marie.

"Isn't that just like men!" Marie was disgusted that Hal had treated Trudy so badly, adding, "Hal should have taken better care of you than that! I'm sorry Trudy, I've been thoughtless. I will see to it that you get some rest, and we can see how you feel after you're rested and then talk further."

Marie took Trudy into the adjoining suite, which looked just like Marie's with a seating area and a balcony that opened over the airport tarmac, and a separate bedroom. Marie guided Trudy to the large queen-sized bed with its ample pillows and a soft downy quilt. She took the pink terry-cloth robe, handing it to Trudy, and told her to put it on and get out of her clothing. As Trudy went into the bathroom to undress, Marie pulled the heavy drapes closed and turned back the comforter and sheets. Trudy returned to the bedroom, and Marie tucked her in as a mother might do. Trudy began to tell her that she didn't think Faust would allow her to sleep, not while he was waiting.

"I'll take care of Hal," insisted Marie, "I'm already irritated with him for not taking better care of your needs. Get some sleep. I will make sure that you are not disturbed. I'll order a nice dinner for later. We can eat in the room. Get to know each other better. Leave it to me, Trudy, now go to sleep."

Trudy felt like a little girl being put to bed. She was exhausted and glad to be in a luxurious bed. She wanted nothing more than to sleep. Closing the adjoining door, Marie went down to the lobby to find Faust. Seated in the cocktail lounge, Faust was enjoying his noontime Perfect Rob Roy while Tony drank iced tea. Faust grimaced, "Where is Trudy?"

Marie answered coolly. Still upset with Faust, she was determined not to let him take the upper hand as he often did as their counselor-at-law, the one giving advice, not taking it.

"Trudy was exhausted. She is getting a much-needed nap, and she complained about the hard bed you've had her sleeping in."

"I need to keep a close eye on Trudy. She's getting very near her due date, and now is not the time to have unnecessary interruptions," Faust was purposely vague. No way did he want to explain to his clients his concern of being tailed.

"I will 'keep a close eye' on Trudy, as you put it, and I can do a much better job of seeing to her needs. She looks exhausted; her clothing is shabby. She is obviously in need of getting cleaned up, with her hair styled and a change of clothing."

Marie turned to go back to her room when Faust stopped her.

"You have no idea what I've gone through to get Trudy here, and I am going to set the parameters of Trudy's stay at this hotel."

But Marie was not about to let Faust tell her what to do. She glared at him and turned to her husband, "Dear, I'm going back to the room — you work it out with the attorney as to what he thinks needs to be done. I'm going to take care of Trudy."

Faust understood the ultimate insult. This wealthy client could be very difficult. He watched as she brushed her hair back over her shoulder, turned abruptly, and left the cocktail lounge.

Tony picked up where Marie left off, asking Faust what he meant by "gone through". "Gone through what?" Faust, growing irritated, sipped his Perfect Rob Roy and prevaricated a story of half-truths.

"Trudy has been working for an overbearing woman named Jackie who has a boyfriend: a motorcycle gang member who does whatever Jackie tells him to do. The two have been pestering Trudy all the way through her pregnancy. I had to get Dr. Wellstein to grant Trudy medical leave before this woman would give Trudy the time off she needed. If that wasn't enough, this employer is still trying to get Trudy to commit to a return date. Her gang-banger boyfriend has been following me."

Tony frowned. "Are you being followed now?"

"No, but you can see why I'm insisting on keeping tabs on this."

Faust drained his glass. "Tony, I've had to work hard on your case. I can't have Marie, who I know means well, expose Trudy's whereabouts."

"I could get more security if that's what is needed," offered Tony, "What kind of job did Trudy have? What would cause an employer to push a pregnant woman to work like that?"

Tony was skeptical of Faust's explanation. It wasn't plausible for a college kid to have a critical job where someone would insist on keeping track of her.

"Look, I'm not going to try to get into the mind of an unreasonable employer. You'll have to take my word on this. You know we have a court hearing right after the birth in order for you and Marie to take the baby home on temporary placement. This is all very delicate right now, and we don't need to have Trudy going through anymore turmoil than she already has."

"Trudy is safe with us. If, as you say, no one knows where Trudy is, this is the best place for her, right?"

"I want you to remind your wife that we have legal requirements ahead. Marie can't just take over, telling Trudy what to do. That will not look right in court, and it could jeopardize the consent that Trudy will be required to give. Her consent must be freely given, without payment or compulsion," argued Faust.

"Alright, what else do we need?" asked Tony.

"Trudy stays with you for now, in her room. She does not leave this airport or the hotel, and I am, at all times, in charge of where Trudy goes. Do you understand that?"

"Yes, I will tell Marie."

"I expect you to contact me every day. I will be the one to keep Trudy safe. This is my responsibility. Also, don't forget you have an appointment on Friday. But Trudy is to stay here, at the hotel. Are we clear?"

"Clear." Tony shook Hal's hand and said he'd go up to the room and have a talk with Marie.

Faust was satisfied and planned to return to his office. Before hailing the car, he headed over to the bank of pay phones at the far end of the lobby. He needed to check in with Jill and tell her to call his wife and let her know he would be home tonight. Faust knew Jill hated to do this, but he wasn't in the mood to talk to his wife and listen to her bitch that he had not been home for several days. She knew that he was working on a difficult termination case.

Pig called Mac on his citizens' band radio to tell him the green Jag was parked in the back alley behind the lawyer's office, asking what he should do next. Mac told him to stay put. He and Tag would head over directly from the courthouse where they'd gone to ask around about Faust.

Mac had learned that adoption cases were handled by the Probate Courts and had been directed up to the district court, probate division of the courthouse on the second floor. There, Mac had talked to an assistant probate registrar, a bureaucrat who was only able to explain basic, public information. Adoption cases involve minors and are therefore confidential. Mac would not be able to discover if any cases were filed. All adoption proceedings involving infants or juveniles were closed hearings. The only bit of information that was at all helpful to him had been learning that Harold Faust was well-known to this clerk. Faust was a member of the local bar association and chairman of the adoption division of the probate bar. The registrar confirmed that

Faust was one of the lawyers appearing often in adoption and termination hearings.

The roar of the motorcycles reverberated off the storefronts of University Avenue as Mac and Tag pulled up to Faust's office. Faust heard the Harleys just as he was returning from the hotel. Not wanting Mac to spot him again, Faust drove on past his office in Jill's Chevy sedan, a car so ordinary that neither Mac nor Tag paid attention to the car or its driver.

Meeting up with Pig, they first walked to the side alley and observed the Jaguar. Pig confirmed that he had not seen Faust come or go since his early morning arrival. Mac asked Tag to keep an eye on the back alley door. He and Pig would go around to the front entrance, and Pig would watch the front door. He would go inside and try to find and maybe talk with Faust, again. This time he would not be sidetracked.

Mac walked boldly into the office, already knowing the receptionist would not give him any information. As he opened the door and walked in, Mac walked briskly beyond the reception area and headed for the inner offices.

"Wait, Stop! You can't go in there," shouted Jill.

Mac saw the inner office and conference rooms were empty. Mac did see many papers on top the desk, unlike the clean conference table. By now, Jill caught up and insisted Mac was not allowed in Faust's inner office. Mac was tempted to stay and read the documents, but Jill would not be deterred.

"Get out of here. Leave now, or I will call 9-1-1!"

"No need to call 9-1-1, I just want to know where Faust is?"

Jill was not a temp but was a well-trained legal secretary. She was not about to let this guy order her to give him information.

"You are to leave this office, right now. You are not a client and have no right demanding any information from me. This is my last warning. Leave now, or I make the call."

Mac knew she meant business and surmised he'd not learn anything from her. Even though he carried the size of a man unaccustomed to being told "no," Mac was not a man that bullied women. He left without any further conflict. It was obvious that if Faust was in the building, he would have already appeared. His secretary was loud enough for both of them.

When Mac got back outside, he motioned for Pig to walk over to the side alley to talk further with Tag. Mac told them Faust was not in his office even though his Jag was still parked in its space. They were no further along in picking up Faust's trail again than yesterday when Mac had been in The Spot. Mac was growing frustrated. Pig and Tag wanted to know what to do next.

Mac thought for several minutes, he asked Tag to take over watching the Jaguar and office for any sign of Faust. Pig was told to go over to Jackie's Counter, get a quick bite to eat and wait for him there. Mac would check The Spot again and try to talk with the dancer he had seen Faust talking to yesterday.

Trudy woke from her nap late in the afternoon, amazed to have slept so well. Marie found her noticeably refreshed. Trudy's eyes were no longer dark sockets. Trudy looked for her clothing, still wearing the pink robe. Marie told her she had sent them to the laundry but had also ordered a few new things for Trudy to wear and expected a delivery soon.

Trudy continued to feel embarrassed around Marie, who kept fussing over her. But the motherly attention was soothing. She slipped into a little sister/big sister role, going along with whatever Marie thought necessary.

Marie suggested they sit out on the balcony and watch the landing and takeoff of jets and the constant movement of luggage carts, fuel trucks, and fleet cars around the tarmac. It was a beautiful day. Marie ordered a cheese platter with appetizers and drinks, wine for Marie and lemonade for Trudy.

"I'd love to take you downtown, where we could enjoy many lovely shops and find a cozy lounge, but I'm under strict orders to stay here; we will have to make do with this for now," announced Marie.

Trudy knew exactly who Marie was talking about. Faust was still controlling her movements. Trudy resented this momentarily but then wondered how she'd go anywhere without her clothing. She found this balcony overlooking the tarmac fascinating. Trudy had never flown on an airplane but did not want to admit it to Marie, who'd probably think she was a simpleton.

Room service arrived, and Marie set out the cheese and fruit, crackers and nuts, on a small round table. Marie continued telling Trudy she made plans for tomorrow, the last weekday before the long Labor Day weekend. She and Trudy could not go outside the airport, but Marie found a hairdresser in the airport concourse and set up an appointment hoping that Trudy would not mind, adding it could be canceled.

Trudy just went along, knowing full well that she needed her hair trimmed. Marie also booked a time for a facial and pedicure for both of them since she would stay with Trudy.

"Since I'm not allowed to take you downtown, we can at least walk through all the shops in the concourse; they have several lovely little shops, and we can have fun shopping. Tonight I've ordered room service, and Tony will be back to join us for dinner."

Marie continued doing much of the talking. She told Trudy they could watch a movie tonight and have an old-fashioned pajama party. She added, "Both Tony and I want to spend time with you—get to know you a little bit."

Tony finally came back. He pulled up a chair out on the balcony but mostly listened as Marie continued to chatter on about their plans for the next day.

Another delivery arrived. This time it was a drop-off for the clothing that Marie ordered for Trudy. She unwrapped the bags, showing Trudy several lovely tops and a new pair of maternity pants for her to wear. Trudy marveled at how easily Marie seemed to just make things appear, her every wish was at her command.

Marie told Trudy to change into the new clothing and model the items to be sure of their fit. The flowing top was not something Trudy would ever have selected or worn, a baby-doll blouse of pale pink flowers set on pretty green vines outlining the neckline and bodice. The linen slacks were black with an elasticized panel around her waistline, certainly much finer than her old gray sweatshirt and jeans. Tony paid the ultimate compliment after Trudy emerged with her new clothing. "You look wonderful."

Their evening went as Marie had planned, with an in-room meal, and later a movie. During dinner, Tony asked Trudy to tell him more about what life was like on a dairy farm. He seemed really interested, telling Trudy that he had several financial clients in the food industry, not exactly farming, she thought, but Tony was friendly. Marie sat back and listened to her husband and Trudy talk livestock and crops, happy to be their hostess.

After the movie, they all retired after Marie explained their Friday plans to Tony. He was happy the plans did not require much on his part, except he reminded Marie that they had an appointment with Faust the next day. She suggested that he take care of it without her. Tony easily agreed.

On Friday, after a light in-room breakfast, Marie had the hotel coach meet them at the front door of the hotel and deliver them to the main concourse of the Milson International Airport. Marie took Trudy directly over to the Hair Port Salon, where their appointment was booked. Marie sat at the manicure table having her hand massaged and nails done while watching Trudy's hair styling, chatting happily with the beautician.

As the stylists washed and brushed Trudy's hair, she commented how beautifully full and natural Trudy's hair was, noting that pregnant women often complained of brittle hair, but Trudy's was not at all like this. "Must be your youth," she commented. Trudy was embarrassed to have this woman boldly talk about her pregnancy, but Marie made Trudy sound as if she was flourishing with expectant joy, adding:

"We are both so excited!" as if she were indeed Trudy's older sister.

Two hours later, Marie and Trudy emerged from the Hair Port Salon with glowing faces, beautifully applied makeup, and manicured nails. Trudy's long, stringy hair was cut shoulder length and perfectly caressed her face. When she looked in the mirror after the services were completed, Trudy could not help but admire her image. It was not the natural farm girl staring back; it was one of the beautiful people that Marie knew.

Marie literally gushed over Trudy's makeover, telling her how lucky she was to have such beautiful, milky skin, such wonderfully thick amber hair.

"You could easily have been a model." Trudy remained silent but walked with Marie, feeling renewed confidence—feeling less embarrassed by her pregnancy. With her new clothes and makeover, Marie said she looked like a pretty pink flower in bloom.

Mac and his buddies sat at Jackie's Counter. They were despondent, not having picked up Faust's trail and not sure they should keep up their surveillance. Labor Day weekend would be quiet as the many city residents were headed out of town for their last vacation days "Up North." Faust's office remained locked after Jill left late in the day on Thursday. When Tag saw Jill lockup and then drive off in the green Jaguar, he reported to Mac, who now realized that Faust was no longer driving his own car.

Mac's short talk with Tanya at The Spot did not reveal much. He'd already known Faust had talked with Terrek. Mac did consider trying to find Faust's home address and set up a watch there, but his home address wasn't listed in the local White Pages, only the office address and office phone number, typical for attorneys who did not want clients disturbing their family.

Jackie served soup and sandwiches to the men, thankful for their search. But she was becoming more concerned than before. It seemed to her that Faust was purposefully misleading the guys, but she wondered why. Why would he hide Trudy's location and take extra precautionary steps to mislead Mac? Her imagination conjured countless concerns.

Trudy was nearing the end of her pregnancy and would surely need some help. It did occur to her that Trudy could have finally gone home to the farm, but Jackie was not convinced. Why wouldn't Trudy tell her this if she did. All of her recent information about Trudy had been through Faust. Jackie realized every effort to contact Trudy always wound its way back to Faust.

Marna came down to the counter when she heard the motorcycles outside. She hoped she might hear more about Trudy. As she listened to Mac and heard Jackie's concerns, Marna finally added that there was still no word from her niece that Trudy was checked in at the hospital.

Mac and his buddies finished lunch. He told Jackie and Marna that he would go over to the college campus and drive around to see what was happening there and then go over to Trudy's apartment and maybe talk with Leslie. He had no other thoughts. Mac told Pig and Tag to enjoy their Labor Day weekend. He'd poke around some more, but without any leads, there seemed to be no point in having three of them just blindly looking for clues. Pig and Tag told Mac to call if he needed them. All three split off.

Tony and Marie had an appointment with Faust mid-morning on Friday. Faust planned to review the reports with them. He was irritated when only Tony showed up for the appointment.

Faust also wanted to go over the mechanics of the court proceeding and have them sign the various forms required by state statutes, including a formal promise to provide for the infant's best interest. This form included disclosures that the prospective parents understood they had all the legal duties of a natural parent and understood the child would become their legal heir.

Tony told Faust not to worry; Marie could sign the documents later. He explained that Marie thought it was more important for her to spend time with Trudy. Faust was irritated that Marie had her own ideas. Faust wrote out contact information for Dr. Wellstein and the hospital, all written down with strict instructions provided as soon as any sign of Trudy's labor was starting. And most importantly, Faust was to be called first. Tony assured Faust he'd follow his instructions.

⁓ ℓ

While Trudy put her swollen ankles up on the second chair, watching the next jet taxi down the long runway, she tried to make sense of her feelings. Her baby's new family would be far different than her own. She told herself that this could be a good thing. Her life hadn't exactly been ideal. But Trudy's grandmother kept coming to mind. No one could love another more ardently than she had been loved by her mother's mother—unconditionally.

Trudy missed her grandmother. Would her baby know such love? If not, she should keep the infant herself; every baby deserved to be loved. What greater love is there than that of a mother? This was the crux of it, Trudy thought. This is the million-dollar question. Then she admonished herself for putting the adoption in dollar terms. This was a concern without a price.

That was it! Trudy thought, Faust put everything into dollar terms while her grandmother did not. Tony and Marie were wealthy; clearly money could pay for many needs—even a college education, which was Trudy's greatest wish. But you cannot buy love.

Trudy's heart began to race. She still had not taken the well-baby classes and had not prepared for what to expect in labor. She thought about the young heifers on the farm; calving came naturally to them. Trudy hoped her own body would find the natural rhythm. Her body was already programmed to do what was needed. She just needed to control her thoughts, many not helpful. But this would be her first time, and she didn't know what to expect. Her body knew what to do and, without thinking it through, just let it happen. Trudy kept telling herself to just let it happen. But she couldn't block out her thoughts or control her nervous energy.

Chapter 14

Labor Day 1977

Trudy could not find a comfortable position now that the baby had dropped. Lying in bed, she tried to sleep on her side by propping herself on a pillow placed under her enlarged midsection. As she bent her knee and raised her right leg atop the pillow, Trudy suddenly felt a gush of warm liquid wet her inner thigh. Her water broke!

As the sheet became soaked, she threw off her covers, got out of bed, and turned on the room light. Trudy rushed into the bathroom to find some towels. Her sudden movements and the light under their connecting inner door were enough to awaken Marie, who rose from her bed. She gently knocked on the shared inner door, asking if everything was alright.

When Trudy failed to answer, Marie knocked a second time and announced she was coming in. As Marie called out from inside Trudy's room, Trudy finally responded, telling Marie that her water broke.

Marie immediately took charge, telling Trudy to stay put for a moment. She woke Tony and asked him to get transportation to the hospital. Marie got the list Faust prepared. It prioritized the first contact as his office, then Dr. Wellstein, and then the hospital. Marie decided to skip contacting Faust for now. It was only 4 a.m., and she saw no reason to wake him. She would manage this herself for now. She made the other two necessary calls.

Dr. Wellstein told Marie it was important for Trudy not to walk or to be on her feet. She was only to transfer into the car. He explained that once the water breaks, there is concern that the baby's umbilical cord might slip down into the birth canal and choke off the blood supply. Trudy was to avoid walking. Most hotels have a courtesy wheelchair, and the doctor told Marie to use the wheelchair to take Trudy to the car and then to the hospital immediately. Marie assured the doctor that she would see to his instructions.

Marie called to Trudy, still in the bathroom, telling her that she called the doctor and got instructions to go to the hospital immediately. She would get a wheelchair. Trudy asked for her clothing, but Marie told her she should just wear the robe. Tony contacted the front desk for transport to the hospital and a wheelchair.

Marie quickly dressed and found the night bag to take to the hospital that Trudy had kept with her, having carried it around for the last several weeks. Tony, along with a bellhop, came into Trudy's room pushing the wheelchair. Everyone was trying to be super helpful.

Marie instructed the bellhop to roll the chair over to the bathroom, took several large towels, and placed one onto the seat. As the entourage rolled out into the early hours of the day, not yet daylight, Trudy saw that she was going to take another stretch limo ride, this one to her delivery room. The poetic justice of this moment did not escape Trudy's notice.

Trudy was helped into the limo by Tony while Marie quickly entered from the opposite side, placing fresh towels on the bench seat for Trudy. The three were on the way to Milson General Hospital, arriving just minutes later as there was little traffic on the roads. Marie was very attentive to Trudy, who was not experiencing anything other than the slow leakage of warm water between her legs.

Marie's own dreams were being fulfilled. She asked if she could stay with Trudy, who merely nodded. Trudy was afraid, still so much unknown before her, and this was her first time in labor.

As the limo pulled up to the emergency entrance, the orderly on night duty took note of the limo, not a customary emergency transport. But at night, orderlies could expect all kinds of odd surprises. The orderly made a mental note, *the limo mom arrives.*

Another wheelchair was brought to the passenger door, and Trudy was assisted from the limo to this wheelchair and pushed into the hospital and over to the emergency admittance desk. Marie gave Tony the contact information, including insurance information prepared by Faust. She turned to Tony and asked him to handle the admission details. The hospital had already been alerted by Dr. Wellstein's office with specific instructions. Trudy was waved into the maternity ward. Marie accompanied her, staying at Trudy's side.

Dr. Wellstein had arranged a birthing room for Trudy instead of admittance into the ward. These extra amenities were to be paid by the adoptive parents, who had instructed that the birth mother should get the best possible care; they wanted a healthy birth.

As Trudy was rolled into the room, she noted that half the room looked more like a bedroom. While the bed was clearly a hospital bed on large wheels with the usual lift controls and IV post, it was covered in a pastel blanket over pink sheets. Lamp tables, a television stand, and other normal bedroom furniture were arranged around the bed.

The opposite, smaller side of the room was clinical, equipped with metal stands for sterile equipment, a sink, medical counter, and storage cabinets with various medical supplies. The floor was highly polished linoleum; attached to the bare, painted walls were oxygen ports and various tubing. At the time of delivery, the bed could be rolled over from the bedroom side of the room to this hospital side.

Trudy was helped from her wheelchair and into the bed. Two nurses were assisting with the admittance procedures. A heart monitor was placed on Trudy as she was dressed in a hospital gown. Monitors were also placed to pick up her baby's vital signs. The nurse finally asked Trudy for the identification of her companion. Marie answered that she was the adopting mother and had Trudy's permission to stay with her. The nurse only listened momentarily, not wanting a lengthy history. Ignoring Marie, she turned to Trudy and asked if she wanted Marie to be in her room. Trudy simply responded yes.

After about thirty minutes of routine check-in procedures and obtaining Trudy's vital signs, the admittance team finally left the room, after explaining a nurse would routinely check monitors and the progress of her labor. Trudy had informed the staff that other than her water breaking, she had not yet experienced any contractions as far as she knew. The nurse replied she'd know if she had one!

Once all the nurses left the room, Marie tried to make Trudy comfortable. Daylight was just breaking as the sunlight poured into the room. Marie turned on the television and suggested watching a movie. Trudy sat comfortably in the bed with her backrest fully raised. She had no other plans and deferred to Marie's suggestion. Marie channeled through the stations, finding an old western. At this time of day, the choices were either morning talk shows, news and weather, or old movie reruns.

After Trudy was comfortably settled watching an old John Wayne western, Marie left the room to find Tony. She still had not contacted Faust and again decided that there was no reason to contact him this early. She told Tony to go back to the hotel, get himself breakfast and a few things that Marie wanted. Tony was happy to get out of the hospital. He disliked being in this institutional setting. Telling Tony that she would not leave, she hugged him,

"I'm so excited, and so lucky to be here, this is working out better than I hoped!" Tony only smiled, he kissed her goodbye, saying he'd be back later.

Trudy began to relax, paying little attention to the movie, when she felt a constriction around her midsection like the tightening of a wide leather belt. It was not severe and eased soon after it started. She was uncertain if this was the beginning of labor since it had not been painful. Unsure how she'd experience labor, Trudy merely stared out the window. All her needs were being met; she knew that she was in a safe place, but everything was surreal. Nothing was familiar. Trudy wished she could go outside and watch the start of this day, it was Labor Day weekend. Trudy thought, *Perfect, I get to take Labor Day literally*, she nearly laughed at herself, but realized the joke was on her.

As hours passed, nurses were in and out taking her vital signs, checking the baby's heart monitor. Marie also was in and out, seeing to Trudy's needs. After Tony returned with requested supplies, Marie brushed Trudy's hair and rearranged pillows so Trudy would be comfortable. Marie learned that this holiday television programming provided a back-to-back marathon of old westerns. She and Trudy would watch from time to time, laughing at the long dresses of the women.

Dr. Wellstein finally came in. He checked Trudy's pulse and looked at her chart. Marie talked with him in a familiar way, getting the same information he gave Trudy. Dr. Wellstein next closed the privacy screen and examined Trudy's progress for dilation; this took only a few moments. He finally told Trudy that she had started to dilate and that labor would begin more earnestly in a few more hours. His office would be on stand-by, and the nurses would contact him when nearer to giving birth. He asked if she had any questions. Trudy shyly responded that she didn't think so. Dr. Wellstein assured Trudy that she was in good hands and he'd be back later.

Marie decided that there was no reason for Tony to wait if it would be hours before any real labor started. She left the room again to talk with him.

"I did not call Faust, even though he wanted to be informed. Trudy is not going to be in labor for hours, and I'd rather not have Faust in here, there's nothing he could do other than upset Trudy or me. What do you think?"

"We have to call him," Tony insisted.

"Yes, I know, but not immediately. Let's wait, and after we see how Trudy's doing, I'll ask you to call him, please?"

Tony hesitated, but he saw no reason to make a call now. It was mid-morning, and the quiet city was just now rolling out of bed. It was a lazy holiday weekend. No call for now, Tony agreed.

By noon, Trudy's status was unchanged, Marie went to the hospital cafeteria for a light lunch, wanting to bring something for Trudy. But Trudy had been given strict instructions not to eat. She had an IV attached to her arm, and liquids were provided to be sure she did not get dehydrated.

In the afternoon, contractions that had previously started with only mild symptoms became noticeably stronger and more regular. Trudy was allowed to get up and use the bathroom but otherwise had to stay in bed. Trudy and Marie continued to watch the marathon of old Western movies, but the time passed slowly.

Suddenly, Trudy felt as if she had been punched in the midsection as she suddenly lost her breath and felt a long, very tight constriction. Marie began to panic; she was not experienced in labor or what to expect. She alerted the nurse by tugging on the call chord that hung from Trudy's bed. The nurse came in and checked on Trudy. She told Trudy to relax and breathe. By now, the pain had eased and Trudy did catch her breath.

The nurse asked Marie if she was Trudy's birthing coach. Marie wasn't familiar with this concept and responded that she was here to help with anything Trudy needed. The nurse instructed Trudy to take several short breaths in and out when she felt a contraction and demonstrated the technique for her. She emphasized the need to relax as much as possible with the breathing. If Trudy tightened, it would make the contraction feel worse. Trudy was told not to hold her breath but to keep breathing.

The nurse left. Back at the nurse's station, she commented to her colleague, "It's going to be a long day with the Limo Mom. That friend she brought along will be no help."

As Trudy relaxed and Marie sat down again on the chair next to Trudy's bed, they returned to watching the old movie. The scenery was one of breathtaking beauty, deep canyons, red cliffs and table rocks against a backdrop of blue sky with fluffy white clouds. Cowboys were herding cows across the wide expanse. The mooing cows reminded Trudy of the farm; young calves were running along with their mothers in this cattle drive. As the action continued, the clouds grew thicker and turned gray, a storm was brewing over the wide canyon.

Lightning struck, thunder roared, and the cattle were spooked. Trudy felt as if she was being punched in the midsection, again losing her breath just as the herding cows began stampeding. As the stampeding roar filled the screen, running headlong into Trudy's birthing room, she began to panic and hold her breath. As the herd turned, Trudy screamed, her consciousness overtaken by pain. The stampeding throb filled the television screen with smoke and dust. Imagining the stampeding herd overrunning her, Trudy was inundated by pain.

Marie also panicked, unsure what to do, she paced back and forth through the room along with the stampeding herd.

Mac parked his old Harley Panhead motorcycle in front of Jackie's Counter just after 2:00 p.m.; he waited for Jackie to come out for a ride as planned early that morning. Mac had spent his morning hours with Tag and Pig while Jackie worked, as usual refusing to close even though it was a slow Saturday on Labor Day weekend.

Jackie finally came out, no longer dressed in a white uniform or wearing a hair net. She let her long hair down, wore tightly fitting jeans and her fitted black leather jacket for riding. Mac's heartbeat quickened as it always did when he saw Jackie, but especially when she let her hair down. She was beautiful, ready to reclaim her youth. Jackie swung her leg over the cycle. She refused to sit in the sidecar, but Mac loved having Jackie hug him as his rider.

The two took a leisurely ride out of Milson, staying on side streets and heading out of town on the scenic roads into the countryside, following a meandering river. This was a bittersweet day, the end of summer.

Mac loved this ride. He recalled Memorial Day with Trudy in the sidecar as they rode under the draping branches. This day was equally as beautiful, still warm and sunny but now the leaves were turning. The birch leaves had all turned golden, and the maple leaves, though still green, were outlined in an orange senescence, beautiful but foreboding, aging like a fine wine.

Mac remembered Trudy's white scarf tailing behind her, pretending to wave to crowds in a parade. It had been a beginning, the start of summer, the start of a deep friendship, the start of vacation. They had so many expectations then, but now Labor Day became the ending, the end of summer, the maturing of expectations, even disappointment, and with Trudy's ominous disappearance, Mac felt sad. He had failed to help Trudy, as if she was his younger sister relying on her big brother for protection.

Mac pulled into the root beer stand where he always stopped on this river road ride, the same place he had taken Trudy on Memorial Day. Pulling up under a mature sugar maple, Mac retrieved his old army blanket from the pouch and spread it on the ground. Jackie already knew the routine and walked over to the outside counter and ordered their usual frothy drinks. She sat down with Mac and took off her helmet, swinging her hair back and over her shoulder. Mac watched Jackie, she was beautiful, and for once, for a few hours, they could be free.

Jackie and Mac took off their leather jackets. It was warm now that they were not riding on the breezy Harley. Jackie wore a tightly fitting black cotton blouse under her jacket. She had a beautiful figure and Mac never tired of seeing her full breasts, thin waist, shapely legs, and compact hips. He only watched, not telling her how beautiful she was as he usually would have. After sipping the last of the root beer, Mac stretched out, resting his head in Jackie's lap. She stroked his hair and outlined his strong chin with her fingers caressing his face. She was also quiet for a long time, enjoying the remnants of summer.

Jackie finally spoke: "You're quiet today, Mac. It's not like you. I know you wanted to ride today. It's so beautiful. Usually, you'd be constantly chatting away like that mourning dove that coos and coos every morning at our window."

"You're calling me a dove then? I can 'coo' if you'd like," teased Mac.

Jackie laughed. "I just want to know if something's wrong."

Mac looked up from Jackie's lap, seeing her lovely face framed by maple branches. Nothing could have been lovelier in Mac's mind. But Jackie was noticing his somber mood. She could read him like a soul mate, fully tuned in to his moods.

Mac looked into Jackie's blue eyes. Her long hair cascading over her shoulders, he wanted to stay like this and not talk. After a long pause, Mac confessed:

"I feel like such a failure. I should have kept that tail on Faust instead of falling for his ploy that got me to tail Trudy's boyfriend. Had I not done that, I might have found Trudy by now. Who knows where she is—or what's happening to her?"

Jackie bent over and kissed Mac's forehead.

"I've been thinking about Trudy, too. She's close to her due date. I hope she did go home, back to her family, which would be a safe place for her. It would explain why no one has seen her."

"Besides, it's not your fault. Even Pig said he'd have done the same; you were trying to find Trudy. All of us, even Marna, thought you did the right thing," Jackie responded.

Mac sat up and faced Jackie, "You know I was here, in this exact spot with Trudy, last Memorial Day. We were having fun. Then Trudy told me about her brooch, after I thought she had lost it in the sidecar. You remember me telling you afterward?"

"I remember."

"Today, if I had found Trudy, I wanted to give her another ride this morning, before your work shift ended, I had a surprise for her!"

"I know you mean well, Mac, but there's no way Trudy could have ridden in the sidecar. She's nine months pregnant! I can't imagine she'd be comfortable sitting in there, and certainly not in any shape for a long ride into the countryside."

Jackie didn't ask Mac about the surprise. Trudy in a sidecar violated Jackie's concept of common sense. Normally, Mac would have teased her about her institutional sense of propriety, but he was hurt after she cut him short, especially after looking so hard for Trudy.

Mac laid down again, but this time not resting his head on Jackie's lap. He laid on his back with his hands under his head, gazing upward. Jackie realized her tongue had been too short, she had not thought through her comment.

Jackie laid down on the blanket next to Mac and snuggled next to him, finally whispering, "I'm sorry, I know you tried."

Mac finally asked, "What did Trudy see in that young punk? When I finally caught him, he was just a sniveling little idiot. I wanted to punch his face in for leaving Trudy to handle his mess."

Jackie recalled his stops at the Counter. Terrek always came in and watched Trudy, hanging around after her work shift and then walking her over to the campus. Jackie had always tried to cut his lunch short. But she did understand the attraction.

"Terrek is a gorgeous hunk, especially to a young girl just out of high school. He is an unusually good-looking young guy, blonde hair, blue eyes. Plus, he was Trudy's contact on campus. She so badly wanted to be part of college life."

"I saw him come in for breakfast on Saturday morning with a hangover, and bloodshot, puffy eyes. In a few years, if he keeps drinking like that, that kid will be fat, balding and lose his pretty baby-face innocence that currently attracts the girls. I was just like Trudy once, and you know my story."

Mac thought Jackie was right, just as she always was. He just saw Terrek as a sneaky, immature jerk who needed to grow up.

"I felt responsible for finding Trudy. Hearing you and Marna offer to help Trudy the way you did. It really hit me. I made plans, too, you know. Trucking on the road all day, I imagined giving her little tyke a ride in my sidecar one day, taking Trudy and her child places, you know big brother plans."

Jackie lifted up on her elbow and turned on her side, facing Mac. "You're sweet, Mac, really the sweetest man I've ever known. That's why I love you so much."

Jackie kissed him and rolled over on top of Mac, hugging him. Mac kissed her back and wrapped his big arms around her. After a long embrace, Mac quipped, "I don't feel like *your* brother! We better get back to the city. I have plans for you tonight."

"You have a beautiful baby girl!"

The nursing assistant finished cleaning the newborn infant, wrapped the crying baby tightly in a cotton swaddling blanket and placed a small cotton cap on her tiny head. The aide carried the infant over to Trudy, still on the delivery bed and placed the baby into Trudy's arms.

Trudy stared into the little face. The infant stopped crying now that she was tightly swaddled and even opened her eyes. They were large eyes that held the entire world, like the Earth seen from space. Trudy's heart was beating as if tribal drums of welcome pounded.

"Talk to her—she'll know your voice," encouraged the young nursing aide.

"Hello! Little one."

Trudy laughed at herself, saying, "Hello!" to a newborn, but she was fixated on this little face. Time stopped, her exhaustion, pain, and sheer terror of the last twenty-some hours drained away. The whole universe came into focus. It was magical and unexpected, a few seconds transporting both into a mystical universe. Trudy floated out of the room, the building and for a few precious seconds found the gap between finity and infinity. Trudy wanted to stay with the baby right here forever, never return to a world of pain and anguish. Trudy whispered to her daughter: "I love you."

But her bubble burst. "Oh, Trudy, she's so beautiful!" exclaimed Marie, who had just walked back into the room, adding, "I really hoped you would have a baby girl!"

Marie returned to the room after giving an update to Tony following the baby's birth. Marie had stayed in the room with Trudy during the delivery but mostly just observed from the comfortable side of the birthing room. When the nurse told her she would have to leave while the baby was cleaned and Trudy was attended to, making sure Trudy would not get blood clots after the birth. Marie had reluctantly left but returned as soon as she was allowed back.

When she saw Trudy holding the baby, Marie was so excited, and without paying any attention to this precious moment between a mother and her newborn, she interrupted, "Trudy, may I hold her, please! I'm so excited to see her!"

Trudy's mystic universe popped like a fragile bubble, no longer a crystal-perfect world reflecting in an infant's new eyes but the here-and-now of the birthing room and the soiled aftermath of birth.

Tears flowing down her face, Trudy let Marie take the swaddled child. Marie started to cry, too, telling Trudy that she also had tears of joy, mistakenly thinking Trudy shared her joy.

But Trudy's heart was breaking. Every fiber of her being wanted to pull the baby back into her embrace. No one had prepared her for this moment. Nor had Trudy been able to plan for this moment. She cried openly, tears flowing. Trudy was exhausted. Two days without sleep and no solid food, she felt dizzy and unsteady.

The duty nurse returned and saw how pale and tired Trudy appeared. The nurse took the baby from Marie, telling her she'd have to leave so Trudy could get some rest. The baby would go to the nursery for a more complete examination by a pediatrician. Reluctantly, Marie let the nurse take the baby, asking when she'd be able to see her again. The nurse told Marie that the baby could be seen by visitors through the nursery window. Marie didn't like this rebuke, but the nurse insisted that Marie leave the room immediately.

Marie checked her watch as she went into the small waiting room where Tony stayed. It was just after 9 a.m. on Monday. She saw Tony was hungry and growing impatient, and she agreed to Tony's suggestion that they should go back to the hotel, get something to eat and finally call Faust. Tony would have done that already except that Marie kept insisting that he not call Faust while Trudy was in labor.

Just then, Marie remembered another call she had to make. She had asked Trudy if she should contact anyone for her after the baby was born. Trudy told Marie to call her college friend, Leslie, and gave her the phone number. Trudy added that Leslie would know who else to call and that would be the only contact Marie needed to make.

"Hold on one moment, I've got to make this call. I promised Trudy I'd do it first thing."

Marie went to the complimentary phone that sat on a small side table in the waiting room and made the promised call to Leslie. Very little information was exchanged, just enough to tell this college friend that Trudy had a baby girl early this morning and that both mother and baby were doing very well.

Marie realized that she was also exhausted. She had not slept all night. They all needed to get some rest, so she allowed Tony to marshal her back to the hotel. She realized that Trudy needed rest, and the baby would not be available for a while and there was nothing else to be done.

Tony told Marie that he should finally call Faust also before leaving the hospital. But Marie asked him to let that wait until they were back in their hotel room. It might not be as short as her call to Leslie.

Faust sat on his back patio. His wife was rattling on about the cocktail party they'd attend later in the day at the country club. The Labor Day party was always the busiest social occasion of the club, the last celebration before the end of summer. It was a last chance to show off their summer tans, sculpted bodies, beautiful summer dresses before fashion changed to fall colors. Attorney and Mrs. Harold Faust would hob nob with the wealthy doctors, lawyers, judges and corporate leaders of Milson.

Having disregarded his wife's chatter while reading the morning paper, Faust left the patio, telling his wife that he was going to make a quick trip into the office for a few phone calls, ignoring her admonishment not to be home late. Faust got into his car, but as he pulled out of his driveway, Faust changed his mind. Instead of going to the office, he'd drive over to the hotel.

Tony was supposed to call him and give updates about Trudy. Yet Faust had not heard from Tony since last Friday. It irritated him since both shook hands on the promise to keep in touch. Faust knew they had to be at the hotel since Tony's promise included not taking Trudy anywhere.

Faust pulled up to the Grand Hamilton portico and told the porter to leave his car out front, he'd only be a few moments. He walked to the front desk and asked to have Tony paged. While the call was being placed, Faust leaned over the desk to watch the room number being punched into the phone deck, Room 311. No one picked up and the clerk told Faust the room was not answering.

Faust told the clerk that Tony had booked two rooms and to try their second room. The clerk checked the booking schedule, found that Faust was correct and again punched the numbers for this room. Faust watched again and saw 313 was called. The clerk informed Faust that no one was picking up. Faust checked his watch, it was just before 9 a.m. He doubted that Tony was still asleep knowing he had been an early riser.

Faust walked through the lobby quickly and checked the restaurant. Growing irritated, Faust walked outside through the back lobby doors to an outdoor pool area. Several children were playing near the pool and were going in and out of the locked doors of the back stairway that led to their rooms. Faust waited momentarily until one of the parents stepped out of the door, merely nodded as if he were a guest, and grabbed the outer door.

Inside the stairwell, Faust quickly ran up three flights of stairs to the top floor. Now sweaty and gasping for air, Faust opened the top hallway door and began checking the room numbers, growing ever angrier that this was taking so much effort. He noted that the odd number rooms were the ones that faced the airport tarmac. He walked all the way down the hall and found 311. Faust knocked on Tony's door, waited, knocked again. Still no answer. Faust walked to room 313 and tried knocking on this door. Same result.

Faust took the elevator back down to the lobby, looked around quickly one more time. Once again, he went to the front desk clerk and asked if Tony had called or left any messages. Once again, he received a negative reply.

Faust walked out and decided to head over to his office. Within minutes of Faust pulling out of the hotel, Tony and Marie pulled up to the portico in a hotel courtesy car, just returning from Milson General. They were tired and hungry. They planned to catch a quick bite to eat, get a short nap, and then return to the hospital. Marie was bubbling over with enthusiasm, telling Tony about the beautiful baby girl.

～ℓ

After Marie's call, Leslie hurried over to Jackie's Counter. She was anxious to tell Jackie, Mac, and Marna about the baby girl. They had all agreed to keep each other informed about Trudy. After Leslie walked to the diner, she found the front door locked and a sign that read:

CLOSED FOR LABOR DAY

Leslie peered through the glass and saw several people inside. Jackie quickly came and unlocked the door to allow Leslie to enter. Just as Leslie was about to announce her news, Jackie excitedly began first. "Trudy is at Milson General; she's had a baby girl!"

"I know," replied Leslie, stunned that Jackie shared the news first. "How did you already know?" And Jackie was surprised to hear Leslie already knew. "Sit down, I'll get some coffee."

Marna explained to Leslie that her niece called very early this morning. She informed her Trudy had checked in early Saturday and had been in labor since Saturday, then all of Sunday, until giving birth very early Monday morning. "The baby was born on Labor Day!"

"But how did you already know, Leslie?" asked Jackie

Leslie explained that a woman named Marie had called. She told me that Trudy had given my name as someone to contact after the baby was born. Marie added, "Trudy said that I'd know who else to contact." This is why I headed directly over here.

"Who is Marie?" Mac interrupted. He had been observing and listening to the three women, but none of them seemed to ask the important question.

Leslie stopped talking and thought for a moment. Sheepishly she added, "I was so excited to find out where Trudy was and also to hear that she had a healthy baby girl, I never asked her for more information; she only told me her name was Marie and that she was calling from the hospital because Trudy had asked her to call. Sorry?"

Mac thought, *isn't that just like a* woman, *the most essential information and they don't bother to ask.* He shook his head.

But Jackie smoothed it over, telling Mac: "What difference does that make, we can go over to Milson General Hospital ourselves and see the baby and ask Trudy."

Mac immediately agreed to take Jackie, Marna and Leslie to the hospital. Telling Jackie they'd have to take her car.

"When should we go?" Everyone was anxious, especially Jackie who responded, "Now!"

But Leslie declined Mac's offer. She planned to see Trudy's baby, but for now, she was on her way over to campus for a VOW meeting. She would go herself later in the day. But Marna readily agreed to go with Jackie and Mac.

Back in their hotel room, Marie told Tony that they should eat breakfast first, before making the call to Faust. Even Tony began to realize that Faust would be the last to know. He agreed but told Marie there would be no further delays, he had promised to keep Faust posted. Marie gave Tony a quick peck on the cheek and asked him if he wasn't excited—he was going to be a dad!

While Tony and Marie sat down to eat a late brunch, Faust stopped at his office, still steaming that he could not locate Tony, or Trudy. Faust checked his phone messages and then called Jill. No information from either. He headed home knowing his wife would once again be irritated that they were going to be late for the Labor Day party.

After breakfast, Tony finally called Faust's office. No answer. He left a message on Faust's phone service informing the attorney that he and Marie had been at the hospital since very early on Saturday. Trudy had her baby early in the day on Monday. He left his hotel phone extension number if Faust wanted more information.

Chapter 15

September 1977, Post-Labor Day

Leslie walked to Milson General Hospital late in the afternoon. It was less than three miles from her apartment. She enjoyed the beautiful day filled with thoughts of her classes for the new semester. After entering the lobby, Leslie stopped at the front desk to get Trudy's room number. The desk clerk called the ward nurse to clear the visit.

Leslie walked into Trudy's room, surprised to see that Trudy was not alone. Smiling warmly, Trudy introduced Leslie to the couple, Marie and Tony. "I'm the one who called you!" Marie explained.

Marie's quick once-over of the VOW sweatshirt and jeans made Leslie feel uncomfortable. Trudy noticed Leslie's discomfort and understood how disarming a woman like Marie could be. She changed gears, asking if Leslie had seen the baby?

"I wanted to come in and say hello first. But I can't wait to see your baby!"

Leslie then asked Trudy if she'd had a visit from Mac, Jackie and Marna earlier in the day. Trudy explained the nurse told her of the visit, but the head maternity nurse wouldn't allow visitors until Trudy awoke from her long rest after being in labor and without sleep for two days.

"I'm sorry I missed them, but the nurse said they did visit my baby."

Leslie remembered Mac's criticism that she had not asked who Marie was or got any information. Now, Leslie wanted to find out why this Marie seemed to be around Trudy on every contact. Trudy had never talked to her before about anyone called either Marie or Tony.

"How do you know Trudy?" Leslie asked Marie in a friendly manner.

"Trudy picked us to be her baby's adoptive parents!" Marie gushed. "I'm guessing Trudy must have told you she was planning a private adoption." Marie bubbled over, "Trudy even allowed me to be with her when the baby was born. The baby is absolutely beautiful! Isn't she Trudy?"

Leslie just looked over to Trudy, who remained quiet. Confused, Leslie knew that Trudy had been considering adoption at one point, but she had seemed to move toward keeping her baby.

"Come with me, Leslie. I'll take you over to the nursery window. I never get tired of looking at the baby, and the nurses already know which baby to bring forward when I come. I could stand and watch her all day! Tony, please stay here, sweetheart, and keep Trudy happy."

Marie gestured to Leslie that she should follow. Leslie looked to Trudy, who nodded her agreement. She was anxious to see the new baby and went along with Marie's lead.

While Leslie and Marie stood before the large picture window down the hallway from Trudy's room, Harold Faust, Esq. stepped out of the elevator. He was still a bit inebriated from the country club Labor Day gala and had a splitting headache.

While still at the club, Faust checked with his answering service, receiving the information on Tony's call. When he learned that Trudy had given birth and that all three of them had been at Milson General for the whole Labor Day weekend, all without his knowledge, Faust felt he was losing control of his case.

He had sped out without explaining to his wife where he was headed. He intended to reassert control. He had tried to counsel his clients that adoption cases were always sensitive regarding contacts between mother and adoptive parents.

On the drive from the club to the hospital, he recalled his long hours serving as chairman of the local county bar committee on Adoptions and Termination of Parental Rights. It had not been easy to convince judges that private adoptions were becoming the new normal, not like the old agency model where the baby would be placed in a foster home while several months of counseling and investigations took place after the baby was born.

The newer private adoptions were designed to allow the birth mom to select her desired adoptive parents. They would meet one another while the birth mom was still pregnant. The counseling would occur during the pregnancy, speeding up the ability of the adoptive parents to receive an infant into their home during the very early, formative months of the baby.

After the landmark abortion case of *Roe v. Wade*, the Supreme Court of the United States ruled that a birth mother had privacy rights and that during her first trimester and even well into her second, her privacy rights to make choices included abortion. Only in the third trimester did the court hold that states could impose restrictions, using the doctrine of *parens-patriae*, Latin for "in the place of a parent."

With the strong backlash by conservatives to *Roe v. Wade*, adoption agencies were scrambling to find ways to encourage adoption over abortion. Desiring to make the choice for adoption more appealing to women, many new ideas were introduced around the idea of allowing birth mothers to have more choices, not to choose abortion, but adoption. Wanting women to feel comfortable about adoption, they were given greater autonomy to choose the parents that would adopt the baby. These procedures and the law surrounding adoption had been updated.

Faust felt great satisfaction knowing he had played a leading role. Several years after the *Roe v. Wade* decision of 1973, the family bar association had created a dual track for adoptions. One track retained the agency adoption model. This agency adoption might require six months or more to completion before a placement could be made.

The newer, second track was created as an alternative to this traditional model. Modern research in pediatrics dictated that these first months in a baby's life were an important bonding time. New private adoption procedures were created so that much of the counseling took place before the baby was even born.

Private adoptions retained the requirement for a social worker's involvement. But agencies did not control the outcome. It was the judge who'd review the report and determine if an adoption was freely chosen by the mother and if it was in the best interest of the infant.

Faust had worked long and hard to create these new laws. Surprisingly, the conservative agencies became allies in updating the laws. At one time, the agencies held a very strict ban on mother/adoptive parent contacts. Records once sealed could never be opened. It had taken *Roe v. Wade* to change this. Women were demanding more rights. The conservative agencies understood that if they wanted to encourage adoption as an alternative to abortion, they would need to support some of these rights and become allies in the creation of new private adoptions.

Even the religious agencies, while providing services that conformed to their religious and ethical beliefs that prohibited abortions, became supportive of private adoption. Balancing separation of church and state pitted against the denial of individual privacy rights of the woman, continued to be highly controversial. Faust knew it remained so.

Since women rarely had access to power in the hierarchy of religious organizations, abortion rights remained controversial. This also had become a feminist issue. Since the male hierarchy of most major religious organizations were unable to control their female members with bans on contraception and abortion, they had turned to secular government to enforce their church rules.

All of these memories flooded Faust's mind as he was racing over to the hospital. He knew that many of the older judges, more familiar with the old agency adoption, were uncomfortable with these new private adoptions. This political hotbed boiled over into the male dominated judiciary. The judges held their own religious bias even though their judicial ethics required impartial decision-making.

These conservative judges argued private adoption could allow too much opportunity for abuse. Birth mothers tended to be young and often impoverished. Since private adoptions entailed a fair amount of expense paid by the adopting couple, these judges told the local bar they would only hear these cases with extra scrutiny, making sure no illegal enticements were being brought to bear on these young women.

Faust feared that Marie was exactly the type of candidate for drawing a judge's extra scrutiny. Marie was actively seeking to control this case. It was incumbent upon him to reassert his authority. He had already skirted the outer limits of scrutiny by isolating Trudy and getting her out of town for a few weeks before her due date. He intended to make sure that Marie and Tony kept within his set boundaries.

If Marie wanted to take the baby home, she must comply, and Faust was going to convince his clients of the importance of his legal counsel. Faust knew he could not explain all of this history, but as their legal counselor, they'd have to trust his professional guidance. He thought Tony had come to understand. But Tony did not seem able to control his own wife.

Faust quietly swore at Tony. Two days without any contact was not complying with his promise. As he stepped off the elevator, Faust spotted Marie standing next to another woman at the nursery window, his headache began pounding and his temper flared. Faust headed directly to Trudy's room.

Faust paused, took a deep breath, and entered the hospital room. "Good evening! I hear you had a *long* weekend, Trudy,"

Faust gave a dirty look to Tony as he stressed the word, long.

"How are you feeling tonight?"

"Much better now that I've gotten some sleep and finally had some food," replied Trudy.

"That's the benefit of being young—that's the spirit! Trudy, do you mind if I ask Tony to step out for a minute so that we can talk?"

Trudy merely nodded, understanding that Faust wasn't really asking her permission. He was already guiding Tony out of the room. Once in the hallway, Faust asked Tony to go back down the long hall into the waiting room where he had recently spent so many hours.

Inside this room, Faust let Tony have it with both barrels: "I thought you agreed to keep me informed, that was the stipulation. Two days without contact is not staying in touch! Do you realize that you're jeopardizing everything I've worked so long and hard to put together? Do you?"

Tony lost his own hot temper. Marie knew how to avoid such outbursts, but Faust stoked it head on. Having had more than just one Rob Roy at the country club had taken its toll on Faust's usual staid demeanor.

"Who the hell do you think you're talking to! I've spent the last two days taking care of this young woman. Where were you? Why didn't you check on Trudy? You knew she was expecting at any moment. I've been pacing in this room for over two days, and you think you can talk to me like that? Let me remind you who is paying your exorbitant fees! You're fired! Get the hell out of my sight!"

Marie came running into the room, having heard her husband yelling all the way down the hallway.

Tony continued, "You smell like you've been drinking all day! This is how you serve a client, half-drunk and out of control?"

"Please Tony, everyone can hear you all the way down the hallway! Please stop!"

Tony looked at Marie and then stormed out of the room. He was either going to bust Faust in the chops or take off and find a quiet place to calm down. Marie saved Faust.

Stunned, Faust wondered if he'd really just been fired. It left him uncharacteristically speechless.

Marie told Faust to sit down. Still off balance, Faust actually obeyed. She told him that Tony could have quite a temper if sufficiently provoked, and that he was fortunate that she came running into the room. Faust only glared at her, finally asking Marie, "Tony just fired me. Is this all over now? Are we done?"

"Of course not! Tony and I have gotten very little sleep ourselves. Trudy's water broke very early Saturday morning. We had to rush over to the hospital with her. She had a very long labor, Dr. Wellstein was here and told me that it is not unusual for a first-time delivery to take longer, but I stayed with Trudy the whole time trying to keep her comfortable. And Tony waited the whole time, too. Trudy finally had her baby. It's a girl! Did you know that?"

"No," Faust confessed.

"Tony is tired. We've had little sleep."

"Who is the young woman you were with in the hallway?" Faust asked.

"That is Trudy's college friend, Leslie. Trudy asked me to make a phone call and inform her about the birth. Another couple along with an older woman, came this afternoon, too, while we were at the hotel. But Trudy was sleeping and they were not allowed to visit."

"Half a dozen people knew about the delivery! And I'm now just learning of it! If I'm fired, you will have to leave Trudy, immediately!"

"Don't be silly," Marie minimized Tony's words. "Tony is tired and lost his temper. I might add that you had something to do with that. It's late, and it has been a very long weekend for everybody. We should all get a good night's rest. We can meet first thing in the morning and work this out."

Marie chose not to remind Faust that he'd obviously had quite a bit to drink, smelled of alcohol, had blood shot eyes and was unusually out of control. The one trait she had admired in this lawyer was his ability to be in control, always well-dressed, well-spoken and exceedingly polite. The Faust of tonight was a man she had not seen before.

Faust thought about Marie's suggestion and finally replied:

"One stipulation: I will meet with you first thing tomorrow morning at my office, but no one sees Trudy or the baby before the meeting. Is that understood?"

"Of course," Marie agreed, "Just let me say good night to her, you can do so as well. We'll both tell Trudy that we will make further arrangements tomorrow."

Faust didn't like having Marie add the one more thing to his stipulation.

"Do you understand that I must control your contacts with the birth mom? You could be jeopardizing everything I've worked so hard to accomplish, and on your behalf, I might add."

"Yes, of course I do," Marie pampered his ego, adding, "We will just say good night together. There is no reason to alarm Trudy, now, is there?"

Marie stood up, ending their negotiations and headed to Trudy's room. Faust swore under his breath but stood and followed Marie. Both of them went into Trudy's room and wished her goodnight, telling her they'd all be back in the morning.

The duty nurse came into the room telling everyone visiting hours were ended. She had already instructed Leslie to leave.

Faust escorted Marie to the elevator and offered to drive her over to the hotel. Marie refused. She didn't want to get in a car with Faust in his inebriated condition, telling him she'd merely call the airport hotel to send over a courtesy car.

The following morning, Tony and Marie arrived at Faust's office at 9 a.m. as prearranged. The long holiday weekend ended. School was back in session which brought the usual early morning rush hour. Faust was now the well-groomed, polished lawyer that his clients expected to see.

Tony had settled down thanks to Marie but was still irritated with Faust. He intended to fly back to the East Coast today and deal with his own work schedule. Marie insisted that she would remain in Milson and keep Tony posted, he would need to return for their court date on the temporary placement of the baby and completing the interstate adoption compact that Faust advised would be needed in order to take the baby out of state. After this order was signed, the jurisdiction of the case would be transferred to Tony and Marie's home state, with a new agency assigned to monitor the case until the adoption became final.

In the interim, Faust would handle the legal details. Marie was confident that she could accomplish all of this and thought allowing Tony to return home and take care of his own business concerns was best for everyone. They walked into Faust's office with Jill greeting them and immediately taking them into the conference room, indicating that Faust was already waiting for them. Jill offered to bring coffee and all the client niceties were restored.

Faust offered a brief apology for the prior evening but got down to business. He outlined the legal steps that would be required and stressed that the clients needed to do everything he instructed.

Faust had already called Dr. Wellstein and confirmed that the doctor would visit with Trudy today to determine if she could be discharged. He also contacted the foster home. The foster mom was on alert to receive the baby during this interim. Faust would talk to Trudy about this further, but he did not give more information to Marie or Tony.

Satisfied that everything was in place, Faust made one more decision. Trudy would need to return to the lake cottage until the court date, hopefully in only a few days. Maria was upset to hear this. She had kept the extra room at the hotel and assumed Trudy would return with her to wait there for the court case.

Faust took a deep breath, composed himself, and reminded Marie of the stipulation at the hospital the night before.

"Trudy cannot stay with you prior to the court date. The judge might start questioning the closeness of the contacts and wonder if Trudy is really giving consent freely or whether she was being coerced. I know you mean well. But I must maintain this separation between you and Trudy."

Tony spoke out, surprising Faust. "Marie, Trudy must spend time alone. You are getting too close. Once we leave Milson, all contacts are going to be terminated. It's time to start right now."

Marie saw that she had to agree with her husband, especially in front of Faust. It hurt to think that she couldn't be with Trudy. She had really grown to like this young woman. Trudy was fresh and naïve and so tender—it brought out her own maternal instincts. Marie thought about the baby and made her choice.

Tony had already booked his plane out of Milson and was anxiously wanting to move on. Faust reminded his clients that he would complete his final billing statement, and Tony confirmed it would be paid before Marie left town. No mention of Tony firing Faust the prior day was ever brought up, and everyone agreed to the arrangements.

After Tony and Marie left the office, Faust pulled out his checklist and began to check it carefully to be sure everything was in place. As he paged through his yellow pad, he came across the checklist he once made for Trudy regarding her initial concerns in her early months of pregnancy. Faust recalled his promise to Trudy that he would help her address all her concerns.

Faust reviewed the check-off list: late rent, paid. Hospital, doctor, medical bills paid, check. Employee leave, check. Refund from clinic for services not given, check. One item remained without a check: "Left jewelry at pawnbroker, reclaim,"

He considered the unfinished item, remembering that Trudy had hocked her grandmother's brooch when she needed money to pay for the abortion at the clinic but ran away before the procedure.

Perhaps this could be a way to make Trudy accept that she would not be taking her baby home from the hospital. She had been so distracted and even spacey these last few weeks, although Faust felt that he had taken good care of Trudy. She had gotten quality medical care and wonderfully wealthy parents for her baby. Maybe he could get this last item completed to demonstrate to Trudy he kept all of his promises to her. Recovering her brooch might also help cheer her up.

Putting his notes back in the file, Faust quickly decided that he'd first head over to Doc's Hoc Shop before seeing Dr. Wellstein. He quickly left the office, instructing Jill to call Dr. Wellstein's office to inform them that Faust was making one stop on the way to the hospital.

Pulling up to the curb, Faust read the gold-leaf lettering on the front window: **INSTANT CASH**. Faust smiled; he knew he was in his element. He walked into the storefront of Doc's Hoc Shop. The place was filthy, and Faust was careful not to touch the counter tops.

Inside the glass cases, he saw a gold mine. Faust was impressed at the quality and quantity. He stared at a Rolex watch, knowing it was valued at over $5,000. He knew the gold chains and jewelry were 14 K or better. He walked over to the small man seated behind the teller-like window at the end of the aisle. Like his store, he was a dirty, disgusting little man wearing a sweaty, armless undershirt.

The pawn broker eyed Faust, mentally noting the fine Italian tailored suit, the white linen shirt with embroidered initials on the French cuffs, the 18 K gold cufflinks, the silk tie and domestic leather shoes. The pawn broker was a savant, knowing value. He knew this man possessed wealth. Doc smiled.

"How may I help you?"

Faust resented having to even deal with this disgusting little man. He reminded himself why he came and motivated himself to respond to this parasite.

"I came to reclaim a piece of jewelry."

"Do you have the receipt?"

"No. But it's an item left by someone I know. What is your holding time for reclaiming an item?"

"You want to know my terms?"

"Yes," replied Faust.

The dance began. Neither would offer any more information than necessary. They were eyeing each other as if playing a game of poker, each answer was like placing another chip into the pot. The pawn broker eyed Faust. Seeing only his poker face, he continued.

"I hold an item for the first thirty days without being subject to sale, and if it is not reclaimed or sold by the end of ninety day, I can sell it outright."

Faust nodded in a familiar way to the savant, knowing these were typical street terms for holding an item pawned. He played his next card.

"The item I'm interested in would have been brought in about ninety days ago. I do not have the receipt, but I would like to purchase the item."

Doc remembered every person who had ever come into his shop since the first day he had opened. "Give me a description of what it is you want to purchase."

"It is a brooch in a heart shape that opens showing two small photographs inside. It was once worn as a brooch but was later hung on a gold chain and worn as a necklace. It is old."

"Did it have a letter inscribed on the front of the heart?" Doc asked.

Faust realized that Doc was getting the upper hand but also surmised that Doc already knew the piece of jewelry that Trudy had described to him but had never seen. She had not mentioned the initial. Faust knew he would need to proceed cautiously; it was not time to call his hand.

"I don't know, I was not the one who brought the brooch in to hock," replied Faust.

The savant snorted through his nose, crudely responding:

"I know. Not only that, but I do remember the young woman who did bring it in here."

"Well, do you have it?"

Doc wasn't done yet, but he knew the pot was being called. He wanted to let this wealthy gentleman know that he was the same as every other greedy bastard that ever walked into his shop.

"But I do remember her. She was a very, very beautiful young woman. I bet you have quite an interest in purchasing her favors. And she was very naïve. I'm sure you would pay a very pretty amount for her favors."

"Don't be disgusting." Faust grimaced, knowing what Doc was suggesting and growing impatient, raising his voice instead of his next bet.

"Do you have the jewelry?"

But the savant was not done, "I could have gotten a lot of money for that brooch, had I really known its value."

"What are you getting at?"

Doc looked Faust over again, head to foot, stopping at the sinister stare of Faust's steely eyes. Doc's nostrils flared with his untrimmed nasal hair curling out. He was thinking about the value of the piece to such a buyer. He could have gotten ten times the price he had sold it for. Doc now placed all his cards face up to inflict maximum pain.

"I wish I had known the value of that piece before I sold it. I knew its intrinsic value, but apparently not the sentimental value."

"What 'sentimental value'?"

"I sold it after my holding period. I did make a tidy profit, but now I see that I didn't get nearly the value of this particular jewelry. I've already had another person asking about that same piece. But once the thirty days expired unclaimed, I sold it to the first buyer who came in and obviously didn't get the price that I should have gotten. But I have lots of gold, why not buy something else?"

"Not interested," replied Faust.

But Doc persisted: "Look around, I have pieces much more valuable that that brooch."

"Crawl back into your worm hole. You have nothing I would want!"

Doc laughed at the insult, "Your world is no different than mine — you just dress it up more and probably charge a premium. I have more value here than your world, and we both know it."

Faust was struck by the philosophy of the pawnbroker. He was not only street wise, but he did hold more value in this shop than Faust wanted to admit. But he was just a low-life barnacle on the cruise ship of his life. Doc was the keeper of the throw-away world of losers.

Faust realized he was not going to complete the last item on Trudy's checklist. He turned and stormed out of the filthy shop. Doc had nothing he wanted. He was irritated he had ever condescended to the level of this pawn broker. Before he got to the door, Faust pulled out his handkerchief that had been carefully folded in the upper chest pocket of his suit jacket, wrapped it around the doorknob, opened the door, and exited. Doc roared in laughter, watching this grand exit.

Back outside, Faust knew he was starting to lose his cool again. He decided he would head over to The Spot for his Perfect Rob Roby before going to Milson General Hospital. It was nearly noon, and he needed to wash out the bad taste left by his visit to Doc's Hoc Shop. The cocktail would help him reclaim his composure.

While Faust sat quietly sipping his cocktail in a darkened corner of The Spot, he thought of Trudy and his failure to complete that last item on her list. He began to devise an alternative. He would call Marie and ask her to shop for a replacement for the brooch. Faust had never seen the brooch. But he knew it was gold in a heart shape, and now thanks to Doc, he knew that the brooch was inscribed with the initial "T." Marie loved to shop, and it would give her something to do while she waited for the final court hearing, which he hoped to obtain before the end of this week. Trudy could be given the new heart necklace as a memory of both Marie and the baby. It would be a nice gesture, Faust thought.

Faust drained his glass and headed over to his office. He made the call to Marie and gave her the new assignment. She was more than happy to purchase a heart necklace. Faust headed over to Milson General Hospital, knowing he'd be late.

⟿

"Length, eighteen point two inches, weight, seven pounds, four ounces, Apgar nine."

Trudy listened intently, wanting to memorize every word the nursing aide recited, giving the infant's birth weight and height. Trudy was not familiar with the word "apgar" and immediately asked the aide what it meant.

As Trudy caressed her baby, looking intently at her sleeping little girl, the aide responded, "It's a scale, sweetheart. Apgar measures general wellness from 1 to 10 at the time of her birth, measuring observations of heart rate, skin tone, oxygen level, nerve responses, and so on. Ten is the highest and perfect score. I've never seen a newborn score a ten. But nine is a very good number. You should be pleased. It means the baby is healthy overall."

"Where does the word come from/" Trudy persisted.

The older woman smiled at Trudy; it was good to see her so interested after her long ordeal in the delivery. "It's the last name of the woman that devised this scale, Dr. Virginia Apgar. She created the scale; it is not scientific but makes observations and basic measurements taken at birth. After further observation, the doctor will often upgrade the number as the baby breathes on her own and her color improves with circulation. I wouldn't be surprised to see this beautiful little girl get a ten before she leaves! Just like her mother."

Trudy smiled. She was also feeling better now that she had gotten rest and had eaten several meals. The staff insisted that Trudy stand and begin to move about. She began to feel like her old self again. Trudy held her baby close.

Dr. Wellstein walked into the room. He was happy to see Trudy looking so well along with the baby. The doctor asked the aide to take the baby back to the nursery as he was going to make his final exam before signing off on Trudy's discharge.

Trudy was sorry to give the baby to the aide, but she knew that Dr. Wellstein would not be patient with her. The doctor saw babies nearly every day and was not interested in waiting. He did his work thoroughly but was not very communicative nor friendly.

Finally, Dr. Wellstein asked if Trudy had any questions. The doctor had already advised Trudy that she would not be allowed to drive for at least one week and should not return to work or school and recommended that she try to get a full three weeks of rest before returning to normal activities.

As Dr. Wellstein was leaving, Faust finally arrived. He was glad to see the doctor already completed his observations and asked how Trudy was doing. The doctor smiled and greeted Faust, telling him that the patient was doing very well. She was young and healthy. Faust was pleased and asked when Trudy could be discharged. Dr. Wellstein told him that she could go home today. The two walked into the hallway to talk further for a few moments.

Faust returned and told Trudy that Dr. Wellstein did not want her to be alone for the next several days. She had to be with someone to be sure there was no fainting, which might indicate a blood clod or other concern. He also reminded Trudy that her last visit with the social worker was incomplete. For these reasons, Trudy would have to return to the lake cottage for several days.

Trudy frowned at this news and teared up, but before Trudy could object, Faust took the upper hand. "I know you don't like staying at the lake cottage. I promise that it won't be with Jill; the two of you don't seem to hit it off. I've asked the social worker to stay with you, and her agency agreed. You will be in good hands, and I will come and check on you. It is doctor's orders not to be alone. Besides, you will only be there for a few days. Once this is all over with, you can go back to your apartment, back to work, back to school, back to whatever you choose to do. The rest of your life is all before you. You've been a real trooper, and I promise after the court date, you will be done with all this."

Dr. Wellstein hadn't told Trudy anything about the baby or when the baby could leave. Faust told Trudy that the social worker would be along shortly for her own discharge. She'd drive Trudy to the cottage. Faust had then left. *But when does the baby leave?* Trudy was left with unanswered questions as she waited alone in her room.

Chapter 16

September 1977, Waning Moon

The social worker arrived at the hospital as Trudy was finishing her discharge procedure. Faust told her the papers were to complete the discharge for her and her baby, but he added, "Nothing is final, it's all interim until you go to court." Faust then introduced the petite young woman named Mary Hightower. Trudy thought she looked just a few years older than Leslie. Mary apologized that she had not been able to do the final counseling session before Trudy gave birth. She had been prepared to go to the hotel last Saturday, but the appointment had been canceled by a man named Tony. "He told me you had gone into labor."

Mary pleasantly commented that she heard Trudy gave birth to a healthy little girl. "I'm sorry you missed the pre-birth counseling, but I'm told everything went well." But Trudy was in no mood to hear about counseling at this moment and began to dread leaving the hospital.

Leaving the hospital meant leaving her baby. Trudy could not get her head around this separation. She began to panic. Feeling the way she had on the day of the abortion appointment, she wanted to run, run now! Instead, Trudy began to cry uncontrollably, becoming shaky and sweaty.

Mary Hightower was surprised by the sudden outburst of tears. She hadn't gotten to know Trudy very well and searched for a way to comfort her. Just before Faust left, he had instructed her to drive Trudy to a cottage that was over an hour away, and she needed to leave during daylight. Mary sat down across from Trudy, who was sitting on the side of her hospital bed.

"I'm sorry, you should have gotten counseling for this separation. It can be traumatic, but most birth moms preparing for an adoption experience this. You go ahead and cry—let out your fears and emotions. I'll take your suitcase down to the car and give you a few moments." Without waiting for an answer, Mary left the room carrying Trudy's small bag.

Trudy lay down on the bed and cried into her pillow. She did not want to face this. She had no idea what to do. As she cried, Trudy thought maybe she could say goodbye to her baby one more time. She sat up in the bed. Finally alone, she stood and walked out into the hallway and headed to the nursery window. Her baby had always been brought into her room by attendants, and she did not know the routine that Marie had to follow to see the baby.

Trudy stood in front of the glass and saw the many bassinets; she searched the cards that were attached at the foot of the glass container, labeled with the mother's name. Finally, she found her name. The bassinet held rumpled blankets, but no baby. Her baby had already gone.

Trudy sobbed uncontrollably and stumbled back into her room. All was lost. Trudy had been in limbo for months, going back and forth thinking about the adoption. But while she was pregnant, it was never final—her baby was kicking inside her. She ate and drank and slept knowing that she had to be healthy for her growing baby. Now, Trudy thought, *I'm just as I was before the pregnancy, except I'm not.* Trudy knew everything had changed. She'd never again be the same as when she first arrived in Milson. Feeling disoriented and panicky, Trudy couldn't lie back in bed, and she began to pace in her room.

Mary Hightower came back into the room with an attendant pushing a wheelchair. But Trudy's pacing and uncontrollable sobs made her ask the attendant to wait. She called for Trudy's nurse.

The head ward nurse returned and asked Trudy to sit down in the chair. She checked Trudy's pulse and vital signs. Telling Mary that she'd have to clear any medicine with Trudy's doctor, she left the room to make her call. Trudy was barely aware of their presence. She was losing awareness of her surroundings. Her ears were buzzing, and she felt dizzy. The panic attack had fully overtaken her consciousness. If she couldn't run, she didn't know how else to cope.

The head nurse came back in the room and again took Trudy's pulse. She took Trudy's hand and tried to calm her down. She told Trudy that all women experience rapidly changing hormonal levels post-pregnancy, some more than others. The doctor ordered diazepam and the nurse explained to Trudy that this medicine would calm her down. She could not be discharged until her heart rate returned to normal.

Trudy didn't hear any of the instructions, but she was compliant just as she always had been when circumstances spiraled beyond her control. She took the pill and drank the water. Trudy sat on the chair, hung her head, and cried quietly. After a while, her pulse slowed and the panic began to ease. The nurse cleared Trudy for discharge.

Trudy felt sad and wanted to lay down on the bed and go back to sleep. But she was told to get into the wheelchair. Trudy complied. Mary and the attendant wheeled Trudy to the drive-up discharge area. Trudy was told to transfer into the passenger seat and buckle her seat belt. Trudy complied. Mary Hightower got into the driver's seat and drove off.

Trudy paid little notice to the drive into the countryside or the changing of the autumn colors, yet the weather remained summerlike. It was another spectacular day. As Mary pulled into the wooded lot of the cottage, she was a bit concerned. The setting was far more secluded than she had expected and hoped Trudy's mental condition was stable. Mary tried to make small talk with Trudy, telling her that she was a graduate of Milson University and knew that Trudy had been a student there last semester. Trudy didn't correct her. She was a dropout, not a student, but what did it matter.

Once inside, Trudy went into the same bedroom and got into bed and instantly fell asleep. Mary attributed Trudy's silence and sleepiness to side effects of the diazepam. She settled Trudy's things into her room, unpacked the car, and tried to make the cottage comfortable for their stay. Mary had only been on her new job since graduating in spring. Everything was still new to her, but she'd never been asked to stay with a client. Her agency worked regularly with Faust, who paid for this added service, and Mary had been assigned to his case.

Early the next morning, Mary checked on Trudy. She was still in bed. Mary shook Trudy gently, calling her name. Trudy barely opened her eyes. Mary asked her if she was well enough to get up and eat something. Trudy responded that she wanted to sleep longer.

After about an hour, Mary returned and checked on Trudy. She was still sleeping. Mary made coffee and walked outside to enjoy the lovely day. She returned to the cottage an hour later and found Trudy was still in bed. She decided to make her breakfast and then insist that Trudy get out of bed, eat, and get dressed.

Mary knocked on the bedroom door, hearing only silence, she gently opened the door, calling again for Trudy to get up. She entered the room, opened the shades and placed Trudy's slippers on the floor and began to fold open her bedding.

"Trudy, I have your breakfast ready. It is really a lovely day outside. Please, you must get up. You can eat breakfast. If you like, we can then walk down to the lake and just quietly begin to talk. There is a really sweet Lab outside."

Trudy opened her eyes; she remembered the dog. But then she also remembered her little baby and wanted to turn over and go back to sleep. But Mary was insistent. Finally, Trudy complied. Mary handed the robe to Trudy and asked if she needed help to walk over to the bathroom and freshen up. Slowly, Trudy followed directions.

Mary had to keep instructing Trudy, first to eat, then to try the lovely fruit, and asked if Trudy wanted coffee. Mary was patient, sat down, and watched Trudy slowly begin to eat. As Trudy finished the piece of toast and ate a small bit of the scrambled eggs, Mary tried to get Trudy to talk:

"Are you feeling better now that you've gotten some food into your stomach?"

Trudy merely nodded, choosing not to engage.

"I know you don't really know me well, but as I said yesterday, I'm here to complete the adoption report. You are still recovering from giving birth and probably need to sleep and catch up a bit more, but we do have some work to get done before you go back to Milson for court."

"Do you have any questions, Trudy?"

Trudy merely shook her head but still remained silent.

"It's okay if you don't want to talk to me right now. Finish eating some fruit, and then you can get dressed. We can go outside and walk down to the lake. I'll clean up the dishes while you dress."

Finally, Trudy dressed, choosing to put on her old jeans and the gray sweatshirt. She left the pretty clothes that Marie had purchased in the closet. But Mary was pleased to see her finally dressed. She opened the door to go outside and led Trudy down the path to the lake.

The two sat down in the Adirondack chairs. The yellow Lab was so excited to see Trudy again, that she came over and placed her head in Trudy's lap. When Trudy failed to greet her, the dog whined just a bit as if talking to her. Only this sweet gesture by the Lab got Trudy to respond. She gently patted the dog on the head and began to cry again.

Mary was moved. She saw how sad Trudy was and was thankful the Lab had gotten some response. Mary hoped Trudy would not lose control again. Fortunately, she had a few more diazepam pills, but she didn't really want to give them to Trudy since they seemed to make her so sleepy. Mary was patient and let Trudy cry for a bit. The yellow Lab whined a bit, too, as if she were quietly talking to Trudy, sensing the hurt.

A loon cry echoed over the surface of the lake, there had been a slight fog over the surface since the night had gotten so cool. The trilling call echoed through the fog sounding the mourning for a last departure. Little wavelets caressed the sandy edge also echoing across the shoreline.

After a long silence, Mary saw that Trudy finally stopped crying, "May I tell you what we must do while I am here?" Trudy only nodded yes.

"If you like, we can sit here and do it. I don't think I've ever worked in such a lovely place and the loon call is so beautiful. Would you like that Trudy?"

Trudy saw how patient Mary was being. She was grateful that Jill was not here, bitching at her as before. Mary wasn't much older than she was and was so petite that Trudy felt she should be her helper. She finally gathered herself and answered Mary:

"Yes, I'd like to stay out if the Lab can stay with us. The loons won't be here much longer." Mary agreed, "We can watch for a bit longer."

Trudy and Mary listened again as the loon trilling echoed through the foggy veneer. As the fog began to evaporate, the sun was well south now, but finally burned away the gray veil over the lake, and it became another clear, sunny day.

Mary explained that she needed to complete an interview for her report to the court. It was mostly background information about Trudy and the course of her pregnancy. She explained that she would need to know more about Trudy's contact with Tony and Marie and how the meeting had gone at the hotel. Trudy agreed to answer her questions. Mary went back to the cottage and retrieved her papers.

And so the work of the day began. The two young women remained outside looking over the lake. Mary carefully went through her questions and made notes for the report. Trudy cooperated, merely answering questions that Mary asked.

Several hours later, Mary was satisfied with the progress she was making. She saw Trudy was getting tired and suggested that they go back inside, and Mary would prepare sandwiches. She said Trudy could take an afternoon nap if she liked, and afterward they could finish the work.

As Trudy slept after lunch, the green Jaguar pulled up to the cottage. Faust walked into the cabin, and Mary informed him that Trudy was resting but that she had made good progress on the report in the morning. Faust was pleased to hear it. He told Mary that he had gotten the expedited court hearing. It would be on Friday of this week, just two days away. He asked if Mary could finish the report by Friday.

"It's not much time, but if I finish my interview with Trudy by this evening, I could work on the report tomorrow and have it ready in time for the court hearing."

Mary then asked Faust, "Doesn't the guardian ad litem for the baby usually want the social worker's report in advance of the court hearing?"

Mary had been told the Legal Aid Society attorneys who served as the GAL wanted the report in advance. This court-appointed attorney represented the interests of the baby. Mary feared this attorney might object to such a late receipt, "I'd basically have to hand it to her as we walk into the courtroom."

Faust chafed at being questioned by this young social worker. He curtly responded, "I'll manage that concern. This is a private adoption and the adoptive parents want to take the baby home this week. Getting the baby in their arms is in the baby's best interest. The GAL will have to cooperate, she'll look incompetent in court if she is putting impediments in the way. And I hope your report will show how much the birth mom wants this adoption completed, do you understand?"

Mary didn't like the indirect instruction telling her what to write, responding, "I'll accurately report what Trudy tells me."

"Well, let's get Trudy out of bed and find out."

Mary didn't like the idea of disturbing Trudy, but she had been napping for over two hours since lunch. Faust told Mary to go in and tell Trudy to get up. "Tell her that I have a surprise for her. I can't stay all afternoon, so the sooner I can see Trudy, the sooner I can leave and allow you to get your work finished."

Mary hesitated.

"Or do you want me to go in and wake Trudy?"

"No, you might startle her. I'll go in."

Mary went into Trudy's room. She gently opened the blinds and let the sunlight pour into the room. Trudy began to stir. Mary told Trudy that Faust was waiting to talk with her and said he had a surprise.

Trudy slowly awoke and began to question what kind of surprise, but Mary told Trudy she didn't know. She asked Trudy to get up and get dressed. "I'll wait in the kitchen with Faust."

As Trudy stepped out of the room, Mary noted her color was returning and Trudy seemed more composed. Faust told Mary that he wanted to talk with Trudy in private and suggested she should go down to the lake. This time, it was Mary that complied.

As Mary walked out of the cottage, Faust turned to Trudy. He greeted her kindly and told her that she looked much better today and would be back to normal in no time. Faust directed Trudy to sit at the kitchen table with him as he pulled out a file and also a small jewelry box, setting it on the table.

"I went over my office notes, Trudy, and found our original checklist. Do you remember the list?"

Trudy only shook her head in the affirmative, barely recalling what was on the list. It just didn't seem to matter now. But Faust continued with some enthusiasm.

"Here it is, Trudy, and as I checked over your six items, I saw that we completed all of the items except that last one."

Faust pushed the yellow paper with his handwritten checklist over to Trudy, pointing to the last item, "Left jewelry at pawnbroker, reclaim."

"You can see the first five are all checked completed, but not item six. And since I promised we'd accomplish all the items on the list, I wanted to finish it."

Trudy wondered where Faust was going with this. She remembered going to see the pawnbroker with Leslie. Doc had laughed at them, telling Trudy that he had sold her grandmother's beloved brooch.

Trudy's eyes widened as Faust pushed the jewelry box over to Trudy. She wondered if he had somehow recovered the brooch.

"Open it, Trudy!"

Trudy took the leather-covered box and slowly lifted the top lid. Inside, a golden sheet of tissue paper covered the contents. Trudy lifted the tissue gently, hoping for a miracle.

But instead, she found a gold heart with the letter *T* inscribed on the face. The gold heart was attached to an expensive 18 K gold chain precisely matching the pendant, not like the one on her grandmother's brooch.

Trudy became teary-eyed. She closed the jewelry box. Faust was disappointed in her reaction and commented, "I know it's not your grandmother's brooch, Trudy. I did go to the pawnbroker's shop. Doc was a disgusting little man, and I hope you never go in there again. He is not someone you should be dealing with. But Doc said he sold your brooch."

Trudy did not respond. Faust continued: "Did you hear me, Trudy? Don't go back in there! When we are finished with your adoption, you will be able to go back to your apartment in peace. Your rent is paid through October, your bills are all paid, the hospital and doctor are all paid."

Faust pointed to the list of unpaid bills and items of concern and told Trudy that it had all been taken care of as promised. Tears rolled down Trudy's cheeks as she spoke through her tears. "I already went back for my brooch with the money refunded by the abortion clinic and tried to reclaim it. I knew Doc sold it," Trudy cried.

"You see! Just as I said, he can't be trusted."

Faust reclaimed his role as a father figure, trying to comfort a child just learning the harsh ways of the world. He softened his tone. Faust opened the jewelry box and pulled out the heart attached to the sparkling gold chain. He reasoned with Trudy,

"I know this can't replace your brooch or the memories. But look how beautiful this one is! Marie bought it for you; she shopped carefully, checking with many jewelers. They don't sell brooches anymore. They've gotten too old-fashioned, I guess. But Marie wants you to know this heart represents all the love for your baby. The love you gave her by giving birth and the love Tony and Marie will give her as parents, fully capable of providing everything the baby could need and more."

"Turn the heart over." Trudy followed his directions. Through her tears, she took the heart from his hand and turned it over. It was inscribed with a date, *September 5, 1977*.

"Isn't it a coincidence, Trudy? You actually gave birth on Labor Day, September 5, 1977. With this heart necklace, you will never forget the wonderful gift of life given to your little girl. You can wear this heart necklace to remember her. Marie sends it with her love, and she wrote a small note card to go with the heart." Faust handed Trudy a small envelope.

Trudy pulled out the card and read the message. "Thank you, Trudy! This heart represents our love, for you, and for our daughter. We thank you from the bottom of our hearts. Love, Tony and Marie."

More tears ran down Trudy's cheeks. Faust walked over to the roll of toweling paper that hung under the cabinet and tore off a sheet, handing it to Trudy. "You can't see Tony and Marie anymore until the court hearing, but Marie did ask me to tell you one more thing. She wanted to come to say goodbye on Tuesday as you were being discharged." Faust added, "But I'm the one who told her that was out of the question, not with a private adoption. Contacts must end after birth."

But Marie insisted that I tell you one more thing. "She and Tony will love your daughter and promise to be wonderful parents." Marie added, "Tell Trudy not to worry about anything with the baby. We wish and pray that she'll have a wonderful life, too."

"I told Marie not to overdo it, but I think you can see how sincere she is being. This gesture of buying this heart locket was meant to symbolize all of their feelings."

Faust took his yellow note paper and marked item six with the final check-off. He handed it back to Trudy. "Everything is completed."

Trudy did not respond. She knew her beloved brooch was gone. She had been so stupid. But she didn't blame Faust. Nothing would ever be the same again. But all of Marie's wishes for her were just more fairy tales. Marie didn't even really know who she was.

Faust then got down to business. He explained that on Friday she would appear in court, and Mary would file her report. He told Trudy to show the checklist to Mary so that she could see how much help Trudy had gotten. He encouraged Trudy to be kind in her comments about Tony and Marie since the court needed to know that the adoption was in the best interests of her baby. Finally, he told Trudy to remember that she had been the one to select this file for these birth parents. Also, she understood that they were paying all of the costs for her living expenses during pregnancy, medical and necessary legal costs of the private adoption.

"I will see you on Friday very early and drive you back to Milson for the court hearing on the termination of your parental rights so the baby can be adopted as you planned. Mary Hightower will finish her report and file it as well. By the way, Terrek did sign the consent, but don't worry, he will not be in court, his appearance is not necessary."

"Do you have any questions?"

Trudy was puzzled about one thing. She wiped her tears, and asked, "If Terrek doesn't have to be in court, why do I?"

Faust smiled, answering, "It doesn't seem fair, does it? But the guy is only a 'putative father,' meaning only named a father, but his paternity has never been proven by blood tests or admitted to by the father. It is obvious who the mother is—you gave birth. You clearly have legal rights as a mother, and the court requires the birth mother appear in order to terminate those rights."

"Leslie is right, then. Women get the short end of everything, while men just skate by," argued Trudy.

Surprisingly, Faust agreed, telling Trudy she was right but then pointed out: "If Terrek wanted to father this child, and you didn't want to marry him, he is the one that would have to prove his fatherhood. The law only gives the father the same rights that you have as the birth mother if he is married to the woman. So any man wanting children better marry the woman before she gives birth."

Trudy thought about that for a moment but didn't say anything. She found this new twist on her rights interesting. Now it seemed her grandmother, and not Leslie, knew how serious being a mother should be. Faust stood up to leave and reminded Trudy to cooperate with Mary so she could get her report finished.

They both walked outside. Faust said goodbye, and he also gave Mary final instructions about meeting on Friday for court. He would arrive very early to drive Trudy to court. They'd have some time during the drive to go over last-minute preparations.

⟋⟍ ℓ

On Thursday, Mary completed her report on the primacy of the adoption. She encouraged Trudy to shower and get ready for her court date. She needed to look "proper," telling her that she would need to dress up the way she would for church. Trudy thought about Marna and decided to wear the blouse Marna made. Trudy had packed it in the hospital bag that she carried everywhere during the pregnancy.

Early Friday morning before dawn, Faust pulled up to the lake cottage. He went inside the cabin and accepted a cup of coffee, drinking it as he talked with Mary briefly. She needed to return to her agency to print copies of her report and would meet Faust and Trudy at the courthouse.

Trudy walked into the kitchen wearing Marna's blouse over the black pants that Marie bought for her. Faust complimented her but then saw that Trudy was not wearing the heart necklace. He asked Trudy to put it on so as not to hurt Marie's feelings. Trudy complied.

Faust escorted Trudy to the Jaguar and opened the passenger side door. This was the day that Trudy had been dreading. It was finally before her, but she was so disengaged from this momentous occasion, it barely registered for her. The car door opened, the car door shut. Nearly nine months of worry and preparation were barely noted now. Trudy had slept so much in the last few days that she was barely present to the moment. Her mental processes disengaged.

Faust at first made small talk about the weather; just after dawn the forest was magnificent. The autumn colors were already nearing peak color.

Faust repeated how lovely Trudy looked today, complimenting her hair style that hung perfectly around her pretty face, thanks to the stylish cut that Marie had arranged. Trudy's surging post-birth hormones flushed her cheeks in pale pink. She wore no makeup, but Faust noted it was advantageous to her youthful appearance. Trudy ignored the compliment.

Faust got down to business as they drove along the quiet country road: "In court, just listen to my questions, Trudy, and make a direct answer. My questions will mostly seek a simple, 'yes.' But you must say it out loud, not nod your head. There is a court reporter that takes precise dictation of all testimony."

"The judge will want to hear you explain in your own words why you are choosing to do an adoption and terminate your parental rights. Tell him what you've said to me many times, you know, that you want your baby to have both a mother and father, that you're not ready to be a parent, that you want to go back to school and finish your studies. Okay?"

Faust waited for Trudy to respond. She had mostly been watching out the window, barely listening to Faust and his legal instructions. She was tired of all of this preparation. But Faust insisted on an answer,

"Trudy, do you know what you are going to say?"

"About what?" she responded.

Faust grew impatient. He saw that Trudy hadn't been listening. Faust lectured her, "Trudy, this is serious—today is your day in court! As I was saying, the judge will want to hear you answer why you're asking to terminate your rights as a parent. You have to tell him in your own words. Do you know what you are going to say?"

"I guess so," Trudy replied.

"Well, what will you say? Pretend I'm the judge for a moment. Tell me why you are doing this private adoption, giving up your rights to the baby?"

Trudy didn't respond.

"Damn it, Trudy! Are you listening? You will be in court in about an hour!"

Trudy turned to Faust and meekly responded, "I know."

"Well, what do you say?"

"Like you said, I'm not a parent, I'm a student and want to go back to my apartment. I want my life back; sort of what you said before."

Faust shook his head but didn't push it. He hoped Trudy would regain her composure once she got in the courtroom. This always motivated the client to be on their best behavior and comport themselves to the solemn surroundings. Faust drove on quietly for a bit and allowed Trudy to think about where they were heading.

After driving many miles, Faust started again, "One other point. When we are in court, I am going to have to tell the judge that I am appearing as the attorney for Tony and Marie. The hearing will start with your termination of parental rights, and Tony and Marie won't be present then. The next part of the hearing is approval of the interstate adoption compact and temporary placement. Tony and Marie will be in court for this part, and I will sit with them at the counsel table."

"During your court appearance, you will be sitting with the guardian ad litem for the baby and with Mary Hightower at the second table. I will introduce all the participants at the start of the case, but you will be introduced as appearing *pro se*, that's Latin, meaning, 'for yourself.'"

Puzzled, Trudy asked, "What do you mean, 'for myself'? Isn't everyone for themselves?"

Faust chuckled at Trudy's play on words, "Of course, but in court, it simply means you are not being represented by an attorney. Trudy, still confused, asked, "Do you mean I don't have a lawyer with me?"

"That's it. Now, you get it," replied Faust, still chuckling. But Trudy saw no humor in this. "Well, who are you, then? You have been my lawyer all these months, haven't you?"

"I've been your counselor, Trudy," Faust replied with some sarcasm.

"This is a legal technicality. I cannot go into court and tell the judge that I am representing two different parties in the same adoption. I must represent just one, as the lawyer of record."

"Why don't Tony and Marie represent just themselves, then?" Trudy was being earnest.

Trudy thought that they certainly had enough money to get a lawyer if they wanted one, why did they have to use her lawyer?"

"Come on, Trudy. Don't make this difficult. Tony and Marie are paying all the bills. I can't tell the judge that I represent everyone in court. Yes, I've been your counselor, and at your request, I might add. You picked Tony and Marie to adopt your baby in a private adoption. You knew that I was bringing files for you to pick from. I can act as a counselor for all the parties during your pregnancy with everyone's consent. Tony and Marie know that I've been counseling you. They've consented as well. But in court, I can't be an attorney for everyone."

"In court, I represent just one party as the lawyer of record. It won't look right if I say I'm your lawyer while Tony and Marie are paying me. And don't forget, I have a lot of other legal responsibilities to finish, the interstate adoption compact to finalize the actual adoption, and all of the court work to finish. For you, today is just about the termination of your parental rights. You are an adult, and you will appear *pro se* to give consent. For Tony and Marie, there is much more work to be done after your hearing that they need an attorney to complete."

Trudy didn't see the fine distinction that Faust was trying to draw, but she stopped trying to object. She had always been alone in this, nothing changed.

Trudy stared out the window and unconsciously moved her hand to grasp her brooch. She instantly felt the unfamiliar heart necklace, the one Faust insisted that she wear. Trudy pulled her hand away from the new heart necklace. Her old habit of reaching for her grandmother's brooch, this comfort. The gesture now only reminded her of all the misery. Her own heart was breaking.

Pulling up to the courthouse, Faust pulled into a reserved parking space in the attorney's lot near the front entrance. Trudy looked at the behemoth of an ugly cement block building. The pseudo-architecture suggested a neo-Roman structure with faux Corinthian columns stretching skyward at the entrance. The columns only reinforced the ugly massiveness. Architectural critics had called the Milson Courthouse a monument to man's stupidity and ignorance, and while Trudy was not privy to this criticism, she saw the ugliness and feared it.

Faust led Trudy inside and over to the elevator that carried them to the second floor. Stepping out, they entered a long corridor dimly lit and lined with ugly gray granite, trying to imitate marble rising from the gray terrazzo flooring. Along the walls, long wooden pews were lined up, not unlike those in church. Mary had mentioned to Trudy to dress as if she were going to church. Trudy hadn't taken it literally then but understood now.

Faust waved to Tony and Marie who were sitting on one of the pews next to a courtroom door. As Marie approached, she remarked enthusiastically, "Oh! Trudy, you look lovely," Marie wiped tears from her eyes on seeing Trudy wearing the new gold heart. Marie hugged Trudy in a friendly manner, but Trudy didn't reciprocate.

Faust took charge. He told Trudy to sit down on the pew and directed Tony and Marie to follow him into a small antechamber at the back of the courtroom that was assigned for client preparations by officers of the court. Once inside, he instructed Tony and Marie that they would have to wait in this room during the parental termination. They would not be allowed to attend the first hearing. All terminations were closed hearings, not open to the public, not even the adopting parents.

Without the termination, there could be no adoption to follow, Faust explained.

Faust told Tony that neither he nor Marie should be talking with Trudy before this hearing, all the counseling is done. Tony said he understood. Faust wished that they had not seen Trudy at all. He went back into the hallway to get ready for this first hearing and to find the guardian ad litem that would represent the baby's interest in court.

In the hallway, he found Mary Hightower sitting next to Trudy on the bench. Faust approached her and asked if she had the copies ready. Mary handed Faust his copy, and he sat down to read it.

Mary gestured to a woman alighting from the elevator, telling Faust that this was the guardian ad litem. Faust looked over momentarily but returned to the report. It was Mary who greeted the GAL and introduced her to Trudy.

"Trudy, this is Atty. Susan Hagerty, who is representing the baby. Attorney Hagerty, this is the birth mom, Trudy."

Trudy merely looked at the middle-aged woman wearing a matching skirt and suit jacket, but clearly not tailored like Faust's suit. Mary handed another copy of the report to Attorney Hagerty, who complained that she did not like getting the report as she was walking into the courtroom, she had not had the time to read it properly and prepare.

Faust stood up: "Look, I just got the report this morning as well. You know how these private adoptions are expedited. I'd suggest you sit down and read it right now, like everyone else has to do."

Faust did not introduce himself, expecting he was already known by other lawyers. Attorney Hagerty did not like his tone. She took the copy from Mary's hands but replied, "I'm going to talk with the birth mother first." Not waiting for permission, Hagerty turned to Trudy, "Walk down the hall with me. I haven't had a chance to talk with you, and I will not go into the courtroom without having an opportunity to hear from you first."

This second part was said directly to Faust instead of Trudy. Faust smiled. "Of course, I expected you would talk with the birth mom. Please, take your time," as if Faust was magnanimously granting her request.

Faust nodded to Trudy as if giving permission for the interview. He had completely taken charge of the proceedings before they ever entered the courtroom. Trudy turned and began to walk down the hallway with this unknown woman.

As they began to walk slowly down the long, dark hallway, Hagerty explained what her role would be in court and even complained to Trudy that she did not like getting the report just before calling the case. Trudy didn't care and barely listened to her ramblings. Hagerty abruptly stopped once they were out of earshot of Mary and Faust and faced Trudy.

"You can ask for more time, you know. If you want to think this over some more, we don't have to have this hearing now, no matter what Faust says about an expedited hearing date. He is representing the adopting parents, not you."

"I know," Trudy responded, adding, "No, I want to get this over with."

"And you understand that you are about to terminate your rights as a parent?"

"I guess so," replied Trudy.

"Tell me, why?" Attorney Hagerty persisted. Trudy tried to remember the rehearsed lines that Faust suggested, but she couldn't remember all of it. Trudy just blurted out:

"I'm not ready to take care of a baby. This was a mistake; I didn't want to get pregnant."

"But you were pregnant—you did have a baby," pointed out the GAL, adding, "You could keep the baby, get assistance. Just because you got pregnant doesn't mean you have to do an adoption. Do you know that?"

Trudy thought about Leslie and all her suggestions. This woman reminded her of Leslie. Not that they looked alike, but both talked about the same rights of women. "Yes, I know all that. I got that kind of information," responded Trudy.

"And did you get counseling? Would you want more of it?" "I did." "No, I don't want more counseling." Trudy responded, adding, "I just want this over with, I don't need any more counseling." She thought about Mary Hightower, who was very nice, but Trudy didn't see how she was going to give her any more help.

"Okay, are you agreeing to the private adoption?"

"Yes," replied Trudy.

"How did you meet these adoptive parents?" Hagerty looked at the report for the first time and added, "Tony and Marie, and how did you pick them?"

"I guess, I picked them from a number of files that were given to me by Faust," responded Trudy. But the GAL wasn't satisfied.

"Well did you pick Tony and Marie?"

Trudy answered, "I picked their file."

"And do you think they will give your baby a good home?"

"I'm sure they will, better than I could," Trudy said honestly, remembering the lovely descriptions of not one but two homes that Marie had given her.

Hagerty checked her watch. It was time for the court hearing on the termination. She turned and headed back to the bench and told Trudy she needed to sit down and read the report.

The GAL was being curt, and Trudy wondered if she had done something wrong. As they headed back toward the courtroom, Faust rose and told Trudy to follow him. He would show her around the courtroom and get her settled before the judge arrived.

Faust suggested that Mary follow them as well so that Trudy would have someone to sit with at the counsel table and again told Attorney Hagerty to take her time, and when she was finished, she could join the other two at the counsel table.

Faust directed Trudy to her chair at the front counsel table on the left side of the courtroom and asked Mary to sit next to her. He pointed to his seat at the plaintiff's table to the right. Faust then left after Trudy and Mary were settled to check on Tony and Marie, explaining that he would return shorty.

In the small anteroom where he had left Tony and Marie, Faust reported he finally got a copy of the social worker's report, adding that the report was positive, and the social worker was recommending approval of the private adoption and termination of the parental rights. He added there were no surprises and that the guardian ad litem for the baby was reading the report and the hearing would begin soon. Marie was overjoyed with this progress.

"One last item, when the approval of the temporary placement is heard, I do have to account for fees and costs to the court. I prepared my legal statement for today's hearings, here is a copy." Faust handed his fee statement to Tony.

Tony looked at it momentarily and then objected: "Wait a minute, we're paying you over $100,000 for your services. Why is the statement only showing $10,250?"

"You don't understand," began Faust. "That statement is just for the termination and temporary placement hearing. It is not a complete breakdown of all my fees on your client matters."

Tony didn't like what Faust was suggesting. As an investment counselor, Tony knew money. He thought Faust was trying to pull something by not disclosing his entire fee to the court and again objected.

"Are you trying to cause a new problem, now!" retorted Faust. Marie grew nervous. She wanted to get this hearing done. Marie placed her hand on Tony's arm and sweetly suggested that they permit Faust to manage the court procedure, telling Tony they know full well how much they were paying for the adoption.

Marie won the day. Faust went back into the courtroom after telling his clients to sit tight; he would return in roughly thirty minutes to begin their placement approval, which was the next phase. Attorney Haggerty would also stop in to talk with them before the next phase.

With Faust out of the courtroom, Trudy looked at her surroundings. The courtroom was dark, with walnut paneling on the walls and heavy, round wooden columns interspersing the large open spaces. The judge's bench at the front was on a raised wooden platform with heavy wood paneled sides. Directly behind the bench was a wall mural depicting a blindfolded woman holding up the scales of justice in one hand and a sword in the other. Dressed in a white flowing gown, she appeared as an ancient goddess of the Roman Empire. Trudy wondered why the goddess of justice wore a blindfold. Shouldn't she be able to see to provide justice?

Faust came to the front and sat down. With all parties present, the clerk, sitting in front of the judge's bench, notified the court reporter to come into the room. Next, the bailiff seated off to the side behind an old metal desk, called out as the judge walked into the courtroom, "All rise," and introduced, "The Honorable Michael Riley, presiding."

Like everyone else, Trudy stood up as instructed. Her knees felt weak, and she began sweating. A small, diminutive man dressed in a black robe with wire-rimmed glasses walked up the few steps to the raised bench and sat down.

"You may take your seats," instructed the bailiff.

Everyone sat down. The clerk called the case into the record: "In the matter of the Termination of Parental Rights to Baby Girl Doe, born September 5, 1977, in Milson County to birth mother, Trudy."

Attorney Faust stood and warmly greeted the judge and then introduced all the persons present in the courtroom, identifying the roles each played in this case. He merely identified Trudy as the birth mother and informed the court that his clients were waiting in the back antechamber for the second phase of the hearing.

Faust next took all of his prepared legal documents along with the report prepared by Mary Hightower and handed them to the court clerk, who stamped each document and turned to hand them to the judge. While all of this was proceeding, Judge Riley observed Trudy closely.

The judge merely listened and quickly reviewed the papers that Faust filed. After several minutes, the judge looked to Faust and stated, "All right, counselor. Proceed."

Very formally, Faust began: "Thank you, your honor. If it please the court, I would request that the petitioning birth mother, Trudy, be called to the witness stand."

The clerk then called Trudy's name to rise and come forward. She instructed Trudy to remain standing and to be sworn under oath for her testimony. Trudy's heart was racing. Faust knew she was nervous so he merely stepped over and politely helped pull her chair out and gently directed her to the witness stand, reminding Trudy to remain standing.

"Raise your right hand. Do you promise to tell the truth, the whole truth and nothing but the truth, so help you God?"

Barely audible, Trudy said, "Yes."

The clerk told her to take her seat and to pull the chair forward so that she could speak into a microphone situated on a small shelf in front of the chair. She also admonished Trudy to speak up so that everyone could hear her answers.

The clerk asked her to state her first name, her birth date, and current address for the record. When Trudy finished giving her answers. The judge told Faust to proceed, and Faust took over.

"Trudy, you are in court today to ask the judge to terminate your parental rights to your baby girl so that she may be adopted by parents you've selected, is this correct?"

Trudy remembered Faust telling her in the car this morning that most of his questions would just call for just a yes. Trudy answered, "Yes."

"And is it correct that you understand that my office is representing Tony and Marie, the parents you selected in this private adoption?"

"Yes."

"And is it correct that you understand you could have an attorney in court if you wanted one, is that right?"

Trudy scowled at Faust and impatiently answered, "Yes."

"And is it correct that you have filed a Petition for Termination of your Parental Rights to baby girl Doe, born September 5, 1977?" Trudy relaxed a bit and joined in the routine, answering, "Yes."

Faust and Trudy continued dancing in this way, Faust reading the elements of the Termination Petition into the court record with Trudy responding in the affirmative to each leading question. Since there was no real controversy, the court allowed Faust to ask direct questions to merely complete the court record with all the required elements to make a complete record.

"And who is the baby's father?"

Trudy scowled again at Faust. He knew perfectly well, but she answered, "Terrek."

Faust began to ask questions that he knew would be embarrassing to Trudy but proceeded in a matter-of-fact way, "Did you have sexual intercourse with Terrek?"

Sweat began to roll down her back under the linen blouse, which was now clinging to her body. Trudy responded, "Yes."

"And did you have sexual intercourse with any other male during the time period of November 1996 through February of 1997, the statutory time frame of conception for a baby born full term?"

Trudy did not like this question. She hesitated. Faust repeated the embarrassing question and explained to her that it was necessary to ask the question to eliminate any other persons of interest. Trudy wanted Faust to move on. He repeated the same uncomfortable question and now she answered adamantly. "No!"

"And during this same time frame, was Terrek the only male you had sexual intercourse with? Was Terrek the only male?" "Yes!" Faust then added, "And there was never any other male, is this correct?"

Again! Trudy thought, wondering how many times Faust was going to ask her this question. She remembered the New Year's Eve celebration in the limo and wished she had never agreed to go out with Terrek, but she never really knew where he was taking her. It was all so innocent at the time. But here she was. Not Terrek, no, he never had to answer for his part, only she had to testify. It was unnerving, and Trudy firmly stated, "Yes. That's correct!"

"And you believe Terrek is the father of your child, Correct?"

"Yes."

"How did you meet Terrek?"

Trudy wanted Faust to shut up about Terrek, but she pushed on. "He was a student at Milson U. He came into the place where I work, and then I would see him on campus. We started dating after that."

"How would you describe your relationship with Terrek at the time you became intimate?" Trudy said, "I don't know, friends?"

"Only as a friend?" Faust countered. "Would you say more than a friend, after you got to know him better?"

Trudy answered, "Maybe at that time, I might have called him my boyfriend, but not anymore."

"And during that time period when he was your boyfriend, did you spend a lot of your time with him?"

Trudy agreed, "I guess so."

"How much time?" Faust asked.

"Nearly every day."

"And as the school year moved on and it began to get cold, let's say all the way through the holidays and the start of this year, you were seeing Terrek nearly every day, is that correct?"

"Yes."

"And is this the time when you would have gotten pregnant?" "Yes."

Faust then asked, "And did you have any other boyfriend during this time frame?"

Trudy scowled but answered adamantly, "No!"

"Do you still see Terrek now?"

Trudy shifted in the witness chair, answering, "No."

"Why not?" Faust countered.

Trudy was getting more upset. All the things that Faust prepared her for, he never said he was going to keep asking all of these questions about Terrek. Faust had told her that she'd just have to tell the court who the father was, but not like this. Trudy was flushed and began to feel the perspiration around her face and neck. Her hands were wet, and she wiped them across her slacks.

Faust repeated the question, "Why don't you see Terrek any-more?"

"He took off, that's why. When I told him I was pregnant, he didn't want to hear about it, and he just left!"

"Did Terrek ever give you money?" Faust asked.

"No, never," Trudy answered adamantly.

"Did he ever ask you about your well-being or ask about the baby after she was born?"

"No."

Faust continued, "To your knowledge, has Terrek ever seen the baby?"

"No. Never that I've known about."

"Do you know where Terrek is now?"

"No."

"Would you say that Terrek abandoned you?" Trudy considered the question, "Maybe. He did say he was going to California."

Finally, the judge interrupted Faust.

"Counselor, I'm satisfied. I think you have established a sufficient record on paternity. You may move on."

"Thank you, your honor. I also have a signed consent by said named, Terrek, and it is filed with the documents."

"Yes, I did see it. Move on. Paternity is established and a consent of the so called, Terrek, the putative father's termination is part of the record.

"Thank you, your honor. Just a few more questions for the peti-tioner."

"Trudy, is there any chance that you and Terrek might reconcile with each other and maybe even get married so that one day, you might want to parent this child?"

Trudy thought Faust was crazy for asking. Did he believe in those old fairy tales? She wanted absolutely nothing to do with Terrek, did not want to see him again or ever talk with him, and responded, "Absolutely not!"

"Trudy, is it your request that your rights to parent the baby be terminated and also that all your rights and the birth father's rights be terminated by this court?"

Trudy wasn't grasping the import of Faust's question, she just wanted him to be done. She quickly answered, "Yes."

"You understand this is final, you can't change your mind later?"

Trudy didn't think it was fair to be equating her termination of parental rights with those of Terrek. What did he ever do to even deserve to be a father? But she kept this to herself and responded: "Yes, I know it is final."

"And did you receive counseling?"

"Yes. I did."

"Do you think any more counseling would help you?"

"No."

Faust turned to the judge and told the court that Mary Hightower had filed a report, and this report summarized the facts and recommended in favor of the private adoption. He asked the judge to accept the report as part of the record. The court granted his request that the report be received and accepted as part of the record.

Faust then went through a litany of rights that a parent has with regard to their natural child; the right to raise the child, to make decisions on education and health matters, and more. Each time, he would stop and ask if Trudy understood that she had such rights and was agreeing to give up the right. Trudy did her part, answering yes each time.

Faust next turned to the adoption decision. He asked Trudy direct questions about reaching her decision to give her baby up for a private adoption. Trudy merely answered yes to each one, including that it had been her decision to come to his office and to receive prospective parent files in order to select adoptive parents.

To conclude, Faust asked Trudy if she believed that Tony and Marie would be good parents for her baby.

"Yes." Trudy confirmed that she had concluded Tony and Marie would be good parents. She added, "Tony and Marie would be able to offer her baby more than I could."

Unexpectedly, the judge interrupted. Trudy had nearly forgotten that the judge was even listening. Now he spoke directly to her.

"Do you understand that I will not accept a termination of your parental rights if it is just because you don't have money?"

Trudy honestly responded, "No."

Faust broke in. His voice was strained, "Your honor, the witness did not understand your question; she would not have said this!"

Faust then directed a different question, "Trudy, you are not giving up the baby just because you have no money, is that correct?"

Trudy understood that he wanted her to say yes. But before she could answer, the judge interrupted again.

"Wait a moment, counselor! I let you go on for quite a bit here to make your record, but I want to see what this mother says. I will now ask a few questions. Sit down!"

Looking back to Trudy, the judge repeated, "Do you understand that I will not accept a termination of your parental rights because your reason for terminating them is that you have no money?"

Trudy looked at the judge. His bright green eyes focused, waiting for her response.

Trudy looked back at Faust. He sat down as commanded but also stared at Trudy. Everyone in the room sat at attention, now waiting for her reply.

"Yes?" Trudy answered as if it were a question to the judge, whether yes was the answer he wanted.

The judge continued: "Do you want more time to make your decision?"

"No," Trudy responded.

"And you understand that your decision here today is permanent, is that right?"

"Let me ask you this way: If you had enough money to pay your rent, and food and all the needs that you and the baby would have, would you keep your baby?"

Trudy thought about this again. This was the question she had been thinking about for months now. But she'd finally come to grips with her decision; she knew that she couldn't offer the baby the kinds of things she'd need. Trudy knew that she wasn't ready to be a mother. She would not want her daughter to be without a mother the way she had been as a child. Trudy hung her head, concluding she wasn't even doing a great job of taking care of herself, much less a baby. She meekly offered, "No."

The judge prompted her, "Tell me why you want to have your baby given up for adoption."

"I wouldn't keep my baby even if I had money. I am not ready to be a parent; I'm still trying to find my own way around. I think my baby deserves better."

Trudy satisfied the court. He turned to Faust and said he could finish.

The court allowed Faust to complete the record on the advantages of a private adoption and began to lead Trudy through another set of direct questions, but the court stopped him and told Faust he had made a sufficient record on the termination.

Next, the guardian ad litem was allowed to ask questions in her role representing the best interests of the baby. But Attorney Hagerty basically repeated the questions already asked. It was all getting so repetitive. Trudy confirmed again to the GAL that she understood she was giving up her legal rights to her baby and had selected the adoptive parents. She confirmed that she needed no more time or counseling. The judge then told the GAL that her record was also complete so they could move on with the next phase.

Just as Trudy thought she was going to be excused, Judge Reilly looked to Trudy and told her that he always asks one more question before finishing. "After everything that's been asked here and with all of your answers, I want you to stop and really understand that if you want, you can still change your mind. You can keep your baby, even if she is placed in a temporary home for a while. You could get your life back together and then, later, keep your baby as her parent."

"Do you understand that?"

"Yes."

"Now think for one moment before you answer. Really think. Do you want me to terminate your parental rights, today?"

Trudy began to cry. All of this was overwhelming. The judge waited. Faust tried to stand up and talk. The judge admonished him, telling Faust to sit down and be quiet.

Trudy really did try to stop and think one more time about what she was doing, as the judge instructed. But she really didn't see any other alternative. She just wanted this to be over.

Through her tears, Trudy replied, "Yes, I want to give the baby up for adoption."

Judge Reilly replied, "Thank you, Trudy, I am relieved to see your tears. I get concerned when a young woman just consents to give up her child showing no emotion. I know this is hard, and I am relieved that you do understand the gravity of what you are doing here, today. Do you have any questions you would like to ask me?"

Trudy saw how kind the judge was being. She thought he was very wise. She looked up at him through her tears and responded: "Thank you! No, no more questions."

"Finally, do you understand that you have six months from today to appeal my decision. Has anyone told you about these rights?"

"Yes, the GAL and Mary Hightower, both told me I have appeal rights." The judge was satisfied, "You may step down and return to your seat."

Trudy went back to her seat next to Mary Hightower. Faust and the guardian ad litem made concluding statements to the court. Trudy did not hear any of it. She hung her head and wanted this to be over. Finally, she heard a loud bang. She jumped slightly in her chair.

The judge ordered: "The parental rights of birth mother, Trudy, are herewith terminated. Mr. Faust, you may proceed with the next phase after the court takes a fifteen-minute recess."

Faust left the courtroom and returned with Tony and Marie, instructing them to sit at his counsel table. After waiting several more minutes, the judge returned, and the second phase began. Trudy did not listen to the testimony or the proceedings on approving a temporary guardianship pending the final adoption, which could not take place for six months. Exhausted, Trudy waited for permission to leave.

The court then excused the birth mother before taking up the interstate agreement for placement in a separate jurisdiction since this involved much personal information about the adoptive parents, including last names. Faust escorted Trudy to the back of the room. Mary Hightower had been instructed to drive Trudy back to her own apartment. He bid farewell to her. Trudy left, totally spent.

Chapter 17

September 1977, Crescent Moon

Trudy slept through the remainder of her court day, through most of Saturday, rising to eat a few crackers and drink water, returning to bed and finally waking on Sunday, late in the afternoon. When she woke, it took her several moments to realize that she had returned to her own apartment. It had been so long since she slept in her own bed that it seemed strange more than familiar. Still drowsy, Trudy wondered if she'd had a long nightmare, like Sleeping Beauty.

As she regained consciousness, Trudy admonished herself for thinking of fairy tales again. Phony fairy tales where the damsel in distress is saved by the handsome prince are cruel parodies of real life; Trudy reminded herself to swear them off. She finally sat up, remaining on the side of her bed. Slowly, she regained the full impact her current reality.

Trudy broke into a sweat and felt like she was having another panic attack. She stood and began to pace, felt dizzy, and sat down in her rocking chair and began to rock back and forth. Rhythmically, she calmed herself—began to breathe normally.

She would never rock her baby in this chair. Tears overwhelmed her. She crossed her arms and hung her head, crying over the loss.

Trudy was emotionally drained and rocked back and forth, trying to find her equilibrium.

Leslie walked through the long hallway and stopped to unlock her apartment door. She stopped, hearing the creaking floorboards coming from inside Trudy's room. Leslie walked over to Trudy's door and knocked.

"Trudy? It's me, Leslie. Are you inside? Trudy? Open the door, please!"

Trudy stopped rocking, looked around as if she was again just waking. Leslie called again, pleading that Trudy open the door.

Trudy finally obeyed. She was beyond rebellion, beyond hiding. Trudy rose from her chair and complied with the command to open her door.

"You're home! We've all been waiting to hear from you! Where have you been?"

Trudy ignored the questions and, leaving the door ajar, returned to her rocking chair. Watching her, Leslie stood momentarily. It was getting hard to see in the waning light. Leslie flipped on the light switch. The overhead light washed over Trudy. She squinted. Having been accustomed to only the dark for days, it was like arising from hibernation, except Trudy wanted to stay in her cave.

Leslie took inventory of the room and Trudy. Only her bed had been disturbed. A small suitcase stood next to the door. Leslie looked for a baby or maybe a crib. She didn't know what to expect, only that Trudy appeared to be alone in the room.

As she looked at Trudy, Leslie saw that she had lost nearly all of her pregnancy weight. Her hair hung uncombed, and she was dressed in a wrinkled blouse and black pants that looked as if they had been slept in. Trudy didn't seem to focus on anything in particular, her eyes vacuous orbs.

"Trudy, how long have you been home?" Again, Trudy did not answer. Looking around, Leslie decided to take charge.

"I have some homemade soup from Jackie. I stopped at the restaurant yesterday to check in with her. We have all been waiting to hear from you. We didn't know what happened after you left the hospital. Jackie wanted you to have soup when you returned so she sent a big bowl."

Leslie stopped talking and waited for Trudy to react in some way. Still, Trudy did not respond.

"I'm going to get the pot of soup and bread and bring it here to heat. Promise not to move until I come back. Okay?"

Leslie couldn't tell if Trudy even heard anything she had said. She left Trudy's door wide open as well as her own. Leslie quickly retrieved a pot of homemade beef vegetable soup from her own refrigerator and an uncut loaf of homemade bread that Marna had given her. Leslie kept peering into Trudy's room to see if she would leave her door open. But Trudy just sat in the rocking chair.

Leslie returned and went into the tiny kitchen to heat the soup. She turned on the light in the kitchen and the one lamp in Trudy's efficiency apartment and switched off the glaring ceiling light. As the soup heated, a fresh aroma of vegetable soup came from the kitchen. Leslie opened a few windows. It was still quite warm outside, and the room was stuffy. Trudy started to focus on Leslie, watching all her activity.

As the soup heated, Leslie flipped on the bathroom light and directed Trudy to go in to brush her hair and freshen up. At first, Trudy did not comply, but Leslie went over to her rocker and extended her straight arm out. She took Trudy's hand, offering to help her rise. Leaving her no choice, Trudy merely took Leslie's hand and got a boost out of the rocker. Leslie walked Trudy over to her bathroom and told her to rinse some water over her face, brush her hair, and wash her hands, as if Trudy were a mere child needing adult supervision.

Trudy complied. Leslie waited to hear Trudy turn on the water in the sink and, once confirmed, returned to the kitchen to stir the soup and prepare a simple meal. Leslie found some tea bags and boiled water to make tea. She saw Trudy had no butter and again ran into her own kitchen to get the butter, leaving both doors wide open.

Leslie set a small table with soup bowls, bread, and butter, and she poured the tea. When Trudy emerged from the bathroom, Leslie was relieved to see that Trudy's eyes were beginning to focus. She pulled out a chair and directed Trudy to sit down, asking her when she had last eaten something. Trudy only shrugged.

As Leslie ladled soup into Trudy's bowl, she made small talk, telling Trudy about her new classes for the semester, about the new VOW project getting ready for the November elections. She cut Marna's bread. She told Trudy that everyone at the Counter was concerned and waiting to hear from her.

As Trudy began to eat, she tasted Jackie's wonderful soup. No meal could have tasted better, full of hearty beef, potatoes, carrots, beans, celery, and onions and spiced so perfectly that it tasted better than an expensive cut of steak. Leslie commented how delicious the soup was, and Trudy agreed. She had not eaten a regular meal in many days and realized that she was famished.

Like the soup, the bread was wonderfully fresh, like the bread her own grandmother made. Trudy ate one, two, and asked for a third piece as Leslie sliced more bread and poured another bowl of soup. Finally renewed, Leslie watched Trudy eat and asked again, "Trudy, how long have you been in your apartment?"

"I don't know. What day is it?"

Leslie shook her head: "It's Sunday! What day did you get home?"

Trudy thought for a moment and answered: "I came home Friday, right after the court hearing."

"You had a court hearing?"

Leslie looked around the room again. She saw no sign of any baby items, clearly the baby was not with Trudy.

She asked, "Where is your baby, Trudy?"

Trudy's eyes began to tear up again. She stopped eating and hung her head, not answering the direct question.

Leslie began to connect the dots: "You were in court on Friday, the baby is not here, was the court hearing about the baby, then?"

"Yes."

"Will you bring her home later? Is she just waiting in a foster home?"

"No!"

Trudy began to cry openly, explaining: "My rights as a parent were terminated by the court," Trudy cried, remembering the words used by the judge.

Leslie was stunned. "That fast! The baby was just born on Monday and your rights were terminated on Friday? I didn't know it could happen that fast! How did you have time to even think about it?"

Crying, Trudy told Leslie she didn't want to talk about it anymore. She knew Leslie wanted to help. But Leslie kept insisting that she didn't see how a young mother could lose her baby like that in just one week. She asked Trudy again, wanting her to explain.

"It wasn't just one week, Leslie. I've had most of last summer to think about this. Tony and Marie are adopting the baby."

Leslie remembered Marie from her visit to the hospital. It was obvious that this woman and her husband had money—their clothing, the east-coast accent, the way they took charge. Marie was the one that suggested they go see the baby. They left Trudy's room shortly after her arrival. Marie kindly showed Leslie where the baby was. She also remembered Tony and another man arguing, then Marie running off. Visiting hours ended, and Leslie was told to leave by the ward nurse. It all happened so quickly that she never got to talk much with Trudy.

Leslie told Trudy she was going to leave the soup, telling her that Jackie made it to give to her, and also the bread from Marna. She asked if Trudy would be all right for the night. Trudy looked at Leslie and thanked her for making the meal. She said she felt much better, now that she had eaten. She would be fine. Leslie was satisfied. Trudy seemed normal again, but she wanted to hear so much more. But Leslie also understood that this was not the time to start asking more questions.

"I'll check in with you tomorrow."

As she left, Leslie decided it wasn't her place to second guess Trudy. It was rough either way. But she kept wondering how a termination of parental rights could happen that fast. She would ask the public defender she knew from the VOW office if all this was on the up and up. Leslie said good night to Trudy and left. She closed all the doors as she returned to her apartment.

Trudy walked quickly away from her apartment early the following morning. She had been up most of the night since she had slept so much all weekend. The soup and bread refreshed her. She showered, changed her clothing, unpacked her small suitcase and then sat in her rocking chair to sort out her thoughts.

Wanting to reach a sense of finality, Trudy decided that she needed to see her baby one more time: to kiss her sweet cheeks, say goodbye properly, hoping this might help her resolve her conflicted feelings. Trudy felt so unsettled. She thought about her decision in court, about the judge's words, about her baby's welfare.

Remembering the Robert Frost poem she had admired from her high school poetry and creative writing class, she thought about standing before two roads and having to choose one. It was a good analogy. In the end, Trudy thought that no matter her choice, she would always wonder what it would have been like to choose the "one less traveled." Was she choosing the easy road? Or was it the road that was better for the baby, even if it wasn't her better choice? But Leslie's exclamation about everything happening so fast during the last week, put into her head that she'd never really had a chance to kiss her baby one final time.

Trudy knew the baby was in a temporary foster home awaiting the termination and approval to be taken out of state by Tony and Marie. She thought her baby may still be in Milson. Tony and Marie had stayed for the court hearing on Friday, and she knew they had more to do after this hearing was completed. She might have time for one more visit. She sat up all night thinking about seeing the baby.

Not long after sunrise, Trudy walked to Faust's office, passing the front door of The Spot on her way. A bar stool standing on the sidewalk held the door wide open to air out the stale smoke-filled bar. An acrid smell of beer, smoke, and sweat wafted outside; the vapors filled the air with invisible graffiti. Giving the open doorway a wide berth, Trudy winced, finding the place disgusting and wondering why anyone would want to enter.

Trudy quickened her step as her pulse started to race. She would have to be firm with Faust. He always had a way of steering things to his way, instead of letting Trudy make a choice. All night long, Trudy vowed to be strong-willed for her baby's sake.

Trudy got to the lawyer's office and was pleased to see the office lights on. She knew that Faust was an early starter. She opened his office door and walked into the waiting room. Jill saw Trudy.

"You can't come in here! Not now!" Jill was nearly shouting.

Faust heard Jill and hurried out of his inner office. He saw Trudy with Jill glaring at her. Trudy had prepared herself to standup to Faust, but Jill's reception was unexpected. She was nearly hysterical.

"No! No! This is not going to happen. You promised!"

Faust told Jill to calm down. "Finish the Vegas reservations—nothing has changed. I'm going to talk to Trudy, that's all."

Faust told Trudy to follow him. He walked into his inner office, but Trudy saw that he was not dressed in his usual attorney's uniform of a suit, tie and white shirt. Faust looked like he was dressed for vacation, wearing a sport shirt open at the collar, casual khaki pants and sandals.

"Trudy, I'm just on my way for a much-needed vacation. Why are you here?"

"Vacation?"

"That's right, a vacation. I get a break once in a while, you know! Now, why are you here?"

Trudy was caught off-guard. Her own life was in turmoil. Taking a vacation was a non-starter. There was no vacation time in her world. But she regrouped, reminding herself why she had come and wanting to show Faust that she had her own mind about things:

"I want to see the baby one more time. I never got time to kiss her goodbye. I want to hold her and kiss her and tell her I love her before she leaves!"

Faust stared at Trudy. He saw that Jill was at the door listening. He got up and shut the door, telling Jill, "Go make the reservation—

nothing has changed." Jill walked back to her desk as Faust closed his door.

"Trudy, you terminated your rights in court on Friday. The baby doesn't know how to say goodbye. It will only make everything harder for you if you see her again."

Trudy was prepared for his rational arguments, the didactics of his reasoning. She rehearsed this part in her rocking chair last night. She mustered her courage and began again, insisting that she be heard.

"I insist. I want to see my baby before she leaves Milson."

Faust saw that Trudy was going to stand her ground. This was not just a young, confused girl. This was a woman who had given birth and was here, a mother standing her ground, guarding her baby.

Faust did not argue with Trudy. He thought momentarily and then began again.

"Alright, Trudy, I'll drive you right now. I have to get back soon and can't spend a lot of time, but let's go."

"Really?" Trudy was not prepared to win so easily.

Faust stood up, telling Trudy, "Let's go."

Faust opened the office door and led the way. Jill scowled, but Faust prevented her next objection.

"I'll be back, finish our reservations, nothing is changed."

He led Trudy out of the office and over to his sleek Jaguar. Faust opened the passenger side door and allowed Trudy to step in. Faust got behind the wheel and started the engine, squealing the tires as he hurriedly tore off down the street.

Trudy didn't ask where the baby was staying and just trusted Faust to drive her there. She was surprised to see him take the freeway ramp onto the interstate. She just assumed the baby would be near the hospital, or the airport, both close to his office. They drove on. Neither talked. After many miles driving away from Milson on the interstate highway, Faust finally broke the silence.

"Trudy, there are some basic facts of life that you need to learn. I'm going to help you, out of the goodness of my heart, no charge, so listen carefully. There are two sides in life."

"I know, like standing at a fork in the road and choosing which one to walk down," replied Trudy thinking of her Frost meditation in the rocker.

Faust sneered. Trudy resented his sarcastic laughter.

"Don't be so naïve, Trudy. There are thousands of roads to go down. No, I'm talking about two kinds of people: the losers or the users, the sellers or the buyers. The chumps or the swindlers. Those two sides!"

"Everybody has a price, and everybody will pay a price. You need to learn what side to be on, that's all. Are you going to let people use you or will you use them? Take Tony and Marie, for example. Tony is a very successful asset manager, and Marie chose a winner. But they wanted something so badly and needed to find a way to get it. They would pay any price to have a family, a baby. They wanted that so badly that they were willing to pay dearly. And I'm the one helping them buy that dream. There are a lot of couples out there just like Tony and Marie."

Trudy was getting angry with Faust. This was *her* baby that he was talking about. There is no price for her own flesh and blood.

"What price?" objected Trudy, adding, "Tony and Marie promised to love the baby—this wasn't about money!"

Faust laughed again, even louder than before. "Trudy, you are so naïve, I just hope you wise up before you have nothing left to sell."

Trudy was getting hotter. "I'm not selling anything," screamed Trudy, hating Faust for even suggesting that she was.

Faust continued laughing. "I know, you just give it away, first to Terrek, then to Tony and Marie. That's being not only a loser but also a sucker."

Trudy stopped talking. She was too angry to reply. She looked out the car window as they continued to drive away from Milson on the interstate.

Faust finally stopped laughing, taking a more serious approach, he continued. "I like you, Trudy. You're still young. You have your whole life ahead of you. I don't want to see you spending your life one day after another working some manual job at minimum wages, letting guys like Terrek just use you."

As Faust drove on, he continued his soliloquy on life: "Or worse, besides the users and losers, there's a whole group of people that just never get in the game at all. They are the vast majority, really. The bystanders, people that just watch life pass them by—they live vicariously, idolizing the so called rich and famous. They live in a dream world of Hollywood pretty people, the sporting team greats, the famous, but they never get in the game themselves."

Trudy hated what he was saying. But then she thought about Leslie telling her the same thing, not to get caught working in a white dress slaving for others, warning her about getting caught in a dead-end job.

Faust drove, continuing his lecture: "You get used up, until you reach old age on Social Security as your future, never having saved one thin dime. You get in line for handouts. Trudy, someone with your talents deserves much better."

Trudy thought about her own grandfather. He swore he'd never take the handouts, but he died never having saved anything. The farm was nearly foreclosed even after all the years of hard work. And her own mother and father getting used up, fighting a war she had never understood. But her grandmother, she didn't seem to fit. Trudy thought about the unconditional love, given freely. That's who Faust wasn't talking about, not her grandmother.

Faust continued: "Trudy, you are a beautiful young woman. Don't give yourself to the Terreks of the world, not for free, not with your assets. That lucky bastard had a couple of wonderful months with you. He won't amount to anything because he's lazy and spoiled. His own parents are already getting tired of him. Maybe he'll find a few more girls who think he's a pretty boy, but Terrek will get fat and old, sitting in bars and leeching off whoever he can find. Then, he'll end up just being another street bum with addictions."

Trudy tried to remember Terrek as she first met him, the Prince Charming who took her to the castle, the university building with turrets on a rolling green campus. It was all just another fairy tale. She hated that Faust's reasoning began to match the world that she had been walking through.

"Trudy, you can't give yourself away for free like that!"

Trudy again objected, not screaming this time, but saying, "I'm not selling anything!"

"Exactly, you gave it away for free. Trudy, I really do like you, and I don't usually help like this, trying to explain how the world works. A poker player doesn't show his hand. He keeps a poker face. I don't go around explaining the rules, it takes years of practice to know when to play, and when to hold the cards and more importantly, when not to play. But you can't keep walking into my office expecting me to solve your problems. You need to grow up. I'm trying to help you see how this world really works!"

"Then what's *your* price?" asked Trudy.

"Ha, ha, ha! I was waiting for you to ask. You're starting to get it, Trudy. Forgive me for laughing, but it is the right question, isn't it?"

"I'm a lawyer. I'm the middleman. I make the deals for those that want to pay the price and those that are selling. The middleman is the ultimate winner! He gets paid, even when everyone else loses; he is the ace poker player, the winner of every pot."

As Faust turned on his right blinker for an exit off the interstate onto the next ramp, he finished his thoughts, "In your case, Trudy, Tony and Marie paid handsomely while you just gave what you had for free. It is the easiest deal to put together, and I'm doing something that society finds admirable: a baby finds a good home, new parents finally realize their dream, and the mom is supported during an unplanned pregnancy so that no abortion is performed. The ultimate win-win for society. The lawyer provides a good service. You saw the plaques in my office. I'm the hero."

Trudy watched Faust pull onto the ramp and finally asked him what location they were driving toward. She mostly saw farm landscape and only a gas station with an attached truck stop, including a diner. It had an extended outside parking area for long-haul stop overs by truckers.

Trudy thought they were making a stop for gas. Faust then asked: "What do you think I got paid by Tony and Marie?"

"The GAL said your fee in court was $10,000 some dollars," Trudy replied.

"Do you think that's a lot of money?" "Yes," replied Trudy.

Faust laughed again. He was enjoying this conversation. "I got more than ten times that number, so far."

"You lied to the baby's guardian ad litem?"

"No, I didn't lie. An attorney takes an oath. As an officer of the court, I cannot tell a lie to the court. I could be disbarred if I ever did that, and I am a very careful lawyer."

"Then, how did she think you got paid $10,000 if you didn't lie?"

"Trudy, you've got to know the question being asked. In this case, my fees were clearly spelled out, very accurately I might add, with an itemized timesheet. This was my fee for your Termination of Parental Rights. I was not disclosing the entire fee for all of my services. My entire time sheet would disclose ten times the total hours spent, but the GAL was only asking for my fees for the proceedings on termination. My time sheet only disclosed services for the termination, not the full adoption or interstate compact or all the other work. And that is the question that I was asked, nothing more."

Trudy never played games like this. She had always taken questions at face value and answered honestly. Yet she felt foolish. She realized how little she knew of how Faust's world worked. As he pulled into a parking area for the diner, Faust concluded.

"Trudy, you were never in the game. I'm trying to show you this. I want you to wise up so you don't get taken advantage of like that again. Don't give yourself away for free. Someday you will thank me for this. Also, remember that the advice from a lawyer is not free either. Abraham Lincoln, a great lawyer who worked for the railroads during the days of the big rail barons said it best: 'A lawyer's time and advice are his stock in trade.' We all have a trade; we are all buyers and sellers except for the bystanders who never have a life."

Trudy sat shaking her head. She wanted Faust to be wrong—the world was not all like this. She didn't want to live in the world Faust was describing. But she could not refute anything he was telling her. Faust was indeed a skilled lawyer. She'd never understood how completely he had been in control.

Faust got out of the car and walked around to the passenger side. He opened Trudy's door and told her this is where she gets out. Trudy was confused. Her baby wasn't here, was she?

Trudy noticed that Faust left his engine running when he got out. She looked around and saw mostly trucks, large long-haul trucks made for carrying a great deal of cargo. Faust's Jaguar was clearly out of place among these road giants.

In front of their parking space was a long glass window. Men were sitting on stools inside at a lunch counter. Most were drinking coffee from large 16-ounce foam containers, the to-go kind. She thought momentarily about Jackie's Counter. It was nothing like this sleezy, dirty-windowed lunch counter next to a gas station. Just a place for grabbing a greasy meal, filling up coffee for the long haul and moving on. The men inside also looked grizzled and unkempt.

As Faust took Trudy's elbow to help her alight from the sleek car, he quipped. "This is where you grow up. Nothing like learning to swim by jumping right into the deep end of the pool. You will have an easy time here. No need to walk the streets or find a middleman to do your bidding. These guys are all horny; you'll have an easy time asking your price. When you learn your trade, move on, Trudy. Go to California the way your boyfriend suggested. Lots of money there."

Faust lifted Trudy out of her seat. She was trying to understand what Faust was telling her. By the time she was standing in the parking lot, Faust slammed the passenger door and walked around the front of his car. A trucker walked out of the counter as Faust was opening the driver's door. He shouted to the grizzly, overweight trucker, "She's all yours."

Looking at Trudy, Faust added, "We had a great time last night, didn't we, Babe!" Looking back to the trucker, Faust smirked, his final remark intended for him, "Ask her for a quick date before you roll out! She won't be available for long!"

Faust got back into the car and drove off. Trudy was stunned. Was he going to turn around and come back for her? Frozen in place like a young doe at the side of the road mesmerized by the headlights of oncoming traffic, Trudy watched the Jaguar as it sped off, taking the ramp on the opposite side of the interstate back toward Milson.

The fat trucker also watched and then spoke to Trudy: "Where you heading?"

Trudy ignored the man. She was still standing in the empty parking spot. Another trucker stepped out the door and observed momentarily. The fat man stepped into the same parking space with Trudy, purposely standing in front of the second trucker and asked Trudy, "Need a ride, I see your sugar daddy left you behind. I've got a really nice rig out here. Or if you don't want a ride, we could just talk for a while, see what happens."

"Give it up, she's way out of your league," quipped the second trucker wearing a blue work shirt with an embroidered truck logo. He was taller and much more fit.

The fat guy responded, "I saw her first, shove off!"

The second trucker only laughed. "You're lucky it's early Monday morning and I've got a deadline. I can't stay." Turning to Trudy and also stepping into the empty parking spot, he added, "I'll be rolling back in here tomorrow afternoon. If you are still around, I can show you a really great time."

Trudy didn't understand why these men were talking to her, much less trying to outdo one another. The fat trucker didn't appreciate the interruption. As the second trucker turned to leave, the fat guy took Trudy's left arm and tried to lead her in the direction of his truck, telling Trudy they should get out of the parking lot.

"Let go of my arm!" yelled Trudy.

"How much do you want? Okay? But we can't just stand here—the management doesn't let girls pick up truckers out front. Come on, I'll take you to my cab before you get in trouble."

"No! No!" screamed Trudy.

A third trucker stepped out from inside the counter. He observed the struggle and walked over to the fat man as he was grabbing Trudy's arm trying to drag her over to his cab.

"Let her go!" He grabbed the fat man by the collar of his shirt and yanked him closer and then grabbing his neck, got into his face, finishing his comments: "I suggest you go to your truck before I shove your face into the blacktop."

Fatso looked up at the big man and decided it was not in his interest to fight further. He had already let go of Trudy's arm. He turned and walked away before he got shoved away.

"Trudy? What the hell are you doing here?"

Mac got no response. Trudy was frozen with fear. Mac saw Trudy's vacant stare and was incredulous that Trudy was at his truck stop. He was just picking up his truck and storing his motorcycle as he did most Monday mornings, getting ready for his long-haul assignment. After weeks of having looked for Trudy, Mac was nearly as stunned as she was, everything was out of place.

"Trudy! Trudy! It's Mac. Are you okay? Trudy, It's me, Mac. I won't let these lechers hurt you! But what are you doing out here?"

Barely hearing anything, Trudy finally recognized that the trucker was Mac. She mumbled, "Mac?"

"Yes, What are you doing here?"

Trudy looked around. She looked at the interstate, still half-thinking that Faust was going to come back for her. Mac repeated his question, and Trudy turned back to him.

"I'm going to see my baby."

"Trudy, you're not making sense! This is a truck stop; you won't find your baby out here!"

Trudy broke down, hearing Mac tell her she wouldn't see her baby. Somehow the last week flashed before her eyes: she was in the Milson hospital having labor pangs and giving birth. Tony and Marie were there, then she was in court, testifying to the judge, a loud gavel banging and then in her own room, rocking and rocking. Her head was spinning. Trudy began to have another panic attack.

Mac saw that Trudy was becoming hysterical. He had no idea what was going through her mind, but he knew she needed help.

"Come on, Trudy, I'll drive you back into Milson before I start my next run."

Trudy's knees collapsed as Mac caught her. He lifted Trudy up in his arms like a baby, again telling Trudy he would drive her home.

"No! Mac, No! I can't go back to Milson, please, No!"

The scene was drawing a lot of attention. As Mac picked up Trudy, some of the truckers called out lewd comments, jeering and whistling, telling Mac to have a good time but to share his prize.

Mac ignored them and carried Trudy over to his rig. In order to open the door to his cab, he had to put Trudy down to climb up and help. The door was nearly four feet above ground level and required stepping onto a foothold. Mac gently set Trudy down, hoping she could stand. But the whole time, Trudy kept sobbing, insisting that she would not return to Milson, hysterically telling Mac she would not go back.

Mac had no idea what to do. Trudy wasn't steady. The truckers inside the counter were ready to take advantage, but not help. Trudy kept sobbing that she would not go back to Milson.

"I can't have passengers, Trudy, it's against at least three rules that I can think of just standing here, probably more, but I'll get you back to Milson, that's all I can do."

"I won't go back! I have to keep moving Mac, I think I'll lose my mind if you take me back there. Please, I'll just ride with you wherever you're going. Mac, please, please! I need to keep moving for now! Please!"

Trudy was hysterical. Mac looked around. He decided there was only one thing he could do. He would give in to Trudy's demands, at least until she calmed down. He'd have to figure out the rest later.

"Alright, Trudy, I won't go back to Milson. Will you get in the cab? We can't stay here."

Mac stood on the foothold with his cab door open. He extended his arm and pulled Trudy up into his rig. Mac opened the curtain behind the seats and told Trudy that she could lay down on his back bunk while they pulled out.

Trudy was still crying, but on hearing that Mac would let her ride with him, she stepped up while being pulled by Mac. She crawled into the back of the rig and laid down on the bed. Mac gave her his fleece blanket and pulled the curtain shut, telling Trudy to lay low while he pulled out.

Trudy felt exhausted. She had not slept last night. Her hormones were raging, and she was still in a panic from being abandoned at the dingy diner. Mac was one person that she knew she could trust. Trudy thought that if she could just keep moving, she might be able to sort things out. Mac started the truck, let it warm up while he checked his route. Soon, he began rolling.

Trudy fell asleep before Mac pulled out onto the interstate. He was supposed to be headed toward Charlotte, North Carolina. Not knowing what he would do with Trudy, Mac just started driving his route. He'd figure it out along the way, hoping Trudy would calm down enough to make sense.

Chapter 18

September 1977, New Moon

Astorm of questions streaked through Mac's mind, wondering what the hell Trudy was doing at a truck stop. He wanted to lecture her about the kind of women that hung out around such places. How did Trudy end up there? He and Jackie had been to the hospital to visit, but they only saw her baby; the nurse wouldn't allow them into Trudy's room so soon after giving birth. He thought about all the time he and his buddies spent looking for Trudy. But now she shows up out of nowhere in a place where she shouldn't be and asking for her baby, no less! That's crazy, Mac thought—a newborn baby at a truck stop?

Mac drove on. Trudy slept. He finally pulled off the interstate after driving many hours, now near Indianapolis. Normally, he would have just driven through, but he wanted to see if Trudy was waking. Mac left the truck idling and stepped out of the cab; he did his usual check routine—tires were good, doors locked, nothing dragging under the truck. Everything was normal. Mac climbed back in and this time opened the curtain of the cab and checked inside. Trudy was wrapped tightly in the fleece blanket, curled up in a fetal position, sound asleep.

He thought about calling Jackie. He always called her from the road, but this was still too early. Jackie would be working. He knew she'd have even more questions than he had answers. He decided to call Jackie at his usual time, later in the day, after she closed the Counter. He hoped Trudy would wake and give him some explanation. Mac checked his route and decided to drive on for now.

Civilians were not allowed to hitch rides. Mac's insurance policy would not cover any mishap, not only for personal harm but could void his entire liability coverage. He also knew that the Federal Highway Administration prohibited commercial truckers from taking on passengers. Then there was the policy of the company he was driving for, even though he was an independent and owned his own rig. As soon as he signed a cargo agreement to carry a load, all of the merchant's rules would have to be followed. Mac knew he was violating at least all three and probably many more. Every state he drove through had its own rules.

Mac normally complied with rules. He was not looking for trouble, and like most independents, he needed to stay in good standing to keep his commercial driver's license. But Trudy was a friend, and Mac did not abandon his friends. He followed his conscience but knew he'd need to be very careful. He also needed to get Trudy educated as soon as she was awake and cognizant.

Mac drove on. Trudy slept. He pulled out a sandwich and ate on the road. He listened for sounds from the back, nothing. Mac knew the route well and mentally checked off the usual wayside markers. It was a beautiful September day. Somehow post-Labor Day meant a return to a sense of normalcy. Kids were back in school, family vacations ended, a normal workweek marked time, whatever normal meant to the majority of people. As a trucker, Mac felt more like an observer of the routine. But his trucking job became a bit easier with all the vacation traffic off the roadways.

Mac followed I-65 south to Louisville, picking up I-64 East, through Lexington and on to I-75 south. He was making very good time. Usually, Mac listened to the radio to pass the time or talked to other truckers on his CB radio. But today he kept the cab quiet, hoping Trudy would sleep and feel rested. They needed to talk, and he needed to figure out what to do with this illegal passenger in his truck. But the quiet was a welcome change. He enjoyed the fantastic autumn weather. Today was not a routine day, and it made him pay attention. The flat-lands changed to rolling hills, and the beautiful green grass morphed into tree-lined roadway.

As Mac rolled on, Trudy slowly began to awaken from her deep sleep. She did not know where she was, and at first, hearing the tires humming along on the road surface, thought she might be in a truck but was still unsure. For a short time, she began sleeping again, rocking with the low hum. Slowly, she became more cognizant, opening her eyes to look around.

The small cabin had only a dim light filtering through the front curtain. Trudy saw that she was lying on a large cushion about the size of a queen-size mattress with a fleece quilt. The entire platform was covered with this cushion, and the sidewalls were covered in blue shag carpeting. She saw a built-in shelf with a sound system, a few books and maps, playing cards, and two speakers installed into the wall near the shelf.

Trudy rolled over onto her back and saw the ceiling was covered in the same blue carpeting; on the opposite side of the cab, Trudy saw a small built-in refrigerator and microwave oven. It reminded her of all the built-in amenities of the limo, but this was peaceful blue like a cloud instead of the hot red hellhole of Terrek's limo.

Slowly, she remembered the morning events, the fear of being abandoned with unknown men pawing at her. Then, she finally re-called Mac. He appeared out of nowhere and carried her away from the danger, talking about going back to Milson. Trudy remembered her panic, knowing she could not go back. She finally figured out that she was being carried along in Mac's rig, but where were they going?

Trudy felt the truck slowing, heard the downshifting of gears, a slow, very slow turn until the rig came to a full stop. Mac slowly opened the curtain and saw Trudy's eyes open and then meet his gaze.

"Hello, Sleeping Beauty!"

"Mac, don't say that. I'm done with fairy tales!"

Mac laughed and apologized, telling Trudy he was just glad to see she was awake, commenting that she must need to use a bathroom and had to be hungry. Trudy agreed to the bathroom stop but didn't think she was hungry.

"Come on, I'll help you down. We're at one of my favorite road stops just outside of Charleston, West Virginia. I got off the interstate a while back just to get a good meal, I figured you'd be hungry. I know I am!"

As Mac helped Trudy down out of the rig, they were in a very small town only a few blocks long. Trudy saw a café, hardware store, and tavern on the nearest corners. Mac escorted Trudy into the small café. Red gingham curtains hung on brass rods. A little bell rang as the door opened, bringing an elderly woman out of the back kitchen.

"Mac, you ole' hound dog, what the heck you doing here this time of day, I usually see you at breakfast time!"

"Agnes, you know I'll eat almost anything you make, 'cept for those grits, never did get a taste for grits!"

"Ain't you lucky, Honey, grits is my blue-plate special tonight."

Agnes laughed heartily and pulled out a few paper placemats and utensils wrapped in napkins and took Mac over to a table, wiping off what looked like a perfectly clean Formica top and placing the mats and utensils down, making two settings.

Mac introduced Agnes to Trudy, telling her she was a new apprentice, learning how to be a trucker. Trudy's eyes widened. Agnes greeted Trudy warmly, telling her that she figured women could do most anything these days, not like when she was young!

As they sat down, Mac winked at Trudy as Agnes told them her actual special tonight was Southern fried chicken, peas, and fresh corn muffins with mashed potatoes and gravy. Mac told Agnes that would be perfect, Trudy never saw a menu. After Agnes went back into the kitchen, Trudy excused herself and went into the bathroom.

As Trudy returned, Alice was pouring coffee and bringing glasses of water. She was an older woman well into her sixties. Alice wore a flowered house dress with an apron over the skirt. Looking around the café, Trudy wondered if they had been driving in a time machine, back into the fifties. Everything was homey with pretty pictures of the rolling hillsides. The Lord's Prayer, hung and framed, was on the back wall.

"Trudy, such a lovely name," commented Agnes, adding, "Don't hear many girls named Trudy nowadays."

Embarrassed having her name commented on, Trudy wondered if she really did belong in this throwback world. In high school, she had spent her senior year trying to convince herself that she didn't belong in her small farming community. But here again, Agnes thought she belonged. But Trudy thought if Agnes knew her, she'd be a girl to be gossiped about, the way the small-town folks spread news about everyone's business. Trudy was glad for the anonymity of being on the road. But her sadness overwhelmed her.

"Come on Trudy, cheer up. We've got a lot to talk about. What am I going to do with you?" asked Mac.

"I don't know?" was all Trudy could say.

As Agnes walked back to her kitchen, Mac called out, telling her to bring one of her homemade chocolate malts for Trudy. He then turned his attention back to Trudy, telling her that he was serious. He wasn't allowed to take passengers while picking up cargo. He explained to Trudy that they were headed to Charlotte. He was picking up a load of small dinghies to haul west into Las Vegas, and he laughed about a desert community needing small boats, but Mac added that the area had a large reservoir where the locals thought they could have water sports in the middle of a desert.

"That's the nature of my trucking business, pick up most anything from anywhere and haul it somewhere."

Mac got serious. He told Trudy that he thought he could get a bus ticket for her on the Greyhound bus and send her back to Milson.

"I shouldn't have brought you this far. But you were nearly hysterical this morning and insisting that you'd not go back to Milson. Then, you just kept sleeping all day. I kept driving, but now we have to figure out how to get you back."

"I'm not going back. I can't go back there," Trudy insisted.

"What were you doing at the truck stop? We were looking for you, all of us: Jackie, Leslie, Marna, Pig, Tag. Then Leslie tells us you're in the hospital one day having your baby. Jackie and I had gone to see you there, but the nurse told us you were sleeping. Then we kept wondering where you were after leaving the hospital last week. One mystery after another. But the truck stop? I would never have looked for you there, not in a hundred years."

"Mac, please don't make me talk about it now. I know that I've got to figure this out, but I need to keep moving, it's the only thing I can think of doing for now."

"Go back to Milson, think about it there."

"No, I'm not going back. I'm sorry. I know you're trying to help. But the one thing I know for sure right now is that I'm not going back to Milson!"

Mac sat quietly, thinking about her refusal. Finally, he told Trudy that he thought he might understand where she was coming from. He explained that when he got back from 'Nam, all shellshocked and grieving for the men his unit lost, he, too, had to keep moving. He'd been home for a few months, drinking heavily, smoking weed, and really messed up. He told Trudy that Tag called, telling Mac he was going to end it all—that he couldn't find a job. After his years of service, he was right back in a heavily segregated Southern city, and no one respected a 'Nam Vet, especially a Black 'Nam Vet.

"I just got on my Harley and rode all the way to see Tag. I called him every day, telling him I was on my way and begging him to just hang on until I got there. I met Tag in the unit that I got assigned to. We made it through 'Nam together—he was in my unit for two years, even saved my life. I wasn't going to lose him.

"When I got to his home outside of Greenville, we more or less saved each other. I taught him how to ride my Harley and then I helped him buy one of his own. We just started ridin' through all the small towns along back country roads. But as long as we kept ridin', we felt free. I stopped my heavy drinking, can't ride drunk."

"We met Agnes on one of those trips. I wouldn't stop in any café that made Tag leave, if my 'Nam brother couldn't eat in a place, I wouldn't eat in that place. Agnes was kind and said she didn't 'cotton to no discrimination.' When Tag asked her why, she told him that she was a God-fearin' woman. That's all she said. But Tag and I found a friend that day. Best food in the South. I stop if I'm near when I pick up cargo."

"What about Pig?" Trudy asked.

"Pig's my buddy from high school. He was in Vietnam too, but not in our unit. After Tag and I spent about six months on the road just ridin,' I talked Tag into coming north to Milson. Lots of factory jobs were hiring, so he said he'd give it a try. When Tag and I came back, Pig asked if he could meet up with us. He knew we were 'Nam Vets, and when he got discharged, Pig said he needed to join a "band of brothers."

"We were all angry as hell. The generals lied, Nixon lied, LBJ lied. The college kids were all demonstratin' against the Vietnam draft. They acted like all the returning vets were just a bunch of fools for goin' or worse, part of the lyin'. Next, Watergate broke; it was bad, and we were angry. But we had each other. Then Pig wanted to buy a Harley, too. We all got jobs and settled down a bit, but still ridin' whenever we had a chance and just hangin' out with each other."

Agnes came over with two plates loaded with half a chicken fried up in cornflake breading, and a mountain of mashed potatoes indented with a lake of gravy. She placed a basket of warm cornmeal muffins in the middle of the table. Trudy could not believe the size of her portion. Her plate was filled with as much food as Mac's plate. Maybe he could eat that much, but for her, it was enough food for a whole week.

"Anyway, as I was sayin', I understand what you're feeling Trudy. Going through trauma somehow makes a person want to keep runnin' away from it."

Mac dug in, telling Trudy to eat; they'd figure out what to do after they had some food in their gut. Trudy tasted the chicken and understood why Mac wanted to stop here. She realized she was hungry and buttered a cornmeal muffin. It was the best flaky muffin she had ever tasted. Agnes served her the chocolate malt. Trudy thought she'd just have a sip until she realized the silky chocolate malt was too good to put down and drained it until the straw slurped at the bottom of the tall glass.

Mac laughed at Trudy and asked if she felt better now that she had eaten. Her plate was nearly empty, and Trudy realized that she had been hungry after all. Good food cures almost anything, Mac told her.

Mac walked over to the counter and paid Agnes, gave her a big kiss, and told her he brought something for her. Mac told Trudy to wait for a minute, maybe use the bathroom again before leaving, but he'd be right back. He walked out to his rig and took out two large shopping bags from the back of his empty truck.

Walking back inside, he gave Agnes two full bags of freshly picked ears of corn, explaining, "Corn crop is nearly done, but this is probably the last of it for the season. It was just picked yesterday. I stopped at a farm stand and bought it from the farmer."

Agnes was nearly beside herself with the gift, telling Mac that the whole town would show up tomorrow for some grilled corn on the cob laid right on the grill still in the husk, well-soaked. Agnes put it all in a big pail and started to run water over it, telling Mac she couldn't get corn in the husk anymore, it was all picked and processed before she could get her hands on it.

Trudy stepped out of the restroom in time to watch Mac get a big kiss and hug from Agnes, who asked when he'd stop again. Mac didn't know. She turned to Trudy and told her it was a pleasure to meet her, hoped she'd learn the trucking business, and told her she had a good teacher in Mac. She invited Trudy to stop in anytime she'd be on the road. As the two customers left, Agnes called out to Mac, reminding him to say hello to Tag.

It was nearing dusk. Mac said they'd stay in a small motel nearer to Charlotte after they'd ride a few more hours. First thing in the morning, he was scheduled to pick up his cargo. At the motel, they'd figure out what to do next. Mac helped Trudy up into the cab, as she asked if she could sit in front this time. Mac agreed but told Trudy to stay low. If he did get stopped for any reason, she'd have to scoot in the back and not make a sound. Trudy agreed.

Mac started the engine, telling Trudy he had to let the big diesel engine warm up for a bit before heading out. He was going to make a few phone calls to check on his cargo, scheduled for pick up the next day. He turned on his FM radio and found a country music station for Trudy, telling her he'd be right back.

Stepping down from his rig, Mac walked over to the small phone booth situated on the corner of the café's parking lot. Inside the booth, he dialed Jackie's number.

"Hello, Babe, love you, how was your day?"

Mac started with his usual greeting, and Jackie asked the question she always asked,

"Love you too. Where are you calling from?"

"I'm in West Virginia, just finished eating at Agnes's café. You'll never guess who I picked up at the truck stop in Milson as I was beginning my run today!"

"I thought you couldn't take passengers?"

"Come on, that's not a guess, you can't ask another question before you answer my question first!" Mac teased.

"I don't know, Pig or Tag, maybe?"

"Not even close!"

"Who, then?" Jackie didn't like the game, which made Mac laugh.

He just blurted out, "Trudy!"

Dead silence. After several seconds, Mac asked if Jackie was still on the line. Jackie repeated the name "Trudy?" Adding, "You're kidding?" Mac assured her that he wasn't kidding around.

Mac described the scene at the truck stop and how hysterical Trudy had been. He told Jackie that he had no choice but to put her in his rig. Jackie asked why he hadn't brought her back to Milson. He replied that he suggested this to her, but Trudy refused to go back—begged him to take her, insisting she'd not go back.

He told Jackie how Trudy had slept in his back cabin through the whole day. She finally woke, and they had just finished eating. Trudy settled down a bit but was telling him that she had to keep moving and would not return to Milson. He didn't know what to do and wanted Jackie to help him come up with a solution. Mac described Trudy as badly shaken and that she had not explained much, but he would try to find out how she got to the truck stop and more. So far, he was just happy to report that she had finally eaten and settled down.

"I wish you were here, Babe! I'm no good at this. I don't know what to do with Trudy. It's like when Tag and I were ridin' our bikes all over the country after 'Nam, tryin' to find ourselves, like that. But Trudy is not one of the guys. I don't know how to talk to her."

"Sounds like you saved her," replied Jackie, adding, "Try to keep her calm, Trudy's been through a lot, and she could have post-partem depression, or something like that. Did she tell you where her baby is?"

"No."

"Where will she stay tonight?"

Mac explained they'd be pulling into a motel in a few hours, and he was picking up his cargo in the morning and heading west toward Vegas. He would let Trudy sleep in the motel, and he'd stay in the cab. Jackie responded that she needed to think about this. She told Mac to keep Trudy calm.

"Be good to her, Mac. See if she will open up."

Jackie asked Mac to call the next day and to try and find out more about how Trudy got to the truck stop.

Mac knew that was probably all they could do for now and felt relief that Jackie now knew Trudy was with him, safe for now. He hoped Jackie would help find some way to get Trudy to go back to Milson.

Jackie reminded Mac to call the next day. Mac agreed and hung up the phone, walked back to his rig and continued the drive to the motel. Sitting in the dark cab as Mac's passenger, Trudy asked Mac if she could ask him a question. Mac agreed, told Trudy to go ahead, ask him anything that she wanted.

"What's your price?"

"My price?" Mac was surprised by the question and confused.

"Yeah, I was told everyone has a price. I'm wondering if you do?"

"Like what would I give up everything I own for a price? Like that?"

"Yes, something like that. I'm probably not explaining it the way I was told, but I think that's it," replied Trudy.

Mac was quiet for a while. Lights from the interstate bridge washed through the cab as they passed under; the cab got dark again, only a few dashboard lights illuminating the passengers inside.

"Okay, well, I'd give everything I owned for the benefit of people I care about: My woman, which you know is Jackie, and my two 'Nam brothers, Pig and Tag. They could have anything I own if they ever asked. I'd give it to them."

Under most circumstances, Mac would never tell anyone these things. But Trudy was being so earnest, he could tell she really needed to know if he had a price. Somehow it seemed important to her.

Trudy nodded as she listened, thinking Mac was a man complete within himself. He knew who he was and he knew who he loved. Trudy respected that and wondered if she'd ever mean something like that to another person. Jackie was a lucky woman, she thought.

Mac completed his thought for Trudy's benefit. "While I'd give everything in the world for these three, they'd never ask for it. I'd give what I have completely, but they would do the same for me. That's what real friendship is about. It's not exactly right to say that something like this has a price—it's priceless. You could never put a price on real friendship."

"Thanks, Mac."

Mac wondered why he was being thanked. Driving on through a few more illuminations, a few more underpasses, Mac finally asked Trudy:

"Who told you everyone has a price?"

Trudy simply replied, "Attorney Faust."

Mac laughed with a sneer, responding, "He would—that's just the world Faust lives in, Trudy," then added, "But it's not my world, and it is not the world Jackie lives in either."

Mac wondered if Faust had anything to do with dumping Trudy at the truck stop. But Trudy was relieved by Mac's answer, thanking him. Yet Mac noted her sadness remained as a deep unresolved loss or maybe something she was running away from. For Trudy, she knew that she could trust Mac as they rode together through these unknown places. She'd never been so far from home, wherever that was.

Early the next morning, Mac left to pick up his cargo and returned to the motel. He and Trudy grabbed a quick bowl of cereal and coffee at the complimentary breakfast bar in the motel and soon left to begin a very long day of driving, heading west. Mac told Trudy to grab some fruit to eat along the route.

While still in the metro area, Mac told Trudy to get in the back and stay low through the city. He'd let her know when it was okay to ride in the front passenger seat. He had to be careful in the large cities with regular sheriff patrols. Trudy apologized, telling Mac she was sorry for being a nuisance. He laughed, telling Trudy it was an interesting way to describe a ghost rider.

Mac turned on his citizens' band radio for road conditions and information from other truckers. Trudy lay low, but today, she lay with her head forward so she was directly behind the curtain and could listen to the chatter on Mac's radio. After about thirty minutes, Mac called Trudy to the front seat, reminding her that she'd have to scoot back if there was a need to stop, or if he told her to for any reason. If Mac did have to come to a full stop, she was to cover up and get down behind the front seat and the back platform with the fleece blanket over her, but Mac explained that this was unlikely to happen, just a precaution.

Mac followed Interstate 40 west. Next major city ahead was Nashville, TN. After Mac called Trudy to come forward into the passenger seat, they drove on for a long time without talking. Trudy watched out the window; she had never been so far from home. Everything she saw was new and quite fascinating.

Trudy finally broke their silence, "I guess you're probably wondering what I was doing at the truck stop, yesterday?"

"Bingo!" Mac exclaimed, adding, "I've been waiting for you to tell me that!"

Starting from the truck stop going back to Milson, Trudy told her story in reverse. Once she started, the story just poured out. Mac didn't interrupt. He knew Trudy needed to talk, to get it out, just like his 'Nam buddies. Once the floodgates open, it all gushes out.

Trudy was soon telling Mac about being in court to terminate her rights, about Tony and Marie, about going into labor, about her stay at the cottage for weeks and going through adoption files. Then she doubled back to yesterday morning, about how she got to thinking about saying goodbye to her baby one more time since everything had been so rushed after the hospital. She knew that Tony and Marie had to arrange final plans with the foster home and finish getting their permission to take the baby out of state.

Trudy told Mac that she was upset that she never really said goodbye. It all seemed like a dream. She explained why she decided to go over to the lawyer's office on Monday morning and insist on one more visit, one final kiss for her baby.

Early Monday morning she walked into Faust's office. To her surprise, he was dressed to go on vacation and his secretary was making reservations to go to Vegas. She expected an argument, but Faust actually agreed to take her to say goodbye. Instead, Faust tricked her and drove her to the truck stop outside of Milson.

"Faust lied, Mac." Trudy began to cry again, not hysterically, but sadly, adding, "You must think I'm terrible?"

"No, I don't," Mac was adamant.

Not saying any more, Mac was angry. How could Faust do that to a young woman, one that had just given birth and gone through what Trudy had gone through? Leave her at a truck stop to get picked up, suggest that she sell her body? Mac never had a good opinion of Faust, but now he truly hated the man. He wanted to hunt him down and teach him a lesson.

Mac looked over to Trudy as they drove on for many miles. Finally, Mac told Trudy that while she was going through her final weeks of pregnancy, they had been looking for her, wanting to help. Mac now told Trudy his side of her story. He explained how Jackie and Marna had made plans to help with her baby so Trudy could work and care for her child. He explained that Pig and Tag were helping him look, trying to tail Faust. They knew that he had something to do with her disappearance but didn't know how.

After Mac finished, Trudy thought about all her friends looking for her. She now understood why Faust wanted her out of Milson. The lake cottage had always seemed so far away, and she had always thought that she was alone. Trudy was very grateful to learn that someone else cared.

"Isn't it ironic that Faust was heading to Vegas? Just like we are, Mac?"

Mac was still seething. He thought for a moment what he'd like to do to Faust if he did find him in Vegas.

"You have to go back to Milson," Mac finally replied to Trudy.

"No, promise you won't make me go back. Please, I can't go back," Trudy pleaded.

Mac feared an argument would force Trudy back into her hysteria. After telling her story, she was on the edge of that same brink of losing her sanity as she had been when he found her. He said nothing further for quite a while, letting the road slip along under them. Trudy watched the rolling hills and felt that she'd like to do this forever, just let the world flow on by. She could be a passenger—participating in life was too painful. She did not want to be part of this miserable world, one without her own baby.

Mac decided to be practical for now. He had a lot to tell Jackie but still had no plans for Trudy. He told her that after the long morning drive, they'd be passing through Nashville, Tennessee. She'd need to go back behind the curtain, even though he would be taking the bypass around the heart of the city. It would still be busy with traffic.

Trudy went in the back and fell asleep. She only started to wake as she felt Mac's truck downshifting through the gears. Finally, Mac's rig came to a full stop. She stayed low as promised. Mac was the one who finally peered through the curtain. He told Trudy it was well past noon, and he had pulled into a truck stop. He gave her instructions to wait while he got out of the cab; he'd make sure no one was around to see her getting out.

Trudy followed instructions. Mac said they'd go inside and eat but that first he would need to get fuel and check the truck over. This would be a good place for Trudy to shop for a few items that she might need: toothbrush, toiletries, whatever.

"Trudy, promise me you won't run away again!"

Trudy stared at Mac. This was the last thing in the world she would consider. She didn't really know where she was except for what Mac was telling her.

"I don't even have any money, Mac. Where would I go?"

Mac grinned. Trudy was being practical. He pulled out his wallet and gave Trudy two twenty-dollar bills, telling her if she needed more to let him know.

"Trudy, you got to know how pretty you are. You could hitch a ride with any trucker in this place."

Laughing now, Mac added: "But no one as nice as I am!"

Trudy apologized, again, as she took Mac's forty dollars, promising she'd pay him back. Trudy stressed that she had no idea where she was and needed Mac to lead her.

Mac put his hands up to stop Trudy. "I'm hungry! We can talk later. Heck, we have all day and night to talk. Let's not do it here. Okay? You go shop, I'll take care of the truck. When I'm done, I'll come and look for you in the store and we'll grab a quick lunch. Remember, don't talk to any of those truckers in there."

Trudy promised. Mac pointed to the door for the store and told her to head over. After watching Trudy, Mac took care of his truck. He decided he'd call Jackie after eating. Mac knew Jackie would be disappointed to hear that Trudy's termination of rights had already happened. She kept holding out hope that maybe Trudy could still keep her baby. This new baby meant new hope.

After eating at the lunch counter, Mac told Trudy to go wait in his cab—he'd be right over but needed to make a phone call. Asking her if she thought she could climb up without his help, Trudy assured him that she was used to climbing up on farm tractors. He told her to be sure no one was around when she got in. Trudy understood her need to keep low.

Mac watched Trudy go over to the cab. It was already after 2 p.m., and not many truckers were around. She got in easily. Mac walked over to the phone bank in the back of the store and dialed Jackie's number.

Jackie was relieved that he called; they barely greeted each other before Jackie asked if Mac had gotten any more information from Trudy. Mac paused, trying not to get angry again. Finally, Mac told Jackie that it had been Faust who dropped her off at the truck stop on Monday morning. Faust had told Trudy that she could get picked up by a trucker and earn money.

Jackie had barely absorbed this shocking news when Mac blurted out the next bit of news: the termination of Trudy's rights to her baby was already done. She was in court last week. Mac explained that the couple named Tony and Marie that Leslie had been talking about meeting at the hospital were the adoptive parents, selected by Trudy. She'd said something about going through files and picking them out.

Jackie was silent. She was incredulous. How could a baby just born about one week ago already be taken away from her mother? Mac knew this was shocking news for Jackie. He softly asked,

"Babe? Are you gonna' be okay?"

Jackie responded, "Wait, Faust wanted Trudy to be a prostitute or something like that?"

"You heard right. That's what Trudy said," Mac replied.

"Her baby is gone? But where?" Jackie's voice was cracking. Mac knew she was near tears.

"I'm sorry, Babe, I'm tellin' you what Trudy told me. She just blurted this all out when she was explainin' how she got to the truck stop, which is sort of what I had asked her. I was afraid she'd get hysterical again, so I didn't ask a lot of questions. I don't know too many more details about what happened to the baby."

Jackie knew Mac wouldn't ask many questions, just like a man. But she didn't ride him for more. She was so outraged about Faust dropping off Trudy at the truck stop that she wasn't thinking straight herself right now.

Tears rolled down Jackie's cheeks. She dabbed her eyes with her apron. It would take her awhile to process what Mac was telling her. She wanted to talk with Marna, to get her wisdom. But Jackie knew that Mac couldn't stay on the phone for a long conversation. Besides, Mac was not good with talking through something that didn't have a plan of action. Jackie got to the point.

"Trudy needs to come back to Milson. What's she going to do with you on the road? What's the plan?"

"I know that! But Trudy doesn't have a plan. That's the problem!"

Mac was short. Jackie knew that he was without a plan. He wasn't trying to be unpleasant but didn't know what the solution was,

"I need you to tell me how to get Trudy to come home, Babe. That's why I called. She needs a woman."

"Sorry, I know. Please take care of Trudy, I'll talk it over with Marna. We'll put our heads together and see if we can think of a way. Love you! Please call again tonight, Okay?"

"Love you, too. Of course, I'll call tonight!" Mac tersely hung up the phone because he was also frustrated.

Mac headed over to his truck without any other plan. He'd continue to drive west. Once inside the cab, he told Trudy that she'd be seeing the great Mississippi River in a few hours. He described it as the great divide between the east and the west.

After Jackie hung up, she just sat for a while. She wondered if Trudy could still decide to keep her baby. She had done all of her thinking around helping Trudy realize this choice. *If only I had talked to her more*, Jackie thought ruefully.

Was it really too late? Jackie knew that Trudy meant more to her than just an employee, but did Trudy know that? Jackie admonished herself for being so closed-up, but she knew it was her own life-saving decision to be independent that had once saved her. She had been deeply hurt once and at about the same age as Trudy. Jackie had decided to fend for herself, not rely on others. She now lived by this creed.

After meeting Mac, she resisted falling in love—again, too much hurt. Starting her little business and through pure determination, Jackie had made it work and determined she wasn't going to be needy.

She knew it had taken her a long time before she admitted to herself that she did love Mac. As for Mac, he said he knew from day one and would keep coming back till Jackie decided to love him back. It made her smile to think of Mac. She had a hard time trusting anyone. Yet she knew Trudy couldn't just keep running; it led to nowhere.

Jackie finished cleaning up and headed upstairs to talk with Marna. She rapped on the door, called out her name and then walked in so Marna didn't need to get up to open the door. Once inside, Jackie related what Mac told her. It shocked Marna as well. Both women knew the score when it came to the abuse of young women. They had all been through different versions, Jackie more than most.

"Mac wants to know how to get Trudy to come home, but Trudy insists that she can't come back and just wants to keep moving. Mac says she is heartbroken and on the brink of a mental collapse. After all she's been through, I don't think Mac is exaggerating."

"If only she had family," Marna counseled.

"I think we are her family," Jackie posited.

"I'll pray for Trudy." But Jackie wanted more, wondering what Mac could do with Trudy after delivering his cargo?

"He can't just abandon her in Las Vegas—he'd be no better than Faust," Marna replied.

"Mac's eventually going to come back to Milson, and if Trudy keeps insisting that she won't come back, he's left with a mess on his hands. Will Trudy run again? But where? Mac tells me she's never been out of state, much less in Las Vegas!"

"Trudy's not in her right mind. She's not thinking this through," Marna concluded.

Marna made tea and cut a piece of coffee cake. She talked about the past, how young women were always protected by their families. Those girls that ran off wanting freedom often met with tragedy. Jackie agreed, knowing that only too well.

But Jackie observed that young women like Leslie were trying to make some progress, get an education, show they can make it without a husband. Marna agreed that getting an education was important, and until recently, most women could not go to college unless they had wealthy families supporting them. Since women won the right to vote, everything started changing, and it seems like what Leslie stands for will bring needed changes.

"I like to listen to her; it gives me hope," added Jackie.

"I had so much hope for Trudy, too. She was so excited to start at Milson U. But the age-old problem destroyed her plans, an unwanted pregnancy! I just wished that I'd have helped her more." Jackie was despondent.

Marna sat down and sipped her tea, "Maybe an adoption wasn't a bad decision," replied Marna. "The baby has two parents. Trudy still has her life before her, she could come back and finish school, older and wiser. We all make mistakes."

The two sat together going over the known history of women raising babies, men continuing on their chosen career paths while the woman stayed home, cooked, raised the kids. Marna shared some stories from the old country. Jackie listened quietly but finally grew impatient.

"Marna, how do we get Trudy to come back?"

"I think you have to go to Las Vegas and talk to her. Mac can't do it; I don't think Trudy will be totally open with Mac. She needs to talk with a woman."

"What would I say?"

"Just be honest, talk to her the way we are talking, tell Trudy that we love her and want her to come home. Tell Trudy Milson is her home now. She could go back to school, start over."

Jackie was quiet, thinking about Marna's wise advice. She knew Marna was right but asked, "What will I do with the restaurant?"

"You put a big, fat sign on the door: CLOSED FOR FIVE DAYS. Problem solved. You're entitled to get away once in a while. Your customers will live without you for a few days."

Jackie laughed, "You make it sound so easy."

"It is! Mac needs you. Trudy needs you. You need to go—get away. Help them!"

Jackie felt immediate relief. Here was a plan. If she did follow it, she needed to start making it possible, make plane reservations to fly into Vegas, start notifying customers that she'd be closing. Jackie gave

Marna a big hug and told her that she'd better get started. Marna smiled and watched Jackie rush off.

Chapter 19

September 1977, New Moon, second day

Trudy was glad they were moving again. The endless miles required nothing of her. Somehow, she was getting on with her life. They were heading toward the mighty Mississippi. The truck, heavily loaded, didn't bounce along as before. Mac had to downshift going up hills.

Mac flipped on his citizen's band radio to pick up the truckers' road talk. Trudy learned the wonderfully colorful language of the road. Mac had a road name, or "handle," as the truckers called it. With familiar handles, they'd greet others warmly. Mac's handle was "Mac-Mack," and he was a good buddy or a good ol' boy. He also called out to familiar buddies when he heard them: Hot Dog, Snoopy, and Talking Tom. Trudy asked why he had to say his name twice for his handle. Mac laughed, explaining it was because his name was Mac and he drove a Mack truck, so other truckers made his handle Mac-Mack.

He explained truckers shared important information or road tips, traffic warnings, or if there was a "plain wrapper" taking pictures, which, Trudy learned, was an unmarked patrol car with radar. But more often, the truckers shared stories along the road, describing cities with colorful names: Chi-Town for Chicago, Beer Town for Milwaukee, Tiger Town for Detroit, Jazz City for New Orleans, and many more.

As the truck passed over the long bridge on the Mississippi River, Trudy remembered how the river looked much farther north, near her farm. Here, it was so much wider, with many more riverboats. It was a dirtier brown here, and the banks were populated with much port activity. They were passing into the western states.

After they crossed, Mac suggested that Trudy get a nap in the back since they would have to take turns sleeping. There'd be no motel tonight. He explained he'd take shorter naps, three hours or so, and Trudy would need to wait in the front cab while he slept. At the next stop, she should find a book. He had some reading materials, but nothing she might want to read, just motorcycle catalogs and maps. As Trudy climbed in back, Mac reminded her not to come out if they did stop, unless he told her it was all clear.

Trudy went in the back and listened to Mac talk on the CB for a while. She felt like a little girl again; this was a big country, and she had not seen most of it. The movement of the truck was comforting, like being rocked in her chair. The steady hum of the tires helped lull her to sleep.

The truck inched forward, then stopped, then inched forward. Trudy was jarred awake. She remembered Mac's admonition not to come forward without his giving an all-clear. She wondered what was happening and became frightened when she heard men's voices. This continued for many minutes, and Trudy wrapped herself tightly under the fleece blanket and stayed very quiet. Mac got out of the cab, slamming his door. Trudy panicked; he hadn't called her to come out, but she didn't know where he was going. She stayed down as he had warned her. Trudy would just have to trust that Mac wouldn't leave her. She listened intently but could not make out what the voices were saying with the truck motor idling.

Finally, Trudy heard someone open the driver's door and get back into the cab. The truck pulled forward slowly at first but then picked up speed as the gears shifted into higher speeds. Finally, Mac gave the all-clear. Trudy opened the curtain cautiously, saw an open road ahead and nothing out of the ordinary. She climbed into the front passenger seat.

"Is everything okay?"

"Yup, just a routine stop for a weigh-in. I was a bit heavy," replied Mac.

"I don't think you're heavy, Mac, muscular maybe, but I'd never call you overweight!"

Mac burst out laughing. After he enjoyed the unexpected joke, he explained to Trudy that the Federal Highway Administration requires long-haul trucks to get weighed since there are penalties for an overweight load. It helps pay for road repairs, and the trucks that move the heavy loads help pay the costs along with all the gas taxes that are paid.

"But thanks for the compliment, Trudy!"

Trudy was briefly embarrassed to find out it was not Mac who was being weighed, it was his truck and cargo. But she shared Mac's laughter, realizing her gaffe. She asked Mac where they were now.

"We're near Little Rock, and after that, on to Oklahoma City, but still on the same interstate. We take it all the way west."

Mac suggested that Trudy eat some of the fruit she'd brought from the motel, telling her they'd stop for food after a few more hours of driving. Then he'd get one of his naps.

Once they started rolling again, they'd stop for an evening meal and Trudy could sleep the rest of the night. He hoped to make Vegas by tomorrow if the road conditions were good and traffic not heavy.

"I like being on the road with you, Mac. And for the first time in many months, I'm starting to feel like myself again."

Mac looked over at her and smiled but didn't ask her a lot of questions, which Trudy appreciated. She watched the miles pass by as they drove through some small towns with more exit ramps. The cars and trucks coming and going, everyone going somewhere.

The miles washed over Trudy. She was gaining a new perspective and reflected on her sorrow. Had she known more about life, would she have been able to perceive how devious Faust had been with her? Trudy hoped so. But she knew life begins with innocence, like her own baby. It saddened Trudy to think she would not be able to protect her baby's innocence through the early years. This was the role of a mother. With all the multitudes of people that come and go along the highway, each had once had a mother who cared, she thought.

Mac's call on the CB radio interrupted her meditation. "This here's Mac-Mack lookin' for a country boy coming out of Oklahoma City. How's it looking over your shoulder? Come back?"

No response. After a short wait, Mac repeated the question. This time, he got a response: "Hey, good buddy, Long John here heading east out of O.C. It's clean-green all the way."

"That's a 10-4, Long John. Clean green into Little Rock as well."

"Time for lunch and my short nap. I'm going to pull into this truck stop, get a sandwich, then go in the back for a couple of hours' sleep. You can come along, get a book and something to eat. You'll sit up front, I'll park in the back lot, no one will see us." Trudy nodded in agreement.

After his nap, Mac started the truck, then headed over to the phone booth. He called Jackie and, after explaining where they were, asked if she had come up with any ideas. They'd be in Vegas by tomorrow, and Mac was getting concerned about what came next with Trudy.

Jackie didn't need Mac to say more. She told him that she was flying out tomorrow and would meet him in Vegas. Mac was uncustomarily dumbfounded.

"Say that again? You're comin' out to Vegas?"

"Yes. I'm coming to Vegas. I know that I have to talk to Trudy. I'm going to get her to come back with me."

"What about the Counter?"

Mac was puzzled; Jackie never closed down on days she worked. He knew since he had begged her many times. She always refused. Mac had often told her that she was more driven than he ever was, never deterring from the work at hand. Was this his same Jackie?

"As Marna suggested, I am going to put a big, fat closed sign in the front window. I'm flying out tomorrow. We need to plan how we meet up, okay?" Jackie took over the conversation. Mac was still incredulous. Would he actually be seeing Jackie in Vegas, tomorrow? Mac never quite got beyond the unexpected announcement as Jackie asked him if he'd gotten the name of the motel.

She had to repeat the information, and she asked him to write it all down. Jackie had booked two rooms at a motel on the outskirts of the city. They could have a nice meal, even take in some of the sights in Vegas, but her main objective was to talk with Trudy. Jackie told Mac that she wouldn't leave Vegas until she had talked Trudy into coming home.

Mac finally understood Jackie was determined. He copied down the motel information as she repeated the instructions, and then he told her that if she was in fact coming to Vegas, he had one thing for her to do.

"Go into my top dresser drawer. You will find a plain envelope marked 'Trudy.' Bring it with you. This is important, don't forget that envelope."

Jackie didn't argue, telling Mac she was packing things tonight and would get the envelope first thing after they hung up. Mac finally told Jackie that he loved her and would see her tomorrow. He was starting to get excited to think that he and Jackie would be in Vegas together!

Mac finished pumping the diesel gas as Trudy returned from her bathroom stop. As they pulled out, he asked what she was reading while he napped.

"I found a Thomas Hardy novel," Trudy said, adding the title, *Tess of the d'Urbervilles*.

Trudy rambled on. She couldn't believe her luck in finding a Thomas Hardy novel in a truck stop. She conjectured that some college student must have sold it. She got it for a quarter.

Mac saw his opening, "Trudy, you have to go back to school. I saw how excited you were about starting last semester, and now, just finding a book got you all excited again."

"It was only a dream, Mac. I have no money now and no way of going back. But I can still read—no one can take my love of reading away. It's not all bad."

Mac said no more. They rode on for a long time not talking. Finally, Trudy asked Mac, "Can I ask a personal question?"

Mac teased, "Another one?"

"You don't have to answer," replied Trudy, adding, "But I'd like to ask."

Mac gave her permission, telling her that she already knew most of his history and adding that he wasn't a complicated man.

"Mac, you always tell me that Jackie is 'your woman,' as you put it; why have you never asked her to marry you?"

Mac smiled, "I have, and if I've asked her once, I've asked her a hundred times. Jackie is the one that won't marry me!"

"Doesn't Jackie love you? I don't believe that. I see how much you mean to Jackie,"

"She says she loves me," Mac replied. "Jackie just says that she can't marry me; she has her reasons. But we might as well be married," Mac argued. "She's my home base, the reason that I always go back to Milson. We are as good as married, that has to be enough.

"Is it?"

"No, not for me. Every year, I ask her again, but it's always the same answer, Jackie says that she's not good enough for me!" Mac concluded, "If you have any other questions about this, you need to ask Jackie,"

Trudy saw that Mac didn't want to discuss it further, so she stopped. Yet she wondered if happiness was within reach, why didn't Jackie choose happiness? Maybe, it was like her own decision. She still didn't know if choosing adoption was right—maybe she'd never know. Trudy thought she'd always want to choose happiness, though. But now she also understood that a decision can be right there in front of you, but you don't understand if you're making the right choice.

Mac turned on the CB again, listening to road chatter. Traffic and weather were both favorable. Mac wanted to be through Oklahoma City before stopping again and knew he wasn't making very good time. Too many distractions with his passenger. Now that he knew Jackie would be in Vegas, Mac wanted to get some sleep, or he'd lose any chance of enjoying this unusual opportunity.

Trudy watched the road, mile after mile. As they drove through a few more urban areas, she began to wonder if Marie and Tony were still in Milson with the baby. Even though she felt confident that Marie would do everything she could for her baby's well-being, Trudy still thought that only a real mother could provide instinctive love for her own flesh and blood. Would Marie love her baby the way she would?

If sacrifice is required, would this wealthy couple move heaven and earth for the baby? These thoughts bothered Trudy until she got to the ultimate question: Would her baby be loved by adoptive parents as much as by her real mother?

Trudy had no answer. A tiny tear overflowed and dropped down her cheek. She wiped the tear with the back of her right sleeve, and Mac saw the gesture. He observed Trudy going from emotion to emotion, laughing and enjoying the sights to a deep sadness. Mac knew this was normal for anyone recovering from trauma. He still had his 'Nam moments. But over time, the deep pain had eroded into simple sadness. He'd learned not to struggle against sadness but to grasp it and finally cherish it because it made him remember his lost brothers, those who did not return. Yet his memory kept them alive in some way. Most combat vets knew this. Mac compared Trudy's loss to his own loss. He allowed her time to grieve.

The day was losing light. Mac gave Trudy an update, telling her that as soon as they drove through Oklahoma City, he would need to stop and take a nap before driving on through the night. He told her that he had one of his favorite stops coming up after Oklahoma City. Jackie's closest friend lives there.

"Remember Sandy who runs Sandy's Dude Ranch and Supper Club? She was at Jackie's Christmas party." Trudy remembered. Jackie had introduced her as a woman who once saved her life. Trudy never understood what Jackie meant, but saw they were very close.

"Sandy's too pretty to be a dude. How come it's a dude ranch?"

Mac laughed heartily. "She's definitely a cowgirl and takes no crap from any cowboy. But the restaurant's name was after her late husband, also named Sandy. That's another long story."

"We'll eat supper there, but I'm goin' to have you stay in the bar with Sandy while I get some shut-eye. I have to drive most of the night if we are to make Vegas by tomorrow."

Trudy began to worry. She did not like the thought of being a woman left alone in a cowboy bar with strangers. She didn't know Sandy very well.

"Is it safe?"

"Of course! I wouldn't leave you in a place that wasn't safe. Don't worry, I'll talk to Sandy and she'll take care of you."

"But Sandy doesn't know me very well, she might not even re-member meeting me!"

Mac smiled: "You're young and pretty. That's all Sandy needs to know, plus the fact that you're my friend and Jackie's. She'll take care of you just fine. In fact, if you watch Sandy, she can teach you a few things about handlin' guys."

Trudy frowned at Mac, which made him laugh:

"Don't give me *the look*, I know you get my drift."

"Of course, I get it. All women know about men coming on too strong, which is why we don't hang out in bars alone," Trudy shot back.

"Dang, I'm sorry, but I've got to sleep. I'd like to watch along with you and Sandy myself, since you're goin' to be the prettiest little gal in there tonight," teased Mac.

"Yea, like raw bait," objected Trudy. "Maybe I'll just stay in the front seat while you get your nap. I can read my book."

"No you don't, I need real sleep. I can't have you lightin' up the whole damn cab reading. Listen Trudy, don't worry. I will talk to Sandy, and she will see to it that you are taken care of in her place. Sandy will have a band, some dancin', lots to enjoy. It is much better than waitin' for me while I sleep in a dark truck."

Trudy stopped complaining. She knew that she was imposing on Mac, but this was not something that she wanted to do. Besides, she was shy around new people. Mac was asking too much of her. Maybe she'd sneak back out after Mac fell asleep and just quietly sit in the truck.

By the time Mac pulled into Sandy's Dude Ranch and Supper Club, which was just a mile down the road from the freeway ramp, it was already dark. Mac pulled into a huge gravel lot and went all the way to the back, where he could easily take the truck in and out. Mac reached into the back of his cab, opened a small wooden chest, and pulled out two shirts. He put on a cowboy shirt right over his gray tee-shirt. The other shirt he threw over to Trudy and told her he'd step out of the cab while she took off her sweatshirt and put this one on.

Trudy thought she'd drown in one of Mac's shirts. But she quickly realized that this was just about her size and was cut for a woman's frame. Mac explained it was one of Jackie's blouses that he kept for her, just in case. As Mac climbed down and closed his door, Trudy pulled the sweatshirt off over her head and quickly put her arms into the long-sleeved shirt. It was a bit loose, but close enough. She'd just take the shirt tails and tie them around her waist. The shirt had mother-of-pearl snaps instead of buttons, so tying the tails was done easily. She rolled up the sleeves and got a fairly good fit once the shirt was tied and sleeves rolled. It was a colorful calico shirt and had double stitching around the yoke. It matched the one Mac was wearing.

She opened her passenger door, and Mac helped her down, telling her they were now appropriately dressed for the dude ranch. Trudy looked at the building as Mac escorted her through the parking lot. It was well-lit and looked like a long hacienda with a low wooden porch at ground level surrounded by corral posts. Once inside, she saw a huge open room with a long wooden bar surrounded by stools with leather horse saddles instead of seats. Another corral surrounded a floor area covered in wood with a raised stage against the wall. Mac led Trudy to one of the booths in the bar room.

"It's still early here. The music won't start for another hour when the cowboys start rolling in after their workday."

Mac handed Trudy one of the menus and told her this was a red meat place so get a steak or ribs, not much else on the menu in any event. As Trudy looked at the selections, a young man came over and greeted Mac as he poured water into their glasses. Mac told him he wanted to talk with Sandy, and the waiter said he'd send her over.

After a few moments, Sandy walked over to the table, and on recognizing Mac became quite demonstrative.

"Look what the tumbleweed blew in! Mac, you ole cowboy. How you been?"

Mac stood up and hugged Sandy, saying it was good to see her. Sandy was tall and slender with long blonde hair that hung beneath her cowgirl hat. He asked Sandy if she remembered Trudy. Sandy greeted Trudy in a friendly way and replied to Mac:

"I don't forget a pretty face like that. Does Jackie know you're here?"

"Don't you worry. You know Jackie's still my woman. I'm just helpin' Trudy out, that's all."

Sandy laughed, telling Mac that's the only reason she lets him in her place. Mac then asked what he should order. Sandy told him that they just finished pulling some ribs off the outdoor grill after slow-cooking them all day. Mac ordered two. He grabbed Trudy's menu and gave them to Sandy. Before Sandy went back into the kitchen, Mac asked if he could talk with her after they ate. Sandy agreed, saying she'd be back later.

As Sandy walked away, Mac explained to Trudy that Sandy had been Jackie's best friend growing up. He got to know her through Jackie and the yearly visit over Christmas.

Trudy wondered how Jackie's best friend was a cowgirl from Oklahoma.

Mac explained that Sandy was from Milson but married a cowboy, also named Sandy. She moved here when he opened this place. Her husband was a rodeo cowboy and rode the circuit, which meant he traveled all over for competitions, even Milson in the summer. That's how he'd met Sandy, in the first place. She had run off with him, got married and stayed in Oklahoma and helped run the restaurant. According to Jackie, it had been an impulsive decision, but it was a happy marriage. Until her husband died riding a bull. He suffered a broken neck!

"Sandy and Jackie compare notes all the time about runnin' a restaurant. In fact it was Sandy who had helped Jackie get back on her feet and open the Counter when she was getting over her own romantic fling. These gals were wild in their youthful days. But Jackie's guy ran off. She didn't have happy days like Sandy's marriage."

Trudy noted that the two restaurants weren't very similar, one was more like a tavern and Jackie's was a cozy little breakfast and lunch counter. Mac agreed, but he reminded Trudy that Sandy ran the place with her husband and a lot of cowboys. Sandy had been a widow on her own for over five years. She'd had to learn how to be tough to handle this place.

Mac told Trudy that Sandy has some big, bad cowboys who she employed as bouncers. She pays them well, but everyone knows Sandy's the boss. The place gets really busy at night.

As Trudy looked at all the rope lassos hanging on the walls alongside the cowhides and longhorn steer racks hanging behind the bar, she remembered the Labor Day cowboy movie marathon that she and Marie had been watching while she was in labor. The stampede overrunning her when she gave birth, at least, that's how she recalled it. She felt she'd come full circle in just a few weeks. Trudy found it strange the way life had a way of doubling back on itself.

Trudy's attention was diverted by the food being served. The waiter put down a metal platter filled with a full rack of ribs, along with cowboy beans, potatoes and a side of slaw. Mac told the waiter they'd have sarsaparillas to drink.

"How come we never order off a menu?" Trudy asked.

Mac was already holding a rib and mumbled his reply: " 'Cause you're just a rookie, that's why. Now eat!"

Trudy laughed but followed Mac's lead. Ribs are too hard to eat with utensils, anyhow. Trudy knew she'd never finish a full rack. They enjoyed the meal, the ribs so well cooked the meat merely fell off the bone. Mac asked Trudy if she was going to finish hers. Trudy bantered that she was finished! Mac grabbed her unfinished half-rack and wrapped it in a napkin, telling her they'd have a snack for the road.

As their plates were cleared away, Sandy came back as promised. Mac suggested that Trudy go wash up and use the rest room for a few minutes. Trudy could see that Mac wanted a few moments to talk and quickly left.

Once safely out of ear shot, Mac explained to Sandy in a very brief, thumbnail sketch about Trudy's status as a runaway. Sandy quickly became an ally in the saga. She'd heard her share of stories about women used by men and had her own share of hard luck stories as well, especially knowing Jackie's history. She asked how she could help. Mac explained that Jackie was coming to Vegas to talk Trudy into going back to Milson. He needed to sleep for several hours and wanted someone to watch Trudy. Make sure she didn't run away and not to let the men hassle her.

"Don't worry, I'll handle the cowboys," quipped Sandy, adding, "And if I ever see that Faust guy around here, I'll dump him at some cowboy truck stop. What a jerk! He's probably never been to an Oklahoma stop, they can be pretty rough, not like your polite midwestern stops where everybody apologizes for just stepping on your toes!"

Mac laughed but stressed that she couldn't tell Trudy that she knows her story. Sandy told him not to worry, she'd be discreet. She kissed Mac quickly on the cheek telling him she was proud of the way he was taking care of the girl, adding that she was a real pretty thing. Cowboys will hang around her like bears to honey. Sandy said she was tending bar tonight. She'd teach Trudy how to manage unwanted attention.

Mac got up and left, waiting momentarily for Trudy near the bathroom marked, Cowgirl." When Trudy came out, Mac told Trudy he was going out to sleep and had talked to Sandy. He told her to go sit on the last stool around the corner of the bar. Sandy would be sure that Trudy was taken care of. Before Trudy could object, Mac left quickly, knowing that she'd be skittish.

Trudy walked over to the stool that Mac pointed to. As she sat down, Sandy wiped the bar in front of her and filled a large mug with beer and placed it in front of Trudy. Trudy frowned but didn't say anything. But Sandy picked up on Trudy's body language.

"Not to worry, you don't need to drink it, this is to let the cowboys know you already got a drink."

Trudy smiled. She saw that Mac was right, Sandy knew the score. She watched Sandy for a bit. The bar was filling up, a band was setting up on the stage and the house lights were dimmed. Sandy greeted most of the cowboys by name. She kept an eye on everything that was happening and from time to time came over and asked Trudy how she was doing and asking if she needed anything.

Sandy explained that a band called The Hollering Five would be starting soon, and she told Trudy she could watch the dancing and enjoy the music. Larger groups of men and women now started to fill up the empty booths. They were dressed in fine western outfits with fringes, silver buckles, and cowboy boots. The women all wore tightly fitting jeans and their leather boots were brightly decorated with red and turquoise, enhancing their silver jewelry.

Within the hour, the band was playing Country/Western music with a comedy routine during the break, between songs. By now the tavern was crowded, all the booths and stools filled, with very little standing room left, except for the dance floor which was slowly gaining dancers.

The band took a short break and came back for a second set, telling the crowd they were going to play some cowboy classics. For an hour they played songs like, "Timber, I'm Falling," "I Dreamed of a Hill-Billy Heaven," "Hello Walls," "The Blackboard of My Heart," and "My Past is Present." Trudy found the lyrics corny but was enjoying the fun.

An uninvited cowboy who had too much to drink had been watching Trudy and saw that no one was with her. He came over and offered to buy her another drink. He found an unoccupied stool and soon pulled his uncomfortably close to hers. Trudy became self-conscious, but Sandy didn't miss a beat. She walked over and told the stranger to move on. He objected, telling Sandy that he was just going to talk to the pretty lady. Sandy nodded to a muscular cowboy, who alertly walked over.

The guy was politely removed from his stood and escorted out the door. Trudy did not see him again. When a few others had too much to drink and tried to order another, Sandy would pour them a cup of hot coffee instead. Most accepted the coffee. If any cowboy did object, he was quickly escorted out. Sandy did not allow anyone to get too drunk and certainly not rowdy.

Watching Sandy, Trudy was reminded of Jackie, who also knew how to handle the few drunks that walked into her place for breakfast after drinking all night. Both were polite, not insulting the drunks so as not to escalate the tension, but like Sandy, Jackie was firm. Most of the men listened much like a naughty boy listens to his mother. Trudy respected their feminine charm, apparently as did the men. Both women knew when it was time to call in the cops or the bouncers. Trudy also saw that the groups of women kept near each other or the men they trusted. Terrek wouldn't last long in this place she thought.

It was getting late; the band was playing the last set. Mac walked up quietly behind Trudy and asked if he could have this dance. Trudy was momentarily surprised but glad to see him. Mac took Trudy's arm and said they'd have one dance for the road. He led Trudy to the dance floor, fiddle music playing a moderately slow waltz as the evening was winding down. Mac held Trudy at arm's length as if dancing with his sister.

After the dance, Mac walked over to Sandy, thanking her. She told him that Trudy was well cared for and warned him to watch the road, lots of drunks out at this time. Mac bent down and politely kissed Sandy on the cheek. She told him to give her best to Jackie. They were soon on the road again. This time Mac told Trudy to get in the back and sleep the night away. She was tired and gladly complied.

Mac took advantage of the night hours; he was making good time, trying to make up for the many lost minutes. Mac anticipated meeting Jackie in Vegas, giving him renewed energy. As the first light of dawn poured through the cab, Trudy finally woke. She had slept better than she had in many months. The rolling truck was an elixir.

Trudy finally climbed into the front and told Mac she'd need a bathroom stop soon. Mac never made such stops, having his trucker's techniques which he'd not explain to Trudy, but he could see that the delays were about to begin again. Mac told Trudy there was a truck stop not too far ahead; they'd stop there, but it would be short, no time for breakfast. He told Trudy he planned to buy a few hard boiled eggs and get some coffee, and she should get something as well.

Mac slowed, took the exit ramp, in and out, and back on the road. He rushed Trudy along stressing that they'd need to make up time today. Once back in the truck, Mac pushed on. Trudy saw Mac wasn't interested in her chatter. She pulled out her Hardy novel and began reading. The hours and the miles faded behind them.

As they drove near Amarillo, continuing west, Trudy noted the terrain was getting hilly and saw mountains in the far distance; they were in the foothills of the Rocky Mountains skirting around the Southern states into New Mexico.

Mac finally broke the silence telling Trudy that he'd need another cat-nap soon and needed to gas up. He added, they'd be through Albuquerque before noon. Once through the busy interchanges, he told her they'd make a stop. "I'll gas up. You can read while I get a couple hours of sleep."

Trudy put her book down, watching the mountains getting taller. She was fascinated by the skyscape around the peaks, so different from the forests of the north, the rolling farmland or green hillside meadows. Most of the land here was arid; instead of green, mostly brown tones. The mountain range made Trudy feel small. This was a big country, and she barely knew it.

Outside Albuquerque, Mac stopped as promised. Trudy stretched her legs, went inside the truck store; purchased a ready-made sandwich and a drink. When she got back in the passenger seat, Mac had already gotten in the back and laid down. She quietly ate her sandwich and began reading her Hardy novel again. Mac kept the truck engine idling; it was too hot to turn off the air conditioning. Trudy was absorbed by the story of Tess, like a sister in many ways. She read on for a few hours while slowly eating her lunch. Finally, Mac climbed back into the front. He told Trudy to take a quick break with him since they'd not stop again for many hours.

Always take advantage of a stop even if you don't need to, trucker's wisdom," he explained. Trudy smiled, knowing what Mac meant and went into the store again to use the rest room.

They were quickly on the road again. Trudy asked Mac if he had gotten enough sleep, having had only a few hours. Mac explained that just a few hours was enough for another eight-hour drive. He got about four hours last night and was used to doing this on the road. He told her he couldn't keep up like this for a whole week, but for three to four days, he was used to trucker's hours. He'd make up for the lost hours over the weekend, often getting two, twelve-hour sleep periods back-to-back.

Mac asked Trudy about her book. She told him that Thomas Hardy was a great writer, and she was spellbound by the plot, even though it was sad. She could relate to Tess's predicament. She explained to Mac that she had always been fascinated by Elizabethan and Gothic novels. Mac asked why.

"I guess I'm a romantic, I enjoy love stories, but these novels always entail a mystery and usually some working-class person interacting with a wealthy person or even royalty. It gives the characters an interesting dynamic when they intermingle, their language, dress, even their common sense is contrasted, sometimes the poor governess has more wisdom than her employer or the farmer is more cunning than the baron. The poor are always trying to survive while the wealthy care little for their predicament."

They rode on quietly for a bit, and finally, Trudy asked Mac if she could ask another question.

Mac laughed, "Again? I always get in trouble with your questions."

Trudy also laughed, telling Mac not to worry, it wasn't too personal. "I'm just wondering what you like to read?"

Mac answered earnestly that he was not a well-read man, just a simple truck driver. But Trudy told him it was just like her novels: "Mac the truck driver has more humanity and is more chivalrous than…" Trudy trailed off, not finishing the sentence.

"Who? I'm more chivalrous than?" Mac insisted that Trudy finish her thought. She hesitated but answered:

"I was going to say, than a wealthy lawyer like Faust!"

Mac was quiet, he was very touched by Trudy's sweet comment. Trudy continued telling Mac this was why she didn't want to go back. But she did have one more question.

"Yeah?"

"Mac, do you think our country, the United States, has classes? You know, like England with royalty vs. the commoners? We're supposed to be a democracy, no kings, but I wonder?"

"Well, not royalty, but classes? Yes. I do think that. We have poor and rich, the powerless and the powerful."

"Who are they Mac? The powerful I mean, this is the upper class, right?"

"Yeah. I learned who they were in Viet Nam by learning who they were *not*. Those that got out of the draft. They're the powerful ones. The *commoners* included anyone who did get drafted. They are the poor, anyone who didn't go to an Ivy League schools out east or universities, and anyone who is not white, Tag taught me that."

Mac thought for a moment and added, "Females also don't count for the draft, so no females. Just look at our US Senators, the rulers, that'll show you what the upper class looks like, or the big names on large corporations' board of directors. Women only make it if they marry these men or their fathers are wealthy. From history, it's people like Carnegie, Rockefeller, DuPont, even Kennedy."

Trudy thought for a moment. She agreed with Mac, knowing his knowledge came from hard-won experience; she finally asked, "Knowing all this Mac, how do you accept your lot in life?"

Mac laughed, "See, now you're gonna' to get me in trouble again with these kinds of questions."

"It's just us, Mac. You can't get in trouble with me, I'm powerless, too."

"Damn, I'm rollin' with a philosopher."

But Trudy was serious and insisted on getting Mac's answer, repeating her question: "How do you accept it, Mac?"

"I don't, that's how. No one judges me, except me."

Trudy thought about Mac's answer. He was wise not to let anyone else's opinion become his ultimate identity. "I wish that I had your confidence, Mac."

"You will, you just have to grow up. Everyone gets kicked around before they wise up. It took me going to 'Nam to get it, and Tag, too. As a Black guy, he got kicked around even more than I did. But we both understood that if we kept together, not let the powerful divvy us up, we could save each other. Jackie knows that, too."

"Trudy, you will learn this, I just got to save your raw hide from the road that Faust tried to kick you onto. Jackie and I will not let you drown out there. That's why I got this rolling daycare all week."

"I love you for it, Mac,' Trudy responded. "You're a good man. I just wish Jackie would give you a break, too."

"You tell Jackie that, Okay?"

"I will!"

Trudy began to cry. Mac was surprised, "What the heck, it's nothing to cry about!"

"Mac, I sold my baby to wealthy East Coast elites!"

"No, you did not! That's not the same thing at all!"

"No, but it feels like that," replied Trudy. "Faust is the one that got all the money, and I was the sucker. Faust even told me, and he's right."

"Stop it, Trudy. Stop beating yourself up!"

"Givin' a baby up for adoption isn't a bad thing. Most people would say you did a good deed. You went through nine months of hell. A lot of girls might have had an abortion. Not you.

I ain't judgin' anyone about that either, but you got to stop beatin' yourself up. For you, that was what you needed to do. You are your own worst judge, no one else. And you got to get over it!"

Through her tears, Trudy replied meekly, "I know."

Chapter 20

September 1977, Harvest Time

Las Vegas, Nevada, was short-changed by Lady Luck, Mac thought as his truck rolled into Vegas much later than he had wanted. Before the gamblers moved in, this was a long, flat valley between the mountains, now taken over by the Strip and nightclubs. His cargo was as much out of place here as the gamblers themselves. He was delivering a load of dinghies to be used on Lake Mead, which was actually a reservoir. Mac was sorry that Trudy was missing the canyon scenery, but she had been sleeping in the back for the last hour.

Trudy will have a chance to see it in the morning, Mac thought, that is, if she's still talking. He never told Trudy that Jackie was waiting to meet them. Mac pulled up behind a motel on the outskirts of town, at the address Jackie had given him. He parked in the back, knowing he'd have to leave his truck in this paved lot. He'd deliver his cargo the next day; it was already too late for anything except checking into their room, grabbing a bite, and sleeping.

Mac pulled open the back curtain to wake Trudy. "I know I can't call you Sleeping Beauty; is Goldilocks off limits too? Time to wake up!" But Trudy had just settled into a deep sleep; she could barely open her eyes. Mac called again.

"Let me sleep here, Mac, I can't open my eyes!" Trudy pleaded.

Mac thought for a moment and had a brilliant idea: "Okay, but you have to promise not to get out of the cab!"

"Fine!" was the only reply.

"Trudy, I'm serious," Mac shouted, "I have to have your promise. I'll come out for you at the crack of dawn, but you can't move from here during the night until I say it's okay!"

"Yeah, I promise," Trudy said meekly and rolled over and went back to sleep.

Mac restarted his engine and turned the air conditioner on low. He opened his window just a crack to allow fresh air in, although the cabin was well-ventilated and equipped to allow sleeping inside safely, not like a passenger car. The truck was in the back and far enough away so as not to disturb anyone. Mac made sure the curtain was fully closed and darkened the interior lights. He exited the cab and locked the doors; Trudy could open them from the inside, but he intended to reopen them himself, well before she woke.

Walking across the wide parking lot carrying his small duffel, Mac thought this was a stroke of genius. Trudy could sleep in the truck while he tracked down Jackie and give her an update. He didn't know how Trudy would react in the morning, but he was glad Jackie would be there to help him figure it out. All Trudy had talked about was how she wanted to keep moving. She kept insisting that she would not go back to Milson.

Inside, Mac went to the front registration desk and gave the receptionist his name, telling her that a woman named Jackie should have checked in earlier, reserving a room for him in his name. She checked and confirmed Mac's information; Mac asked her to page Jackie and tell her he was at the front desk waiting. Before Mac finished filling out his registration form, Jackie was standing next to him.

"Where's Trudy?"

"Let's go to the room, I don't want to talk here,"

Jackie nodded as Mac told the receptionist that he had parked his long haul truck at the very back of the lot and would remove it first thing in the morning since it was already too late to make a delivery. The receptionist approved a waiver to park his truck, one night only.

Jackie unlocked her door, and they both stepped inside. Barely taking time to fully shut the door, Mac swept Jackie up into his arms and gave her a long, passionate kiss, holding her in a tight embrace. Jackie wrapped her arms around Mac's neck and kissed him back, greeting him with the same passion. She then gently pushed him back and repeated her question.

"Where's Trudy?"

Mac smiled, so happy to see Jackie, but he saw that she was anxious for news. "Trudy fell asleep in the cab about an hour before I rolled in. We should have been here well before dark, but a trucker gets really delayed by a passenger. Anyway, when I tried to wake Trudy to come in, she begged me to let her sleep. I had a brilliant idea, let her sleep while I go find you. She still doesn't know you're here! But I made her promise not to leave the cab until I came back for her."

"Is it safe?"

"It'll be okay for now. The truck's locked, and she's slept back there a good part of the week anyhow. Trudy's gotten quite comfortable sleepin' on the road. But I have to go out there before the light of dawn. Trudy promised to wait for me before gettin' out."

"You didn't tell her that I'm here?"

"Nope, I didn't know how. I'm still worried she'll run again. I need you to help me with that, Babe."

Jackie only nodded; she understood Mac's dilemma. He repeated how happy he was to see her and told her it was too bad that he was so tired or he'd make love to her right then and there. Jackie smiled at his teasing and objected, telling him he smelled like he hadn't bathed in a week.

"No kiddin'. I haven't! You always get to see me when I'm nicely showered, shaved, and baby talcum all over my sweet bottom just for you," Mac teased, adding: "And well-rested with plenty of energy."

"Enough!" Jackie pushed Mac into the bathroom, telling him to shower. She'd think about how they'd meet Trudy in the morning. While Mac showered, Jackie called room service and ordered a sandwich and cold beer for Mac with a glass of wine for herself. She thought about their dilemma.

Mac got out of the shower, shaved, and put on a fresh shirt. He stepped out of the bathroom fresher than a Cub Scout ready for Sunday church. On seeing the cold beer and sandwich, he told Jackie that's why he loved her and sat down to eat while Jackie sipped her wine. Together, they devised a plan for the next morning.

Mac told Jackie he hadn't slept for twenty hours and the beer had made him sleepy. Jackie kissed him, told him to go to bed, and she'd be sure that he'd awake first thing at the crack of dawn. They had come up with sort of a plan, both hoping it would be a way to convince Trudy to come back to Milson

Jackie woke Mac; he had barely slept six hours, not nearly enough to catch up on his sleep. Jackie had not slept well as she tossed most of the night thinking that Trudy would awaken in the truck and run away again. Trudy knew Vegas was the end of their trip, and Jackie worried that she might run into the city.

Jackie encouraged Mac to get up and check on Trudy. The light of dawn was already breaking over the mountains. Jackie reminded Mac that he and Trudy should eat a quick complimentary breakfast before coming back into the room. She would wait for them here. Mac nodded and dragged himself out of bed.

Still yawning, Mac walked across the blacktop lot, unlocked the driver's door, and turned off the ignition. He made a quick check of all his gauges and saw everything was normal. Before he could call out, Trudy opened the curtain. Mac said good morning, asking how she had slept.

"I slept like a baby," Trudy responded, adding, "Did you sleep in the front all night?"

"You did sleep soundly. No, I'm already checked into the motel and slept in a real bed last night. I tried to wake you, but you begged me to let you sleep. Your every wish is my command!" Mac teased.

Trudy yawned and answered, "Oh, yeah, I remember."

"You must be ready for a bathroom stop and a bite to eat. Then, I'll take you to the room we're checked into, and you can take a shower and clean up. We do need to talk a bit, but I have to get this truck into the terminal for unloadin'; I can't leave it sit here all day. I had to get special permission just to leave it overnight."

Trudy merely complied; she climbed out of the back and followed Mac across the parking lot. Mac told her that he had to check in with the clerk about moving his truck but pointed to the women's restroom and told Trudy he'd wait for her in the lobby. They'd grab a bowl of cereal or whatever and some coffee before heading to the room. Trudy agreed to all of it, glad to follow his lead.

As promised, Mac was waiting for Trudy after she had splashed some water on her face and combed her hair, looking a bit more presentable for the complimentary breakfast. But no one was around to see them. Trudy and Mac grabbed a quick breakfast, sharing unimportant information about their location and the weather.

Mac was satisfied that Trudy was fully awake and had something in her stomach before taking her to the room. He knew she would be either in shock or very upset in just a few moments, but he acted as if they were just going about their routine as travelers.

Jackie had been pacing in the room, trying to figure out a gentle way to talk with Trudy. Out in the hallway, Trudy followed behind Mac. He stopped in front of the room door and put the key into the lock.

Jackie heard the key, stopped pacing, and stood waiting for Mac and Trudy to enter. As Mac opened the door, he stepped to the side and motioned for Trudy to enter in front of him. She absently obeyed, not anticipating anything other than stepping into an empty room. As soon as Trudy took her first step through the doorway, Mac quickly stepped behind her.

Once Trudy stepped into the room, she realized someone was already inside. Her first reaction was thinking Mac had taken them into the wrong room, someone else's room. Slowly, she recognized the person, a woman wearing tight jeans and a casual yellow blouse. She was very pretty and familiar.

"Good morning," said the familiar voice. It was Jackie!

In a panic, Trudy turned but bumped directly into Mac. His tall frame was entirely blocking the doorway. Mac gently put his arms around Trudy, "You can't keep running away."

Trudy began to cry and wanted to flee. Mac gently restrained her. He looked up to Jackie, who also had tears in her eyes. She realized how frightened Trudy was, or maybe how hurt she was, but Jackie saw how badly Trudy wanted to run again. Mac gently lifted Trudy inside the room and closed the door as he continued to stand in front of it. Both Trudy and Jackie were now crying, Jackie gently telling Trudy that they needed to talk.

"This wasn't exactly how I planned to shower this morning," Mac teased, trying to ease the tension with humor.

Mac nodded to Jackie to come forward and take Trudy from his embrace. Since she could not run, Trudy just hung her head. She was embarrassed, confused, and her sadness resurfaced; she was getting that panicky feeling again.

Jackie took Mac's cue. She stepped forward, took Trudy's arm and tried to coax her over to the side of the bed to sit down.

"Please Trudy, I came a long way just to talk. Please talk to me for a while. We need to figure out what you're going to do."

Jackie's words made Trudy realize Las Vegas was a long way from Milson. But why was Jackie here? But then, that didn't make sense either. This was Friday, or was it Saturday? Trudy had lost track of the days, but she knew it was still a workday for Jackie; she couldn't be here in Las Vegas. Could she?

Trudy allowed Jackie to coax her over to the side of the bed to sit down. Jackie pulled the small desk chair over and sat facing Trudy. Still hanging her head, Trudy mumbled,

"I'm sorry,"

"Don't be sorry, Trudy. There's nothing you have to say you're sorry for to me!"

Mac quietly left the room. He would tend to his truck and deliver his load while Jackie and Trudy had a heart-to-heart talk.

"Yes, I do. I'm sorry." Trudy repeated stubbornly.

"Okay, I'm sorry then, too," Jackie replied.

Jackie slowly rose and sat next to Trudy on the bed. She put her arm around Trudy's slumping shoulders and hugged her. Both began to cry fully. Trudy's sadness unleashed emotions Jackie thought she had buried. She was normally so stoic, so single-mindedly standing alone against all the injustices of the world. Jackie had learned that a single woman had to be strong, grappling with many injustices, which she had met head on almost daily.

Trudy was trying to regain her composure after the shock of seeing Jackie. She finally asked, "Why do you have to say you're sorry to me?"

"Because I should have had a real conversation with you a long time ago. I saw you needed help, but I just kept waiting for you to tell me what you wanted or to share your planning for the baby."

Jackie continued, "I should have been much more thoughtful than I was. I should have offered to help instead of letting you think you had to do it all on your own. That's why I have to say, 'I'm sorry,' Trudy, and I am, I am so truly sorry."

"But why aren't you working today? This isn't your off day, is it?"

Jackie smiled through her tears. She knew everyone kept telling her she was driven to the point of making everyone else crazy with her schedule. She answered softly, "A wise woman gave me some good advice."

Trudy looked at her, wondering what she meant. "Marna wanted me to make you understand that you have to come back to Milson. She's worried about you, and Leslie, too. When I told Marna that I had to work, do you know what she told me?"

Trudy shook her head, no. "Marna said, and this is a direct quote: 'Put a big, fat closed sign in the front window.' It was that easy, Trudy. I just tell my customers that I'm closing for five days, and I'm closed!"

Now Trudy smiled through her tears, "You've always been good to me, gave me a job, shared tips with me even though I know a lot of dishwashers don't get tips. Then you made my work a meal job."

"But you're a waitress, too, and a very good one!" Jackie argued.

"You've always been only good to me; you have nothing to say you're sorry about, not to me!"

Jackie smiled again and stopped crying. "You don't know how special you are, Trudy. I've never had such hard-working help as you. Everything that I ever taught you, you learned after just one demonstration. You always took care of the customers just the way I would have. You never complained, you didn't cut corners. Do you know how special that is? I've had lots of employees. I get that being a dishwasher is a menial job, but you always did it as if you were in a family kitchen helping with your own family."

"Then when you wanted to start school, I was really proud of you! You have ambition and intelligence. I was cheering you on, Trudy. I wanted to see you go places, be someone."

"You were?"

"Now you see! Even you didn't know. I was too harsh, too strict. Mac is right Trudy, I'm too driven."

"Mac said I could only go as far as Las Vegas," said Trudy on hearing his name. "But I didn't know he was going to bring you here."

"Mac asked for my help, but it was Marna who first encouraged me to come. But I saw that she was right, and Mac agreed, too. Marna knew you needed to have someone bring you home."

"I thought Mac was just going to leave me here," Trudy replied.

"Mac wouldn't do that to you," offered Jackie, adding, "He doesn't just abandon a friend in need of help! But he didn't know what to do. We talked on the phone every day, worrying about whether you were going to run away again."

"Mac is my friend, isn't he, a real friend?"

"Yes," replied Jackie.

Trudy thought about Mac for a while. Then gave voice to her own thought: "You know what Mac called me on the road?"

"No, what?"

"A philosopher!" laughed Trudy. "But do you know what? I think Mac is a minister, a truck-driving minister! Everyone he meets seems to love him, and he finds good in almost everyone, even old Agnes, who also runs a restaurant."

Jackie smiled at Trudy, agreeing that Mac was a very special person.

"You know what else?" Jackie played along, letting Trudy lead her: "No, what else?"

"Mac loves you, Jackie!"

Jackie was touched, "I know. He calls me his home base cause he's on the road most of the time, but when he comes home, that means me, his home base."

"Maybe you don't think that's very romantic, but Mac really loves you. Mac and I saw your friend Sandy on the road. She got concerned when she saw me with Mac, but Mac told her she had nothing to worry about. Mac said, 'Jackie's my woman,' and at the end of the evening, Mac even danced with me to show Sandy he meant it. He danced with me just like I was his little sister!"

Trudy got serious. "I did make one promise to Mac that I'd tell you how much you mean to him. Why won't you marry Mac? He said he's asked you many times. If you're trying not to be so harsh, as you say, why not marry Mac? You do love him, don't you?"

"Yes, more than anyone."

But Jackie changed the topic, "I'm here to help you, not Mac."

"Trudy, let's fly home to Milson together. You still have an apartment, and your job."

"I can't, I really messed up," Trudy hung her head. "There are too many bad memories for me in Milson."

"It might not be too late. We can go back to Milson, find out about your baby. Leslie did ask the public defender about your rights after everyone learned you went to court so quickly. The attorney said you had six months to appeal the termination decision. The final adoption can't take place until after the appeal time is expired."

"This time, I am here to help you. You don't have to do it alone. Let us know what you want to do. We'll stand behind you, help you figure it out."

Trudy saw Jackie was being sincere about her offer. Jackie's world was one of hard work, hard reality. Just like her grandparent's world, day in and day out, hard work, hard reality. Trudy didn't want to live her life under those terms. After all the problems and heartaches, her grandparents on the brink of losing everything more than once, and in the end, they just died. She ran away from that once, and she didn't want to go back to it again.

"I was so foolish when I left home after high school," Trudy admitted, "I thought going to the big city was the fix for living in a harsh world. But I didn't even make it a year before I got myself into trouble."

"Mac and I will help this time. Come back, we'll help you fight for your rights."

Trudy was conflicted. She thought about the past week, two weeks, nine months. She didn't want to repeat any of it.

Jackie stood up and went back to the chair so that she could face Trudy. She waited as Trudy seemed to consider her options. Jackie wanted Trudy to understand that everyone makes mistakes when they are young. She knew she needed to share her own story so that Trudy would see that she really did understand.

"I don't talk about my life before owning the restaurant and then meeting Mac since it is a painful story for me," Jackie began, adding, "But I'm going to tell you, Trudy, so you know that I really do understand."

Trudy looked into Jackie's pretty green eyes, noticing that she looked wonderful. She wasn't wearing her white dress and usual hair net. She wore makeup, looking as fresh in her yellow blouse as a new butterfly just emerging from the cocoon. Trudy saw how sincere Jackie was being. She was trying very hard to confide in her.

"I was young and foolish, too. I left home full of big plans. I didn't want to live in the dull world of my parents. I won't bore you with all the details of leaving, but I found my escape with a boyfriend. I'm not saying his name. I promised myself that I would never again utter his name. I first met him when I was a sophomore in high school, and he was a senior. After he graduated, he began living on his own, working. He took me to places that I've never seen before: nightclubs, drive-in movies, dance halls. It was wonderful and I fell madly in love, at least I thought I did."

"After I graduated, we made plans to move to the big city, get out of our small world. I got a job at the telephone company. I also got what I thought was good pay. I was on my own, a new apartment, new clothes. And I was in love."

"He bought a car, and we went places. We traveled around the Midwest for a while, especially in summer. It was wonderful, and I thought that I was really making a new life for myself."

"Anyway, you get the picture! Long story short: I got pregnant, just like you did." Jackie stopped for a moment. She saw that Trudy was listening intently.

"In the days of my youth, women mostly did not even consider keeping a baby as a single mother. There was a societal stigma if a woman did. She'd become something of an outcast. This seems to be changing a bit now. But I think there is still a bias against being a single mother, at least it seems so to me," Jackie surmised.

"What did you do?" Trudy was now vested in Jackie's story. She was shocked to hear Jackie had lived through this and wanted badly to know how she had managed it.

"I hoped my boyfriend would marry me," replied Jackie. "I thought he was the man of my dreams. I loved him and wanted more than anything to be with him and to please him. I thought having sex meant that he really did love me, too, just like I loved him.

"I learned men don't see having sex as equal to being in love, like many women do. I learned that the hard way."

Trudy nodded to tell Jackie that she understood and confessed, "At least you were having sex with someone you thought loved you. My only excuse was drinking a couple glasses of champagne and letting my guard down."

Jackie laughed. She hadn't heard Trudy open up so honestly before, and she offered her own rebuttal. "Well, at least you weren't trying to rationalize being young and foolish by thinking you were in love with someone who was not willing to make any commitment."

"As I said, to make a long story short, the guy got really mad when I told him that I was pregnant. He acted like it was completely my doing, as if it doesn't take two to tango."

"Same as Terrek."

Jackie smiled at Trudy and continued: "My boyfriend did not want me to have the baby. He said he wasn't old enough to be a father. He strung me along, saying maybe in a few years down the road, but not now. That was enough to keep me trying to please him. He said he wouldn't leave me."

"At least he didn't accuse you of sleeping around," posited Trudy.

"No, he knew better, we were together all the time," Jackie concluded and added, "We talked about what to do. I wondered about carrying the baby full term and giving the baby up for adoption, like you did. But he didn't like the idea, saying I'd have to drop out of life for a good part of a year, arguing that at our age, that was like an eternity. We'd miss out on too much fun. He wanted me to end my pregnancy, and we could go on just like before."

"I wanted to please him, still worried that he might leave me. I had convinced myself that I could not live without him, that I should do what he wanted. I gave no thought to my own feelings."

Trudy nodded and remembered her trips to the VOW office and actually going to a medical clinic to make an appointment for the abortion but then running away. Terrek had abandoned her from the outset, at the first news that she was pregnant. She realized that his abandonment allowed her to think only of herself and the baby. Trudy thought Jackie wasn't so lucky—her guy strung her along. In their sorority of womanhood, Trudy was arguing for Jackie's cause.

Jackie took a deep breath; these were difficult memories to share. She tried to keep her tears at bay. Trudy saw her emotion and understood, while also trying to ease Jackie's discomfort, asking, "What did you do next?"

"Don't think badly of me, Trudy. I was just a foolish young girl who was trying to be so grown up and sophisticated. Looking back, I realize now how little I really knew. But I made a life-altering decision.

"My boyfriend got the name of a massage therapist who also did abortions. He took me to meet her. We set up an appointment. He encouraged me, saying he'd pay for the procedure and would go with me, take care of me afterward."

"I was nervous. It also went against everything that I had ever been taught. My parents raised me going to church. I felt deep down that what I was doing was wrong, but then I convinced myself that my parents were wrong. I wasn't living at home, and I shouldn't let them dictate to me. They were old-fashioned, I was not, and on and on. My boyfriend totally agreed, telling me that my parents wouldn't understand. 'Just don't tell them,' he said."

"He took me to a 'clinic' as he called it. It was really a back room in a massage parlor. Looking back now, I think she was mostly doing illegal abortions, but I don't know. She wore a white dress, used clean white sheets, and wore latex gloves. She assured me that everything was very clean. Her back room had a surgery table. She gave me something to drink that she said would calm me. All I remember was falling asleep for a short while, and when I woke up, the woman told me she was all done and that I was fine. I should expect some bleeding. She told me to go home and rest for a few days."

"My boyfriend took me home, was very attentive, walked me into my apartment, and told me he'd check on me in the next few days. I cried myself to sleep that night, alone and frightened."

This time, Trudy reached out and touched the side of Jackie's arm as she sat in the chair. She saw how hard it was for Jackie to share this story. Trudy nodded to Jackie as if to say that she understood how hard this was.

Jackie continued, "After a couple of days, I started to feel sick to my stomach. I thought it was just something I had eaten. But then I started to run a fever. I did bleed as she predicted, but it got heavier, not lighter. I called my boyfriend. He came over, but he got really scared when he saw me. He went back to the clinic and told the woman what was happening. She told him that if he ever led anyone to her door again, she would deny everything and that he'd be in more trouble with the law than she was. But she finally told him to get me to the hospital immediately.

"He came back to my apartment. I nearly passed out from the loss of blood. He carried me to his car and got me to the emergency entrance of the local hospital. As I was checked in, he took off. I never saw him again after that."

Tears were running down Jackie's cheeks. "You see why I never tell my story. I can never tell it without crying. Besides, it makes me feel so very angry and ashamed."

Trudy also had tears. She wondered if this might have happened to her had she not run away from her own abortion appointment. Trudy felt personally involved in Jackie's story.

"What happened?"

"I didn't remember anything once I got to the hospital. I passed out from lack of blood. Apparently, it was touch-and-go for a while. I was admitted to the emergency room, given a blood transfusion. Later, I was told by the medical staff that I'd been near death. They contacted my family."

"My parents came and after several weeks, took me home. I don't know if they were just hurt or angry, probably both. But as I slowly recovered, my mother told me the full extent of the diagnosis. The abortion had left me sterile! I'd never be able to have children, again."

"I was barely twenty! Just a young girl, really, and I'd made a miscalculation that would change the rest of my life! And for what? That guy that I thought I couldn't live without? He left and never came back. I've lived my life without him, after all. I ruined my life for a nameless nobody."

"Trudy, do you see how I really do understand?"

"I do," agreed Trudy, adding, "But you did go on, you have your café, you have Mac."

Jackie smiled as she wiped the tears. She agreed, adding names to her list of blessings, as she called them, "Sandy, my best friend, and Marna, Tag, Pig, all the regulars."

"I have all my people, and the regulars that have no one, they are my family. Do you remember the Christmas Party?"

Trudy nodded as Jackie continued, "This is my family, now. I have blessings even though I don't deserve to have them. And you are part of my family! Now, do you see why you have to come home?"

"We can help you, Trudy, help you fight for your rights. You were braver than I was. You had a beautiful baby girl. And you can still have more children if you want."

Trudy objected, "I wasn't brave."

"I have so many unresolved concerns. Riding in the truck all week has given me some time, but I'm still just going over and over the hurt. I haven't resolved anything."

"I've seen my baby, actually held her. But I've also met Tony and Marie who wanted so badly to adopt the baby. Tony and Marie were really nice people and were so helpful to me. I know it would break Marie's heart if I changed my mind now!"

"Jackie, you tell me that you will help me fight for my rights as a parent, but I really did agree to the adoption. In court, the judge told Faust to be quiet and sit down. He would ask me if I really understood what I was doing. I did think about this, not just in court but the whole time I was pregnant. I did get counseling. In the end, I did tell the judge that I wasn't ready to be a parent. I'm still not. I'm a mess and can barely make it day to day, much less take care of a baby. But I know that I'll always wonder if I made the right decision."

Jackie saw how hard this was for Trudy. She'd gone through the whole nine months while her own pregnancy had only been for about ten weeks, never even looking pregnant. But Jackie did understand the permanency of the decision.

"I do understand. And you're right; you never stop second-guessing yourself. I learned that the hard way. But one thing I do know, you have to learn how to keep going, to get up every day, not let the pain be the only emotion you feel."

"Come home, Trudy. You can't stay here."

But Trudy insisted that she wanted to think about what she should do, and going back to Milson, would bring back her most painful memories.

"What will we do now, today, just today!" emphasized Trudy.

"I get it, you need time to think. Well, I took off work. I'm going to have a few days of vacation in Vegas. That's what I'm doing today. Mac will come back after he drops off his load. He will leave his truck at the truck stop. I have a rental car from the airport. I'll go and pick up Mac and bring him back here."

"Maybe you'd like to clean up. I know how grubby you can feel after being on the road driving in a truck all week. Take a really hot bath, pamper yourself. There's an outdoor pool and spa!"

"And Mac needs a nap this afternoon. Maybe you do too, but tonight, we can see the Strip. We are in Las Vegas, after all! Vegas is not a place to call home—it's a place to escape! Can you do that just for today?" asked Jackie.

Trudy considered the offer; she did need to clean up, and a hot bath sounded wonderful. She agreed, "Yes! Just for today!"

But Jackie wanted a promise from Trudy that she would stay put. She was planning to drive out to pick up Mac at the truck terminal. She wanted to hear that Trudy would not run away, "Promise me, you'll stay put!"

"I promise," Trudy responded on Jackie's insistence.

She pointed out that she really had no idea where she was—had no money. Trudy also felt like she was still rolling, as if she were still on the road, moving. She had a slight dizzy feeling. She knew a hot bath was exactly what she wanted, and a nap in a real bed on solid ground might help settle her motion sickness.

Mac and Jackie returned to the motel after Jackie drove out to the truck terminal as prearranged. On her way back, Jackie told Mac about her talk with Trudy. Mac knew Jackie's story, she had always been honest with him. But he also knew how hard it was for Jackie to talk about it. He knew sharing with Trudy would not have been easy.

"Nothing is resolved," Jackie told Mac. "We agreed to enjoy Vegas for just one day."

Telling Mac, both she and Trudy were looking forward to a night out in Vegas. Jackie asked if he'd be their escort. Mac smiled and readily agreed. As he unlocked the room door, he turned to Jackie and asked, "Did you know this is the start of a harvest moon?"

Mac closed the door and kissed Jackie passionately. Mac could not believe his turn of luck. He was in Vegas with the woman he loved and the great fortune of an unplanned afternoon.

"Do you know what happens with a harvest moon in autumn?" continued Mac.

Jackie smiled, wrapping her arms around Mac, "I could venture a guess, but you tell me!"

"The Druids would bring in the harvest and then lay in the furrows of the freshly harvested field and hold a celebratory orgy, right there, under the light of the harvest moon!"

Mac began unbuttoning Jackie's blouse, kissing her while running his free hand up her back, under her blouse, unhooking her bra. As they both undressed each other, Mac continued the tale, telling her that first the farmer plows the fields, then the farmer sows his crops, taking good care of them, fertilizing the crop. Mac caressed Jackie's breasts gently and walked her toward the double bed.

Mac continued his narrative, whispering to Jackie, telling her of the spring rains gently watering the crops as it falls on the plowed field. Mac laid Jackie down and ran his hands over her hips and legs as if his fingers were the spring rain. He continued telling the story. The crops begin to grow and with proper care, blossom into beautiful wheat fields waving in the wind, big white cumulous clouds overhead shining in the moonlight.

Mac took Jackie's hand and encouraged her to feel his crop in the beautiful field, moving a white cloud pillow gently to support her head. The farmer began passionately kissing the love of his life, and the farmer knew every square inch of the harvest field, the familiarity of it, the erogenous zones so ready for his plow.

"And when the crop is ready for harvest," Mac continued, "The crops yield to the lover, and the farmer begins to harvest."

Mac, fully erect, entered Jackie as she sighed with yearning pleasure. Between kisses, Mac whispered, "As the farmer cuts the stalks of wheat, he bails and binds, bales and binds."

The orgy of the harvest moon reached climax. Two lovers were now fully spent, pleased with the crop they harvested.

Jackie found the familiar crook of Mac's right arm and curled her body into his, resting on her side. Mac knew her creamy curves, coupling his own body into hers with his hand around her breast. The two lovers fell asleep, deeply entwined and dreaming as lovers in the furrow of their field.

Chapter 21

September 1977, Autumnal Equinox

After a long afternoon rest, they set out to enjoy Las Vegas in the early evening, Mac calling themselves the three amigos. The end of September meant the hot days were cooling by day's end. Jackie's rental car provided transport to the edge of the city. From there, they'd walk the Strip.

Arm-in-arm, Mac began crowing about escorting two beautiful women, one on each arm. He puffed out his chest as men passed by, staring in admiration, with Trudy and Jackie laughing at his display.

The neon lights from the marquees reflected in puddles after a rare, late afternoon storm. The Strip was awash in color and flashing lights. Vegas, like a circus, held no limits on garish neon or over-the-top billboards. Stopping in the many casinos and gift shops, they looked at all the bangles. Trudy was amazed at the size of the gambling rooms, larger than football fields with wall-to-wall slot machines and gaming tables.

Mac insisted Trudy try a slot machine. He stopped at a "one-armed bandit," as he called it and gave Trudy a quarter to put in the slot. Trudy inserted the coin and pulled the large lever on the side. The three rollers flashed logos, sometimes matching, mostly not, until they stopped. Trudy lost, and the house won.

. "Is that all it does?"

"Yup," said Mac, adding, "The house never loses."

"I could have more fun playing bingo, and I don't even like bingo!" Trudy quipped. Jackie suggested they move on, as there was much more to see than just slot machines.

"Well, now Trudy gets to say that she gambled in Las Vegas! Or as we say in road lingo, she gambled in Lost Wages!"

"Mac's right! This whole road trip has been about new experiences, seeing this big country."

Jackie saw it was stacking up to be two against one, but she stood her ground, also smiling and half-teasing Trudy, "Just don't forget what stock you come from!"

After walking miles and miles under neon signs and flashing lights with music flowing out onto the sidewalk, venue after venue. The amigos decided to eat supper in one of the many nightclubs.

"We can enjoy a good steak," Mac insisted, "And watch one of the shows while we eat." He led the way to a horseshoe-shaped booth with overstuffed cushions and ordered a cold beer. Jackie and Trudy ordered iced tea. They enjoyed a four-course meal and watched the comedian entertaining the crowd, mostly with halfhearted insults and gambling jokes.

It was growing late, but Jackie suggested they walk a bit more to digest the heavy meal, which she argued was ridiculously large-portioned and not up to her standards.

"If I had been preparing this meal, it would have been made with the best lean meat and freshest vegetables."

But Mac reminded Jackie that this was a vacation. "No one would eat like this on a daily basis."

"Want to bet?" she retorted. "The soup and sandwiches I pack for your road trips are always healthy, not like this stuff in 'Lost Wages.'"

"And that's why I love you!" Mac got in the last word this time, and Jackie just smiled as the three amigos finished their walk to the end of the strip.

"Come on, one more casino, before we call it a night," Mac insisted.

He led them through the doors of Caesars Palace, the Romanesque casino advertising that everyone is treated like Caesar himself. The interior was massive, with thousands of machines in brightly lit gaming rooms and separate entertainment venues the size of theaters, all within one spacious palace.

Trudy found that once inside, it did not matter whether it was daytime or nighttime. This was a world unto itself and always bright. Mac led them through the halls, stopping from time to time to watch some of the gaming. He explained this was the casino where serious gamblers played, but it still included the small-time slots as well as the serious blackjack and poker tables.

As they walked on, Trudy was in disbelief, seeing someone she thought she knew. She stopped, causing Mac and Jackie to pause. They followed her gaze. Sitting before one of the many slot machines, Jill was feeding coins and pulling the lever, over and over.

Jackie was surprised as well to see Jill. It took her a moment to place her, a familiar face in an unfamiliar setting. Mac, unable to identify the woman, asked if it was someone they knew.

"It's Attorney Faust's secretary," replied Trudy.

She then recalled Monday morning and told Jackie and Mac about overhearing Faust tell Jill to make Vegas reservations. Trudy thought nothing of it at the time, but this was serendipity, rather a stroke of misguided luck or misfortune, perhaps.

Trudy asked if they could move on; she didn't want Jill to see her. But Mac asked if Faust was planning to come to Vegas as well.

"I'm not sure," replied Trudy, adding, "He was dressed like he was going on vacation."

"Well, maybe he's here!" Mac replied.

The mood of all three changed, the frivolous fun of the evening becoming one of dreaded apprehension. Mac got quiet, but he was now a man on a mission. He knew Faust wouldn't be sitting in front of a slot machine.

Mac started to step into the serious gaming rooms, checking the tables. Jackie became alarmed. If Mac was looking for Faust, she knew it would mean trouble.

Just as Jackie started to ask Mac if they could leave, she watched his gaze focus on a single gaming table. She followed his stare and saw Faust sitting at the poker table, a large stack of chips in front of him.

Mac made a move toward the players. Jackie grabbed his arm. "Please, Mac, let's just leave."

Trudy saw what was happening when Jackie grabbed Mac. She also looked over to the table and recognized Faust's distinctive glowing white mane. Trudy began to feel panicky.

Mac took another step into the room. Jackie quickly stepped in front of him. "Please, Mac. It's not worth it, let's leave."

Mac's temper was flaring as he recalled how Trudy had been left at the truck stop. Faust deserved to be torn limb from limb and thrown into the lion's den to save other innocents.

Jackie stood her ground. She knew how serious this could get. Mac would have to knock her over; she would not yield.

Trudy calmed her panic. She saw that Jackie needed her help. She feared Mac would get into serious trouble if he acted on his temper.

Trudy also stepped in front of Mac, next to Jackie. She pleaded with him. "Mac, Jackie's right! He's not worth it! Mac, you're worth more than a thousand men like Faust. Please turn around and come out on the street with Jackie and me! Please!"

Mac diverted his gaze and looked at Trudy as she cried, pleading with him. Jackie quietly repeated Trudy's plea.

"Please, Mac. Trudy's right, he's not worth your trouble."

Mac took a deep breath and began to regain control of his temper. He thought for a moment, finally turning around and quietly telling them,

"Let's get out of here. I've had enough of Vegas."

Faust never saw them, never knew of his danger. But Jill, sitting close to this gaming room so she could play the slot machines while at the same time watch Faust, did see what was happening. Jill watched as the three of them turned around and walked out, slowly at first, but then quickening their pace, leaving this palace of other-worldly delights.

By the time the three arrived back at the motel, it was nearly midnight. They drove back in silence. Once out of the city, the lights dimmed under a starry sky. At the stroke of twelve, their chariot ride to the palace became a cheap sedan ride back to reality, as they became, once again, the working-class tourists of the stratified world that kept this country humming. All three had had enough of Lost Wages.

As Jackie parked the rental car, Mac asked, "Trudy, would you come to our room for just a moment before you turn in?" Adding as an afterthought, "I have something that I want to give you."

Jackie knew that Mac wanted to talk seriously to Trudy, she knew it was getting late, but Trudy's intentions were still in doubt. As they neared the motel door, Jackie told the two of them that she had forgotten something in the car. She knew Mac wanted to give Trudy the envelope he had asked her to bring and wanted to give Mac this moment alone with Trudy.

Trudy was tired and more than ready to go to bed. But she wondered what Mac would want to give her at this time of night. Tomorrow would be soon enough for everything, she thought. But Trudy was also dreading the end of her road trip with Mac. She didn't voice her objection and followed Mac to his room.

Once inside, Mac walked over to his duffel bag and pulled out the small envelope that he had asked Jackie to bring from Milson. He had been waiting for an appropriate moment to give it to Trudy.

Mac handed the white envelope to Trudy. She took it from him and looked into Mac's eyes for a clue. He only nodded for her to open it. Her name had been printed on the front, but no other notation. She hesitated.

"Open it, Trudy!"

She slowly pulled up the tip of the flap; it was not sealed. She opened it slowly as if something might spring out. She lifted the flap fully to look inside. Trudy saw white tissue paper but didn't pull it out.

"Go on!" Mac encouraged.

Trudy drew the white tissue paper free of the envelope and set the envelope down on the desk. She could feel the weight of something wrapped inside. It was well-wrapped in several layers of tissue. She slowly peeled each thin sheet back as if she were unsheathing a pearly onion.

Mac watched intently as Trudy finally unwrapped the last sheet of tissue. He watched as her face changed from quiet despair to unbridled glee. Tears of joy fell freely down her cheeks as she cried, "Grandmother's brooch!"

Trudy drew the heart-shaped brooch to her bosom, where it had hung before she took it to the pawnbroker. But just as suddenly, she pulled it away to look at it intently. It really was the same one, but was it still intact? Trudy quickly slipped her thumbnail between the small slit of the brooch opposite the small hinge and opened the heart.

The beloved picture of her grandmother was still inside opposite the handsome soldier, the love of her grandmother's life and her own grandfather.

"The pictures are still in here!" Trudy cried. Mac just shook his head, understanding everything.

Trudy looked again into the face of her beautiful grandmother dressed in her white wedding dress and the handsome soldier still dressed in his WWII officer's uniform. Trudy was overwhelmed to have her brooch back, her dear grandmother's brooch! Tears of joy filled her eyes.

Trudy was overwhelmed to have it returned but knew she was different this time. Her thoughts of fairy tales were misplaced. She now knew their lives were not lived happily ever after. This time, her thoughts were replaced with knowing how difficult their lives really were. Somehow, they'd raised a family, including Trudy's own mother. She knew how her mother had disappointed them and now, how she would have disappointed them, too, had they still been alive. Trudy also thought about how her grandmother had the fortitude and wisdom to keep going, keeping her family together to survive. She finally understood. This woman, her grandmother, had saved her family.

The memories no longer seemed so youthfully romantic. But Trudy had an even deeper respect for her grandmother, finally understanding what her struggles had entailed. Trudy closed the brooch with the pictures safely inside and caressed it once again.

"Thank you! Thank you! I can't say it often enough, but how did you get it, Mac? I thought it was gone forever!"

Mac reminded Trudy of their Memorial Day motorcycle ride. She had been sitting outside the sidecar. He asked how she had lost the brooch and began frantically looking through the sidecar until Trudy admitted that she no longer had it and that she had taken it to the pawnbroker.

Mac asked if she remembered how quickly they returned to Milson afterward.

"I went right over to Doc's Hop Shop, that same day and reclaimed it. But I didn't want to give it to you right away. I was afraid you'd hock it again—so I kept it, waiting for the right moment. I think this is a good time, don't you?"

"It's perfect!"

Jackie knocked on the door, "It's me, Jackie. Is it okay to come in now?"

Mac didn't answer; he walked over to the door and opened it. Trudy stepped forward, holding her brooch, showing it to Jackie.

"Look what Mac gave me! I got my grandmother's brooch back!"

Jackie stepped forward. Seeing the tears and knowing how much this meant to Trudy, she hugged her. She then offered to help Trudy put it back on, where it belonged, where Trudy had first worn it when she came into Jackie's Counter. Trudy nodded and turned to allow Jackie to clasp the gold chain around her neck. While Jackie clasped the brooch, she looked up through her tears, seeing Mac watching both of them.

Fresh tears started to roll down Trudy's cheeks. After Jackie finished clasping the brooch, Trudy went to Mac and gave him a hug, standing on her toes to reach him. Trudy thanked him over and over, telling him she thought it had been lost forever. She didn't know how she'd be able to thank him enough.

She reached for her brooch, her old habit, but this time, she found her heart where it belonged.

Mac got serious: "Trudy, I don't want to give you a lecture now, but pawnbrokers are not a trustworthy bunch. They take advantage of you, just like the gamblers, or even…"

"Even what, Mac?" Trudy noticed that Mac had not finished his last thought.

"I was about to say, 'like those truckers at the truck stop that pick up women,' but I'm a trucker, too. But not me, Trudy!"

"Not you, Mac. I know. Not you. You're one of a kind!"

Trudy hugged Mac again as she buried her tear-stained face into his chest. Mac looked at Jackie, also in tears, so deeply touched watching them.

Mac pulled Jackie into their embrace. Trudy opened her own arm and pulled Jackie into their hug as well.

"One more piece of unsolicited advice," Mac continued, "Trudy, don't ever sell your heart again."

Trudy smiled, answering: "I won't, Mac."

Still in their hugging triangle, Trudy thought that she wanted somehow to return Mac's favor.

"Mac, I'll never be able to repay you, but what was that one question that, if you've asked once, you've asked a hundred times?"

Jackie frowned, still encased in their arms, wondering where Trudy was going with this question.

"You mean, 'Jackie, will you marry me?' That one?" Mac answered.

"Yup, that one. Now ask it again."

Mac put his arms down, releasing both of them. He took his cue from Trudy and turned to face Jackie.

"Woman, will you marry me, once and for all?"

Jackie backed away slightly. Mac and Trudy were both staring at her intently.

Jackie answered Trudy, not Mac. "You know that I can't marry Mac!"

"Why not?" Trudy challenged.

Like earlier in the evening, Jackie saw that this was getting to be two against one.

"Trudy, be fair!" Jackie complained. But Mac stepped closer to Jackie, making her turn to him:

"I'm the one that's asking—Why won't you marry me?"

"Oh, Mac! You know why," she pleaded, but Mac repeated, "Why?"

"Because I cannot give you children, that's why! I am not worthy of your love, Mac!"

Jackie was in tears. She never said these words out loud to anyone, not even Mac, though he knew her story. She had always been honest with him.

Mac took Jackie in his arms again, this time to comfort her. He knew how much hurt it took for Jackie to say this out loud to him.

"I love you. I will never love anyone else," Mac pleaded, telling Jackie to please see how much he did love her.

Trudy watched; she was on Mac's side. She encouraged him.

"Ask her again, Mac."

"Jackie, please marry me!"

Jackie looked over to Trudy. Jackie was shaking her head back and forth as if to say, please stop.

But Trudy didn't see any of this from Jackie's viewpoint. There could be no excuses, not with love.

Trudy stepped forward as Mac held Jackie in his embrace: Trudy pleaded, "Jackie, you want me to come back home, as you call it, as if Milson was my home. At least let me know that I can still have hope! Forgive yourself, Jackie. You're even harder on yourself than you are on the rest of us! Mac loves you, give him a break."

Trudy looked to Mac and said, "Mac, ask Jackie again."

Mac saw what Trudy was doing. He smiled brightly at her. Mac took Jackie's face between the two huge palms of his hands and made Jackie gaze into his eyes.

"Show Trudy, hope is still possible. I still have hope, every time I ask!"

"Jackie, I love you. I will never stop loving you." Mac got down on one knee. "Please marry me!"

Through her tears, Jackie looked into Mac's pleading eyes and quietly answered,

"Yes! I will marry you!"

The next morning, Mac went to Trudy's door and knocked gently, asking if he could talk to her. Trudy was dressed and fully awake. She opened the door.

"I need to drive my rig back to Milson, and Jackie needs to fly back home, but we need to know once and for all about what you'll do. That was quite an accomplishment last night, but now, what are you going to do?"

Mac stepped into her room. "Trudy, it's crunch time. I know it's tough with everything you've gone through, but running away is never the answer. I know that from helping Tag, and all my 'Nam buddies. You can't run away from things that have already happened."

"I know," Trudy answered. "After last night, I came back to my room and thought about everything. Mac, it's so wonderful to hold my brooch again; somehow it helps me think things through."

Trudy went on, telling Mac about all her indecisions, as she called them. Her list included her window of time to appeal the adoption, and whether she'd disappoint Tony and Marie. But really, she wanted to know what was best for her baby.

"And after this big one, what does life hold for me? Could I still go back to school? Should I stay in Milson?"

"I just don't know Mac, but through all of this, I kept thinking that for right now, I wanted to hold my brooch and rock in my rocking chair. Somehow rocking helps me think better. I finally decided I want to go back, at least for a little while, and hold my brooch and rock in my chair. That chair is just like my grandmother's rocker, the one she used to hold me in, and read to me."

Trudy saw Mac was listening but still waiting for an answer to his question. "I will go back with Jackie, okay. For now, but it may not be forever."

"Great!" Mac was relieved. But Trudy quickly added, "But it might only be for a short time. I don't know if I'll stay. But I know that I have to think things through, by myself, without anyone taking me away and trying to tell me what my options are. That's for me to decide."

"Trudy, I agree, you don't have to convince me! I know, but remember last night, there's always hope."

Trudy smiled, "We did gang up on Jackie, didn't we?"

"Yup, the same way I did for Tag after he lost hope. Sometimes, you just don't see it."

"But while you're spending all that time thinking in that rocking chair, remember one thing. You can't go back and change things."

"It's hard, Mac. How do you know if you're making the right decision?"

"You don't. But hopefully you've gotten wiser. Don't try to forget your problems; wrap them up in your life and learn from them. Jackie tells me she can't give me a family, but she's wrong, you know."

"How is she wrong?

"It's because both of you are being hard-headed. A family is whoever you make your family. Jackie is my family. I'm thrilled that she will marry me and be my wife. But she is and always will be my family, even without that piece of paper that makes it official. You will always be my family, too. That's why Jackie and I cannot leave you stranded here. We don't do that to family."

"And whatever you decide, Jackie and I will respect it, Trudy. You are family to us and always will be."

Epilogue

The Rocker, previously published in *Bramble Literary Magazine*, Summer 2020, audio recording, https://www.wfop.org/bramblesummer-2020issue-14/2020/6/16/the-rocker

The Rocker
Finding the rhythm of rocking on
the rocking rocker takes a few spins
like a gyroscope wobbling on tight wire
seeking the balance, but finding the
rhythm of rocking on rocking rocker

puts the reflex response on hold so the
psyche keeps time with the flowing blood
pulsing through the veins, or suckling baby
on mother's bouncing breast while
her tapping toes keep the timing

of rocking on the rocking rocker.
The nursing newborn finds the balance
reminiscent of cavernous waves in womb
with the ebb and flow echoing the rhythm
of the cosmos, and time is kept by timing

the rhythm of rocking on rocking rocker.
In cradled arms measuring her sleep,
baby leaves off nursing but measures time
by moving her pursing lips as still suckling
until mother's tapping toes suddenly

Stop! The rhythm of the pulsating ether
interrupted. The cosmic ebb and flow
strangely, unexpectedly suspended until
finally falling fully and unconnectedly
AWAKE!

~Patricia Carney